DATE DUE

JAN 05 1999	
JAN 29 1999	
FEB 16 1999	

DEMCO, INC. 38-2931

a novel by
TATIANA LOBO

ASSAULT ON PARADISE

translated by
Asa Zatz

CURBSTONE PRESS

Acknowledgment
The reconstruction of these events would have been impossible
without the collaboration of the staff of the Archivo de la Curia
Metropolitania de San José, and without the generous support of so
many friends.—Tatiana Lobo

Curbstone wishes to thank Barbara Rosen for her editorial work
on this book.

Printed in Canada on acid-free paper by Transcon Printing & Graphics/
          Best Book Manufacturers
Cover design by Stephanie Church

          This book was published with the support of the
          Connecticut Commission on the Arts and the National
          Endowment for the Arts, and donations from many
          individuals. We are very grateful for this support.

Library of Congress Cataloging-in-Publication Data

     Lobo, Tatiana.
          [Asalto al paraíso. English]
          Assault on paradise : a novel / by Tatiana Lobo; translated by
     Asa Zatz.
               p.   cm.
          ISBN 1-880684-46-2
          1. Costa Rica—History—to 1821—Fiction. I. Title.
     PQ7489.2.L58A7313   1998
     863—dc21   97-47572

published by
CURBSTONE PRESS   321 Jackson Street   Willimantic, CT 06226
     phone: (860) 423-5110   e-mail: curbston@connix.com
               www.connix.com/~curbston/

CONTENTS

"What stupidities are you trying to tell me, miserable savage? I cannot understand your murky language."

> —Francisco Pizarro,
> translated by Felipillo in
> "La muerte de Atahualpa."

In his book EL PARAISO DE LAS INDIAS, written in 1650, Antonio de León Pinelo maintained at great length that Biblical Paradise was situated in America. Others believed the same, many went in search of it, and among them they set about laying it waste.

ASSAULT ON PARADISE

Pa-brú Presbere dreams of Surá, Lord of the Nether World

Before beginning his spirit journey, he ate the last permissible bit of banana, and fed the last sweet-cedar twigs into the fire. The cave lit up. The sacred tapir had perhaps walked nearby, perhaps far away. He hearkened to the Kapá's final words. "This is how it is..." the Kapá said, "The order of things has been so determined: there are three worlds above with rocks, clouds, winds, and stars. Sibú dwells there. And there are three worlds below where Lord Surá dwells. Looking up or looking down, counting from above or from below, we inhabit a fourth world, a dual world, the world of appearances. Actual things are in the nether worlds: it is from below that life springs, man has his root there, and his head, as well, because we return below when we die. This is the mystery that the men with moss upon their jaws are unable to understand. Their order of the universe is backwards. They have but one God in the sky and do not see that Sibú without Surá is an impossibility. Deceived by their only god, they walk about in their long garments here and there, to and fro: they never sit down, are never satisfied..."

The Kapá finished speaking in his old man's voice and then broke into a long monotonous song. Pa-brú asked no questions; he already knew all there was to know. This was not his first spirit trance but it was of special importance. The fire slowly expired and the shadows fell, the darkness good for thinking and meditation but not about the external things that anguish us in the officious light of day, rather about the secrets of the womb. Pa-brú thought about Sibú whose breath gives life. He saw him, impalpable as the wind. Sibú thought of Presbere as a cacao berry and Presbere's blood as chocolate. Surá, guardian of the underground world to which the dead return, dwelt below. Surá molds people as the potter shapes a vessel and, when he has finished them, Sibú exhales the breath of life, and the children leave the safe haven of their mother's womb to open their eyes upon a world of facade and deceit.

Sibú breathed upon man's understanding and taught him to sing and dance, to use vessels, and light fires. Surá tends the seeds that Sibú caused to sprout and brings all that decays back to life.

The Kapá sings the song that unlocks the portal of the underground world, of that which is not thought, nor seen, nor understood when the eyes are open and one is occupied with the little things of everyday. He is insistent and repeats his call, the melody rebounding from the walls of the cave, dispersing itself in the darkness. How much time has passed? How big or how small is space? How long is time?

Sibú-Surá are one and indivisible. It is no more possible to separate them than it is to separate the cloud from the rain or the rain from the damp earth that gives birth to the greenery that is food for the deer which in turn is food for the puma from whose excrement the fruits and flowers sprout which feed the hummingbird whose chicks are eaten by the hawk whose decaying flesh nourishes the bushes which are food for the deer on whom the puma feeds. The cycle of life and death has no end; an eternal death is the same as an eternal rebirth. Life-death veers in Kapá's song and Pa-brú veers; his bones melt, his elbows, knees, jaw, and all his body parts that end in an angle disintegrate. Muscle dissolves and flesh as well, yet he is perfectly aware of his innermost parts, liver, kidneys, lungs. His blood circulates slowly causing him to feel heavy and at the same time light. His heart beating quietly, imperceptibly, Pa-brú transcends the frontier of the impossible; he joins together the separated, leaves this level of appearances and descends to the real world, the origin of all things. He would succeed were it not for an error that obliges him to go back to the surface of deceptive appearances and so lose the opportunity to understand the order within disorder. His body once again encloses itself within its narrow confines, his bones harden, the borders that separate him from the other establish his difference and the voyage to origins collapses like a broken vessel. Pa-brú had left one eye open. He opens the other. His spirit trance has been broken.

His spirit trance was broken because of a perverse idea that entered through the window of his opened eyelid. The Kapá has stopped singing. How to resume his journey now if the Kapá is no longer guiding him? Pa-bru is beset by uneasiness. What had been the dual god's purpose in bringing the bearded men? Or is it that they were only in Sibú's plan? Did Surá also have something to do with it all? Was it a joint plan or was one of them alone responsible? Then Sibú-Surá are not indivisible...each has his own will. And they might not have been in agreement... Perhaps it was Sibú, the one who looks upon people as cacao berries... The foreigners who used a long garment tied around the waist with a cord said that God lives above, precisely where Sibú lives. They went in and out of the jungle, their faces covered with hair, skinny and pale, and they said that Surá was a devil, because the devil dwells under the earth. Walking one behind another, they conversed in their barbaric tongue and talked to a small piece of white cloth. Their bony heels and bleeding feet showed from under their garment the color of ticks. They appeared to be very ill, decrepit, but they did not stop anywhere to seek help from the healers nor to gather medicinal herbs. They came as far as Recul in search of the Kapá. Presbere clad himself in the gaudy colors of the macaw and went up an annato tree. Perched there he watched them running away from the women who, he was gratified to see, were throwing stones at them and noted with satisfaction how they tugged at their hairy jaws and wailed as they stretched up their arms. Spat upon, stoned, and insulted, they went away looking up into the sky, unmindful of where they trod.

They never returned to Recul but did not depart entirely. They built strange-looking houses that in no way resembled Sibú's cone-shaped house and, on top where there should have been an upturned tub on the roof beam to catch the rainwater, they placed two crossed timbers and said that it was God, the one, true God of all people.

The houses of that god were built in the air, detached from the earth. And they wished to sow the souls of the Indians in the air, as well.

The Kapá's breathing had stopped entirely. He was no longer in the cave, that uterus of grandmother earth, old, ancient, yet ever fertile.

Pa-brú Presbere searched for another idea that might console him. And he came upon it: the lords of the air and the earth had given him life in order for him to put a stop to the terrible harm being wreaked by the foreigners through their cruelty and greed. That was his destiny, his great, important destiny. He felt better, consoled. He was still young and had a long road ahead. There was no hurry. The Kapá had told him: slow as the sloth, relentless as its claws.

Pa-brú Presbere lay face down, arms spread out, the better to feel the voluptuous contact of the earth against the skin of his genitals. His doubt had not been resolved but he would soon find the answer. Serene and at peace, he put off till later in his journey the mystery that had distracted him, shut his eyes, and gave himself up to the descent. The roots of all that lives, is born, and dies could be seen in the layers of the world below. He saw the seeds not yet sown interspersed with the roots of the avocado, the sweet cedar, and the bitter cedar. He saw his mother's roots and those of the maternal clan, which was also his, and he saw the spirit of the macaw, his protector; the macaw, named Pa-brú, like Presbere. He saw all the worlds and understood all things, and he also saw a little girl with eyes like two pools, who made the stones fall silent: a strange child floating, adrift in life.

Of Pedro Albarán's first days in a part of the West Indies where the inhabitants impress him as being gossipmongers, backbiters, and troublemakers

Bárbara Lorenzana and Pedro Albarán arrived at the city of Cartago at the same time, slept under the same roof, made love to the same woman, and had not spoken to one another for the past ten long years. Because of the peculiarity of her neck he never could forget the first time he laid eyes on her, though it is highly unlikely that Lorenzana took any notice of Pedro in the atrium of that parish church. First, because she was then going through a very difficult moment in her life and, secondly, because he bore the indecorous signs of dusty roads, his beard was matted, and the only thing noteworthy about his appearance was that there was water dripping on his frayed jacket. Pedro had bathed in the stream of the monastery that gave him lodging and just moments before emerged from the icy water bleating and shivering, with nothing to dry himself on. Finally, he made do with a Franciscan cassock in a heap of dirty clothing upon which a cake of yellow soap had been left lying. He lamented the garment's stench but consoled himself with the thought that the clothing he was about to put back on stank even worse, perfumed as it was by the sweat accumulated since he left Cádiz. He pulled on his ragged underdrawers and trousers, shrouded mercifully with his shirt the bites of fleas and lice that has tried to devour him during the night, and threw on the black jacket formerly the property of a Sevillian doctor from whom he had obtained it in an untoward manner.

His blood sent racing by the cold bath and a vigorous rubdown with the rough cassock made him feel better and more sanguine about the Governor of the province giving him the scribe's job that the Superior of the monastery had requested for his guest. Pedro Albarán anticipated doing work of that nature until such time as fate could come up with something more in keeping with his expectations when he set sail from Cádiz. Meanwhile, there was no call to lament, for the Superior of the San Francisco monastery had given him a roof overhead with bed and board in exchange for bookkeeping work. The roof was not bad with its red tiles still intact. The food was very good, abundant, and the beef excellent. The bed, however, hard, narrow, and habitat of noxious bugs, could not have been worse. He even woke up with a huge tarantula sharing the bed, a revolting light-brown, hairy creature with two small horns on its head, which he killed without much trouble because the spider was as sluggish as it was ugly.

All in all, he couldn't complain. He, a Spaniard without name, lineage, or fortune was already assured only three days after arrival of the basic necessities, thanks to the letter given him by Servando García, an erudite Franciscan friar of Seville, man of science, theology, and other clandestine callings to be gone into later. The Superior of the monastery had accepted the letter and, despite its scruffy appearance, the paper wrinkled and the ink faded from the rigors of the voyage, read it through respectfully, folded it carefully, and making no attempt to return it, laid it aside. Pedro found this regrettable, for the lack of Servando's recommendation would constitute a serious disadvantage should he be obliged to continue his wanderings about the New World. That letter had been of incalculable benefit to him. From the time he landed in Veracruz it had enabled him to leapfrog from monastery to monastery, eating gratis, attaching himself to mule trains of goods from the Orient, convincing an occasional ship's captain to allow him free passage in the hold in exchange for swabbing decks and other such menial work.

The Superior had kept the letter but on the strength of it provided him lodging which Pedro repaid with work on the friars' account books. That was already a big favor.

Bathed, his hair and beard still dripping, his body clean but wearing the same borrowed clothes he had on the day he had escaped and fled, Pedro Albarán, alias Pedro de la Baranda, headed for the main door and the street to be interviewed by the Governor for the post of scribe to the Governor's office and the city council. The Superior with his cauliflower nose, rubicund old Christian's countenance, and trencherman's potbelly, stood waiting for him beside the brother doorkeeper. He took him by the arm, and repeated the advice he had already given him, "Be prudent, Don Pedro de la Baranda...discreet and prudent. His Honor the Governor is a very busy man who must deal with a host of problems and cope with disputes that plague him constantly." He let go of Pedro's arm to address a monk who was also on his way out, saying, "See to it, Brother Lorenzo, that the material be of good quality and low price. Check through what is left over, carefully examine the remnants, and purchase the one that seems to you most appropriate for the purpose we intend it."

Pedro and Brother Lorenzo went out together, the monk growling and complaining because he was being sent to buy the most expensive material at the cheapest price, "He expects a miracle not forthcoming in these times, and who's to know what manner of goods were seized from *Nuestra Señora de la Soledad*? That's the frigate that was caught in a typhoon on its way from Panama to Peru and ended up a wreck in the port of Caldera with no papers or documents, and so everything in its holds was sequestered."

Pedro listened with one ear as they walked and with the other picked up the few street sounds to be heard on the deserted thoroughfare: the sobbing of a child, the noise of a receptacle being emptied into the drainage ditch, a load of wood dropped in the square, wagon wheels squeaking in the distance. They walked three blocks to the Royal Square where an auction had been in progress for some time and little merchandise remained on exhibit in the city hall corridor. Pedro, who went there because he had to wait for the auction to end before he could see the Governor, climbed the stairway to the atrium of the parish church where he stayed to watch the women in their colorful skirts, some with their heads covered. Mules grazed, pigs ran about loose, chickens strutted among the crowds. Erstwhile companion of peddlers, itinerant tradesmen, and unfrocked priests who drifted from place to place, their way of life cheating and roguery, Pedro had grown accustomed to the motley panorama of the West

Indies with its chromatic scale of myriad castes, a mélange bred of the union of Europeans, Africans, and American aborigines, its surprising results to be appreciated in women the color of molasses, of stewed quinces, of peaches in syrup, a full range from slate black to the warm softness of brown sugar, full-fleshed with protuberant front and rear, ample-bottomed and buxom, slim and willowy. There were tall, short, and middle-sized, too, even midgets. He had never seen such a sampler of women in Seville, and that was a cosmopolitan city. In Pedro's appreciation of this variety none was spared his close attention. Therein lay the pleasure, his eyes gladdening at the sight of this one and that, notwithstanding the weariness that had settled in his bones during the tedious crossing of the Atlantic and the fact that he was ill at ease in this city of which he had seen little, but enough to feel that he was in the remotest corner of a land lying close to the edge of nowhere.

The hubbub of the crowd was something phenomenal. Up in the trees of the square, boys perched astride the branches were having great sport spitting down on people and interrupting the bidding of the auction by whistling and shouting rowdy remarks. A woman standing a short distance from him, let her rebozo slip down over her shoulders as she turned to whisper into her companion's ear. She was young, probably not more than fifteen, with long braids, very dark eyes, and thick eyebrows. Her uptilted little nose and smooth white skin indicated that she was of pure Iberian ancestry. In time, Pedro would learn that the girl's father was from Marbella and that she, Nicolasa Guerrero, was the source of enough gossip to keep the entire province entertained. The youth to whom she was whispering bore such a resemblance to her that obviously they were brother and sister. Ten years later, he, Juan Guerrero, was to displease Blas González Coronel, Deputy Director of the Royal Bank, who at this very moment was leaning over the railing above the corridor of the city hall observing the progress of the auction with a scornful eye. None of these personages, however, knew Pedro Albarán as yet, and the only thought that entered his mind as he gazed at the profile before his eyes was that he would not have minded finding that girl in bed with him instead of the tarantula he woke up with.

Above the corridor, a short, gray-haired, fortyish man was bellowing his lungs out, repeating the words: "Who bids more? Who bids more?" each time after singing the praises of the items seized from the frigate *Nuestra Señora de la Soledad.* He was known as Captain Fajardo to the bidders who waved their caps above their head to catch his attention. A soldier in an ill-fitting uniform stood next to him, an anxious expression on his mulatto countenance. He was Lázaro de Robles, the aide to whom Pedro had spoken the day before, and from whom he expected a call when the auction was over and the Governor able to receive him. Pedro did not know him by sight but none of the other Spaniards in the corridor had such a look of authority.

The onlookers, mostly men and women without the wherewithal to acquire such luxuries, applauded each time a higher bid was made, and when a smiling winner carried off his acquisition, while the loser made faces and shook his head or slapped his thighs in irritation. Climbing the stairs was a priest with a rather worldly air, impeccable white stockings beneath his short cassock, his hair slicked down as though by a cow's tongue except for two curls at the temples. He hurried to examine the remaining articles as a voice behind Pedro remarked, "What's Angulo doing here? That priest already has more than he knows what to do with." Casting a practiced eye on the goods under Lázaro de Robles's increasingly anxious glance, he picked up several items, and called out to the auctioneer in a childish, piping voice, "I bid three hundred pesos for these four pieces." Captain Fajardo knocked it down to him immediately, giving other bidders no opportunity and the priest trotted off with his acquisitions. Crossing the square attended by a lancer, he made his way through the muttering populace towards the side of the atrium, leaving a wake of fragrant French perfume that did not quite succeed in overpowering the stench of the shit-stained straw under the captives waiting to be auctioned off.

The sale proceeded. Captain Fajardo placed on the block a young, well-built African slave encased in a shapeless garment of sackcloth which did not succeed in concealing the prominence of her swelling breasts and the insolent thrust of her rump. This imposing figure of a woman stood a good head above the auctioneer and several inches taller than the mulatto Robles who now wore an expression of satisfaction rather than one of anguish as he held one end of the rope tied around the black woman's neck. Her head bent to one side gave her a wary, disdainful expression quite similar to that of Blas González Coronel, the Deputy Director of the Royal Bank. His cynical, mocking gaze was fixed upon her, his shapely head turned to one side as well, a faint, undefinable smile on the finely turned lips beneath his closely clipped mustache. The difference between them, as Pedro could see from where he stood, was that the man's neck was bent because he felt like bending it while hers was permanently frozen. The condition was evident from the scars on that long neck left by the iron ring to which she had been chained on the slave trip that took her from her native land. The black woman seemed a prisoner of war, vanquished after a prolonged struggle, neck bent over one shoulder, looking at the world, like a spectator at a parade of outlandish madmen crossing the ring of a circus. People stared at the captive curiously, uncertain whether to reject her for the deformity of her neck or to value the high quality of her other attributes. Pedro watched brother Lorenzo push his way through the crowd of onlookers and climb to the top of the corridor stairway to examine the black woman close up. The friar looked her over from head to foot, opened her mouth, counted the teeth, measured the girth of her hips, felt all her bones to check whether they were intact. He tried to straighten her neck but desisted when she grimaced with pain. Lorenzo shrugged his shoulders and spread his hands indicating that nothing could be done about the defect. He made a close inspection of the injury, stepped back a couple of paces, scratched his beard, and again approached her. The onlookers held their breath. Lorenzo leaned over and ran his fingers over the woman's abdomen. The youths in the trees shrieked enthusiastically. He finished his scrutiny, straightened up, and shouted, "I bid fifty pesos for this Negress."

"I have fifty pesos," announced Captain Fajardo. "Who bids more? Who bids more?"

A man took off his hat, waved it in the air, and shouted, "I bid seventy-five."

Locating the bidder in the crowd, the auctioneer said to him, "Don José de Mier, is your honor not aware that this Negress's neck is broken?"

"Babies are not made through the neck," he responded.

Pedro could not see his face but he had the impression of a man in the prime of life. The boys in the trees howled with laughter. Don José de Mier calmly continued, "I want her for breeding and she seems to be healthy."

"Not really," interrupted Lorenzo, "her hips are too narrow. Check for yourself."

"Seventy-five," insisted Don José de Mier, donning his hat.

"Eighty!" shouted Lorenzo. "Not a peso more." This was said with such vehemence that a startled buzzard flying over the roof of the building came to rest on the handrail of the corridor where it remained perched near Blas González Coronel, its greedy little eyes fixed on the bags of bones rejected from the auction: an old black woman, almost a skeleton, and a boy of perhaps seven standing on one foot clutching his surrogate mother, for the other foot had a spike driven through it from the ankle to the sole. The old woman looked at the child with anguish, perhaps wishing to take him in her arms but without strength to do so, she herself hardly able to stand.

José de Mier made a gesture in Lorenzo's direction that said, "Take her if you want her."

Captain Fajardo, hoarse from shouting, croaked, "If I have no further bids, the Negress is going...going once...going twice...going thrice...and sold! And may she produce bouncing offspring for you!"

The voice behind Pedro spoke up again: "I'd myself invest if I had the brass."

"Need a bed warmer, do you?"

Pedro turned to have a look at the speakers. One identified himself as a tailor by a pair of shears hanging over his chest. The other, who had spoken first, wore a leather jacket, was exaggeratedly pug-nosed and had watery, light-colored eyes, replied, "I was referring to the little black fellow."

"And what would you be wanting such a little black fellow for?"

"For one thing! To have that spike pulled out of his leg." The pug-nosed man was indignant.

Friar Lorenzo went off to the monastery with his slave in tow. From the woman's finely chiseled features it was hard to know her lineage. She could have come from somewhere like Arara, the Congo, Cape Verde, or Angola.

"You made a good buy," said the tailor to the friar. "What can they do to straighten her neck?"

"No need to," answered Lorenzo. "The Superior wants her as a cook and cooking is not done with the neck." And he continued down the street, followed by the black woman and her proud rump.

Above the corridor, the auctioneer and Lázaro were pulling on the little boy in an effort to loosen his hold on the old woman's ragged skirt while she, too timid to shield the child, had no choice but to yield him up. When Lázaro stood the Negro on the highest step so that all might see him, an animal-like shriek streaked like an arrow through the square, causing even the youths up in the trees to fall silent. The boy fell silent, too, and a woman with a black shawl over her head bid twenty-five pesos for him on condition that he be turned over to her with the spike removed and with a few days' grace to ensure that he was going to remain alive. Lázaro de Robles picked the child up and pulled on the spike, cries of protest coming from the crowd as the victim howled. The pug-nosed man standing behind Pedro bawled: "Don't be so stupid, Lázaro! Let me take care of it. I know how it should be done!"

"Let the shoemaker do it," agreed the woman with the shawl, a typical Spanish matron, turning towards him.

"I'll take care of it, Doña Mariana," the shoemaker replied as he hurried to snatch the slave child away from Lázaro, leaving the man with his arms hanging foolishly. Doña Mariana de Echeverría and the shoemaker, bearing the boy in his arms with great care, rounded the corner of the city hall and disappeared. Captain Fajardo drew a huge handkerchief from his pocket and mopped his sweaty forehead. Only the old black slave remained to be sold but nobody wanted her. The square emptied and the people on the atrium came down. Even the buzzard took flight to philosophize on the bell tower of the church. Lázaro de Robles, Captain Fajardo, and the man with the clipped mustache went into the city hall. Somebody finally bought the old black woman, and Pedro Albarán found a seat on a bench to await the Governor's summons, his back to the tall, lichen-stained walls of the church, nature invading its chinks with tendrilly fingers, tiny leaves sprouting to take possession of the masonry as well as the adobe of the houses stretching down the hill. Little flowers grew everywhere and weeds and wild plants lined the edges of the roughly paved streets. On the sidewalks, chickens, cryptographers skilled in the preparation of hidden messages, scratched gibberish in the mud with their little witch's feet. A great mountain looming beyond the tiled roof of the city hall, its peak wreathed in clouds, mounted guard sleeplessly over the grand homes facing the square, as well as the small mud-and-wattle houses on the outskirts, an arcadian cluster of bucolic harmony. Anyone arriving there without having witnessed the slave auction would have believed himself at the very heart of idyllic serenity.

Pedro stretched out his legs, feeling compassion for the torn boot making a wry grimace that exposed his big toe and long nail, a deplorable sight that clamored for a cobbler. Without stockings, his last pair having evolved into a fistful of shreds bulging like a handkerchief in his jacket with all its buttons missing, he was a cartoon of wretchedness. His long and hazardous voyage and desperate flight appeared to have come to an end in the city of Nueva Cartago, on a narrows and an inlet, where all the hopes that had soared when he made his escape with the fleet of galleons at the port of Cádiz plummeted to earth. Harsh reality had so throttled his illusions that for the time being his greatest concern was to impress the Governor favorably enough to give him work. Otherwise, he would be obliged to become a peasant or remain a rogue wandering the face of this broad continent, living on his wits.

On the atrium, an irreverent and rowdy cock, strutting his arrogant plumage in conquest of the hens pecking away at kernels of corn, passed above the spot where Pedro sat, and dropped his contribution to the tribulations of the former Cordovan resident of Seville. Under the impact of the warm, gray gob, Pedro felt his cup of anguish, rage, and fear brim over. Removing the mess with his fingers and leaping to his feet, he glared murderously at the offender regretting that he lacked a sword or, if he had one, the skill with which to skewer him from breast to tail. Perfectly unconcerned, the miscreant continued his amorous advances with a seductive beating of wings, followed by the syncopated steps of a buzzard who had flown down from the bell tower. As it grew late, the birds departed, leaving Pedro more humiliated than ever and impatient, for, apparently, Lázaro de Robles had no intention of calling him. He considered going to the city hall and making an approach on his own but, remembering the Superior's counsel, he sat down again, lifting the skirt of his jacket to keep it from getting damp, the very same jacket he had taken off the Inquisition prison doctor in Seville after leaving him lying stunned on the floor in a puddle of milk.

His spectacular escape was accomplished not a moment too soon, for it spared him an interrogation that could hardly have gone well for him. The Inquisition, expert in tracing genealogies, would soon have discovered that Pedro was the grandson of a man who was put to death in a splendid auto-da-fé for professing the Mohammedan faith. It was attended by large crowds at the pronouncement of sentence and those—accusers and accused— who took part in the ceremony, complete with platform for the authorities, podium for the Inquisitor, the great cloth panels bearing the elegantly painted emblem of the Inquisition. No other theatrical detail was missing to make the auto-da-fé a mass spectacle more elaborate and sophisticated than a Roman circus in the days of the martyrs.

There were the condemned in ritual conical cap and gown. Those with the flames of the pyre painted upward, who had recanted at the last moment, were led from the square of La Corredora to the platform of the gallows where they were garroted and the bodies consigned to the pyre. Pedro's grandfather did not recant, and the child perched on his father's shoulders saw how he was tied to a huge stake and gagged so that those at the execution should not hear his curses. Pedro was four years old at the time and thought at first that it was a game they were playing with his grandfather. He learned later that the old man was a family disgrace kept hidden by all its members. On the day of the auto-da-fé, the child Pedro saw how they trussed up the old man and how some men set the logs afire while others fed the flames with dry faggots until the blaze leapt up to the edges of the condemned man's shirt. Pedro's father then left with his son and soon after moved the whole family to Galicia, never to return to

Córdoba, but Pedro returned to Andalusia because he could never get used to the Galicians' underhanded way of life.

Pedro could never banish the memory of his grandfather from his mind, associated as it was with the odor of burning flesh, and as soon as he was of age he left to study at the University of Seville. He came into contact there with Servando García, his professor of philosophy and theology, a member of the Franciscan Order. The rebellious young student with an aversion to fire was dazzled by his maestro's dialectical discourse which opened fresh vistas for him. His was a questioning approach, wise and daring but, at the same time, cautiously concealed behind a mantle of unassailable orthodoxy. In contrast to his classmates, content with copying down and memorizing the teacher's words, he wanted to know what underlay them. Questioning, investigating, curious, even prying, he sought to get closer to Servando who soon recognized in the youth a questing spirit that could not be ignored. After careful probing, enquiry, and appraisal, he took him under his wing to prepare him for the delicate task of countervailing the ignorance and obscurantism that enabled the dictatorship of the Catholic faith to keep Spain crushed and paralyzed under the ironclad censorship imposed by the Holy Office of the Inquisition.

Pedro had no inkling of just how powerful this institution was until he had a mishap. He was able, however, to escape the dangerous consequences facing him just before "they" would have wormed all manner of unconfessed secrets and mysteries of the soul out of him at a fearsome trial, exploring labyrinths of whose existence the very possessor of the soul was himself ignorant. That's what "they" were like, experts in ferreting out crimes buried below the level of consciousness, occult desires, larval heresies, embryonic sins. And so, pitiless and tireless, "they" fought to maintain their omnipotence despite the indignant voices clamoring throughout Europe and even in Spain itself for the cessation of their activities. Unfailingly patient and tenacious in their interrogations, they poked into darkest interstices, leaving the spirit of the interrogated wounded and scarred by the unrelenting probing.

Even now, at this very moment, safe in Cartago, Pedro

Albarán, alias Pedro de la Baranda, did not feel safe; pronouncements were posted right behind him on the church door threatening shunned excommunication, *latae sententiae ipso facato icurrenda*, for all who did not pay tithes in full and when due. The subject of tithes had been of considerable concern to Servando, who considered that the arrangement reached by the Holy See and the Spanish king was clearly immoral, a dirty business that endangered the Church's independence. At a time when he was certain not to be overheard, he remarked, "It cannot be that the church's worldly goods should be dealt in as though they were a priest's underdrawers." To Servando, the income from papal bulls, tithes, canonships, primacies, and everything concerned with material wealth should be returned in hospitals for the poor, food kitchens for the needy, and schools where, at least, the abc's were taught. That the king should appropriate assets contributed to the Church by Catholics for the salvation of their souls from hellfire and, furthermore, use them for purposes of war, was obviously a grave misdeed.

Those were Servando's convictions and he confided them to Pedro, who never asked where he had gotten such ideas, for he knew. Servando was one of the few intellectuals permitted to read books banned by the Inquisition and had a library of British utopians and French rationalists in his monastic cell. Not many were aware that the Franciscan was translating those texts into vernacular Spanish and having them printed in a place only he knew about hidden somewhere in a cellar or the castle of some nobleman who was above suspicion. Pedro never asked about that press because it was a secret he was not permitted to share.

The organization of the illicit traffic in banned books was compartmentalized in such a way that nobody knew what the others were doing, what their names were, nor where they carried out their activities. Pedro never found out where the books were printed or how they were distributed. He and a few others checked galleys against Servando's original translation. He had been doing this for a relatively short time out of a sense of obligation to disseminate new ideas in unenlightened Spain; he worked from a room in a pension where for the time being he was the only occupant, the owner having gone off to the town of Castilla la Vieja to attend to property she owned there, leaving him in charge. He labored under candle light, the candles supplied by the organization, for he had no income other than a modest allowance from his father which sufficed only for his barest needs.

Pedro and his maestro observed strict caution in their contacts at the university since it was infested with students turned informers, eager to pick up a few pesetas selling information the Inquisition was hunting for.

Nobody, however, distrusted Servando, belonging as he did to a family of noble lineage and impeccable reputation. When he was certain of not being overheard he would talk to Pedro of his high hopes in the territories overseas, particularly the Americas, where republics would spring up even though monarchies continued to flourish in Europe. Carried away by his euphoria, he leapt centuries ahead and centuries back, hitching his wagon to the theology propounded by Bartolomé de las Casas, a priest of the Dominican Order who was born two hundred years before in Seville and who had devoted his life and passion to the defense of the downtrodden, and, based upon his personal experiences with the exploitation of the Indian masses in Latin America by the *encomenderos*,[1] proposed a new interpretation of the gospel which favored the most bitterly oppressed.

There was no doubt that the new world discovered by Columbus would certainly be among the lands targeted for forbidden books. Servando himself, in a rash moment, had hinted to Pedro that they were being passed through customs inside wine barrels, camouflaged as collections of inspirational thoughts for the faithful, bound as works of Aristotle or Saint Thomas Aquinas, or simply concealed under virginal skirts.

During the early hours of that ill-fated day when Pedro Albarán anticipated none of the indiscretions customary in the night, master and disciple were strolling along chatting of this and that, exchanging gossip, discussing the latest talk of the town; this concerned the Archbishop of Seville who had climbed the Giralda Tower to placate the winds and exorcise the devils that rode the storm clouds of the tempest which had lashed the city unmercifully all the previous week. The two goodhumoredly

---

1. Settlers in colonial Latin America granted lands and control over the Indian inhabitants by the Spanish Crown.

mocked the folly of the Monsignor's exploit, for he had insisted on walking barefooted to the top, accomplishing nothing thereby but catching a terrible cold that nearly did him in.

"How wanting in common sense are our prelates," observed Servando after they had laughed their fill. "If they are not dull-witted as donkeys, they skulk about the palace corridors reeking of intrigue." Then, lowering his voice as he took Pedro by the elbow, he added, "I am told that Cardinal Portocarrero and the King's confessor are subjecting His Majesty to a treatment of exorcisms and spells to cleanse him of the effects of a potion of deadman's brains dissolved in chocolate that was sloshed down the royal gullet... King Charles is convinced that he has been bewitched and submits to this torture at the hands of the two of them and a certain Dominican brought in from Germany who is said to be a specialist in exorcism."

"The King is such an idiot that it wouldn't be farfetched to believe he really had been bewitched," offered Pedro. "Spain has never before had a ruler as inept at governing as he is unadept at procreating."

"Here's the nub of the matter," said Servando, his clever eyes sparkling, as he loosed Pedro's elbow and bent over to whisper in his ear. "The King has no offspring. Logically, upon his death the succession will come into dispute. I'm afraid that Cardinal Portocarrero has taken it on himself to hasten his sovereign's demise, inasmuch as he has already picked his successor and it seems to me that it will be..." As a group of students neared, he raised his voice, saying, "I've heard word going around that His Majesty said to Inquisitor General Mendoza: 'I think this confessor of mine should be denounced to the Holy See for he insists on bearing tales about devils to me every morning.'" Nodding respectfully to Servando, the students continued on their way, as he lowered his voice again to mutter, "That's what's being bruited about and I also heard that Inquisitor Mendoza had the King's confessor secretly arrested. That, of course, made Portocarrero very angry. So he, in turn, demanded that Mendoza return the exorcist-confessor to his Majesty's bedside, alleging that if canonical law was to be observed, the future widow would also have to be declared an accomplice in the confessor's crime. That was an argument which put the Inquisitor General on the spot, he being, as everybody knows, an intimate friend of the Austrian Queen."

"And so Austrians will continue as the inheritors of the Spanish crown," proclaimed Pedro, separating himself by a good pace from his maestro, whose breakfast each morning consisted of a head of garlic and a chunk of bread.

"Yes, the future King of Spain would have to be the Archduke of Austria, unless Cardinal Portocarrero has another candidate in mind and..."

A pair of preceptors deep in conversation were now walking by. Servando waved a greeting and called out, smiling, "Greetings, colleagues, may Aristotle sponsor a fine morning for you." And he resumed his conversation with Pedro, talking in a loud voice. "Indeed, I've heard rumors that the King's condition has become increasingly unstable as a consequence of exorcisms being applied to him by that imprudent confessor of his and may the Lord grant him good health and the new confessor assigned him by Father Mendoza bring repose to his soul."

He stole a glance over his shoulder and seeing that the two colleagues were out of earshot, continued in a discreet tone: "They say that Inquisitor Mendoza is in Seville conducting highly confidential investigations regarding the colonies, especially with respect to the Viceroy of New Spain who, rumor hath it, is in league with Cardinal Portocarrero."

Pedro made no attempt to stifle his hilarity. Mimicking Servando's gossipmongering tone, he asked, "Isn't it rather that Inquisitor Mendoza, the Queen, and the Archduke of Austria are fearful that Cardinal Portocarrero is plotting with the Viceroy of New Spain to put Don Quixote de la Mancha on the throne of Madrid and that he is now on his way from Chihuahua to claim his right to succession?"

The maestro was annoyed. "Don't be flippant, man, this is no laughing matter."

Pedro, in no mood to be chastened, persisted in his good-humored raillery. "Or could it have something to do with the delicate affair of the Archbishop's having climbed Giralda to plot with devils mounted on the clouds?"

Accepting defeat, the other said goodhumoredly, "Would you like me to let you in on a secret, a terrible secret? The Archbishop climbed the tower..." he paused with mock gravity "...to mount his altar boy!" And the august maestro slapped at his cassock and tugged on his noble beard laughing like an urchin at his own joke.

Pedro then set out for La Chamberga's tavern, skipping over the university courtyard cobblestones, gay and unconcerned, being as yet unaware that the very same night his loose tongue would give his life a new turn and that La Chamberga's breasts, the numerous flagons of wine, and the oaken barrel bearing the inscription "Piss For The French" put him in a more precarious position than he could ever have anticipated.

A shrill whistle interrupted Pedro Albarán's thoughts. It was Lázaro de Robles waving at him from the doorway. The mulatto's attitude was unbearably disrespectful, his fingers arrogantly signaling a command to approach.

Pedro left the atrium, crossed the deserted square, and headed towards the stairway where Lázaro de Robles stopped him with another authoritative gesture to tell him that the Governor was tied up at a meeting with the Deputy Director of the Royal Bank and Captain Fajardo, admonishing him to wait right where he was until they left. Resigned, Pedro sat down on the first step of the stairway and Lázaro went on his way, undoubtedly to have his lunch, the sun being at the zenith. Voices raised in anger could be heard through the thick walls of the building, causing Pedro to cock his ears but since the words were muffled and unintelligible, he turned his attention inward to browse among his reminiscences.

La Chamberga had the handsomest pair of breasts in all of Seville. It was this and nothing else that explained the success of her tavern. And well did she knew perfectly well how to exploit them with low-cut blouses of red satin open to the level of the nipples. In addition, she affected the soft, broad-brimmed *sombrero chambergo*[2] together with a long black skirt. Consequently, the eyes could settle nowhere but upon that décolletage. Pedro felt very welcome at the tavern since the proprietress permitted a pinch from time to time and extended credit to him for wine and Extremeño sausage, considerations

2. Of the uniform of the regiment of King Charles II.

not given to other guests. Pedro, in turn, was always ready to do her little favors, such as laying out posters and signs listing the prices of wine, by the barrel, pitcher and jug. The day he made mockery of the Archbishop, it was done because she asked him to. It would never have occurred to Pedro on his own. She had brought out a little keg from her private stock—on the house, of course—put it in his lap and began to egg him on, chanting "Up on the table...go on...up, up...!" The sherry was top quality, no question about that. In any case, it soon went to his head, heated his brain, and clouded his judgement, leading thereby to folly. Although the tavern's regular customers were from the neighborhood, plus an occasional irreverent and blasphemous student or two, the majority, carpenters and masons, were sympathetic to the ideas of a certain architect who used a compass as his emblem and was organizing workmen into a brotherhood of universal solidarity; these were matters obviously quite contrary to the Catholic faith and there could very well have been an Inquisition informer among them.

In any case, what happened was La Chamberga's fault. She sat on his lap, stuffing a sausage into his mouth and making graphic allusions to it the while, and then, oh! the wild drinking and carryings on, with her instigating him: "Get up on the table, Pedro! Get up on the table and do the Archbishop!" The two of them laughing like crazy, making fun of that fool of an Archbishop, Pedro stuffing down sausage the while.

Finally, one of the customers yelled, "You shouldn't be eating sausage, it's Friday!" To which Pedro replied, "How could anything that goes in through the mouth and out through the asshole possibly cause harm to the soul?"

That started it for Pedro, now emboldened by the raucous reception that greeted his sally. La Chamberga laughed so hard she wet herself and his trousers. And she then rewarded his wit with another tankard of wine—on the house, of course. When he was deep into it she began goading him again, "Come on, Pedro, up on the table with you, and tell the story of the Archbishop. Let the customers in on it."

"Yes, yes, give us the story!" they all shouted.

Now, well-oiled and unable to resist popular clamor and the urging of La Chamberga, ever the innkeeper, all sense of prudence and decorum fled at the view from the table top of her flushed cheek shaded by the brim of her trademark headpiece and half a luscious breast bulging from her red-satin décolletage. And, as she reached him the tankard of wine to the accompanying shouts of the audience, "The story! The story!" he began telling the tale.

To begin with, he recalled to them the days of the terrible storm they had all just lived through and how in the teeth of the gale and under the pouring rain, the Archbishop had climbed the Giralda tower... Then, in a dramatic pause he drained the tankard, turned his hat around on his head to mimic an archbishop's miter, and continued in a singsong tremolo: "Soooooooooo, the Archbishop cliiiimbed the toooower, and he cliiiiiiiiiiiiiiiimbed the toooooooooooooower with an altar boooooooooooy... Oh, Dolores!"

"Can't understand you," complained the audience.

Pedro then switched from song to straight narration, telling how the Archbishop of Seville had climbed the Giralda tower in his bare feet together with an adolescent altar boy who carried a flagon of holy water and His Eminence's satin slippers. "And he took him to the tower thinking he was a virgin," said Pedro, and all split their sides laughing till tears rolled down their cheeks. And up on the tower, Monseñor, olé!, all night long was spent exorcising downpours and gales and frightening off devils mounted on the clouds. This until, by one of those freaks of nature, the storm moved out on its way to the Guadalquivir, and the Archbishop with the altar boy "whom moooonseñoooor took up to the toooooooooower, and olé!" came down with satisfaction written all over his face to be met by the board of elders of the cathedral who made the announcement that a miracle had taken place and that the cathedral would be lit up with tapers to celebrate the supernatural occurrence.

When his story was over and the listeners had collapsed upon the benches and chairs catching their breath, Pedro, delighted with the ovation from his audience, began to bless the wine barrels and to sprinkle the drunkards with the vintage sherry as he exorcised the devils of continence, prudence, and sobriety from the premises, where pleasure and carousal were ensconced as the closest possible approach to bliss that existed on this earth. By that time, La Chamberga had taken hold of his legs in an effort to pull him down from the table top, warning him, "That's enough of that, Pedro, get down, now!" But Pedro, on the crest of the wave of adulation, carried away by the daring of his heresies, enjoying his every minute as the center of attention, let loose his tongue to denounce the Archbishop as an ignoramus who had no understanding of natural phenomena since storms and tempests were expressions of nature which had nothing to do with the forces of Hell, because there was no such thing as devils mounted on clouds, and the only one actually mounted was the Archbishop himself on the altar boy... La Chamberga desperately tugging at the overwrought drunkard's legs, yelled at him: "Stop it, Pedro, and get down from there! Stop that nonsense, you're going to get us all into trouble with that stupid talk. Come down, now, immediately!"

She could neither shut him up nor get him down for he had now taken to recalling the famous words of Philip II when the Invincible Armada was sunk before reaching the English port. "Is it possible that God sent the Archbishop to do battle against the elements?" After this rhetorical question, he began to skip irrationally from one subject to another. Not knowing what he was talking about anymore, he began to rail against Philip II unconscious of the fact that the listeners had lost interest because Philip II belonged to the distant past and many of them had never even heard of him. This, however, discomfited Pedro not a whit since he felt like a professor at a lectern in a university with absolute freedom of expression, explaining to the students that the Emperor himself had on the wall in his bedroom at El Escorial a daring painting quite on the suspicious side of the sensual and carnal, depicting young men with flowers in the ass, and that such exotic tastes of the Emperor along with his passion for the paintings of the Flemish Bosch had never been investigated by the Inquisition whose duty it was to purify morality even in the palace itself, and who knows whether Philip II in addition to being Emperor of the Spains wasn't also a sodomite and maybe even a converted Jew... Clearly unfair, justice should be equal for all, and the Inquisition should keep an eye on the Bewitched King Charles II at whose deathbed his confessor was switched so that his sins could be concealed—or revealed, which was all the same; and should stupidity and inept governance ever be considered crimes of heresy, if justice were to be done, as ought to be the case, then the Bewitched King should be burned at the stake in time for his soul to be delivered up to the Creator duly tidied and burnished by the flames.

Pedro, delighted at hearing himself talk and say such clever things, had not realized that the silence around him was deafening and that La Chamberga, rooted to the spot, her mouth open, was pale as a ghost. And so, he continued merrily on: "Now that Carlos II has left us, God should take advantage of the situation to give us a new royal family, because I'm sick and tired of those idiotic, degenerate, lantern-jawed Hapsburgs. Enough of the Austrians! Spain should be under more cultivated and spirited people, such as...such as... We should be grateful to God if...if God would favor us with a king... of a king (I was going to say Genovese because of the intrigues of Cardinal Portocarrero who came from Genova, but who on account of being nearsighted sat down on an old barrel upon which some Spanish patriot had written 'Piss For The French')... a French king! Because the Kings of France are much more amusing than the Austrians, who live in a perpetual masquerade ball, wear comical powdered wigs, have voluptuous mistresses, and..."

He was unable to go on because the onlookers' catcalls drowned out his voice. They were outraged at the last part of his diatribe, spat olive pits at him, and yelled, "Get off that table, you traitor! Down with the French!"

La Chamberga emerged from her haze, gave Pedro such a push that he lost his unstable balance and tumbled off the table, disconcerted by the disfavor into which he had fallen, his skinny body sprawling onto a bulky customer who roared furiously, "Damn you, either replace my wine or return my money!"

Without a second thought, La Chamberga, with the aid of several customers, picked him up like a sack of potatoes and threw him out on the street, shouting, "...and don't set foot in this tavern again! You're getting me into trouble, you good-for-nothing, drunken traitor, sonofabitch, and disgrace to the mother that whelped you!"

Pedro returned home thoroughly confused, torn between the euphoria of his initial success and the final ridicule, seeking a middle ground between self-satisfaction and humiliation, drunk as a lord, furious at having to live in Seville rather than London or

Paris—Seville, center of tradesmen, politicians, thieves, and ruffians, bridge to a better life in America for those without hope, and obligatory way station for those returning to the Old World without knowing which was worse.

On reaching the Dominican convent, he stopped at the gate and shouted at the top of his lungs that he wanted to see the inseminator nun. The story of the inseminator nun was as racy as that of the Archbishop, if not more so. It circulated in the halls of the universities, markets, reception rooms of the palace, the Chamber of Commerce, the notarial offices, and wherever more than two persons gathered to comment on the case of the nun inseminated by the Holy Ghost, according to the Mother Superior of the convent and the Archbishop himself who was seeking to promote any miracle in which he could play a role of some consequence. However, the Inquisition, remote from poetic metaphor, found that the matter smelled suspicious and stuck its prosaic nose into the cloister. And so, it became known that the Holy Ghost had become incarnated in another nun with hair on the chest and a regulation cock that hung in its proper place, who had infiltrated the sacrosanct premises by what satanic subterfuge nobody knew. The pregnant nun gave birth to a healthy and robust infant who was turned over to the authorities, the mother was confined to an enclosed convent, and the father locked up in a secret Inquisition prison for having committed the heresy of passing himself off as the dove of the Holy Trinity. Nobody answered Pedro's summons and so he left and went staggering on his way thinking that there was much to be learned regarding monastic heterodoxies. He arrived home not knowing when or how and whether the bed was his or if it belonged to a Dominican nun. The following day when, despite a dreadful headache, he was able to get up, he went to the University where Servando took him aside and upbraided him for his imprudent behavior. A student who was present at the tavern the night before had made known the deplorable incident of the revelation about the Archbishop and the altar boy, and all the rest about Philip II and King Charles the Bewitched, and Pedro's foolish act could have long-lasting consequences because—it is also known, he said, that the Archbishop had caught cold climbing the Giralda barefooted and that people were commenting that there weren't handkerchiefs enough to sop up the flood of Archiepiscopal mucus.

Servando added that while the anecdote as told by Pedro was certainly amusing, he had nevertheless stepped over the line with his mockery, and that the security of his mission concerning the illegal traffic in banned books precluded indulgence in carousals and drinking sprees and the possibility of attendant indiscretion. He then ordered him to turn over to him immediately the proofs of the Spinoza book he had been correcting and advised him that he would give him no further work until he had demonstrated his ability to stop drinking.

Pedro went home ashamed and repentant, gathered up the pages, and returned them to Servando. He locked himself in for the next several days, humiliated and admitting that his imprudence deserved expulsion from the organization. For that reason he was unaware when the Archbishop died of galloping pneumonia. Also, his having delivered the Spinoza proofs to Servando when he did turned out to have been a great stroke of luck for when the Inquisition arrested him the first night he went out to beg La Chamberga's pardon, the only mildly incriminating material he had at home was a lampoon lent to him by Servando that was written by an anonymous author a hundred years ago bearing the provocative title *"On the Perverse Order Given His Class by Francisco de Vittoria to Take Notes of His Lectures as a Result of which His Students Became Increasingly Dull-Witted and Forgetful."* Servando had given it to Pedro so that he would learn to think as a rational person and not allow himself to be seduced by the sluggardly custom of copying like a monkey.

Shortly thereafter, with a few pesetas in his pocket, papers under a fictitious name, and a letter of recommendation from his Franciscan teacher to his brothers of the Order, Pedro disembarked in Veracruz after a three months' voyage, a dreadful experience that left its mark on him for life. He continued on his way overland as far as the city of Cartago where he was now to be found seated on the bottom step of the stairway to the City Hall, exactly two steps below where Bárbara Lorenzana, the black woman with the wry neck and body like a palm tree hidden under a burlap sack had been standing.

From where he sat, he had a clear view of the notice board on the door of the church to which was affixed the threat of shunned excommunication. Suddenly, there was a loud sound of a blow on wood, the door of the City hall opened, and out stepped the man with the clipped mustache and sardonic expression he had seen leaning on the railing watching the slave auction. Banging his heels with rage he ran downstairs two steps at a time and without a glance at Pedro stamped across the main square to disappear inside a big seigniorial house on its west side. Obviously, he was the official with whom the Governor had been closeted. Thirtyish, hair cut short, shoulders slightly stooped, dressed all in black, tall boots and stylish trousers, he gave the impression of a crow.

It was the first and only time that Pedro saw Blas González Coronel, Deputy Director of the Royal Bank, in a rage; as time went by he was to learn that this man could vent his anger in very different but more effective ways.

The mulatto, Lázaro de Robles came out to summon him. He jumped to his feet and accompanied him to the office where His Honor, Governor Serrano de Reina, would be receiving him. As he crossed the threshold, he stepped aside to allow Captain Fajardo to pass and heard him say as he went by: "Blas González is very headstrong. He refuses to admit that things in this province cannot be done in a straightforward manner." A pleasant half-light filled the room, in the center of which was a massive table with half a dozen chairs around it; against one wall stood a cupboard jammed with papers, and on the opposite wall alongside the window a stained, dust-covered desk. There was a portrait in the rear next to the Spanish flag, its likeness unmistakable because of the disproportionate size of the jaw which the painter, despite his best efforts, had been unable to disguise. The Bewitched King was observing him as he entered with the same imbecilic expression as in all his portraits (and in real life, too according to all who had had the honor of seeing him in person). Below the painting, on a heavy wooden armchair with a leather back and seat sat the Governor in an outlandish green silk dress coat with shiny silver buttons. He was cleaning his nails with the point of his ceremonial sword. Middle-aged, he had the air of a retired soldier, small shrewd eyes, and a peevish expression.

"Good day, Your Lordship," Pedro greeted him ingratiatingly, as he handed him his papers. The Governor laid his sword aside on the table, took the papers, glanced at them perfunctorily, and asked: "Don Pedro de la Baranda, can you write a good hand, rapidly and neatly? I have no need for a lawyer but I can use a scribe with a good memory. There is no lack of people in this city who know how to write, but they have jobs in business or farming. The regular official scribe is always in poor health and very sick right now."

"My father gave me a good education, Your Honor. The pen and I do well together."

"There's no more to be said, then. You may begin work tomorrow, Monday, at 9 o'clock in the morning. Your desk is over there. What we're lacking is ink. It will be up to you to procure it."

The Governor rose, thrust his sword into his belt, came out from behind the table, and walked towards the door. He was wearing brown velvet trousers, high-heeled shoes, and red stockings that bulged out over his heavy calves. Feeling as though he were at a carnival, Pedro was gratified that the Governor's choice of clothing should be in such sharp contrast with the funereal sobriety of customary Spanish dress.

Out in the square again, Pedro was not sure that he was happy about the result of his interview. True, he had work but there was no indication as to salary or conditions. However, the hot sun was at the zenith in a bright blue sky and the square's greenery shone with the brilliance of Governor Serrano's picturesque silk dress coat. The doors of the church with the notice of excommunications had remained open. Seeking shade and a place to reflect quietly, he entered and took a seat in the last row of benches of the empty nave at the same time that a pair of pious old biddies, bundled up to noses that had sniffed the smoke of a million candles, turned their eyes in Pedro's direction as they made their way out. There was a small chest with two big locks next to the rough carved stone of the holy-water fount. Massive redwood columns supported a ceiling of broad planks running from one plain whitewashed wall to another on which there were boards that had a Way of the Cross painted on them. Several statues decorated with fake tinsel observed it, their glass eyes staring as though nothing was escaping their vigilant surveillance.

Uncomfortable at the feeling of the officious eyes of the saints upon him, Pedro left the church, putting off reflection to a later time. He hurried along the street because he was hungry and had just remembered that meals at the monastery were very early. He walked towards the south, leaving behind him the square, the city hall, and the great mountain with its cap of clouds. He met the tireless rooster flapping his wings over his hens, the pigs snuffling about in the malodorous drainage ditches, and buzzards scavenging the garbage flung from windows. Refusing to step on the manure and other filth in his torn boots, he decided to seek out a cobbler the very next day and ask him to repair them on credit. With his first salary he would buy himself a shirt, trousers, a new jacket, stockings, and, of course, there was no lack of other things upon which to spend the money. He had heard that some neighbors had shops in their homes where anything from a hoe to a silk handkerchief could be bought. It was not long before Pedro discovered why Cartago's wealthy citizens dressed in bright colors, satins of Florence, lace of Milan, Breton blouses, French velvets, Chinese silks, and Manila shawls, and also why so many private homes became veritable warehouses crammed with all manner of useful and useless goods available from pirate vessels.

Eager to spend the money he had not yet earned, Pedro set out for the monastery, his steps hastened by the odor of broiled meat that sharpened the edge on his appetite even more. On the way, he nearly ran into a tall, well-built young man who was coming out of an open doorway in a thick stone and plaster wall. He was quite a handsome fellow with a Roman nose and unusual bright red hair, arrogant in his bearing as he strode by unconcerned about his velvet coat, fitted with gold buttons and a captain's insignia, getting spattered with mud. He was José de Casasola y Córdoba, an illustrious nobody possessed of a most audacious ambition, unwavering in its tenacity, which soon would bring him high position in the military and the administrative hierarchy and the promise of a brilliant future not dreamed attainable even by him at this time. Pedro had no idea then who that young man could be, redheaded as an Irishman, his intense pallor and black eyebrows contrasting so vividly.

He watched him as he put his fingers to his mouth and whistled shrilly. A mulatto boy appeared at the south corner leading an exceptionally beautiful chestnut horse, a pure-blooded Arab with a rebellious head, powerful hindquarters, and delicate legs. The mulatto could barely hang on to the restive animal's bridle as the redhead seized the reins, his arms lengthening out of all proportion in so doing, giving the disturbing impression of an ape attempting to ride horseback. But no, his owner was not trying to mount but only to overcome the animal's resistance and force him to go through the doorway in the stone wall. Man and beast each fought to impose his will upon the other, the horse rearing and dragging the man along despite being lashed by a rawhide quirt which subdued him only momentarily. Though anxious to be on his way Pedro's curiosity got the better of him, and he paused to look through the gateway.

He saw a broad patio of orange trees, Andalusian-style, with a carriage in the rear, and a young woman in Morocco slippers approaching swiftly over the cobblestones. He stepped aside to let her pass but the woman remained at the door to watch the battle of wills. She was slim, of medium height, and wore a satin dress picked out in silver and gold, a plush shawl lined with scarlet taffeta over her shoulders, and a small beaver hat with silken ribbons atop a crown of blond curls. The chestnut was now kicking furiously sending up clods of mud. The startled woman, on lifting the hem of her skirt, showed her white silk stockings and, in turning to take refuge behind the wall, exposed, with a swish and a swirl, the turmoil of her linen and lace lingerie. Pedro, disconcerted by the blinding sunlight, was unsure whether the sight he had seen was an optical illusion or whether such a lovely, exquisitely dressed woman was really to be found in this remote rural setting. The horse, finally vanquished, gave up the struggle and let his owner and the groom lead him through the doorway. The door shut behind them and Pedro continued on his way still dazzled by the vision of the incongruous beauty's intimacies and the small, bejeweled hand holding up her skirt.

The brother doorkeeper, a grouchy, rheumatic old fellow, opened the door of the monastery, grumbling at him about guests who do not respect the institution's schedules.

There were a few friars, actually four, in the refectory finishing their meal and conversing animatedly under the tolerant eye of the Superior who also joined freely in the chatting as he reached into a big bowl filled with mangoes in the center of the table, a fruit that tasted to Pedro like a cross between peach and melon and which left greedy eaters smeared from head to foot. He sat down at his place where a clay plate and wooden spoon were set and waited for the elderly black cook to bring out the stew. This was one of her few duties for she was so old that she often mistook sugar for salt thereby making the roast beef and potatoes come out tasting like frogs'-legs marmalade. She had already been declared superfluous and would be farmed out to an outlying parish to serve the clerics there in light duties until her death. As far as Pedro could see, the followers of Saint Francis in the city of Cartago had spared themselves the task of cooking and left it in the more capable hands of women, which had caused tongues to wag. When he first arrived at the monastery, Pedro heard the brother doorkeeper, a *criollo*[3] whose entire life had been spent opening and closing a door, declare that putting black women into the kitchen was tantamount to introducing the devil himself into the holy residence.

As Pedro spooned up the soup with cabbage leaves and succulent chunks of beef swimming in it, he listened desultorily to the friars' table talk. One was saying, "Rebullida was put out of the monastery because his company was unbearable." Another offered the opinion that, "Father Pablo de Rebullida has the balls to survive in this God-forsaken land of savages!" "Rubbish!" said the first, "Rebullida is a coward for he believes in arms having the sole power of persuasion." And he went on, "Where did you ever hear of having to preach the holy gospel over pistol shots and musket fire?" To which the other replied, sucking greedily on the pit of the mango he had just devoured, his mouth stained yellow with the delectable juice, "If love doesn't work...try fear, then."

The conversation languished. Friar Lorenzo who had kept silent, was shooing away flies that were buzzing around the plates. They flew off towards the flame of a candle set before the effigy of Saint Francis on the wall, close beside that of an anonymous monk whose fleshless hands rested on a skull hanging from a cord around his neck, a sort of mystical Hamlet given over to deep necrophiliac introspection. The wall opposite held a

---

3. Person of Spanish blood born in America.

pleasant painting of the Child Virgin Mary seated upon Saint Anne's ample lap, both framed in a profuse entangled orgy of gilt volutes and arabesques. The flies, after singeing their wings in the flame of Saint Francis's candle, returned to their jurisdiction of the mango bowl.

Lorenzo was irritated. "Where's that black girl I bought? If she's off loafing, she'd better get busy swatting flies."

"You didn't acquire her for purposes of that nature," observed the Superior in annoyance.

A thin little adolescent friar who had not opened his mouth since Pedro arrived at the table choked and the mango pit he was sucking fell to the floor. The thud seemed simultaneously to wrench an explosion of hilarity from the lad. His apple-pink cheeks puffed out like bellows, and the guffaw that burst from him bounced off the table and irreverently onto Saint Anne's volutes to splash over the sinister prelate with the skull. The other monks, infected by the laugh, were unable to contain themselves and filled the refectory with their impious howls until the Superior rose to his feet and put down the rebellion. One by one, the friars shuffled out except for Pedro and the youth who had touched off the outburst and, now, in shame, hid his hands in the enormous sleeves of his ill-fitting, oversize cassock.

"You, Juan de las Alas, may go also," scolded the Superior, "Retire to your room and meditate upon prudence and discretion and do not come out until you have purged your heart of moral impropriety."

The youth slunk out, ears flaming, and Pedro, too, rose to go, but the Superior detained him. "Directing this house is a mission for the saints, and I am only a poor sinner from Burgos," he began. "My father had a bakery there and brought me up strictly. I know about bread and about prayers but must admit that I cannot cope with the direction of this monastery of rascals. What can one expect of these mestizo *criollos*? And the example the Spaniards set does not help, no, does not help... Some more, some less, they all take advantage of religious celebrations to commit improprieties... The papal nuncio is an east mark who looks the other way and pretends not to be aware that his priests, instead of shepherding souls, are devoting themselves to card-playing and dice and making advances to women in the confessional... He makes no effort to defend the faith and is satisfied with punishing wrongdoing by impounding cows and mules... Alas! What these colonies lack is—how can I say it?—Spanish steadfastness...will power, integrity, spiritual devotion, yes, spiritual devotion. Here, even the most upright wilt because of the races less blessed with courage and daring. Indians and blacks pollute the Hispanic lineage with their pernicious characteristics; slothful mestizos and mulattos of dubious moral stability."

Drained by his tirade, he brushed out a few crumbs of white bread that had got trapped in his beard.

"This life is hard for an old Christian like me... Even our holy father Saint Francis could understand what it means to be abandoned by Catholics who prefer a dark-skinned Virgin simply because their processions and worship lend themselves to licentiousness at a level impossible for a good Christian to imagine. Besides, nobody can be certain that this Virgin really appeared to a young Indian woman or if it was the priest at the time who pretended that she had really seen the image that she worshipped... In short, I am not without worries. The Recollets[4] and friar Pablo de Rebullida, in particular, challenge doctrines seek to monopolize the huge region of Talamanca which contains some seven thousand unbaptized Indians. I am too late myself in repenting! I'm very much afraid that the black girl with the wry neck that Lorenzo bought at the auction is going to cause me trouble!" He ended with a sigh and went off to take his siesta.

Understanding nothing, Pedro left the room to walk in the hallway that led to the few cells and an attempt at a garden where somebody had planted roses, with meager results. The poor plants were surviving largely to serve as a feast for plant lice and ants, a battlefield on which a red bud occasionally won out, lost in the midst of disaster. He drew up a plan for his life. Before anything, he would keep himself at a point equidistant from all problems, shut his eyes, and stay out of trouble. His watchword would be like that of the dog playing dead: be all ears. He would never set foot in the kitchen for fear that some evil-minded person would accuse him of having designs on the black girl with the wry neck.

---

4. A sect of Franciscans within the order who accept nothing but the most austere, total dedication to worship.

And the moment a favorable situation presented itself he would take off for another spot in the Indies where life offered greater attractions and where he could find some way of continuing his education.

For the time being he felt unthreatened. The Superior had mentioned that the Inquisition in Cartago was largely concerned with impounding the property of prisoners and Pedro possessed nothing impoundable, not even a respectable pair of boots, which was precisely his immediate and most pressing concern. He had asked the Superior to recommend a cobbler and was informed with some pride that there was in the city an abundance of capable weavers, tailors, carpenters, blacksmiths, potters, silversmiths, and dyers, to say nothing of fine shoemakers, as well as rough and ready cobblers. And so, until such time as he could afford a new pair Pedro intended to look up one of the latter kind and request that he wait to be paid till Pedro received his first week's salary.

Having checked his bed and straw mattress for tarantulas, he nodded off with satisfaction, thinking that having succeeded in landing a job so quickly, he might also be able to dream up a way to meet the beautiful girl with the lace petticoats.

Sick and tired of seeing his big toe poking out of the toe of his boot, he was out and at the cobbler's shop early the next morning. Poking his head in at the doorway, he saw the maestro at his bench in the midst of an indescribable clutter of sandals, shoemaker's knife in hand cutting into a hide. It was the same pug-nosed man he had seen in the atrium of the church who had bought the boy in order to remove the spike from his leg.

* * *

I believe I was the first person in the city who really paid any attention to the fellow. I was cutting out a sole when I saw him come in and recognized him immediately. I'd seen him in the atrium during the slave auction, and one didn't have to be really sharp to notice that he was a very scared individual beneath his growth of beard and dirty clothing, which made him look like a tramp and not to be trusted. But I don't let surface impressions influence me. I have a gift for reading character and that one seemed to me to be a decent person.

"Come in and have a seat," I said, motioning to him with my knife. He took some lady's slippers off the chair and sat. "I saw you yesterday in the square. Where are you from?" Because he had the smell of someone on the run, I quickly introduced myself before he could answer so he would feel at home and not have to give me some cock-and-bull story. "They call me 'Smiles,'" I told him, "because I'm such a gloomy cuss."

He was distrustful. I was hoping to squeeze a little smile out of the fellow, at least. How old could he be? Judging from his hair—curly Moorish on his head and lank in his Christian beard—I figured him for a couple of years younger than me, and I had just turned twenty-seven.

"I'm a master shoemaker," I explained, "but one without a single apprentice. Lázaro de Robles's brother takes them all for himself. Family privilege, I guess. Lázaro is Serrano's right-hand man and runs the contraband business for him, so he owes Lázaro a lot of favors."

He sat down, pulled off a boot that was an authentic disaster and said that his name was Pedro de la Baranda. I see a lot of outsiders over at The Mother of Visitors. The mule drivers on their way to Panama, the peddlers coming from Panama, all stop for a bite to eat and a little recreation, decent folks some, and the majority the other kind, but never one like this. "How long you been in our fair land?" I asked. "In Cartago, you mean?" he answered. "Yes, where else would I be meaning?" I retorted. "Three days," he told me.

I took the boot and gave it a close look, as I do with all my work. "I'll have it for you tomorrow, like new," I told him. "No," he objected, "I need it right away. I have to report in by nine o'clock at the city hall, and I have no other shoes." Ah!—I said to myself—then this has to be the new scribe they say Serrano just took on. I could see he had soft hands, not cut out for man's work, which I take to be soldiering and farming or the like, and my own. And so I figured he must be sitting on interesting stuff, and I liked that. Besides, I must have cottoned to him because I'm a no-nose and he's a big-nose. I also got the message that his pockets were empty and that he would be asking to pay me later (in cocoa beans, I expect). Seems like he read my mind because he hurried up to let me know he was living at the monastery and would be staying on as their bookkeeper. "You know," I told him, "it so happens I fix their sandals for the brothers."

And I set to work on that sorry piece of footwear, putting in a reinforcement, not much to look at, but good and strong. I had a pair of French boots stuck away under my bench, suede. I'd got them as a bargain, confiscated from a smuggler who came from Matina. You couldn't help seeing they were contraband, so Serrano confiscated them and disappeared the merchandise into his son Bruno's hands, who sold them out of his house, which was how I got them. But I didn't offer those boots to the *gachupín*[5] because he obviously couldn't pay. So I settled for mending his old ones, figuring he'd settle up one day. I noted some Andalusian influence in him from the way he softened his z's, but not as much as I do since many generations before me were born in Cartago. He asked me how I'd pulled the spike out of the boy's leg and what happened to him. I explained that I do that kind of thing with pincers and then treat the wound with herbs and stanch the hemorrhage with a plug made of spider webs. I told him that Doña Mariana de Echeverría—the highest-caste woman in these parts, being a descendant on the Retes side of the upper-class courtier Juan Vásquez de Coronado—gave me a good fee, and that was it. After I did the surgery she took the little black fellow away with her. She called him José Canela and told me that he was a present for her daughter Agueda, who married Captain José Casasola y Córdoba a short while ago.

I took to the practice of medicine because that is my true profession. I do shoemaking for the simple reason that I am not authorized nor have I any title to act as a doctor. Nevertheless, a lot of people call on me, and I am happy to take care of them in exchange for a chicken, a suckling pig, a turkey or whatever. As I poked my needle and thread through the old holes that had been left from before, I warned him to have a care with the plagues and diseases that strike this province from time to time. He made an anguished face when I told him that the pox wiped out the whole town of Ujarrás a short time ago, and that there were many

5. Pejorative name for a Spaniard.

deaths from consumption that makes the lungs fill up with blood
blisters and at the same time brings on coughing fits so bad that
the person's eyes nearly pop out, and then ends up settling in his
bones until he is left dried up and yellow. Then I told him about
'pinta' in which white, coffee-colored, red, or violet spots break
out all over the skin, and the purple disease that causes lumps to
form under the scalp and the person goes blind, and bloody
diarrhea and rabies. I also cautioned him to not to lie with the
Indian women because they say that it leads to damage of the
balls worse than the French disease. And, as I tied off my thread,
I warned him to beware of lepers... When I glanced up at him, I
saw that his face was absolutely green. So, I took out a wineskin I
always keep under my bench, finances permitting, and held it out
to him, saying, "There's nothing better than wine for preventing
disease."

He took a long swig and I could see that my diagnosis was
right because he perked right up, put on the mended boot, passed
me the other one, and asked for the city doctor. Then I explained
to him that we didn't have a proper doctor but that I knew about
curing sicknesses, that I was also a barber and if he wished I could
trim his beard when I finished with his boots. He liked the idea,
and after I did the second boot, I trimmed his beard with my
same shoemaker's knife. Then I explained that in cases of fever
apparently induced by fits of rage I use red wine with orange and
cinnamon; to treat wounds, washing with wine and aloe leaves;
for newborns, wine with garlic, onion, and lemon; for cold urine
and disturbances of the bladder in general, very hot wine with
ground up earthworms and a few drops of green-banana vinegar.
Before he could interrupt me, because I was cutting off his entire
beard to see what type of person appeared underneath so I could
withdraw my confidence in time if I didn't like his looks, I let go
my whole catalogue of mystical pharmacopoeia at him: Saint
Agueda for chest pains; Saint Apolonia for the teeth; Saint
Raymond for mothers in labor; Saint Lucia for the eyes; Saint
Erasmus for the abdomen; Saint Acacio for headaches. I finished
with his beard and continued to work on the mop on his head as
I talked of the pharmacopoeia of the brothers of the monastery
who have medicines that are difficult to obtain, such as sweet
mercury for the French disease; narwhal water and balsam of

Persia for toothache and for the gums, green vitriol macerated under heat, bile, tartaric acid salt, and Armenian clay. "As far as I'm concerned," I told him when the floor was covered with Arab hair, "the best thing for teeth pitted with cavities is massages with white excrement of black dog while reciting the following prayer:

> By the star of Venus and the rising sun,
> by the Holy Sacrament and the setting one
> let pain of molar or incisor be undone."

I brushed off his shoulder and swept up the hair from the floor. His face was cleared; he had a long nose and lively eyes. He was certainly not a good-looking fellow, not the kind that drives the ladies mad. I would say that he had a rather homely but honest face. Without the beard and long hair he no longer looked like a pirate, and I was glad I left him a few hairs on his face to soften the impact. As I suspected, he told me he would pay me when he collected his first salary. I told him to come back any time he felt like it, that I knew everything that went on in the city, and that he should watch his step because this town was a gathering place for all the scoundrels of the Iberian Peninsula who couldn't make it in other places: down-and-out soldiers, priests defrocked for who knows for what reason? And to be on guard especially with members of the city council and Blas González, the Deputy Director of the Royal Bank, who was shrewd as a Jesuit and, to make matters worse, close to the Holy See. He went off in good shape, making a great effort not to lose heart. Feminine hands notwithstanding, he had balls. I was sorry for him.

*Of the passion that possesses the
scribe, and of the strange life led by
the people of Cartago*

It was late in the year 1700 (after Pedro had been working at the
city hall for some months) that the news arrived of the death of
Charles II, the Bewitched King, but with no indication of who his
successor would be. Governor Serrano had his portrait taken
down, leaving the Spanish flag behind, orphaned and solitary, the
faded rectangle alongside it acting as an insistent question mark
on the wall. Charles II, said to have been bewitched by the draft
of chocolate with brains of a dead man stirred into it, had left the
throne vacant and, incompetent as he was to rule or procreate,
provided in his will—as scandalized rumor had it—that the Sun
King, Louis XIV of France, should decide succession to the
Spanish crown. The news finally arrived that the new king of
Spain was not an Austrian—as had been traditionally the case
since Joan the Mad married Philip the Handsome—but Philip V,
grandson of the Sun King, a Bourbon, a Frenchman, who had
taken upon himself the nickname of "The Bold" in order to
establish that he had absolutely no intention of allowing the
throne to be snatched out from under him, as the Archduke of
Austria was already planning to do. Confusion reigned and in the
bitter debate which followed, people chose sides, some favoring
the Bourbon, others the Austrian, until everyone realized that it
was a no-win situation; who knew how long the Bourbon could
last as King? And if he were deposed, what were the chances for
the Austrian?

From the very first day that Pedro sat down at his desk,

Lázaro de Robles made no effort to hide his animosity, though the Spaniard had done nothing to deserve it—had not put the evil eye on him and feigned only cordiality, for Lázaro was Governor Serrano's confidential employee. Of the two *regidores*[6] at the time, the elderly Nicolás de Céspedes showed a certain regard for him and the other, only indifference. The rest of the public posts were vacant: there were no town clerk, treasurer or magistrate, nor the three *regidores* necessary to elect them. Consequently, council meetings were infrequent, peculiar, and of very little interest because in view of the situation there was no administrative capability to settle any business and the city was left to its own devices, to say nothing of what was happening to the fields in the valley, and the ports on the two coasts, La Caldera on the southern sea, and Matina on the sea to the north. Blás González, who collected tribute from the Indians of the neighboring villages and went about constantly grumbling that the Royal Bank was empty, attended the city council regularly, as did José de Casasola y Córdoba, the man who was struggling with his horse the day the beautiful woman in her lace petticoat dazzled Pedro. The fact that Blas González Coronel was a native of Seville, as well as an officer of the Inquisition, was reason enough for Pedro to avoid him, besides which he wore a nasty little mustache and a sneer on his face that resembled a fox's, and one never had a clue as to what he was really thinking.

Blas González and José de Casasola owned cacao plantations in Matina. So did everybody else in central Matina. "There's more to those beans than meets the eye," Pedro thought. "It must have been the chocolate from those same beans that fouled up the Bewitched King's brains and now they're going to foul me up." Since the coffers of the Royal Bank were empty, wages were being paid in cacao. Sacks of it at a price of one hundred beans for one peso, were piling up in the armory. On his next payday, Pedro had to haul his salary away in a heavy bag and stuff it under his bed where the cockroach infestation became even worse because the botanical medium of exchange attracted the greedy bugs in unbelievable swarms. When he wanted to buy soap or a candle he had to separate the bugs from the seeds and make sure that

6. City council members.

the ones he was going to pay with were good and dry or the shopkeeper would not accept them. Unfortunately, they turned damp and half-rotten and so the wealth accumulating under the bed was rapidly devalued and by the middle of the month Pedro had to throw out half his hoard because he could no longer put up with the stench of fermentation.

Pedro hated cacao, but thanks to it he made friends with the shoemaker, a friendship that sustained him during his stay in the city. When he received his wages in cacao, he brought a bag of seeds to pay the shoemaker, called Smiles, who roared with laughter and refused to accept them because he said he was sick and tired of chocolate, morning, noon, and night. Wine or spirits were his indulgence, and they could be had only for hard currency. However, spirits were dispensed for cacao at The Mother of Visitor's place. That was a blessing. When he wanted to order a new jacket, the tailor also refused to accept the seeds. The shoemaker felt sorry for him and made him one out of leather, which was destined not to last as long as anticipated, but that was a matter of fate and not Pedro's fault. After the gift of the jacket he had no choice but to reciprocate by giving Smiles his friendship and so it was "you scratch my back and I scratch yours," the natural order of things.

During all the rest of that year and into the next, Pedro's was the anonymous hand that wrote birth and death certificates, wills, complaints, a garnishment or two, a few confiscations, and a huge number of routine notices which were then signed by the scribe José de Prado, gravely ill and bedridden at the time, suffering from seizures and various illnesses which did not prevent his receiving his salary in pure silver coinage. Pedro never signed anything (for which reason his name did not appear on any document), nor did he complain on that score, anonymity being the most convenient status for him. Instead, despite working like an ox, taking his pay in cacao beans, and seeing his work signed by somebody else, he tried to do the best job possible so there would be no complaints about him. The slogan he had invented for himself was "undercover efficiency," which fit neatly with the old one of "play dead dog: be all ears." As a matter of fact, all were quite satisfied with this obliging, discreet scribe whose rapid, neat, and elegant penmanship was unmatched in the city except for that of Blas González, who had the finicky, frilly, elaborate handwriting of one who had received a lengthy, leisurely education and could indulge himself in spending ten minutes over the complex flourish of his signature. When a sudden stroke left the scribe José de Prado paralyzed, Pedro had to chase down witnesses in a search of signatures that resembled grapevine tendrils. It was he who came up with the expression "hang your grapevine on the line," which later became a widespread popular saying.

Pedro made his own ink according to a secret recipe given to him by the shoemaker, who had it from an old Indian of the village of San Juan de Herrera where it was originally used in dyeing cloth. Some 400 Indians lived there, from whose ranks came the carriers and firewood, the drummers who accompanied the town criers, and the town criers themselves. There was one crier named Diego Malaventura who was popular because of his powerful voice. Pedro frequently sought him out when an announcement had to be made, such as one regarding an official post persons would want to bid on. That was the case when Blas González was aiming to head the Holy Brotherhood, to be a voting member of the city council, and to obtain the authority to collect fines in the countryside. This coincided with Captain José de Casasola y Córdoba's ambition to become *regidor* and chief standard-bearer.

Pedro looked up Diego Malaventura who, standing in the corridor of the city hall after six o'clock in the afternoon, made the announcement in a faint tone belying his sonorous voice: "Five hundred pesos is offered for the post of chief standard bearer and councilman of this city, payable over three years." And so, he repeated this cry in a low voice for the regulation thirty days. This done, the populace having been duly informed of the auction, and the danger that someone else might be interested in the jobs passed, the announcement was discontinued and the official and legal document, prepared by Pedro, was sent to Guatemala City, the seat of the higher government, for bureaucratic processing.

Pedro disliked the San Juan de Herrera Indians. Humble, servile, they were governed by venal officials who strove to please the Spaniards. Pedro developed an aversion towards them either because he could not abide suffering or because those Indians were so submissive. He was deeply disturbed by their sullenness, their sadness, silence, and their mute rancor camouflaged as servility. He hated the underhanded, sly manner of the Indians, their shifty glances, and their way of never showing their feelings. Particularly irritating to him were the women, small, with short chunky legs, apparently without capacity for love or pleasure, forever hunched over their *metates* grinding corn, unfit even for giving birth, the few children born in San Juan de Herrera coming into the world as downcast as their mothers. When the problem of the corn arose, Pedro saw Indian women standing for the first time because they had no corn to grind. A blight had dried up the cornfields and the Indians were without food. This was of little concern to the Spaniards for they had their wheat fields and bread. And time passed without anybody doing anything about the starvation in San Juan de Herrera and the neighboring Indian villages of the valley until the bread gave out because the slaves were stealing the flour from the storerooms of their masters to sell in the Indian villages. One day, as he was climbing the city hall stairs, Blas González remarked with a touch of bitterness in his voice that he had just breakfasted on yucca pancakes because there was no flour at his house. The wheat fields were simply gone and the people came to complain of the apathy of the authorities who made no effort to deal with the problem. If things continued that way they would be forced to eat wild roots; and who knew then what blights this would give rise to? Serrano, who preferred a good beefsteak to any other type of food paid no attention to the complainants until Father Angulo—the same who had a ringlet at each temple—appeared one day reeking to high heaven of French perfume to grouse about his cook having concocted a disgusting dish of yam cakes fried in lard that caused him a dreadful bellyache, and to demand that immediate steps be taken to remedy the scarcity of corn so that the wheat fields could serve their real owners. "In this city," he said, "the slaves eat bread and the masters eat shit which, obviously, is a reversal of the natural order of things."

This was a lie, however, for the slaves had not eaten the flour, rather they had bartered it with the Indians for drums, ocarinas, and other musical instruments. And so, the worse the lack of bread in the city the louder was the music-making of the blacks at twilight who accompanied the native ocarinas with lutes and rebecs and sad songs that turned smiles melancholy and damped the high spirits in The Mother of Travelers gaming house.

Nor was there bread on the monastery table.

Nor tortillas or rolls in any house. Serrano tried to placate the angry people by saying that man does not live by bread alone. Though the phrase came from the Bible, it was hissed anyway by the priest Angulo, an officer of the Inquisition, who countered, 'Give us our daily bread but now...yucca and yams are not fit food for a Christian.'

The city council met and although the posts on which Casasola and Blas González had bid had not yet been confirmed by Guatemala City, it was taken for granted that they were appointed. That being the case, a minimum of five persons met to settle the question: Serrano, the two *regidores*, Blas González and José de Casasola plus Angulo, the priest who put his oar in with the pretext of feeding the poor. The Superior of the monastery could have attended the meeting as well but deemed it politic to leave acute problems for others to solve. He then busied himself in organizing a cycle of prayers in the San Francisco church as a move to wean away followers of the dark-skinned Virgen de los Angeles.

After a thoroughgoing analysis of the situation, the Governor, the Church, and the city council reached a diagnosis that corn grew better and faster in the region than wheat and so it was essential to organize emergency corn patches as rapidly as possible. And—unavoidably—to eat tortillas until such time as the wheat fields returned to normal. This appeared to end the problem but, actually, it was just the beginning. The matter of who would cultivate the cornfields remained unsettled as the Indians spent their hours and days carrying water and firewood for the Spaniards because there weren't enough slaves, and, anyway, those blacks were a bunch of lazy loafers—they said— who cared about nothing except singing, dancing, and other frivolities. Besides, they were the ones sent off to work in the unhealthy climate of the Matina cacao plantations where there were swamps and swarms of mosquitoes which only they could cope with. Finally, the decision was taken to send the militiamen of the Mulatto Regiment to take over the corn fields so that the

Indians could continue with their usual tasks. However, the militiamen protested, saying that they could not neglect their small farms because they lived off them, nor the two cows that supplied their children with milk, nor the mule with which they fetched firewood for their homes and the thatch for their roofs. Serrano disagreed, saying that the military jurisdiction prohibited using militia as labor for tasks unrelated to military operations. While the question was being settled as to who should cultivate the cornfields, time went by without tortillas and without bread. When it was decided to make a foray into the Talamanca mountains and capture wild Indians for the purpose, Father Fray Pablo de Rebullida and Fray José de San José had arrived to make conversions to Christianity there and nobody dared speak of the matter because the two priests had convinced the Supreme Governor of Guatemala to strictly forbid the Spaniards seizing Indians from Talamanca for their personal use.

Hands to work the cornfields were nowhere to be had. Pedro was convinced that the solution lay in the valley Indians taking over the task of cultivation while the Spaniards fetched their own water and cut their own wood, but he was careful to keep the idea to himself, for it was beneath an hidalgo's dignity to soil his hands with plebeian duties.

The debate was still going on in the city council when, all at once, there was an invasion of Indian women on the streets going door to door offering packets of corn tortillas wrapped in banana leaves, thick and delicious, warm and fragrant from their clay griddles. It then came out that when the corn had dried up and rotted, the Indian women who had cat's eyes would go out at night and poke into the ground with their sharp-pointed digging sticks to plant the sound kernels they had managed to salvage from the blight. Without further ado, closemouthed and tenacious, they tended the growing plants, harvested the ears of corn, and went out to barter the tortillas for used clothing, iron utensils, and other articles impossible for them, in their abject poverty, to possess.

In a brilliant Sunday sermon, the Superior of the monastery made the determination that Saint Francis had miraculously caused the corn to grow so that the lilies of the field and the birdies of the wood should have no concern, for the Lord provides.

And the catechism priest of Ujarrás reported, via a sweaty, dust-covered archangel who galloped all the way to Cartago in the early hours of morning, that the bells of the Sanctuary had pealed of their own accord, without rivers having risen nor pirates appearing, and that the wonder could only be attributed to the sudden appearance of the corn. Other stories rapidly went the rounds and the episode was called the "Miracle of the Corn" which grew between the night and the morning. Unaware of the monastery Superior's sermon and the bells of Ujarrás, public opinion decided that the dark-skinned Virgen de los Angeles, patron saint of mestizos, blacks, and mulattos was responsible for the wonder. The San Francisco church and the one at Ujarrás emptied out to fill the modest hermitage of Los Angeles, and the priest Angulo had no choice but to have a palm-covered shelter made to protect the fervent crowd that came to thank the dark Virgin for the wonder of the corn that grew by itself.

The city returned to its normal routine. There were tortillas on every table for breakfast, lunch, and supper, and the wheat stalks began to raise their golden heads. Pedro worked assiduously at his desk with its ever-growing pile of wills, lawsuits large and small, and dowry pledges of mixed-blood damsels who had managed to snare pure-blooded Spanish husbands. And Lázaro de Robles continued making his life miserable with outrageous pranks like emptying his inkwell into the drainage that flowed past the city hall, or allowing chickens to nest on the copies of the wills, leaving their droppings on the immaculate sheets bearing Pedro's beautiful penmanship. Serrano, with the problem of the corn now miraculously resolved, gave feasts in his house to keep the nobility happy and seldom set foot in the city hall.

The servile and monotonous life of Pedro Albarán, alias Pedro de la Baranda, would have been utterly unbearable were it not for his friendship with the shoemaker and his visits to The Mother of Travelers' gaming house which provided the salt and pepper that enabled him to get through the long days of his work as a scribe and his interminable nights of totting up monastic debits and credits, together with the unhealthy and unending annoyance of the bugs that shared his bed.

But the one who really helped him withstand the bitterness

of his lot was the beautiful woman who in the first few days of his arrival shook out that teasing ripple of lace and ribbons under his astonished nose. Pedro had fallen madly in love despite the fact that she, Agueda Pérez de Muro, was the daughter of the bailiff of the Inquisition and the wife of Captain José de Casasola y Córdoba, the ambitious redhead who wanted to be chief standard-bearer, councilman of the city, and an officer of the Inquisition as well. Pedro had found out that the mansion with the stone walls, carriage, and cobblestone patio with orange trees, where he had first caught sight of Agueda, belonged to her father, Don José Pérez de Muro, one of the richest men in the province. Why he should have allowed his daughter to marry a nobody was a mystery, although old Nicolás Céspedes, wise in the ways of the world, totted up on his fingers and observed that the bulge of her belly and the date of her marriage were not compatible. Whatever the truth, Don José furnished his son-in-law a golden ladder and did everything in his power to help him mount the rungs to power and fortune. The bailiff of the Inquisition had provided a generous dowry as evidenced by the corresponding official document in the files at the city hall in which Pedro ascertained that it included, among an array of other objects, a silver chamber pot, a receptacle worthy of the newly acquired status of the Captain's urinary output. It was not known for certain where he hailed from. His clear enunciation and somewhat affected Castilian accent sounded artificial. On his papers, next to his name, there stood a vague annotation declaring him a "resident of this city" and, as the shoemaker would say (paraphrasing Don Quixote de la Mancha), Casasola "came from a place with a blemish [mancha] there was no reason to recall." Be that as it may, everybody took him for what he was: the son-in-law of Don José Pérez de Muro, a man from Navarra with a Jewish streak (from the sephardic Pérez) but whose fortune was so large it could overshadow any "stain."

When Agueda began construction of her house on the southwest corner of the main square next to Blas González Coronel's and took upon herself the task of personally directing the workers, the signs of her pregnancy were already unmistakable. In the light of that, Pedro saw his dream of love vanish and had to content himself with desiring her from the waist up and at a distance. Not a moralist and blithely unconcerned about his own sins or those of others, he would not have hesitated to pin a splendid set of horns on Casasola's red head, though he could never countenance bedding a woman impregnated by another. He despised the crusades of the priest Angulo, who, as an agent of the Inquisition, went about constantly sniffing out the crotch-transgressions of members of his flock. The favorite topic of his sermons on high holidays, when attendance at the church was at its peak, concerned the sin of "coveting thy neighbor's wife." Thrust into vestments that hung loosely upon him, making the curls upon his temples tremble, his arms outstretched, he would enumerate in his shrill little voice cases of public knowledge and their associated details, without citing names but so specific that nobody could fail to recognize the allusions. It was said that Father Angulo blackmailed kneeling penitents during the sacrament of confession into informing on others who had sinned and was profligate in his absolution of sinners who not only confessed their transgressions but those of their neighbors.

If anybody knew more than Smiles about the underground life of the city that person was Angulo. Relations between him and the bishop, whose episcopal headquarters was in León, Nicaragua, were unfriendly, tense, and minimal. It was said, among other things, that the officer of the Inquisition kept for himself part of the cacao belonging to the bishop, as well as an overly large percentage of revenues from the sale of bulls. He sometimes called upon Pedro to help count the number of cacao beans collected for the right to go to heaven and then invited him to have a cup of chocolate. Upon hearing the whooshing sound of the beater in the kitchen of the priestly residence, Pedro imagined the souls of the faithful being ground up, pulverized, dissolved in milk, and then gulped down by the officer, to finally end up, after a tour through intestines, in the drainage ditch where the slaves and servants emptied their masters' potties. Smiles had assured Pedro that cacao was a specific for the treatment of liver colic, a sickness he was supposed to be suffering from. He, however, despite having been advised to drink it liberally, hated the stuff because it reminded him of what took place in Angulo's chocolate mixer to the souls of purchasers of bulls. But Angulo was grateful for Pedro's assistance and promised him a seat on the right side of God the Father surrounded by cherubs and angels singing sweet little songs to the accompaniment of harps and zithers, celestial delights that Pedro found more tedious and boring than his office in the city hall where he spent the day serving individuals who ended up—in an energy-saving process characteristic of criollo efficiency—by shortening his false name to Pedralbarán.

He avoided the priest Angulo whenever possible but wasn't able to when it came to counting up the contents of the sacks of cacao that came in from the transactions with bulls. And he never passed on any information even though he would have been well recompensed for denunciations. He did not do so because sexual peccadillos and secret love affairs were none of his concern. Nor did sins, in general, mean anything to him. For example, he didn't turn in one of Blas González Coronel's mulatto slaves whom he surprised one day standing on a mound, his rear end bare, in flagrant romance with one of González's mares conveniently in a hollow. In this, he was motivated neither by mercy for the slave nor consideration for Blas González. He remained silent as revenge against the priest, by depriving him of sure prey and of another prisoner in the crowded jail.

He closed his eyes to immorality in the church, as well as to the shady goings-on in the Interior Ministry, particularly with regard to smuggling through the port of Matina on English and mestizo ships. Serrano was actively involved in those deals with letters of marque. His business consisted of giving free passage to the contraband and then disposing of the goods by turning them over to his son who sold them out of his home. All, then, were in the same game together but Serrano's hands were ostensibly clean.

And so, in his monotonous scribe's job paid off in damp cacao beans, assisting the priest Angulo, keeping the monastery books, seeking to maintain himself aloof from gossip, hunting down Diego Malaventura, the town crier, in the village of San Juan de Herrera, sitting near the blank space on the wall where the portrait of The Bewitched King once hung, battling the bedbugs, listening patiently to the endless harangues of the Superior on the subject of the management of the holy abode, consoling himself at Smiles's shoemaker's shop where they stripped all the world naked, obsessed with Agueda Pérez de Muro, he gradually became inured to the interminable rains of the month of May. Sometimes, as he went over the monastery accounts, his hand would stray to the corner of the pages and betray his hidden passion by drawing ankles and lace-trimmed booties, and the like. Returning to reality, he would hide the pages under his mattress, thankful that they were unnumbered and that the Superior did not notice that the ledgers were growing thinner, wasted by the accountant's hopeless passion. In any case, the Superior was well satisfied with him. When he reviewed the accounts, he took note of the neat columns listing cows, sacks of wheat, corn, beans, and cacao; fees for chapel services, masses for the dead, marriage ceremonies, cemetery services, and baptisms; mules, slaves, tapers, wineskins, flasks of honey; tithes, pharmacy services, and consolations of the dying. The only heading that never went into the books was that corresponding to the Superior's losses at dice and cards at the gambling sessions organized by governor Serrano at his house at six o'clock every Wednesday afternoon. These were personal accounts entered by the Superior himself in discreetest privacy. The missing cows or cash shortages were balanced out in the books with fictitious donations that Pedro never verified. He kept the books straight with the data given him.

Haunted by his passion for Agueda, he spent nights drawing legs or scribbling verses from memory, being incapable of creating his own, to assuage the agony of entrapment in hopeless love. To tell the truth, Pedro had become a bit unhinged by his situation. He was not aware of what was happening to him, however, until years later when he discovered that going somewhat daft was the most delectable state a person can hope to attain since excessive rationality can, under certain conditions, lead to total loss of one's wits. At this time, thoroughly mixed up and unable to distinguish between fantasy and reality, he managed to survive and behave normally and even competently in all respects. Except where Agueda was concerned. When, for instance, he caught sight of her through the window of the city hall on the roof of her unfinished house counting the tiles to make sure that the masons weren't stealing, or at high mass with a décolletage so steep that had she not been the daughter of an officer of the Inquisition, Angulo would have excommunicated her for disrespect toward the church. Seized by intense emotions overheated by anxiety, he wrote alongside a column of monastery credits: "frail lamb, whose snowy likeness formed by nature, flake by flake, offers to the valley the purity of its whiteness," without giving credence to the fact that all he had seen and heard of her flatly contradicted those lines. It meant absolutely nothing to Pedro that Agueda was no frail lamb nor would offer her purity to the valley, so long as he could weep with love and feel appeased thereby. And he appropriated another's inspiration without stopping to consider the author's identity or if there was any correspondence between the poet's intention and his own. He plagiarized from the Mexican nun: "Will the day ever come when you write sweet finis to so much agony? When your lovely light will gild my senses with the glory of your sight?" And he wrote this totally glossing over the fact that Sor Juana Inés de la Cruz had shut herself up in a convent of the Sisters of Saint Jerome to think and write poetry and was referring either to a mystical communion with Christ or to another less mystical with her friend the Marquise de la Laguna... Like the poetic nun, Pedro had fallen in love totally and madly with an impossibility. And if a nun spent her time writing poems to a vicereine, a bachelor without ties could, with greater freedom and more reason, do the same to a married woman. When memory failed and he was unable to remember verses, sonnets, or dramatic soliloquies, he would blow out his smelly tallow candle and eagerly give himself over to the expiation of his sins, the torment of fleas and bedbugs, forgetting fear and love to decry, as he scratched with all his might, the weakness of the flesh. When Pedro learned that Agueda, in addition to being a construction boss, could read and write fluently and enjoyed books greatly, he stole a Franciscan "*Florecillas*" with the idea of sending it to her with a dedication composed by him on the flyleaf. Fortunately, it never came to that for the scandal that could have ensued might have gotten him into deep trouble. Depressed by his lack of ingenuity, he returned the book and tore up the notes he had made:

> 1. To the frail lamb whose snow-white
> fleece enshrouded my senses with glory

2. To the little lamb of my sunshine
3. To the sunlight of my snowflakes
4. To the turmoil of my valley
5. To the innocent little lamb of my glory

The sixth and last, which synthesized his passion perfectly, simply said: "to the sunlight of my turmoil." But he did not like it and "*Florecillas*" was returned to its bookshelf pure and unsullied.

"My turmoil" was what he called her from that moment on whenever he thought and dreamed of her but Agueda, of course, had no inkling of this. Who knows what might have happened then—because what did happen happened many years later—if when she was walking on the roof of her new house or when she lifted her skirt to climb the steps of the church, she had known the things that Pedro was writing about her, or that he had called her by so poetic a name. Neither was she aware that in a cell teeming with mice and other noxious species, a young man who had escaped the Inquisition feigned sitting her in his lap and slowly stripping off her hose to entirely expose the pink mystery that lay beneath. For Pedro's thoughts always dwelt on Agueda's intimate parts, the covered and hidden places not open to the eye, and he never paid any attention to, or even really saw, her face, which was always overshadowed by her beaver hats or palanquin. He imagined it as very beautiful but vague, changing, sometimes pale, sometimes blushing, the mouth either small or full-lipped. Sometimes she would have blue eyes, at others green or dark, with a nose upturned or aquiline. The Agueda of his dreams resembled all women but none in particular. And she was the only one in the world whose ankles were swathed in filmy white silk.

Pedro dreamed of Agueda but slept with The Mother of Travelers. Such is life, and nothing remarkable, anyway.

The Mother of Travelers, a *mulata* whose real name had long fallen into complete and absolute disuse, ran a gaming-house in the Barrio of the Coloreds. It was located near the hermitage where the Virgen de los Angeles was worshipped, of whom the kindly Superior of the monastery was so jealous. However, like everybody else he had nothing against gaming. The authorities and community leaders were also very tolerant of it—as they were of the other facilities for relaxation—and the *mulata* had protectors and benefactors who kept her business prosperous. Even the priest Angulo, backed by quotes from famous theologians, asserted that the businesses of The Mother of Travelers benefited public health, protected the chastity of single women, relieved the married ones, and, in general, were excellent for public morale, and very necessary for the well-being of the populace.

The sensual *mulata* relaxed nervous tension, distracted the preoccupied, and as far as Pedro was concerned rendered him a great service in temporarily placating his obsession with Agueda. Effusive, cheerful, generous, and open, with a keen social sense, she had learned that the success of her gaming house lay in insulating it from gossip. She had divided her customers into groups according to occupation and scheduled them separately so that none knew when and for what purpose another was there. Wednesdays were reserved for the clergy; Tuesdays for the military; Thursdays for public servants; Fridays for bachelors and widowers who had nothing at all to be concerned about; and Saturdays for farmers who came in from the distant hills and valleys. The rest of the week was for businessmen, peddlers, muleteers, teachers, and travelers, in general.

The Mother entertained all customers in her gaming house which was well-furnished with comfortable chairs, tables, decks of cards, and ivory dice, as well as a bar that dispensed spirits distilled on the premises. She charged nothing for her personal services and bestowed them in accordance with strict criteria as to the individual's need for consolation. Behind a blue door was the big wide bed, soft and clean, access to which was available to the interested party upon providing proof that he was going through an exceptionally difficult moment in his life and was in urgent need of understanding and alleviation. This unleashed keen competition among the unfortunate and unhappy because the Mother had a reputation that left no room for doubt and whoever entered by that blue doorway returned through it like one emerging from Paradise. At no time did Pedro ever hear anyone refer to her as a whore. The Mother's prestige guaranteed her customers' self-esteem. To insult her would have been tantamount to putting into question the dignity of those who frequented her establishment. To go to bed with her was an honor and whoever did so assumed a lifelong debt of gratitude.

She was the only woman of color who attended high mass wearing a heavy black veil and, although nobody greeted her, all people—including honest women—made way for her with consideration and respect. Conjugal conflicts were settled by lessons from the *mulata* and many chaste women were aware that they owed her thanks. She understood life and knew men better than they knew themselves. She also practiced white magic and her spells to counteract evil enjoyed the same reputation as her gaming house and bed. She refused entrance at her gambling establishment to drunks and when she noticed a customer beginning to sway in his chair, she had one of her two servants see him home and keep him out of trouble. As for those who were misbehaving under the influence, she quietly and very considerately convinced them to leave and would see them to the door. Her behavior toward a customer who became unruly was otherwise. She would simply take down a whip that hung on the wall and drive him out, flogging him unmercifully. By such means did she guarantee the security of her clientele, her own safety and dignity, and assure wives that when their husbands visited her gaming house, they were in good hands.

It was a secret to none that The Mother was deeply in love with the shoemaker and a mystery to everyone why he had not gone overboard for her. Her preference for him was enshrined in a phrase. "I couldn't bear to see a shoemaker cry," she said. "Were he a priest, it would be another matter."

The Golden Gang was the only seriously disruptive element at the *mulata's* gaming house. They appeared out of nowhere, spurring their horses, whooping, and disturbing the players and the entire neighborhood. Handsome, spoiled young men, of upper-class families, pockets well-lined, they would burst into The Mother's patio, shouting insults at those who tried to stop them. Everyone waited for the moment when The Mother would come out on the patio with her whip to take the marauders down a peg, horses and all. Laughing and celebrating their insolence, they would then gallop off, the horses as arrogant as their riders, hooves sending up clouds of dust. The leaders of the Gang were two young captains of the Madriz Linares clan, Asturian youths from the town of Lastre. Since they received their pay from Spain, they took advantage of the fact in asserting their superiority whenever criollos, like the brothers Tomás and Andrés Polo, tried to challenge their position. It was a day for celebration when Francisco, the older brother of the Madriz, left Cartago to fight the English in the Royal Armada. A general sigh of relief was also breathed when Vicente Polo too went to the port of Matina to deal with the English who were entering there with letters of marque. Tomás Polo married soon after and so, to everybody's great satisfaction, the Golden Gang disbanded. However, as long as the two pairs of brothers were on the loose and with nothing to do for the time being or the foreseeable future, they were a source of great annoyance at The Mother's gaming house, where they would insist on entering and she on keeping them out.

If not for those disturbances by the Golden Gang, the gaming house would never have awakened a sleeping neighbor. A barrio of lutes and rebecs, of guitars and colored people, of freed slaves, half-breeds, and quadroons, The Barrio of the Coloreds was proud of having in its midst a social center of such respectability and prestige as the *mulata's* gaming house.

It was evident that Pedro liked black women. He enjoyed watching them as they went by, burdens on their head, swaying their hips to the rhythm of an inaudible, sensual song. His was a generalized taste. Black women were pursued politely and impolitely in courtyards and vestibules, kitchens and stables, and even in the cemetery adjoining the parish church where more than one night owl found a place among the indifferent dead appropriate for giving free rein to unbridled impulses. To say nothing of the monastery, as well. When the black woman of the wry neck, whom they had baptized with the Christian name of Bárbara, for her aspect, and had given the surname of Lorenzana for the friar who bought her, appeared with her swollen belly exhibiting the telltale sign of forbidden incursions into the kitchen, the Superior flew into a rage, but try as he might, despite all his wiles he was unable to pin down the culprit. Lorenzo was the prime suspect, for after the purchase of the black woman it was noted that he had been going about with an air of smug satisfaction. Furthermore, he had volunteered for dish-washing duty which was quite extraordinary, he being well-known as a hardened loafer. However, there was no proof since the black woman, who spoke an unintelligible tongue, refused to give any indication of anything, which annoyed the Superior even more. He therefore decided to settle the problem by putting her up for sale.

She was purchased by Agueda Pérez de Muro but not for the kitchen. Agueda trained her to be a nursemaid and developed a great affection for her. Lorenzana had bad luck with her pregnancy; the child was born premature and dead. Perhaps that was why Agueda grew so fond of her. She never went out again by herself and the city grew accustomed to seeing her with Agueda's little boy in her arms, her mistress alongside. With the money the Superior received from the sale of Bárbara he bought two skinny, undernourished black boys from Blas González Coronel on condition that he have his cook teach them to cook, which he fulfilled only partly because he retired the cook before the two could learn the secrets of culinary art, to say nothing of how to keep themselves clean. The Guardian, fed up with finding mummified cockroaches in his rolls, sent the two boys to a city in Esparza where there was a Franciscan monastery with two friars, to help out in a certain traffic of goods from Peru, which arrived on a regular basis from the neighboring port of Caldera and from there were dispatched on mule back to the big Franciscan monastery in the city of Granada. What the friars there did with the goods that originated in Peru, only God and the friars themselves knew.

Once the Superior had gotten rid of the incompetent black boys, he sent Lorenzo to the kitchen as punishment for his unconfessed transgression. In the presence of all the monks, he said more or less the following: "Brother Lorenzo, you will be so good as to feed this flock, taking into consideration that in the short stay here of Bárbara Lorenzana you acted as her assistant in the kitchen and would, I imagine, have learned something from her."

And so it was clear to all that the Superior knew what everybody else knew, namely, that Lorenzo was responsible for Lorenzana's pregnancy and that Lorenzo now knew that the Superior, as well as the other friars, also knew.

Pedro survived the culinary massacre that followed the Superior's words thanks to a potion prepared for him by Smiles with seven *fines herbes* steeped under the light of a full moon which served equally well for maladies resulting from liver malfunction and maladies produced by love-sickness. It worked only for Pedro's liver. Apart from the large quantities of lard and hot chili pepper Lorenzo put in the food to camouflage his ignorance, despite all his efforts, he was unable to come to terms with the marmite—a kind of hermetic retort which operated in accordance with alchemical mysteries the poor lecherous sinner could not decipher—and the kitchen became an experimental laboratory responsible for the production of colics, intestinal catarrhs, heartburn, and the horrible feeling of having eaten nothing. The friars grew scrawny and the Superior protested the absence of nuns in Cartago which meant that there was nobody to solve the dilemma of the monastic cuisine. This was during the epoch of corn and wheat scarcity.

And so, when the notorious and polemical friar Pablo de Rebolledo arrived from distant Talamanca together with his companion in missionary zeal José de San José, the monastery, instead of grumbling with displeasure—as usually happened whenever Rebullida left his distant mission in the jungle to return to Cartago—reacted with joy. Everybody, and the Superior in particular, was excited, for the missionaries were bringing two Indian women with them in exchange for the altarpiece of volutes depicting Saint Anne and the Child Virgin. They were anxious to have it for they had just founded a new mission which bore precisely her name, Saint Anne, in a most remote and inaccessible spot which the Spaniards knew by the name of Viceita. This was a hamlet inhabited by fierce and warlike Indians, a fact which greatly enhanced the prestige of the missionaries.

The Superior did not hesitate a moment. The deal was struck at once and the two Indians of the Talamanqueña tribe were officially appointed monastery cooks. They came recommended as specialists in fasting and scrimping who were able to prepare any dish provided it was no more complicated than boiled bananas. Although it turned out to be by no means the ideal solution to the problem, there were no complaints and, after Lorenzo's excesses, everyone accepted the insipid but simple and healthful diet. He was shipped off to the wilds of Chirripó to provide catechism in exchange for the current teacher who was brought back. Pedro, observing those desperate maneuvers, thought to himself that it was no wonder the Superior lost every time he played cards or dice. And he feared that without censuring eyes to keep Lorenzo's weaknesses of the flesh in check, he would be regaling his appetite unchecked on the Indian women of Chirripó. The Superior's inability to conduct his affairs now became apparent in the way he was making obvious efforts to ingratiate himself with the two missionary guests while they, recognizing his weakness, took advantage of the situation to such a degree that the monastery came under Pablo de Rebullida's ascetic and authoritarian control. The first thing he did was to order the two Indian women to be dressed in the Franciscan cassock in order to forestall arousal of temptation among the friars, the hood to be worn over the head at all times, with the result that the more robust of them resembled a squat, chunky friar and the other a small, very young novice.

Discipline and order reigned in the monastery throughout Rebullida's stay. Whether the camouflage worn by the Indians dampened all sinful design or they were less toothsome than the blacks, the fact of the matter was that no known forays into the kitchen took place, nor was there the slightest suspicion thereof. The Superior was satisfied and gave Rebullida a free hand to impose his orders. Rules and regulations formerly paid lip service—for example, those concerning fasting, matins, and vespers—were now strictly enforced. There was to be no talking in the refectory and each kept his head bent over his frugal plate more in fear than piousness, for Father Rebullida inspired veritable terror with his tall, angular frame, the bones of which seemed to be striving to force their way out from under the bronzed skin, the feverish eyes set in deep, dark sockets that glared with a determination whetted by contact with the most insuperable obstacles. At night, during hours of repose, the sound of the lash with which he scourged his emaciated body was clearly to be heard. It was said that were it not for flagellation Rebullida would be a dead man because it was precisely the whipping that kept him up and about, invulnerable to death and the countless perils of his stoical life in the far-off mountains of Talamanca.

Pedro avoided him as best he could because to have those eyes boring relentlessly into one was a terrifying sensation for which distance was the only antidote. Rebullida was bountiful in spearing souls but sparing of words.

His comrade, José de San José, however, talked a blue streak, cornering whoever came within earshot to engulf the person pitilessly in tales of his life in the mountains among barbaric infidels whom he referred to out of a select glossary of foul terms, such as spawn of the devil, apostates, louts, filth, and other such epithets. The harried missionary, who arrived in the city devoured by mosquitos and covered with bubos, related over and over again how "with unflagging spirit and intrepid courage, he had crossed those barren wastelands, incredible wildernesses, scaling daunting heights and pushing his way through bristling thickets, completely barefooted, his habit inlaid with patches, and with no guide but the light of the heavens..." After that introduction, which seldom varied, he would recount details of his rounds among Indian palisades, settlements, and camps, entering huts from which the wild brutes, barbarians, savages, heathens, and so forth, fled instantly at the sight of him. Pedro was thinking that the Indians were undoubtedly seeking to escape his implacable harangues and sympathized with them, taking their side against the missionary who seemed more like a knight errant with shield and buckler. By no means gentle nor humble, in contradiction to the Franciscan habit he wore, San José, having recuperated from starvation and the ordeal of the mountains, reverted to his former robustness. As a soldier, he was also the most enthusiastic partisan of the project that had brought the two of them to the city: the obtaining of a military escort to accompany them and help spread the evangelical light in Talamanca. Until now—San José argued—preaching the gospel had been done with love, but with love alone it was impossible to obtain from the Indians all that was necessary. On hearing this, Pedro asked himself if what was good for the Indians was good for the friars, too, but obedient to his instructions not to get involved in what didn't concern him, he made no effort to solve the riddle.

The Saint Anne altarpiece disappeared from the wall just as Carlos the Bewitched did from the city hall. Rebullida whisked it away to his cell together with a supply of candles and other articles that had been stored away to be taken to Talamanca. The friar of the picture in the refectory with the skull hanging from his waist remained completely alone. Pedro missed chubby Saint Anne as he did the former days when everybody felt free to talk and local gossip was bandied about, and he even missed the greasy-spoon cooking of the black boys and Lorenzo's heavy hand with the condiments. He was sick of boiled bananas and the stews of yucca and insipid bits of beef so tiny that he would have appreciated the aid of one of those portentous inventions known as the microscope to find them. The Superior had assigned Juan de las Alas, the little friar who had provoked the outburst of irreverent laughter in the refectory, to kitchen duty, thinking that the novice's very youth would protect him against Satan's tricks. He gave him the order together with an admonition. "From now on," he said to him, "you will help the cooks out by waiting on table because I do not want them in the refectory. And keep in mind what San Agustín said about women: that they are a temple built over a cloaca."

Pedro was certain that the youth had not grasped the underlying meaning of the phrase because he opened his astonished green eyes wide and went off to his duty without replying. By virtue of this prudent measure on the Superior's part, the men would be alone in their monastery at all times, Rebullida's Indians apparently nonexistent, for they were rarely to be seen. The stouter, older one went about with the marmite ladle in her hand at all times while the other one, said to be a mute and somewhat retarded, never ventured out of the kitchen, where she was useless. This was of no concern to the Superior for the older one did the work of three.

This precautionary step served to shield the Indian women from the friars but not the friars from the Indian women and, before long, innocent Juan de las Alas came down with an illness as unavoidable as mumps or measles.

All this took place before La Chamberga had threatened to follow Pedro's tracks to Cartago and, at that time, he didn't even remotely suspect what lay in store for him. Faithful to his slogan of "play dead dog: be all ears," he had fashioned a temperate and circumspect way of life for himself which enabled him to be on good terms with everyone and suffer his passion for Agueda with discretion. His friendship with the shoemaker and his sessions at The Mother's gaming house—where he sometimes had luck and returned to the monastery with a few *patacones* in his purse—jumping the wall Don Juan-style, with the connivance of a small tree that seemed planted there for the very purpose—served to calm his fears, making it possible for him to have pleasant, superficial relations with all sorts of people, and to go unnoticed, which was his main concern. Had it not been for the penchant of people to call him Pedralbarán, his past history and his identity as a fugitive from the dungeons of the Inquisition would have melted into history. The cursed nickname stood in the way, however, impelling him to step up his effort to appear insignificant, a nobody. Skillful as he was in throwing Angulo, the priest with the bloodhound nose for breaches of the faith, off the scent, he unwittingly stepped on a banana skin José de San José slipped under his foot one afternoon in the monastery corridor. Pedro came upon him that day sitting on a bench stroking his beard and looking out melancholically upon the few drooping rosebushes that the brother doorkeeper pompously referred to as the garden. He held a piece of bread with a chunk of bacon on it which he was munching dispiritedly and made no sign or effort to answer when Pedro stopped and said, "Splendid afternoon we're having, isn't it?"

Suspecting that the missionary was deep in metaphysical musing or mulling over some brush with Rebullida, Pedro went on, "What is it, Father? I see you're more downcast than a bird in a cage."

"How could I be otherwise?" he responded. "This waiting is not only tedious but never-ending."

"Waiting for what?"

"Don't you know? Does Your Honor not work in the city hall? Is it possible you are unaware that the Guatemalan Government has not yet deigned to reply to our request for a military escort for the missions in Talamanca? Is Your Honor is also unaware that Governor Serrano intrigues against us because he doesn't want men to be sent to the missions? He wants them all for his own purposes and his contraband business with the pirates."

This was all absolutely true and there was no reason to deny it. Rebullida came to the city hall every day to inquire whether an answer had arrived from Guatemala (a pointless question because he knew very well that when the post arrived, he would be the first to know). That was his way of bringing pressure to bear and Serrano, whenever he saw him about, would slip through a rear door and disappear. Neither Serrano nor Blas González nor very many others were sympathetic to the idea of Rebullida draining off to Talamanca the few militia available and also the Indians of the valley settlements, the manpower so necessary for the little work that had to be done. Rebullida was aware of this and suspected that the Governor was double-crossing him but wasn't sure how. Pedro, however, knew that Serrano had written to Guatemala to the effect that he did not believe in the efficacy of the missions and that it was a waste of money to finance the high cost of maintaining an armed garrison at such a distance. Whenever missionaries were discussed, Blas González would refer to them disparagingly, if out of range of disapproving ears, commenting that the work of the missions should be entrusted to the Jesuits, who were more learned in theology and more intelligent and capable than all those improvised Recollets that were being turned out. He and Serrano would exchange knowing glances at those words because the two of them had prepared a letter in which they told the Guatemalan government that missions were a risky adventure in a risky place, and that it would be an unsound undertaking to send off hands needed for the cacao plantations of Matina and the cornfields of the central valley. "Listen, all of you, if the corn blight recurs there will be no one to plant emergency cornfields!"

On hearing such statements the scribe was convinced that Serrano had absolutely no faith in the missions. And the wild Indians of the mountains, the bone of contention, had absolutely no idea of the rift they were causing. On the one hand, the missionary priests kept hammering away at the idea of the escort being for the greater glory of God and King and all that; and, on the other side of the dispute, Serrano and the members of the council were counting up how many hands would be lost if the friars had their way, and wanting to know how the province could be expected to progress if they couldn't even go into Talamanca to get workers for Matina, and grumbling hat what the missionaries were after was not souls to save but the benefits they would gain out of instituting catechism, money lending, to say nothing of the tribute the Indians had to pay to the Crown. The priest of Ujarrás was doing just that, sloughing off ninety percent of the tribute to feather his nest and in the meantime, the proprietors of the cacao haciendas in Matina were having all kinds of problems getting their products into the foreign market. They were concerned only that the supreme government grant the petition to convert cacao into official currency for domestic circulation. But no, the government had higher regard for projects of crack-brained friars than for the good, faithful, noble subjects whose work was swelling the fiscal coffers, a number of whom were already speculating with cacao, selling not at a peso per hundred grams, but per eighty grams.

These were what Pedro termed "pen-down" discussions, for they were not recorded in the minutes. Not appearing in the record, either, were the fierce, overheated arguments that arose every time the subject of the battle unleashed in Spain between the Bourbon and the Austrian came up (the Pope played dumb and took no sides, though the whole world knew he sympathized with Austria). When the argument on this thorny point began to show signs of ending in fisticuffs or swordplay, Serrano skillfully diverted enmity toward the Indians, consigning those heathens to rot in hell if it turned out that capacity in heaven was limited. When this point was reached, Blas González pursed his lips and came out with his favorite joke: "Spain is hamstrung...it would be preferable if the English, with their practical sense and their sound, businesslike approach, were to colonize these lands..."

At the monastery, Pedro heard surprising things about Rebullida: that his wild appearance was due to his having been born in the mountains somewhere between Aragon and Catalonia; and that during the ocean crossing he had interrupted his Franciscan brothers' prayers with hoarse outbursts of "Let me die a martyr, let me die a martyr!" Then the sea became angry and the poor friars had to take refuge inside the ship among the bales, chickens, and smelly passengers.

San José, not having followed the thread of Pedro's remarks, went on talking. "It is true that venerable Mother María de Agreda has said that in those years Our Father Saint Francis was granted the concession that all infidel nations would be considered converted by the mere sight of his habit, and I see nothing amiss in giving the process a push."

"Are you referring to the escort?"

"That is whereof I speak. The savage barbarians of Talamanca jabbed Father Rebullida with a spear and he still breathes through the wound. I was subjected to terrible insults, my prayer book was stolen, and they tied leaves around their heads as though they were feathers... Ah, but I stun them with the power of God and all immediately disperse."

"Then keep stunning them with those powers because it costs a lot less than the upkeep of an escort."

San José tilted his head to one side, knotted his cordon, took a deep breath, and snapped, "Your honor is perhaps taken aback by the difficulty of the undertaking and, therefore, he mocks."

"Oh! I am not what you might be called a particularly brave man... I was only asking where the monies will come from to finance your request if the Royal Bank, as the Deputy Director says, is empty and Spain is expending funds it doesn't have in a war against itself."

"Souls have a higher value than coins."

"I agree. I agree."

Pedro noted that San José had turned redder than an angry turkey and sought to calm him down by changing the subject."

"And...about those Indians of Talamanca that you are converting? Do they submit to baptism and marriage?"

"Oh!" sighed San José. "Better that we don't open the subject of marriage. I have preached to them that there is no other way than marriage but their response is: 'Father, if I marry only one woman and then I get angry, what do I do if I can't change her? Because, now, if I get angry at my wife, or she with me, we separate, I look for another one, and that way I have no troubles.' 'Tell me, Father,' those villains say to me, 'is it not a bad thing for a person to have troubles? Then, so as not to have troubles I don't want to get married. And, look, Father, if I have only one wife and she turns out bad-tempered and to punish me she takes my children and goes off to her family, you can't bring her back to me! So I am left without a wife or children. That's why, Father,' those sly fellows tell me, 'I am happy with many friendly women.'"

Pedro brought his hand up to his nostrils to hide an irresistible smile and his utter agreement with the Indian attitude toward marriage. Carried away by emotion, San José did not notice, and plunged ahead.

"Besides, the savages are sorcerers and practice witchcraft. They have stones of different colors, as if for a game like checkers. When they are out on the move, the red ones will detect whether there are enemies in the neighborhood, and other stones like marble with lead-colored stripes let them know when to plant, and other infernal things of the sort."

"And what do they do with the stones? Cast them on the ground, perhaps, and see on which side they fall?"

"No, They place them in the palm of one hand, ask them whether yes or no, and then blow on them. The barbarians say that if the answer is 'yes,' the stones dance, and if 'no' they don't. I have burned about two bushels of them..."

Pedro contained his laughter and held back his question as to how he had managed to set stones on fire and let him continue his exaggerations.

"They all go about naked as the day they were born, wearing nothing but feathers in their hair and beads about their neck. These witless creatures live jumbled together in scandalous disorder and sleep in a mass in very large houses like animals. Imagine what sort of animals when some have tails three spans long!"

Pedro, unable to hold back any longer, let out a guffaw.

"So you don't believe me," said San José, getting angry.

"I don't know whether to or not... First you say they have souls and now you come out with them having tails..." Without realizing it he had addressed him using the familiar form. "Furthermore," he went on in a conciliatory tone, "the matter of human reason isn't all that clear... I once saw a man with a monkey who went about amusing a crowd. The people made faces at the monkey and he imitated them. I don't know at what point they changed roles: the monkey made grimaces at them and they imitated him. Sometimes I wonder if man isn't any more than an intelligent ape. Maybe we invented reason so as to build a manageable universe, but we go on being animals..."

"Soul and reason are one and the same," said San José, regarding him curiously.

"Oh!" Pedro had seated himself on the ground and was watching the shadows creep over the rosebushes. He inhaled the perfume, absently. "Soul is put and take. It was said for a long time that the Indians of America had no soul, until Pope Paul III decided that they did..."

"Are you suggesting that it is the Pope who bestows our soul or takes it from us?" San José had leaned over until he seemed like a tiger about to leap, but Pedro didn't notice.

"Not exactly... I was thinking that nobody knows exactly what the soul is... Don't you yourself say that the Indians are animals with tails and yet you waste your time and energy in converting them? Forgive me, but I question the Indians' tails as much as the infallibility of the Pope."

"Heretic!" The friar leapt to his feet. "Heretic!" he shouted again in a triumphant voice. "I've found you out! I suspected strange things about you. To the stake! I shall send you to the stake!"

"Don't be stupid, you piece-of-shit friar. What I said was simple reasoning to make you see your contradictions. You're the heretic, converting individuals with a tail whose rationality you question. Didn't you yourself say that soul and reason are one?"

But San José was so inebriated with his discovery that he threw himself on Pedro, seizing him by the arms as he shouted at the top of his lungs: "Come, brothers! I've captured the devil! There's a heretic in the monastery!"

"Shut up, you friar idiot! I'm not one of the Indian women you fornicate with in the bushes for you to be grabbing me like that!"

Pedro tried to get loose by jamming his knee between the friar's legs but the other, husky and in condition from his daily labors in the harsh mountains, twisted away and pressed Pedro to the ground where he held him in a hammer lock. Attracted by the rumpus, the Superior came running over and set him free.

"Father," the bookkeeper tried to explain, "I was only trying to make it clear to this one that tails on the Indians do not necessarily prove that they lack reason, which is the same as the soul. I just mentioned what Pope Paul III said..."

"What sort of bookkeeper is this for a monastery to have who denies the soul and says that His Holiness Paul III..." San José counterattacked.

"Enough!" roared the Superior. "I don't want to hear another word about Indians' soul or a Pope's tail. All I care about is that there be peace and quiet in this monastery!"

Standing in the rear, Rebullida's eyes bored into Pedro like a pair of red-hot gimlets. He led San José out with him and the Superior accompanied Pedro to his cell where they entered together. Surprised and disconcerted at the inexplicable behavior of his bookkeeper, who was more moderate than the friars themselves, he said, shaking his head, "Frankly...frankly, I haven't the slightest idea of what has happened here... Father San José turns very violent when contradicted, but...in this place and wearing the habit! Something very serious must have happened. I beg of you, Pedralbarán, don't be provocative or put me in a bind with Father Rebullida; he is a very influential man."

From that day on, an hour of after-dinner chatting was devoted to theological discussion on topics selected by the Father Superior, such as in-depth analysis of subtle questions like that of the number of angels that might fit on the head of a pin or whether Christ would have been the same Redeemer had he been born a woman.

On the Superior's advice, Pedro became a member of the Brotherhood of the Holy Cross. The Franciscan's recommendation was sufficient for the organization to waive examination of his pedigree despite Pedro's dark, gypsy-like complexion. He joined against his will in the belief that it would enhance the image he had created for himself to conceal his status as an escaped prisoner of the Inquisition. During the celebration of Lent the following year, he had to appear in penitential robe and hood, whip in hand, lashing himself.

And so, as a consequence of public self-castigation and redoubled caution, he managed to escape the toils of local intrigue and lead a life reasonably free of anxiety until a second mishap placed him in jeopardy once again. This time, however, it was not because of imprudence on his part. Governor Serrano's contraband dealings were to blame, involving, in particular, the slave auction at which Pedro saw Bárbara Lorenzana for the first time. She had arrived on the frigate *Nuestra Señora de la Soledad* whose entire cargo was confiscated because of improper papers and having disembarked by error in the Province of Costa Rica when its registered destination was Peru. Were it not for the vagaries of destiny, which weaves its threads at will—in this case, the effect of the winds of the misnamed Pacific Ocean, Agueda Pérez de Muro would never have come to own Lorenzana to whom she became so attached.

When the captain of the port of La Caldera saw the *Nuestra Señora de la Soledad* approaching in a state of shipwreck, he seized the opportunity fate presented to impound its cargo of slaves and goods, selling off all he could to the people of the port and the city of Esparza and sending the remainder to Cartago for auction. The *Nuestra Señora*, damaged and high in the water, continued on to the ports of Guatemala, where the first thing the Captain did was to file a complaint of seizure of his cargo by the province of Costa Rica. However, Cartago had no inkling of this and when the lawyer of the Supreme Government of Guatemala arrived to investigate what became of the money collected from the sale of the impounded cargo—not a single real in the way of customs duty had entered the coffers—Serrano was suddenly taken gravely ill with intestinal catarrh, the priest Angulo closeted himself in spiritual retreat, and the only one still about was Blas González Coronel wearing his usual unchanging, crooked smile. The matter took a very grave turn when a deficit of over seven thousand pesos sterling appeared on the books of the port. This amount corresponded to the value of the confiscated cargo declared by the captain, and the lawyer was demanding to know what had happened to the money. The captain of the port of La Caldera, supervising the impounding, had fled, taking all his belongings with him, and the lawyer insisted on identifying the responsible party.

Pedro was positive not only that it was the captain of the frigate who had lodged the claim but that Blas González had something, if not a lot, to do with the matter. Smiles, an insomniac, had seen the lawyer emerging one night from Blas González's house on the other side of the square. Seated at The Mother's gaming house sipping rum from a gourd, he explained: "This type of crime is called a 'sausage' because it has many links and looks like there's nothing suspicious there. But everybody knows different, only proving it is impossible. In this case, however...hmm...Serrano is cooked. Contrabanding with the English is still excusable, but not stealing the money from the sale of the slaves. Since the captain of the port has absconded, taking everything with him, the Governor will have to assume the responsibility for both of them."

* * *

That's what I said to him because at that stage of the game we were still close friends and he always paid attention to my advice in everything. I never told him that in trying so hard to appear simple he aroused suspicion since behavior like that was as unusual as seeing a hen hanging out with foxes. He was being careful not to drink enough to loosen his tongue, and he never told me what really brought him to Cartago. I respected his reserve, thinking that some day he would have to tell somebody and that person would be me. It was a howl to see him, pious and repentant, flailing away at himself with the best of them in the bloody processions. With me, though, he didn't hesitate to admit that he wasn't much of a believer. Not that I go bruising my knees, either... I've never had any use for priests and friars, lazy bunch of loafers and parasites that they are, but I do feel devotion for my Black Saint and never miss an August first to let her know so. My pious and repentant Virgen de los Angeles has always been a big help to me with my medicines and I owe her a debt for life. But Pedro...poor lad! It took some years before I realized how much it took out of him to be such a hypocrite.

Regarding the matter of the lawyer who came to investigate the money missing from the port, I advised him to cooperate with him in a disinterested kind of way and gain his confidence. I was up on what happened with the slaves that were confiscated from the frigate and I told him the whole story so that he would be aware of what a difficult nut it was to crack. So as not to string it out, I'll dish it up in two servings. What happened was that Serrano put them up for sale at a ridiculous price or to some people, like the priest Angulo, for nothing. So what little was realized ended up in his pocket. That was the reason Blas González got so angry at them for involving him in such a dangerous business. I figure he must have informed Guatemala so as to keep his hands clean and not lose either his post of Deputy Director of the Royal Bank or his appointment as Chief Magistrate of the Inquisition, for which he had applied. Blas González is, of course, as bad a scoundrel as any, or worse, but he knows how to do things right and you can't take that away from him.

The fact of the matter is that Pedro was shitting green. He was so terrified by the lawyer from Guatemala that you'd think he was the one who stole the money. But Serrano outshat them all. His diarrhea attack was the real thing. He was squatting over his outhouse hole night and day and the stink reached all the way to my workshop. I could have cured him but he preferred using the brothers' pharmacy. Who knows what swill they gave him for he got worse and worse every day. The best thing was what happened afterwards. Somebody turned Father Angulo in and they dragged him out of his spiritual retreat and dumped him into the seat of justice. I have no idea who pulled the plug but I don't believe it was Blas González. It's pretty hard to imagine that a member of the Inquisition would denounce a higher-up of the organization. In any case, Pedro kept me informed and since I'm not lacking in imagination, you can guess what a fine time I had picturing the priest's face when he had to admit that the three slaves he got at the auction were bought for others. For example, who would have thought that two of them went to a couple of council members in the name of the church. I'm at the head of the class when it comes to investigating and checking up, but I never figured that the third slave went to Lázaro de Robles, of all people. I thought he bought him because Serrano made the request to Angulo... The night Pedro told me all that over some of The Mother's gaming-house rum, I enjoyed myself so much that The Mother didn't care to accept me—her favorite—and rather took Pedro to bed, seeing him so unstrung. Of course, consolation is her thing and what she likes best to do.

* * *

Lázaro de Robles kept getting paler as time passed and the day the Inquisition Officer was called by the lawyer from Guatemala to appear in the chapter house of the city council, he turned absolutely green. It did Pedro's heart good to see the mulatto's color change. Lázaro was knocked off his perch, became helpful, humble, no longer emptying Pedro's inkwell into the ditch and making sure the chickens didn't mess on the pages of the official record written in his elegant hand that the lawyer would be taking with him after he concluded his investigation.

The air was heavy with French perfume when Father Angulo finished giving his statement. The lawyer retired to his rented house, the city council was completely deserted, and Lázaro de Robles had disappeared. Smiles figured that he had gone up to the Aguacate hills, where he was looking for gold in an abandoned mine with the help of the slave that Angulo had bought for him. He had undoubtedly taken off in a hurry in order to hide him, for fear that the lawyer might confiscate him.

Taking advantage of the situation, the shoemaker thought up the practical joke of sending anonymous letters to the lawyer denouncing abuses of authority and illegalities committed by the city council. The accusations were that the judges in the countryside were stealing the peasants' cows, that meat prices were going sky high, that contraband from Matina was coming through constantly in the middle of the night, that certain people had set up shop with goods purchased from the pirates, and that the English were coming to Matina and Moín to do business freely and openly with Spanish nobles. In short, a sheaf of papers in different handwritings and inks, some more watery than others, appeared at the door of the lawyer's rented house where they were picked up by the Indian woman who brought the wood and made the fire for him at five o'clock in the morning.

The lawyer put the papers away and mentioned them to nobody, not even Pedro. He paid Serrano a visit at his house, where a servant told Pedro he overheard him tell his master: "Your honor, either you pay up the amount missing from the accounts or you pack your bags and get out of the province."

Later, the lawyer returned to Guatemala with José de Casasola y Córdoba, who was taking advantage of the trip to check if there were any developments with respect to the posts of Chief Standard Bearer and *regidor* that he was trying to buy.

Gossip had it that Pérez de Muro, bailiff of the Inquisition, had sent his son-in-law to sniff out the Palace of Captains in Santiago de los Caballeros and to pick up any information concerning the Serrano matter.

It was public knowledge that the light on Father Angulo's balcony went out late in the night and that as the afternoon shadows lengthened, other shadows passed through the doorway, not to emerge again until the lamp was extinguished. Those involved in the purchase of blacks and other goods put up for auction were deliberating there regarding what they should do when things got really thick, that is to say, when the lawyer had returned to Guatemala. Smiles speculated that given the slow transportation and bad roads, it would allow about two months' grace, long enough for a solution to be found. "Considering all the fluids drained out of him by his diarrhea," he said, "Serrano could well be feeding the worms by then."

Bored and alone at the city council, Pedro filled in the interminable hours strolling the hallways, sitting in Lázaro de Robles's empty chair, contemplating the wheeling of the buzzards, listening to the raindrops that alternated with the scorching sunlight, and hoping that Agueda Pérez would appear with her slave in tow, as usual.

When least expected, he saw her approaching, her legs beneath her thin cotton skirt completely bare, not inappropriately in the almost unbearable heat. She was walking through the grass in the square, the black woman alongside shielding her with a Chinese parasol whose gay colors reveled in the bright sunlight. As she neared, her face in shadow, her arms slender and elegant in the short sleeves of her fine Brittany lawn blouse, her deep inviting décolletage barely covered by a simple baize bodice, short and tight, she was holding up the hem of her lace petticoat in unbejewelled fingers with a charming gesture that exposed her feet, shod in black *alpargatas* tied around the ankles. Pedro could make out the black woman's wry neck as the two women crossed the street. They then proceeded directly towards the corridor of the city hall where Pedro sat, practically glued to Lázaro de Robles's chair. "Arise and walk," he ordered himself and managed to run to his own chair as the two began to mount the stairway. He barricaded himself behind his desk, making believe he was very busy, his hands trembling, unable to raise his eyes. When the source of his turmoil made her spectacular entrance into the room, the poor fellow had dipped his goose quill in the inkwell ten times, dripping along the way upon the original of a death certificate on eight-real stamped paper. Aghast at the sight of the blots, not daring to look at her for fear of something dreadful and irreparable happening, such going blind or having snot leak out of his nose, he watched the exquisitely tied black *alpargatas* approach as she stepped straight to the desk, the colors of her skirt hypnotizing him.

"Good afternoon, Pedralbarán," she said in a voice like molasses being poured out at a sugar mill.

"Ah, Doña Agueda! Pardon me, but I didn't hear you come in. I'm...there's so much...I can't keep up..." he answered without raising his eyes from the paper.

The stripes on her cotton skirt undulated like snakes as she turned in search of another person in the room, broad stripes at the edges of the garment narrowing to where they remained imprisoned beneath the bodice. It was the color of fresh and dewy moss at daybreak and Pedro, not daring to shift his glance towards her breasts, rushed out to find Serrano, who was given over at that moment to the same occupation that had been keeping him so upset and weak for so many days. Bárbara Lorenzana, sitting in Lázaro de Robles's seat, watched him as he went by with a curious expression that made Pedro think she was laughing at him. Serrano refused to receive Agueda, saying that he was in no condition to be attending to visitors "particularly in the case of wives of traitors like Casasola who owes me so many favors, the daughter of a lousy bailiff for whom it would be no problem to give me a boost, a bossy, arrogant bit of work who didn't think to invite me to her son's baptism, a mannish wench who goes about on a rooftop letting the masons have a peek at her ass and pussy, who thanks to my generosity has a black woman to get around with, like a pair of oxen in the same yoke..."

and so on. And when he ran out of insults he came out of the toilet, buttoning his trousers. Calmed down to some degree, he went on, "Women always find the most inopportune moments to bother a man and this one, you can be sure, is here to pester me about some whim of hers, taking advantage of my state on account of this shit hemorrhage that gives me no rest."

He washed his face, changed his jacket, checked his trousers, and came out to attend to Agueda sitting in the meeting hall, the sun streaming through the window full upon her, obliging Serrano to sit facing her with the light in his eyes. Pedro stared in fascination at the golden reflection from the tresses of the beautiful woman of his torment, the blushing skin of her neck, the smooth, delicate line of her head, the hair caught up at the nape of the neck, the ivory tone of her arms, and the deep shadow of the open cleavage between her breasts. A woman of shadows, Agueda seemed to be utterly comfortable with the sun at her back.

Agueda spoke. "Your honor is unwell and I come to trouble you. All the people of the city are worried about your honor and we wish to help you in this difficult moment. My father has entrusted me with the task of paying you a visit to convey his respects and his kindest intentions of contributing to... To get to the point, my father, acting upon his interpretation of the wishes of the nobility of Cartago, has sent me to propose an arrangement that could resolve the problem that your honor now faces."

(The scribe rejoiced: *Oh, sorceress! What a gift for diplomacy, what capacity for negotiation! What rare gifts in a woman! What talent!*)

Serrano shifted uneasily in his seat.

"My father wishes to apprise Your Honor of his deep concern because my husband, now in Guatemala, has notified us that your removal is imminent unless the shortage in the accounts from the impounded goods of the frigate is made good... However, such a regrettable outcome—which the good people of this province are fully justified in opposing, for we feel a debt of gratitude to your honor's capable government—can be avoided."

Serrano crossed his legs and leaned forward, pressing his hands between his knees. "If I should find myself obliged, Señora, to appear before the Captaincy General, many of the good people of this province would be deprived of their slaves and lose their rank as officers of the militia, members of the council, and even bailiffs of the Inquisition..."

"We are aware of it...well aware. That, indeed, could happen."

Agueda raised her tone slightly and then continued, more softly. "And it is truly deplorable that a governor be dishonored by dismissal, particularly at a moment like this, when the Archduke of Austria makes war upon our legitimate monarch, King Philip V, who takes a keen interest in unmasking traitors, sympathizers of the Archduke..."

Serrano stiffened at the threat. "Tell me, Doña Agueda Pérez, what does your father propose?"

"Very simple. Your honor has objects of silver and unpaid salaries coming to you. Put up those assets against the shortage and citizens will cover the difference. And there is one other small matter, a small favor my father wishes to ask of you which is in your power to grant... Some time ago, my father bought a minor quantity of Peruvian wine in Panama which will be arriving at La Caldera in a few days. The shipment amounts to twenty-three jugs of wine and seven of pisco and, there being no captain of the port, well...my father would appreciate it if Your Honor would issue the necessary permit and send a person there to facilitate the unloading and the transportation to Cartago."

"Impossible," shouted Serrano, springing to his feet and causing a disagreeable smell to permeate the room, "In my situation, that would be putting the rope around my neck. You know very well, Señora, that the importation of Peruvian wine is forbidden, strictly forbidden."

"In that case," responded Agueda, coolly, "consider that I have not paid you this visit."

Nobody asked the scribe's opinion but when he saw Agueda making ready to leave, he dove in head first. "If discretion is called for, I could go there myself and disembark the wine."

"That seems to me a very generous offer on your part, Pedralbarán," she said, and Pedro felt her presence so close that a faint whiff of perspiration dispelled by her Brittany blouse reached him. Agueda turned her head and the sun struck her full in the face. The lady was smiling at him, so close, so brightly illuminated, her red lips parted in an expression of amusement, exposing teeth that protruded like a rabbit's. Agueda had buck teeth, long, and yellowed with tobacco. Yes! The lady of my torment, the woman of my dreams, has buck teeth and lusterless eyes in a doughy face.

Pedro was dismayed. Under his mattress lay a collection of drawings of ankles, lacy frills, and cleavages, a sheaf of foolishness that predated the sight of the bailiff's daughter's teeth. A waste of paper...a whole ledger full...sleepless nights, lost hours, a waste of Sor Juana Inés de la Cruz and poets who thought of anything but rabbits when they were writing their poems. What to do with those papers of passion? Whether to save them or dump them in the trash? Where is there a place to store away a passion that has culminated in rabbit's teeth? Tied in knots of silk and ribbons, bodices and cleavages, lambs and snowflakes, he remained standing there like an unwound watch, discomfited, an empty heart on his sleeve in a world with no room for empty hearts.

Then, at that very moment, the earth quaked. Pedro took it for the shivering of a body that had become unstable because of the sudden loss of a vital organ. He did not realize that the earth itself was trembling until he saw a roof tile fall and Serrano running toward the door that led to the street. Pedro made a move to follow him but Agueda's hand on his hand restrained him. "You're not an ass like that Governor, are you now?" she said coyly, not moving from her seat. "It's only one of those little tremors that make this city vibrate...it will be over in a moment."

A second tile slipped down toward the space left by the first, raising a little cloud of reddish dust. The inkwell danced on the table, slid as far as the edge, stopped there and ceased quivering...

"It's over," said Agueda, letting go of Pedro's hand. "I'll have a couple of tiles sent over from my house to replace those."

She rose calmly, went to the window, looked out, and laughed. Pedro glanced at the square and saw Serrano in the center, bowlegged, hugging a tree.

"Oh, that Serrano!" said Agueda, her rabbit teeth glinting in the sunlight. "I'll tell my father to order the mules for you to pick up the wine at La Caldera." And without further ado, she lifted her skirts and marched off with Bárbara Lorenzana. Pedro remained watching as Serrano returned slowly to the city hall, bowing politely as he passed Agueda, and climbed the stairs stiffly. He said to Pedro, "You'd best start preparing your trip. The Pérez de Muro family don't like to be kept waiting."

Pedro set out with the mule train furious with himself for having completely lost his common sense. It had not even occurred to him to borrow proper clothing for the trip from Smiles. After the quake, the sky had turned dark, and it was not long before it began to rain in torrents. Pedro got soaked, caught a cold, and when he reached the Pacific Ocean after a week of trudging uphill and down without letup, accompanied by a muleteer hired along with the mules, he was so exhausted and feverish that he preferred enduring the infernal heat with its onslaught of mosquitoes for another week to undertaking the return trip at once. The red, potbellied jugs stoppered with sealing wax were removed from their bed of straw, the muleteer distributed the load and the dried, salt fish that was to be their food onto the backs of the mules and they set off on the return over the same exhausting road. The mules were bad-tempered because the load was heavy, the terrain rough, and the downpour, between drizzle and cloudbursts, unceasing. On the third night of stopping in roadside huts to sleep, soaked to the skin, so parched from the salt fish that water could no longer alleviate the thirst, the muleteer lightened one mule of part of its load, breaking the seal on a jug and raising it to his mouth. When he lowered it, Pedro's hand was already stretched out to receive it. He had already invented the story about the mule stumbling and smashing a jug. The last of the wine trickled down the throats of one howling sad songs and the other burbling incoherences about rabbit teeth and the earth quaking underfoot.

Pedro had never before drunk spirits distilled from grapes and was curious to find out what pisco tasted like. Each day the fish seemed saltier and the tale of stumbling mules more convincing. The saddlebags were now filled with Peruvian pottery shards and the mules, though no longer weighted down, seemed in no hurry to be back in Cartago.

A boatman on the Rio Grande, wielding his oar, came close to cracking the skull of a drunkard who insisted on trying to get his mouth open to see what his teeth looked like.

Two weeks later, a muleteer, dead drunk, arrived one afternoon at the Bailiff of the Inquisition's home with a drove of mules and a story that the animals had stumbled and broken the jugs. Nothing was left in the saddlebags but shards since all the wine had been soaked up by the road.

Pedro had no idea when it was that he threw up the last of the salt fish swimming in a vermilion puddle. He regained consciousness in prison with his legs shackled and a suit pending for the theft of 23 jugs of wine and 7 of pisco. Snoring beside him was the muleteer, his head in pillory. The city council was deprived of its scribe, Agueda's father of his wine, and Pedro of his liberty.

Smiles paid him a visit bearing a dish of minced *arracachá* root, three tortillas, and a gourd full of milk. He told him everything he had been able to find out. Serrano was confined to bed in critical condition. Pérez de Muro was determined to press for the Governor's resignation. The Superior was praying for Pedro's salvation but had no intention of lifting a finger for him. Agueda was the only one who laughed at the scandal. The shoemaker learned this from Blas González's washerwoman, who did her laundry in the same stream as Agueda's washerwoman.

"She must have sensed something about you to be laughing over the fix you're in."

"I don't know this washerwoman nor ever spoke to her."

"You're still soused. I'm not talking about the washerwoman, I'm talking about the Pérez woman."

Pedro was released after a week because Agueda interceded for him. The muleteer stayed locked up for three more weeks and every time Pedro passed by the jail he could hear him ranting, shouting that Pedro was the one who had instigated the emptying of the jugs.

Pedro felt obliged to pay Agueda a call to thank her for getting him released, and one day when he saw her on the roof of the house she was building he did so, unwillingly. She was inextricably associated with a sense of deception and danger. His reluctance was caused not only by regret for the time and emotion he had wasted on her but by the fact that she had held his hand during the earthquake, making it appear that this was prompted by concern that a tile might fall on his head. Fortunately that did not happen, but it might well have. She saw him approaching and climbed off the roof confidently and lithely on a rickety ladder, showing her white silk hose and the fringes of her tumultuous petticoats. It was a sight that no longer thrilled him. Nor was he gratified by her cordial reception, her excusing him for drinking up her father's wine, and putting all the blame on the muleteer. "It was not your fault, Pedralbarán. You are a respectable, reliable person and the whole city knows it."

She began to pursue him from that time on. She would arrive at the city hall on any pretext, pinning him behind his desk, indifferent to the impression made or the gossip aroused since her husband had not yet returned from his trip to Guatemala. He was pushing his appointment while waiting for instructions from his father-in-law regarding Serrano's deposition.

Pedro had removed all his little sketches and verses from their hiding place and made confetti out of them. He then went to The Mother for a counterspell to keep Agueda out of his hair, but it turned out to be utterly ineffective since the obstinate woman would confront him in the church before everybody, making it appear a casual encounter.

It was during this period of going about looking over his shoulder, ready to dodge Agueda, that the reply arrived for the missionaries. The document authorized recruitment of a complement of seventy mulatto freedmen and valley Indians to make up the escort to Talamanca, as well as any Spaniards who wished to go. It provided four thousand pesos, as well, to defray expenses. Serrano, overwhelmed by debt, bending to the will of his constituents, having no authority or power, obeyed the order without a word. Those opposed to it commented bitterly. Blas González went as far as to tell Serrano to his face: "We in this province are being sent governors with no background, common soldiers unable to command respect" and added that the Bewitched King was in that way rewarding services of dubious merit.

"I fought the French!" protested Serrano faintly, debilitated as he was by the diarrhea, which, fortunately, had stopped.

"Better not bring it up at this time," said Blas González, with a smile. "You Honor forgets that the Pyrenees no longer exist and that the King of Spain is French. The fact of the matter is that the few workers in this valley are going to waste their time and perhaps lose their lives in an evangelizing adventure that will produce little benefit. As far as I'm concerned, Friar Pablo has been allotted a stipend of one butt of wine and forty pesos a year. Let him accept it and leave off dunning me for more altar wine and wheat for the hosts. If he runs out of flour let him make them out of corn. Not a single peso more will be forthcoming from my account."

Seventy men were recruited from among valley Indians, mulatto freedmen, and the few Spaniards disposed to risk their skins in these remote mountains. Pablo de Rebullida removed the Saint Anne altarpiece from his cell together with the candles and all the rest of the things he had been so patiently accumulating. He loaded the mules and with the help of a mulatto named Cristóbal returned overland to his mission in Talamanca, leaving as a remembrance the lame mule on which he had arrived. San José waited until the recruitment was complete, stubbornly insisting on an idea that sounded wild-eyed to everybody but which nevertheless began to be accepted as time went by. It was to reach Talamanca through the mouth of the Sixaola, an enormous river that was swarming with crocodiles. San José's plan was to proceed to the port of Matina and to move the escort from there to the mountains by boat.

While these preparations were under way, with Rebullida gone, the monastery reverted to its former way of life. Theological discussions on whether Adam had a navel were suspended, scheduling of vespers and matins became less rigid, and a fresh breeze of liberality began to blow through the monastery. The Superior, as usual, continued putting his foot in it and laying the blame on the impiety of his children. Nothing, however, caused him as much annoyance as the pranks of the lad Juan de las Alas who had been caught one night trying to jump over the wall—off to where he would not say—by means of the same tree that abetted Pedro's escapades. The Superior, well aware of the nocturnal rambling of his bookkeeper, who had turned out to be considerably less God-fearing than he had at first seemed, gave him the huge key to the monastery's main door, and ordered the tree cut down. What the Franciscan did not know was that there were strange goings-on in the kitchen undetectable at a cursory glance, such as the fact that Juan de las Alas had lost his appetite and was going about ill-groomed, distracted and in a befuddled state. Not a keen observer, the Superior had assigned the youth a task that aggravated his condition. He was to learn the language of Gerónima, the Indian cook, the one who went about with an iron ladle never out of her hand. The other Indian, her younger sister, was small, thin, and unquestionably a mute. Another of Juan's tasks was to deliver the monastery sandals to Smiles for repair. Those trips gave him an opportunity to slip over to the city hall to chat with Pedro and ferret out what he was doing. It was because of this circumstance that Pedro came to be the first to realize that a catastrophe was in the making. It dawned on him the moment that Juan, standing before his desk, bag of sandals in hand, very nervous, asked him if he knew of any system for communicating with mutes.

A few days before that, Pedro had gone down to bathe in the stream that ran through the monastery yard but was unable to do so because the two Indians were there washing clothes. Gerónima, the elder, sturdy and stout, was sitting astride a rock bashing the laundry as though the water were there to destroying. As he approached, she raised her head, and he read such hostility in her eyes that it startled him. Her sister was leaning over with a bored expression watching a leaf floating in the water. She wore a hood, her skirt was hiked up to keep it out of the water, and her slender young thighs were of such elegance that he had to force himself to tear his eyes away and return to the monastery.

Juan de las Alas looked at him intently and blushed. Pedro was about to answer that the hands were used for communicating with mutes but quickly changed his mind, for that was open to grave misinterpretation.

"Why would you want to be communicating with mutes? Theirs is a mysterious world. Even they themselves don't know it."

"Oh, you're wrong. Catalina is no ordinary mute. She knows things...knows things and I would like to find out what they are...I want her to..."

"There isn't much a wild Indian could know if she can't even talk. Forget about her and remember that there's only a short time to go before they'll be sending you to school in Guatemala to become a missionary. Isn't that what you want? So forget about this, it's not for you. Now take off, you're wasting my time. I have to finish making the list of soldiers who will be going along with the missionaries and you're holding me up with your nonsense." He regretted the offended expression with which the boy looked at him as he picked up his bag of sandals and left. That was the first alarm. The second was when he confessed that he thought the mute was very beautiful, saying so with eyes opened wide, as though the kitchen were an immense magical boiler from which unusual and wonderful things came bubbling out.

Pedro then considered that he should play the part of older brother and warn him about life's dangers. He began by reminding him of the Superior's words when Juan was assigned to help the cooks by waiting on table: "Women are a cloaca built over a temple."

"That's not what San Agustín said," Juan corrected him. "What he said was that women were a temple built over a cloaca." Having made the clarification, Juan folded his arms in preparation for continuing to listen to the imminent counseling. Pedro raised an index finger in a gesture that seemed to him appropriate for moral instruction and proceeded to explain that women did not exist, that they were illusory, that they never bear any resemblance to the image that is created of them and that men usually let themselves be carried away by vain dreams and later pay dearly when they discover that women have feet of clay. Pedro then lowered his finger and noted with some satisfaction that Juan had dropped his glance as a sign that he understood. After a moment, he raised it, looked at Pedro out of the deep pools of his eyes, and observed: "I don't know why you're telling me all this. I'm not interested in women. All I want is to be able to communicate with The Mute."

Days went by and Pedro neglected to warn the Superior that the youngest sheep in his flock was about to be snapped up in the jaws of a mute she-wolf. A new concern had clouded the horizon, this time in the atrium of the church. Father Angulo had asked for help in an extremely delicate matter. The Superior could not refuse because the priest had already told Serrano, who could deny him nothing, that he needed the services of a scribe. Pedro, likewise, was not in a position after the wine-jug scandal to refuse anybody anything. When he remembered Juan de las Alas, alone and unfettered in the kitchen, he decided to let things run their course for, after all, did not the poet Arcipreste de Hita say that ladies were necessary except when very small and the mute was quite little. Apart from this, if he wanted to hold on to his job at the city council, he had best concern himself with serious matters and not the flirtations of an adolescent little friar. It was Serrano himself who informed Pedro that Father Angulo was requesting his cooperation in a delicate matter. Serrano, his tail between his legs, was doing his utmost to ingratiate himself with the Commissary of the Inquisition, who was now collecting the funds to make up the deficit in the royal treasury.

* * *

I said to Pedro: "Listen, what those pigs want is for this Governor to stay on. The possibility is very remote that another as indulgent would be sent from Spain. A new, straitlaced one might even take it into his head to go in for controlling smuggling and collecting taxes."

He was getting fed up with Agueda Pérez keeping her sights trained on him and pursuing him even into the city council. I warned him to be very careful with that woman, that she was the kind who stops at nothing and respects nobody. Not even her father could teach her obedience and modesty and the priests weren't able even to get her to cover her head, her husband, who goes about chasing down honorary appointments and lusting for power, least of all.

The Pérez woman was making life unbearable for my sidekick, and I said to him: "Watch your step with that wench, she's liable to make trouble for you. Why not settle down and get hitched? That way, the married ones won't be giving you the eye."

"'I have no intention of sticking my head in the noose,'" was his answer.

I told him: "Marriage is right for you. You're from the Peninsula and the girls don't need to know much more than that to catch an upper-crust scent. You're not taking advantage of your gifts, my boy. Listen to me and hook into a cacao fortune."

"What about yourself?" he asked me. "Why haven't you done it?"

"Because I wasn't born in Spain, dammit! Can't you spot the mestizo in me? A country girl smelling of sour milk is about the most I could aspire to. And that's still in the offing, still in the offing..."

"I don't want to get married. Not me, not ever!" He said that flatly and recited a couplet:

> "Matrimony's a vise,
> A trap in a fool's paradise."

I matched him couplet for couplet:

> "To be kissed by a husband from Spain,
> What greater bliss could a girl attain?"

At least that's the idea of girls in the colonies and they'll give anything for the chance. But Pedro is going to end up entangled with Casasola's wife and when the fellow comes back from Guatemala and finds out he'll skewer him like a turkey on a spit.

*Threats loom over Pedro de Albarán
and the Inquisition enforces its
justice*

"Another task finished," said Pedro to Serrano, as they watched San José moving out at the head of a contingent of sixty motley, ill-shod soldiers and a corporal, carrying with them rations of salt meat, tins of biscuits, pouches of tobacco, and spirits.

"We hope so," replied Serrano. "but my familiarity with military matters tells me that they'll soon be back with us."

Serrano went home. Pedro hoisted his feet up on the desk. Ever since he had been able to afford a new pair of boots, he took great pride in admiring them, neat, smooth, shiny. After Smiles's prodding about marriage, he took to calculating who among the girls he knew might make him a suitable wife. He kept going back in his mind to Nicolasa Guerrero, whom he had seen at mass, always accompanied by her brother Juan. Though young, she was sprouting the forms of a woman, and was perhaps going on seventeen, a good age at which to snare her before somebody else did. Her father owned some land in Ujarrás and although not monied people, they were getting by. This was compensated for by the fact that Nicolasa had the charm and freshness of a ripening fruit. Although she couldn't read or write she was young enough to learn. He was daydreaming about all this, fantasizing educating her, living with her in a comfortable little home somewhere, the two of them having breakfast together on cinnamon buns and fresh water, drinking chocolate at twilight, and frolicking at night in a bed without fleas or bedbugs, when the shoemaker came in, cross.

"I can't understand how you do it, how you make it with the ladies in that getup of yours, looking like a half-starved outcast? What do you do to them that they chase after you like that?"

Pedro jumped to his feet and made for the back door, thinking that Smiles was referring to Agueda Pérez.

"Where are you going? She's not here yet," the shoemaker reassured him, and proceeded to explain what happened. A muleteer on his way from Nicaragua with a train of pack animals to sell in Panama City had stopped off at The Mother's place and asked if she knew of a certain Pedro de la Baranda. It seemed a Spanish woman, from Seville from the look of her, was asking about him. She was resting in the city of León where she was recovering from a fall from her horse. The woman had asked the muleteer to find out on his way through Costa Rica if this Pedro was there or, if he had been and gone, where he was bound for, since she was prepared to go to Tierra del Fuego, if necessary, to locate him. That was what the muleteer told The Mother and she promised to have the information for him on his way back to Nicaragua if she found out anything.

"But give me a clue, give me a clue, what have you got that makes a woman go that crazy, falling off horses and all, searching for you?" Smiles looked at him as though seeing him for the first time. "You've never told me anything about your life, and I thought you were my friend. So, it's on account of that woman that you came running here... Now, you see, she found you, she found you!" The muleteer didn't know her name but said she was wearing a *chambergo*. The Mother told Pedro more or less the same story and added, "Daddy boy, I always distrust mysterious people because I like things out in the open and that woman who's looking for you goes around in a *chambergo*, they say. And so, I let the muleteer know that I would have the information for him on his way back. That way, I can tell him I never heard of you if that's what you want me to do. You've got two months to think it over. It's your call."

Why was La Chamberga hunting him? It couldn't be anybody else. How did she know that his name was now Pedro de la Baranda? Servando was right when he said "Beware the angry woman for she's worse than a snake." How did she know he was in Costa Rica? Who was financing her trip? The last time he saw her was the day she threw him out of her tavern and told him, "Get out, you drunkard, I never want to see you again!" Those were the exact words La Chamberga shouted at him before she slammed the door in his face, the crowd hooting at him. And, determined never to return, he staggered off in search of another tavern-keeper somewhere else in Seville. Now, here she was in Cartago waiting to mess up his life, for God alone knows what sinister reason. She appeared like a ghost from a past that he would have liked to expunge just at a time when he was thinking of marrying Nicolasa Guerrero and settling down Spanish-stye, that is say, with a young woman who possessed a sizable fortune. Well... Nicolasa was no heiress but her father was a respectable person and she was Spanish, a sweet, demure homebody, and a very pretty one, of that there was no doubt. La Chamberga was appearing at the most inopportune moment, just as Pedro de la Baranda was forgetting Pedro Albarán. La Chamberga was putting in question the flagellation he had given himself during Holy Week, ruining all his patient work, all the innumerable fasts...even the humiliations, such as the apologies he had made to San José after mocking him because in one of the theological after-dinner discussions, San José had offered the opinion that even if Christ had been born a bean sprout he would still have been the Redeemer. Two years of forging a new God-fearing personality and La Chamberga was there to throw a crimp into all his efforts! Everything down the shit hole! Great gossip that she was, she would spread it all over town that Pedro's name wasn't de la Baranda but Albarán, a student from Seville who had gotten into trouble with the Inquisition and escaped from one of their prisons. La Chamberga knew all this...she always knew everything.

Lázaro de Robles, an evil smirk on his face, approached the desk as Pedro was pondering the problem of La Chamberga. Lázaro de Robles had returned to the city council after the lawyer of the Royal Tribunal left, and was up to his old tricks of emptying the inkwell and smearing chicken shit on his chair seat.

"The Commissary of the Inquisition wants to see you," he announced, a note of sadistic pleasure in his voice, "and he wants a lancer to go with you."

"Up your ass with the lancer!" roared Pedro on his way to the stairway on his skinny legs, Lázaro's snake eyes following him down.

Father Angulo was waiting for him at a huge table in what he called his hearing chamber, a bronze bell beside him that he used to silence grumblers, and what seemed like enough chairs around the room to accommodate half the city. Pedro sat down in one of them waiting to be told why he was wanted. Father Angulo, twirling one of his curls, looked at him closely, caressed the bell gently and sensually, picked up a sheet of paper, and spoke. "I am gratified that His Honor the Governor has seen fit to collaborate in this particular instance by granting me the use of your services, Pedralbarán. The case is an extremely delicate one, a matter of incest. A daughter who denounced her father has been placed in safekeeping at the home of Mier Ceballos where she will receive indoctrination appropriate for her soul... The poor little thing doesn't know what it's all about. You, Pedro Albarán, will have to go as soon as possible to the western valley to question the neighbors, record the testimony in this painful affair, and conduct a preliminary hearing until such time as I proceed in my position as an Inquisition judge. Since this matter is exclusively within the Inquisition, I have so notified the Governor, in order that he should not intervene. In any case, I have called for two lancers to accompany you, for as long as necessary."

Angulo let his eyes wander over the paper he held in his hands, a heavy gold ring with a purple stone in the center on his right ring finger and on his left hand two smaller diamond rings in silver settings. Pedro let his eyes roam from the priest's hands to the emblem of the Inquisition on the wall behind him. He was able to make out clearly the cross, olive branch, and sword. The same symbols must certainly have been on the door of the carriage into which he was thrown when they took him prisoner but they placed a cloth over his head before he could take note of anything. The Seville Inquisition had arrested Pedro as he walked peacefully down the street with no thought in mind except how to get La Chamberga to forgive him and what excuses to invent to avoid paying the bill he owed for wine and sausages which was of long-standing and substantial. That was why he had sought out the dark and gloomy little-used alleys of Seville. The smells of cooking seeped through the windows. Playing in the doorways were a few children, well bundled up because with summer on the way out, the weather was turning cool. He didn't realize what was happening when they hooded him and offered no resistance when shoved into a carriage which took off immediately in some direction he could not tell. When he heard the roar of the Guadalquivir River he was afraid that they were bound for the bridge to the Triana Castle, the most sinister and dreaded prison of the Inquisition. When the carriage stopped, they led him out, still hooded, stupefied and terrified, to a sound of creaking hinges and locks.

Father Angulo's fluttery, childish voice drew his attention from the Inquisition emblem to the table where the priest was looking at him curiously. He was saying, "They are the symbols of the Inquisition...the olive branch for forgiveness, the sword for punishment... Were you not familiar with them?"

"Of course, I was," Pedro hastened to assure him. "What Christian doesn't recognize the emblem of the Inquisition?"

Angulo laughed goodhumoredly. "Christian or infidel, they know it everywhere in the world. And, now, down to our business. Under your word of absolute confidentiality, read this letter I received concerning the issue at the western valley, a place of perdition where the devil and his cohorts have free rein... The possibility always exists that the daughter is lying. When parents punish children severely, they may invent tales in revenge." Taking out a white cambric handkerchief, he blew his nose delicately and went on, "Yes, the untrustworthiness of an angry woman is taken for granted." He then folded up the handkerchief neatly, pocketed it, took a turn around the table, and approached Pedro, the letter in his hand. "Should that woman be lying," he said, his voice rising melodramatically as he raised a hand to his childish breast, "she will receive her just desserts. If not, punishment will be meted out! Rest assured that God's sword, in my hand, will be wielded, Pedralbarán."

Perhaps La Chamberga was lying to him all along and was an informer of the Inquisition. Where did she get the money with which to open her tavern? Her past was a mystery, her place of origin an imprecise village among vineyards and olive groves... La Chamberga loved money and would sell herself for twenty-five pesetas. There was absolutely no reason for her to cross the ocean in search of Pedro Albarán. Why had such a shrewd person as Servando been so stupid as to pick out a name for him so close to the original? Why not have made him pass for an Italian with a name like Piero de la Barandola, for instance.

But there was no time for further conjecture, Father Angulo was holding out the letter to him, saying. "Once you have taken the statements of the neighbors, bring them to me immediately in utmost secrecy. Nobody must know that you are on a mission for the Inquisition. Let the priest of the western valley conduct the investigation, let him do the questioning. All you have to do is write down what they say. Nothing more."

Pedro took the letter and read: "Señor Commissary of the Holy Inquisition, Francisca Hernández appeared before me to accuse her father Pedro Hernández of illicit solicitation of her, as well as of his other two daughters and, because of this, he cruelly mistreats his wife. The three of them, in addition to living such a shameful life, are completely ignorant of Christian doctrine, do not attend mass, as the said María Francisca, whom I am turning over to your court, will tell you, the offender remains in prison for having attempted to escape upon learning that his daughter had brought charges against him..." The signature was that of the priest with whom Pedro would be working. Angulo concluded the interview and that was all.

Pedro was soon to understand why such a delicate task, one Angulo himself should have been responsible for, was entrusted to a neophyte like him. The road to the scene of the allegations was an absolute calvary. With a table and chair on the back of a mule, his inkwell, pens, and a sheaf of paper in his bag, and the company of lancers who knew the way, he had to climb rugged, desolate mountains to reach the Hernández dwelling and the mission where the local priest was holding the offender prisoner. His worst misfortunes were the mud and swollen rivers, for he nearly drowned in protecting the paper from getting wet. It was unusual to encounter a hanging bridge, or even a simple one of logs, and so most of the time he was forced to wade or swim across. When he finally arrived at the priest's modest dwelling, the man lent him a tattered old cassock until his clothing could dry out. Only an innocent like Pedro, ignorant of geography, would have ventured to make a trip to a remote place like that over such a road.

Standing at the fire where Pedro's clothing were drying, the priest of the western valley felt them and then turned them over, taking his time in doing so for he did not know what to think of this inexperienced young man that the delegate of the Inquisition had sent on such a delicate matter. And he was a foreigner, to boot. It was obvious to him at first sight that this fellow in a ragged cassock had no idea what to do, how to do it, or why, nor the slightest interest in any of it.

"I imagine..." he said reassuringly to Pedro, "I imagine you would like to know the background of the matter before beginning the investigation. Unfortunately, I can't tell you much because I am bound by confessional secrecy. The girl came to see me and told me what was already common gossip among the neighbors, and I had already suspected as much. I immediately sent her to Cartago for the Commissary of the Inquisition, Father Angulo, to decide the matter. I assume that María Hernández would have told him exactly what she told me. And now the Commissary wants to collect the testimony of the neighbors... It won't be easy. The Spaniards in these godforsaken places are very different from those in the city. Here, the poverty of the mulattos and black freedmen and that of the Spaniards, who could only survive by working the land with their own hands, are joined. When the countryside is poor it brutalizes.

There are no iron tools, or very few, the work is exhausting, mornings are freezing and damp, and breakfast often consists of nothing but a cold ear of corn because the damp firewood resists the flame. The climate is no aid to survival; the mud, the constant overflowing of the rivers, the downpours, and the wind... The houses are so unprotected that when storms strike, it makes little difference whether one is inside or out. The cattle, sick all the time, are eaten by worms while still alive. The Lord puts his children to the test by visiting misfortunes of all sorts upon them. Poverty debases. He must know the reason why he does it. Families turn in on themselves, members of the same stock marry, isolate themselves, and become encased like turtles in their shells. They are all ashamed of their raggedness. I reached the extreme of suspending religious festivities because of the drunkenness, abuse, and immorality that takes place. That is the way these poor sheep give vent to the anguish that has festered in them all the year... The city has abandoned us. The Governor is more concerned about tribute from the Indians and the labor of the slaves than about these unfortunates who are free but starving, forsaken by the hand of God and of the King..."

Curled up in the priest's cassock waiting for his clothes to dry, Pedro wondered where the man was heading with this monologue.

"...In the case of Pedro Hernández—God forgive me—I would not have denounced him had the daughter not come out with it. You will ask yourself what kind of shepherd I am who does not keep his flock in order. Were I to do so, the flock would go to pieces... The poor girl was shattered when she came to see me, she had to walk a long way to my house and was covered with mud when she arrived. A pitiful sight, she cried a long while until she was able to tell her story. I already knew it. We all did. But nobody denounced him, nobody did anything...out of fear. Fear is everywhere here, you spoon it up with your soup, it is under the covers with you... There's fear of the lancers and fear of the field judges who, when they come for the cattle to supply the city's meat, steal the mules and attack the girls. If there has been a dispute over a bit of land or parcel of cane, there's fear of a neighbor seeking revenge. Fear is everywhere and it's never certain from where the danger will come. Your hardest job will be loosening tongues. The people here hate words. They hide when they feel them coming... You'll see for yourself...they hide..."

The priest stopped talking. And so—Pedro thought—Father Angulo had sent him on a fool's errand. His clothes now dry, he took off the cassock and got dressed.

"We'll leave the lancers behind and go alone, you and I. That will seem less threatening."

Astride the slow and placid beast Angulo had provided him, Pedro accompanied the priest on the long, tortuous journey into the mountains, visiting the peasants in their mud-and-wattle dwellings lashed unmercifully by the furious winds. Covered with ponchos made of bark, ragged, inhospitable, hostile, suspicious people emerged from the huts like creatures out of an animal refuge. Naked women hid behind bushes in the yards, the men appeared to be suffering from chronic deafness, children fled when they saw them approaching. The priest dismounted and with infinite patience proceeded to open portholes in the walls of blank minds. Pedro took out paper and inkwell from his bag, set out his table and chair, and wrote, filling out the monosyllables emitted as answers.

After three days of arduous traveling little was accomplished, the only information he obtained being that Pedro Hernández was never to be seen at mass, at confession, or taking communion. That was all. He put the scanty testimony in order and had Hernández released from imprisonment in the mission. He was a Spaniard, fifty years old or thereabouts, who swore, blasphemed, and spat in the direction of the altar. An illiterate peasant, an immigrant from somewhere or other, a fugitive from a fiefdom of goats and *droit du seigneur*, Hernández was at the nadir of degradation and seemed to be mentally disturbed. Nudged along by the lancers, he walked the road dragging his calloused, bunioned feet and muttering foul insults against those who had affronted his dignity. Faltering at every step, he kept bellowing that he was a true Christian with no Moorish, Jewish, Indian, or African taint, who was not about to let his daughters be dishonored by getting impregnated with the base blood of a dark-colored male.

In a Cartago prison, Hernández, his head and hands in pillory, blasphemed to such a degree that the bars of his cell had to be covered so that passersby would not have to listen to his foul imprecations.

Angulo, not satisfied with the depositions taken by Pedro, ordered that the prisoner's wife and his other two daughters be arrested. This was done with a great show of spears and cavalry, and the women were confined at the home of José de Mier Ceballos, whose wife covered her eyes at the shocking sight of Hernández's wife. She looked like a horrible, humpbacked witch, a prematurely aged reject of femininity, her legs crooked and covered with varicose veins, the expression in her eyes that of a draft animal brutalized by inhuman burdens.

The Inquisition trial was the talk of the town and expectation high among the people. At the monastery, Pedro was besieged by the friars, who gave him no peace, grilling him about this, that, and the other. Busybodies, trying to make it appear that they were unconcerned, passed by the Mier de Ceballos house in the hope of catching a glimpse of the four woman being held there, who, in addition to receiving religious indoctrination, were doing housework, gratis. Mier Ceballos was furious at the annoyance being caused by the horde of vendors who knocked at the door incessantly, offering bundles of firewood, fruit drinks, sweetened fresh water, eggs, preserves, syrups, brooms, baskets, gourds, cordage, chickens, suckling pigs, rabbits, griddles, clay pots, cotton saddlebags, and pastries. If it wasn't vendors stretching their necks at the doorway hoping for a curiosity-satisfying peek, it was mischievous kids who knocked at the door and fled when it was opened. It was the same situation at the prison where the incestuous Spaniard was locked up. An attempt was even made to knock a hole in the fresh adobe that blocked the cell window. The Governor, then, had no choice but to station a line of lancers before the door and window, not for fear of the prisoner escaping but because the intruders did not obey orders to move on and had to be held off at spear's point.

The Superior believed that the Commissary of the Inquisition had involved himself in an insoluble conflict since Hernández had no confiscable property. He was not alone in that opinion. Blas González also considered Angulo a prisoner of his own court, because if he declared Hernández innocent, public opinion would be against him and if he found him guilty, he would have to assume all the expenses of prison maintenance and, what is more, defray out of his own pocket the long and extremely expensive trip to the Supreme Court of the Inquisition in Mexico.

It seems that Angulo had already realized that he had entangled himself in his own web for he sent a special courier to León to request the bishop to assume charge of the prisoner. The bishop, however, took advantage of the opportunity to rid himself with elegance of all obligations to Angulo, by an immediate response to the effect that it would be unnecessary for it was a case the Commissary would know how to settle. With Hernández being too hot to handle, Angulo chose to hold a trial the like of which had never before been seen in Cartago. He searched his library and came up with a similar case tried many years ago. He reread the "Commissary's Manual" many times, prepared his case rigorously in accordance with established procedure and notified the Bailiff of the Inquisition to appear. Agueda's father, who, to be honest, had no intention of wasting his time over a case of incest, replied that he had urgent business in Panama and went to La Caldera to await a ship. This added fuel to rumors that the Bailiff had a mistress there and explained his very frequent trips to that city. When this news reached Agueda's mother, Doña Mariana de Echeverría, she told Father Angulo that no Inquisition trial could be held in Cartago without her husband's presence and that he must have him located or she would notify the bishop that there were irregularities in his procedures. While this was going on, Hernández remained in prison eating at the Commissary's expense. And time passed. Mier Ceballos's wife was protesting about the hunchback woman's presence in her house, and Mier Ceballos requested an armed guard to protect his entrance, for the continuous opening and closing of the door by busybodies had loosened its hinges.

Beset, Angulo neglected to make the spit curls over his temples and appeared unkempt with two lank strands of hair hanging at either side of his forehead. He set a date for the opening of the Inquisition trial, which was to be held in the hall of ordinary ecclesiastical meetings, observing all legalities, including the participation of a lawyer, an inquisitor, and a scribe. The lawyer had very urgent business to take care of at his cattle hacienda in Bagaces and left his defense—that Hernández was insane—in writing. The scribe was Pedro de la Baranda, hastily sworn in, to enable Angulo to ask for his resignation on the day of the trial's termination. The only bona fide professional taking part in the trial was the Inquisitor; Avendaño was a professional. He came from Mexico and had stopped off in Cartago for a few days on his way to Cartagena to board ship in Matina. When Angulo introduced Pedro to Avendaño he thought there was something familiar about that somber style of dress, those sharp, waxen features, shrewd, piercing eyes, and malicious, calculating expression. Looking him up and down, Avendaño said, "Pedro de la Baranda...Where did I hear that name before?"

Angulo shut the door of the hearing chamber and summoned the main witnesses to the crime, Hernández's wife and three daughters, for questioning. The first to testify was the plaintiff, María Hernández, a good-looking young woman, dressed in castoffs of Mier Ceballos's wife. She made nervous little gestures with her hands and had difficulty expressing herself. The presence of Angulo and Avendaño was inhibiting. Speaking haltingly and choking up from time to time, she strung out the same story she told the western-valley priest: that her father had been harassing her for the last ten years with persistent, indecent approaches and when she refused, which was always, he would tie her up and whip her. Even so, she never gave in. But, on the second day of Lent, on the way back from the village of Brava with her father, he ordered her into a deserted house and there committed the wicked deed.

"Child, why did you let him?" asked Angulo. "Don't you know that it is a double crime? The sin of lust and an offense against nature."

"I know...I know..." wept María Francisca, "but I didn't have the strength... and God tells us we must obey our father, doesn't He?"

"You've not had proper indoctrination, girl. Go on with your statement."

María Francisca went into detail, flustered by the weeping of her sisters beside her.

The mother seemed not to understand anything and did nothing but stare at her bare feet.

Pedro was having a very hard time keeping his record coherent, particularly in the case of María Francisca's statement that she, her mother, and her father shared the same bed and that Hernández made his wife sleep at the foot, leaving him and the daughter in the widest part. Afterward, Angulo questioned María Francisca about the family's religious habits, and she confessed that she had never seen her father go to mass or anything and that on one occasion when she wanted to go to confession, he forbade her, saying that priests took advantage of women at confession and so had no right to give absolution for they were themselves in sin.

Angulo cut the girl off at once and turned to her sisters. Their statements corroborated hers. The mother would not open her mouth no matter how much she was questioned, and the interrogation was closed.

Outside, a multitude had assembled to watch the girl who was raped by her father come out. It was like the day Bárbara

Lorenzana was auctioned off, when the boys climbed the trees to have a clear view of the spectacle. Angulo came to the door with his spit curls mussed, sent everyone packing, and let the women leave the building under escort of the lancers. Trailing behind María Francisca's sobs went the sobbing of her sisters and the hunchback's stubborn silence.

At the monastery, Pedro was under siege to pass on the story of what the witnesses had said. So absorbed were the friars in hearing the last detail that, but for luck, the Superior would never have found out that his youngest friar, he of the green eyes and outsize cassock, had had his senses awakened and his head turned because of the mute Indian girl, so diminutive and gentle, like a chaste Romeo who had transformed the Franciscan monastery of Cartago into a Verona and his habit into a bone of contention.

Pedro had held his peace regarding that forbidden love and turned out to have been quite mistaken in assuming that the first gust of wind would blow out the flame. But the unstable balance of the situation came close to tumbling Juan de las Alas and leaving him bound forever to the unforgettable body of a female. Delighted with the idea that Juan would be learning Gerónima's native tongue, which would then serve him for converting the heathen, the Superior suspected nothing. Pedro had reasoned, very superficially, that if The Mute were not dumb, Juan's enthusiasm would have chilled quickly; that it was the mystery that had gotten him into such a state of excitation. He concluded, therefore, that the most sensible course would be to leave it to the process of time to weary Juan of reaching for forbidden fruit. This is what Pedro had thought, not realizing that he himself never tied of wondering why La Chamberga was looking for him.

Lorenzo, spending a few days at the monastery in recovery from his harsh life in Chirripó, was the one who sounded the tocsin. And he did so with a fury and force that only envy, rancor, and vengeance are capable of producing. Standing in the kitchen, he banged with a ladle upon the kettle over the fire. It was that gong, with a sound like a blacksmith shop, that brought the Superior running. He found the friar smiting the vessel, the mute Indian girl, her hood down, staring in astonishment at the wild bell ringer, and the smallest of his sons, red as the inside of a watermelon, trying to hold back Lorenzo's barrage. The truth of what Lorenzo told was never verified but Juan de las Alas was sent to his cell with a penitence of twenty-five lashes to be self-inflicted with a hair shirt on.

Lorenzo's story was that he had gone into the kitchen in mid-afternoon, assuming that nobody would be there, to have a bit of bread and a cup of chocolate, only to come upon Juan de las Alas there with the girl's face between his hands, kissing it with savage intensity. According to Juan, however, he had no intention ever of doing any such thing and was only trying to read something related to a deep pool and tiny goldfish in the mute's eyes. This defense served him little, for the Superior did no more than reduce the punishment to only fifteen lashes and forgive the hair shirt. That night, in the silence of the vastness of stars that appeared nobody knows from where, Pedro heard a faltering, syncopated whap, whap, that made him shut his eyes and cover his ears. The next morning, the expression in the eyes of the little brother of the sun and moon, ever merry and mischievous, was that of an old man, and he walked hunched over.

Pedro was incensed at Lorenzo but was unable to do anything against him or for Juan because the Commissary's attention was totally centered on the trial of Hernández, who had been removed from prison to confess the day after Juan's flagellation.

Inquisitor Avendaño, who had Pedro accompany him on his visit to take cognizance of the prisoner locked in the pillory, observed the reprobate with the eye of a carpenter measuring a corpse for a coffin. Hernández, given to constant fits of rage, frothing at the mouth, screaming and cursing at whoever came nosing around, upon seeing Avendaño staring at him, kept his eyes cast down, his head pinned in its wooden vise, sensing that this man dressed all in black who glared at him so pitilessly, would be assuming possession of his body, his soul, and his life in this world, as well as the next. Trapped in the silence between the two men, ill at ease, and with an uncontrollable desire to flee, Pedro calmed himself with the thought that the prison at Cartago was a hostel for travelers in comparison to the dungeons of the Seville Inquisition. And that Pedro Hernández, head and hands poking out of the openings in the slab, could consider himself free and lucky compared with that anonymous voice in the San Gerónimo tower: "Ayayay, they're killing me, killing an innocent man with the justice of God."

In his first cell, Pedro had tried in vain to speak to his stone-faced jailer while Hernández was able to talk from his cell to passersby in the street if he so desired. In any case, his cries could be heard all the way to the monastery. Pedro Albarán never knew why he had been arrested nor what crime he was alleged to have committed, while Pedro Hernández was perfectly aware of his guilt, what he was being accused of, and why he was in the pillory at the Cartago prison. Hernández had not endangered anybody in his crime except for the harm he had done his daughter. Albarán was tortured by the uncertainty as to whether or not he had given Servando away or somehow involuntarily exposed the network that was distributing the books banned by the Inquisition. The very idea that his imprudence...

The very idea that his imprudence at La Chamberga's tavern had put the inquisitors on the trail was worse than the danger to his life and his future. The days of imprisonment went by in unbearable solitude, and he tried so hard to figure out the signs around him that he was at the edge of being unable to distinguish between reality and imagination and nearly went out of his mind holding dialogue with mysterious noises of doors and locks, chains and groans. And then the time came when the sounds spoke of blood and the stones of the dungeon made music for sinister instruments to root out sin.

They took him out when he was at the borderline of rationality and walked him, hooded and blind, through long corridors until he was thrown into what turned out to be a spacious room where there were four pallid men who looked at him suspiciously. In view of his recent indiscretions, Pedro refused to talk to them or answer their questions and remained seated on the floor, his back against the wall, looking at them. The other prisoners ignored him and moved away to converse under a window where light from a gray sky entered. Pedro was able to overhear them and to his surprise what they were saying had nothing to do with the calamity at hand but revolved around generalities of an academic nature.

One of them was saying, "As we were just discussing, the comet discovered by Halley proves that comets are wandering stars that continue on immutable paths through the universe. It can be assumed, then, that they are entirely devoid of religious context."

"Then that confirms the theory," another replied, "that God is a watchmaker who wound up the world and then lay down and took a nap."

Philosophizing along those lines kept the four of them occupied until nightfall when each lay down on a straw mattress and went to sleep. Pedro, without bed or bedding, stretched out on the bare floor and spent most of the night wide awake staring into space. When he awoke in the morning he heard one of them saying, "As we were commenting yesterday, the Dutchman's discovery of the tiny creatures with the big heads in the seminal fluid proves that all living beings inherit features that their fathers and mothers inherited from their grandfathers and so on, and so on, until you end up at Adam and Eve."

"And that goes to show," pointed out another, "that Aristotle was way off when he maintained that life begins with the egg."

"Semen is in the egg," said a third man, laughing. "Aristotle was mistaken in thinking of a single egg when actually life starts with four: two from the female and two from the male."

The conversation was interrupted by the entrance of a jailer carrying a pitcher of water and four rolls. The prisoners waited for him to leave and resumed their animated discussion the moment the door closed behind him, each with a roll in his hand. There was no roll for Pedro. Famished, he approached the men in the hope they would take notice of his predicament but they ignored him and kept on talking.

One of them bit a chunk out of his roll, chewed, swallowed, and went on expounding enthusiastically, "The necessary and sufficient condition for Kepler's laws to be correct is that the planets undergo an attraction from the sun that varies inversely by the square of the distance."

"Exactly," said another, "if the oscillations of a pendulum are slower at the equator, as the Cayenne observations showed, it is because gravity there is less with respect to the earth's bulge."

"And so we come down to the fact that comets obey the laws of attraction, as we analyzed yesterday, and their movements are only apparently irregular..." He broke off abruptly and said to Pedro, all of them staring at him, "What do you want? Don't tell me you're interested in what we are discussing."

There was no bread in sight. Pedro went back to his place, back against the wall, wondering how many times a day those prisoners received food and why he wasn't getting any.

The four men continued their animated conversation, jumping from one subject to another. At midday, Pedro started for the door in an effort to be there first when food arrived. Four plates of lentils and bacon appeared but he got none for he was pushed violently out of the way and had no choice but to retreat to his corner.

"Look here, young fellow," said the one who seemed the elder of the group, as he approached him with a plate in his hand. "I have no idea what your case is, but we are paying for this food ourselves, and all we can do for you—that is, if you act a little more sociable—is to let you have a bit of what they bring us." By the time they took him out three days later, Pedro had gotten used to the company of those unusual prisoners and their talk, which he realized was their only way of escaping momentarily from prison. The guard came for him in the middle of an animated discussion on Calderón de la Barca. They were observing that if life really were a dream, it made no sense to suffer, since upon awaking, everything dreamed would be over, absurd, illogical, and nonexistent.

Again, he was forced to go up and down steps, his eyes covered, and when he heard a door close and took off the blindfold, he thought he had lost his sight for the place was plunged in almost total darkness. When his eyes adjusted, he saw a faint light at an open slot near the ceiling. It was not daylight but a glow as though from many candles. He was in a very narrow dungeon, not much wider than a coffin in which he could barely fit sitting down on the wet and foul floor. The ceiling was so high it would have been impossible to see out of the slot even if there were a chair or something to stand on. And, agonizing over why they had moved him from where he was in the prison, he forced himself to be patient.

First, he thought it was the sound of rats gnawing at the walls a distance away, for it was indistinct and faint. He strained his ears, stretching toward the slot, and in that dense, sinister silence, the sound took on the characteristics of a pen scraping on paper. He considered calling out for help to whoever was writing, Before he could make up his mind there was a murmur of voices and the sound of steps at the barred opening near the ceiling. He chose not to make his presence known until he could determine who was there and what they were doing. Then, he couldn't remember what he had done. Or perhaps he had fainted. There were days of silence and days of sobbing and supplication. Confused in the delirium of his impotence, Pedro sought refuge in rolling over and over, covering his ears, getting smeared in his urine and excrement, as though he were removed from time, wanting to tear his head off so as not to have to hear, to think, a regrettable perverse leftover, a castaway among his disobedient guts, with an alien pain deep in the entrails and between the shreds of bad memories, memories of a woman, words as islets in a bottomless lagoon: "Ayayayay, they're killing me! Killing me by the justice of God...! Ayayay...ayayay!"

When Pedro returned from his long voyage of horror, distant and alone, barely emerging from the blankness in which he had taken refuge to escape the unbearable, he found himself in a clean bed before a window that gave on a great tree branch gilded with the colors of autumn. A thin man was leaning over his chest. He was impeccably dressed in black, with a cape around his shoulders, a large, wide-brimmed hat on his head, and spectacles in a gold frame. Pedro fought to separate his identity from that of the woman being tortured in the chamber above. In his mind's eye, there paraded before him La Chamberga's tavern, Servando, the carriage with which they trapped him, his first cell, the men who discussed Halley's comet and the woman whose shrieks came through the trap, "Oh, woe, oh woe is me...!"

The man in black straightened up. Pedro could see his goatee and white shirt collar. A doctor, most likely. He watched him go to a table and pour a stream of milk into a cup from a pitcher. The round and sturdy pitcher, of crude, heavy clay was the first tangible thing he saw, unmistakably real and actual, primitive rough clay bearing the marks of the potter's fingers. He took a sip of milk and vomited immediately. He could not bear the thought that this physician had come from the torture chamber after having closed the eyes of some poor unfortunate. He heard a murmuring and saw the doctor leave with a satchel, followed by the blurry figure of another man. Grateful for the softness of the bed, the pleasant friction of clean sheets, the warm weight of a woolen coverlet, he sank into a deep sleep. This was followed by long days of physical weakness and mental confusion before he was able to realize that he was still imprisoned but under very tolerable conditions. His new cell had light and air and the consolation of an autumn tree branch. The window opened on a narrow yard, enclosed by a very high wall. Indistinct sounds and noises of doors opening and closing could be heard from far away, sure signs that he was in strict isolation. A chair and a table with paper, pen, and inkstand on it were close to the bed. From the moment he saw it he knew that it had been left there for him to write his confession. The jailer who brought his food, which was healthful and abundant, was as taciturn and stone-faced as the previous ones; they came and went without looking at him, without talking, indifferent, mute, and removed.

The days went by, he recovered his strength, and nobody ever came to see him. He sat at the table, examined the paper which was thick, fibrous, but smooth, white, the seal of the Inquisition with its olive branch, cross, and sword in one corner above. The pages were all numbered and initialed. He took up the pen many times and dipped it in the inkwell with the intention of making some innocuous confession, but was never able to think of one. Inevitably, any minor offense led into a major one. He racked his brain trying to clear up the mystery of why he was arrested and what the accusation might be but had no idea whether it was because of the fuss in La Chamberga's tavern, the underground traffic in forbidden books, or both.

Unable to find an answer to the riddle, he would lie on the bed day after day, hands under his head, staring out the window, pondering as he watched the tree begin to shed its leaves. One morning when the doctor appeared, he dared besiege him with questions. The man ignored him, simply going about his routine of opening Pedro's pajama blouse and listening to his heart. At that moment, Pedro's eyes lit on the milk pitcher. Without stopping to think, he seized the heavy handle in one hand and smashed it over the doctor's head. The man slid to the floor and lay there, a baby unconscious in a pool of milk. He then pulled off the man's clothes, lifted him into the bed, and covered him with the blanket. Next, he wrapped himself in the doctor's cape, put on his hat, set the spectacles upon the end of his nose in such a way that he could see over them, picked up the doctor's satchel and, his heart pounding, banged on the door. The jailer, with his usual vacant stare, opened it, let him out without a glance, and immediately shut it behind him. Pedro went out into the yard, saw a stout wooden door, opened it and found himself about to enter a big room crowded with busy friars: scribes, secretaries putting shelves in order, others sewing folios. He had walked into an office in which evidently the Inquisition kept records of its victims. Unable to retreat, he crossed the room, his head down, and went out through a door at the other end. It let out onto a corridor with a staircase. Pedro ran down it and out into a yard where he followed a wall that looked like it belonged to a church until he came to another door which he opened and stepped into a shed where there was an incredible jumble of furniture, household articles, and supplies of all kinds piled up everywhere which a swarm of servants was loading into carts and wagons. At one side of this hubbub, one of them stood holding up the end of a heavy mirror and shouting for help to get it onto a wagon. Since nobody was paying any attention to him, Pedro, without hesitation, set his doctor's bag down and gave the man a hand.

This task accomplished, the servant took his place on the seat of the wagon and asked Pedro if he wished to join him. He accepted the invitation with alacrity and climbed up beside him, after which they waited in line to move out of the shed. Pedro asked him what was going on and the fellow explained that the warden was moving. That his wife was refusing to cook because her kitchen was right below the Saint Jerome tower, and she couldn't stand the screams of the tortured any longer.

"What a sensitive lady," said Pedro, adjusting his spectacles that were slipping further and further down his nose.

"Hard to believe," the fellow observed, "that a warden of the Inquisition should let a woman give him orders. Nowadays, women don't respect officials of the church, let alone their husbands. My wife, for instance, has started locking the door on me when I come home late and I have to climb in through the window. Would Your Honor have a medicine against a sickness of that kind?"

Pedro leaned over the doctor's bag and feigned poking about for a remedy to calm irritable wives, at the same questioning him about other symptoms. The man was delighted to be receiving such attention and talked a blue streak. Finally, the way opened and they moved out on the street and off towards the port of Triana. Pedro apologized for not having the medicine he needed but counseled him that for edgy and bossy wives the best remedy was a heavy hand judiciously applied.

With that he jumped off the wagon and made his way to the monastery where he found Servando bent over a tome by an alchemist named Newton. His friend was unable to throw light on the reason for Pedro's arrest for there was no sign of any interruption in the traffic of banned books. He was inclined, however, to cast the blame on La Chamberga on the ground that a vengeful woman was worse than a snake. He then proceeded to unroll maps and decided that Pedro must immediately flee to America. The province of Costa Rica of the Captaincy General of Guatemala, which had been described to him as a tranquil, underpopulated region with a pleasant climate, seemed a likely place.

"If it's not swarming with Spaniards that means there's no riches to satisfy the greed of our countrymen," he observed, and passed judgment, "so, better bored to death than burned to death."

Then, the long ocean crossing with only the companionship of pigs, chickens, crates, and unrelenting bouts of seasickness to relieve the monotony.

Perhaps Avendaño had made the same voyage, landing in Veracruz, Mexico. Now he was on his way to Cartagena de Indias. Why hadn't he embarked in Veracruz for Cartagena? It was most unusual that Avendaño should choose to undergo such an uncomfortable trip to Cartago with the intention of embarking in Matina, an insignificant port swarming with pirates and mosquitoes. Avendaño had taken a little leather-covered notebook out of his pocket. Pedro glanced at him out of the corner of his eye unable to decipher the notes the man started to

jot down. It was unfathomable why the Inquisitor of the Holy
Office had chosen such an unusual route to reach the Inquisition
Court in Cartagena de Indias. Avendaño, sensing that he was
being observed, raised his piercing eyes and said, "Pedralbarán...
where did I hear that name?"

The incestuous father's appearance before the Church court was
a degrading spectacle. The defendant drooled, showed the whites
of his eyes, and pretended that he didn't understand anything he
was being asked. Angulo could get nothing out of him and
ordered him returned to the pillory. He was then taken out of his
cell once more on the day set by Avendaño for the confrontation
between the accused and his victim, the day final sentence was
to be pronounced. When Hernández saw his daughter face to face
he lost his composure and forgot to feign insanity. He threw
himself to the floor on his knees, grabbed onto the skirt she had
been given by Mier Ceballos's wife so that she might be decently
dressed and, snuffling and sobbing, begged her to forgive him.
And so he remained for at least fifteen minutes, until poor María
Francisca began to weep as well, as she sought to dislodge her
skirt from his grip. The judge ordered the guards to separate him
from the girl and, uncomfortable at the sight of such loss of
dignity by an old man, they set him on his feet. Stammering, his
voice hoarse, Hernández confessed to having abused his daughter,
trying at the same time to explain away his behavior as the act of
a weak and vulnerable man open to temptations of the flesh who
was overcome by an all too human passion. He also admitted
that he did not attend mass and that he cursed and blasphemed.
Avendaño had little trouble extracting a complete confession
from the man—indeed, Pedro, as scribe, suspected that the sight
of the Inquisitor so terrorized Hernández that he would have
admitted anything. However, Avendaño did not go to excess and
confined himself strictly to what was contained in the testimony
and depositions of the plaintiff and the witnesses. When the
interrogation was over, Avendaño had María Francisca take a seat
on the bench being shared by her mother and sisters while
Hernández remained standing, held upright by two lancers, his
humbled head hanging, its bald spot prominent, as well as the
welts left on the nape of his neck by the pillory.

The Inquisitor, after being satisfied that Pedro was taking down his words, launched into a severe criticism of the lawyer for not having been present at the trial, challenged the defense by disqualifying the defendant's plea of insanity and ended by saying, "In view of the fact that all recognized authors and jurists deal with these crimes and assure that they are to be severely punished, I request that your honor see fit to impose punishment on this Pedro Hernández, as an example and a warning to all the city. I abstain from requesting punishment for the daughter, for no other reason than that she committed what she did in a hidden house, forced by her father, though if the opinion of the erudite Villadiego is taken, at least as precedent, the daughter should be severely punished together with the father. I call for justice, and anticipate it, in your Honor's verdict."

Father Angulo, as though acting in response to a prearranged signal, rose and read from a paper unfamiliar to Pedro, which had undoubtedly been prepared at the Inquisitor's instigation. Angulo's spit curls, dressed with the aid of a curling iron, trembled momentarily, then remained still as he began to read. "*Christi Nomine Invocato*! My decision is that I should find, and do so find, Pedro Hernández guilty of incest and public blasphemy, for which reason I order that he desist from committing more such crimes under threat of severe punishment and my proceeding against him with the full force of the law. Considering his advanced age, that he is found to be seriously ill as a consequence of his harsh imprisonment, and that he has shown remorse and pleads for mercy, I commute the punishment he should receive, and pass sentence that he shall, on a holy day, enter and go bodily from the main entrance of the cathedral on his knees to the altar with a lighted candle in his hands and in that condition hear mass. That having been done, he shall place himself at the disposal of the missionary fathers for them to hear his general confession and assign him spiritual exercises and other humble tasks so that through these, serving as mortification of the flesh and punishment for his sins, he shall find reconciliation with God."

Angulo folded the paper and announced that no court costs would be imposed in view of the prisoner's abject poverty.

A row of armed guards had to be sent out in advance to clear the street, for the crowd was refusing to leave. Hernández returned to the pillory and the women to their lodging.

The sentence gave rise to much discussion in the monastery. Juan de las Alas's dalliance with The Mute was forgotten by the friars but not by the Superior who, discharging his tensions upon Hernández, considered that Angulo should have sent the incestuous rapist to be burned at the stake in Mexico, though that would have been a costly proposition, that Hernández would be of no use at the missions, and that Rebullida, who had requested soldiers, not lawbreakers, was not going to like it. Blas González enjoyed Angulo's Solomonic decision and celebrated his cleverness, saying "The guilty party was brought to justice without the expenditure of one real, for Hernández, in his condition, couldn't survive a three-day walk over those mountains."

* * *

It seemed a natural thing to me that Pedro should have taken that decision. He had become extremely nervous after finding out that the woman from Seville was looking for him. Nor did it surprise me that the Father Superior of the San Francisco monastery should have wished to get rid of the dumb girl since it was Pedro himself who told me what happened to Juan de las Alas when he was caught in the kitchen by that rascal Lorenzo, who himself knocked up Lorenzana, something the whole city knew about. I knew Pedro was hiding something, but since he never leveled with me, I didn't know what he was scared of and had no intention of being so rude as to ask questions. That dark side of his life wasn't revealed to me until much later. The question of the hour was who would take Hernández to the Talamanca missions where they were sending him to atone for his sins. It was the general opinion that the pillory had so broken the man, to say nothing of the toll taken by the swill he had been eating, that he couldn't get beyond Atirro. Without a doubt, Angulo wanted him to die fast so as to get him off his hands, which explained the abominable food he was sending to the prison. If all this had happened when Friar José de San José was readying the escort, Hernández would have gone with him, but that was not the case.

Pedro came one day to ask me what I thought. I told him that it sounded all right to me, that a few days' hike in the woods with nothing to do—for the lancer would be taking care of Hernández—would be good for him and clear up the rings under his eyes. He asked for a tonic for Hernández that would give him back some strength. I might have suspected that Pedro wanted to prolong Hernández's life. However, it never occurred to me at the moment and I gave him a potion that would have brought Lazarus back from the dead faster than Jesus Christ. It was prepared from bull's semen and other secret ingredients of my own.

Angulo seem to be satisfied with Pedro's proposal and Serrano gave him permission because, at this stage, with the debt he owed the Royal Bank, he was in no position to refuse anybody a favor. The lawyer from Guatemala had shown no signs of life and that made his uncertainty even greater. Nobody was surprised that the Superior should have wanted to get rid of the dumb Indian by returning her to Rebullida's mission. Her presence was unsettling the monastery, and he could neither sell nor give her away since Rebullida was sure to throw a fit that would be heard for leagues around. Rebullida's furies were known to reach as far as the Royal Tribunal.

I learned from the friar who came to bring me the monastery sandals that when Juan de las Alas found out that they were sending the mute back to Talamanca, he closed himself in his cell, feigning illness.

It was the dry season and the weather was pleasant. The Superior was very pleased that Pedro would be accompanying the mute as far as the mission in Chirripó where Lorenzo was to take charge of her with orders to send her immediately to Rebullida. That is to say, it was Pedro's task to bury Hernández on the heights of Atirro and to leave the mute in Chirripó; a journey of twenty days there and back, a pleasant hike in good weather with no work involved. The Mother of Travelers left a message for Pedro saying that the muleteer who was looking for him at the request of the *chambergo* hat woman, came by the gaming house to tell her that he didn't know of any Pedro de la Baranda and that nobody had ever heard of him.

But, as is always the case, man proposes and God disposes.

Pedro sets out on the dangerous route of the missionaries and lets fate steer his course

The friars at the monastery were laying wagers on whether Hernández would reach Atirro alive or die on the way. Pedro was readying his provisions for the trip. He had convinced the Superior to let him have the lame, one-eyed mule that Rebullida had ridden which must know the way perfectly to the Urinama mission where brother Pablo was baptizing the heathen. He was taking along enough dried meat, salt, biscuits, chocolate, and even a wineskin Smiles gave him. He needed nothing more with which to reach the Chirripó mission where he was to deliver the dumb Indian girl. Pedro dreamily considered taking advantage of being off in the hinterlands with Lorenzo to give him the beating of his life for causing The Mute's banishment and Juan de Alas's consequent depression. With such thoughts racing through his mind as he packed his knapsack, he was notified that he had a visitor. It was Agueda Pérez de Muro, the last person in the world he wanted to see. He had no choice but to receive her, for the brother doorkeeper was waiting to escort him to the entrance where he hung around to eavesdrop. Agueda had outdone herself in elegance, dressed as though for a fiesta with emerald bracelets and beaver hat, the ever-present Bárbara Lorenzana carrying a present for him, a curved machete with a fine steel blade and its whetstone. Pedro, who had never wielded anything but a pen, accepted it without having any idea what he might do with such an article or to what extent it might obligate him. Agueda, after smiling at him with something more than mere friendliness, departed in a wake of rustling blue taffeta skirt and flashing white, silk-encased ankles. As Pedro, machete in hand, watched her disappearing down the street, he could feel his repulsion that the sight of her rabbit's teeth had aroused ebbing and being gradually displaced into a zone that might be described as one of vaguely friendly, neutral empathy. After all—he said to himself— not every woman has to be bedded.

The following Sunday, the Commissary had the first part of the sentence carried out in order to show the people how relentless justice could be. Pathetically unclothed, in deplorable physical condition, Pedro Hernández walked on his knees from the church door to the main altar, before a crowd such as had never before been seen that packed the building to the bursting point. Latecomers had to remain in the atrium craning their necks for a glimpse of the green candle in the penitent's hands that inched its way toward the altar where the Commissary waited for Hernández with an ad hoc sermon on incest, blasphemy, oaths, and disobedience to Church teachings. At the conclusion of the sermon, a thunderous amen plummeted like a chorus of avenging angels upon the penitent's trembling body, shaking the church to its foundations. Never before had such fervor been seen among the faithful who wept with terror as they repented their own sins. María Francisca, her mother and sisters, compelled to attend the shameful spectacle, soaked their black shawls with tears as they sought to hide their faces and their shame and dismay.

The only inhabitant in the city who had no desire to witness Hernández's penitence was Juan de las Alas. In bed with fever, he refused to eat or drink and would see no one. With one day left before The Mute would be leaving for good, he came to the refectory for breakfast, the shadow of adulthood now upon his face, evident to all. The Superior had assigned two friars to watch over the girl. There was a pall over the refectory that evening at supper, abetted perhaps by the stained square left on the wall by the removal of the portrait of plump Saint Anne and the Virgin Girl, causing them all to remember sentimental partings, small thefts, childish mischief, puppy-loves, which every man has experienced at some time. The Mute was leaving, taking along with her without knowing it, a virgin heart, and Juan de las Alas would never see the world in the same way again, for life had ceased being a huge magical cauldron and turned into the everlasting grief of a final goodbye.

After Agueda's machete, Pedro received another present from Smiles, of a bottle of a greenish, ill-smelling liquid. It was a remedy against mosquito bites.

Long before sunrise, Pedro set out with The Mute, who was wearing the same coarse tunic in which she arrived. They passed by the prison where two shifty-eyed, sullen mestizo lancers and the prisoner were waiting for them. They made Hernández walk ahead of them. Frail and feeble, he seemed about to give his last gasp, the only sign of life in his body being his two feet as he staggered along, hands at his neck as though surprised at not feeling the boards of the vise in which his head had been pinned.

Smiles's potion had an immediate effect. A few minutes after the first swallow, Hernández was able to walk without dragging his feet, and as they were passing The Mother of Travelers establishment, closed at that early hour, he was no longer tripping over stones in the road. They moved out of the Barrio of the Coloreds onto the main road to Matina and where it divided set out on the fork to Talamanca taken by the missionaries. The mule, her one good eye on the horizon, trotted gaily without limping at such a clip that it was necessary to pull her ears to slow her down. Hernández walked between the lancers, his hands tied behind his back, and behind them Pedro and The Mute. They descended a slight slope and continued on a level stretch. When they came to a hillside and began to climb, the mule, always in the lead, stopped short, brayed, and refused to go on. They pushed her, they pulled her, they whispered sweet words into her ears, petted her, calling her "Good mule, pretty mule!" Nothing doing, the animal was immune to flattery. Switching to "Get going, you stubborn bitch of a mule, you stupid beast!" didn't work, either. The two lancers walked ahead to see if they could find some reason for her stubbornness. Off to one side a short distance away, they, too, stopped short in amazement. Pedro spied a blurry figure at the crest of the hill in the middle of the road in the dark shadows of the trees raising their tall crowns toward the slowly brightening sky. Hernández took fright and fell to the ground, muttering, "The *zegua,* the *zegua!*" Pedro stared at it and seemed to make out something that looked a horse's head with a long dress hanging from it and possibly the ear of a similar animal and something like a muzzle. The Mute looked at the strange creature with a foolish smile on her face. Pedro crossed to it in a few long strides for he had no fear of the mythological, raised his brand new machete threateningly, and as he was about to decapitate the myth, it cried out, "No, Pedro, don't, it's me, it's me!"

Pedro poked the point of his blade into what had looked like a horse's ear and uncovered Juan de las Alas's frightened face under the cowl of his habit. He lowered the machete to the ground beheading on the way down a bouquet of wild flowers that died without dispensing aroma.

"You? You looked like an imaginary animal to me in this light and I nearly slit your throat! What a foolish thing to do...! Do you mind telling me what you're doing here?"

"Waiting for you, to go along with you. See, I brought my own food. I won't be a burden to you, I swear!" And he held out the leather bag to him that he used for carrying the monastery sandals to the cobbler.

Pedro flew off the handle. "I swear you must be out of your mind! How can I take you without the Superior's permission? Not only that, what excuse have you dreamed up for when we get back? That I took you for a walk, or what?"

"It's that I'm not going back to Cartago... My idea is to go along with Catalina to Father Rebullida's mission and stay there."

"How about that? Aren't you clever? You're passing yourself off as a missionary and what you're really doing is running after a woman, whether her name is Catalina, The Mute, or whoever... Now listen to this. Either you undo what you've done and get back into the monastery without being seen or I'll slice up your head with this machete! That's it! Now, get a move on!"

"Wait a minute, Pedro, you didn't understand me. I just wanted...I'm afraid that...I'm worried about what Lorenzo might do to Catalina...you know how he is! If you don't want to take me, at least, promise me that you'll take her yourself as far as Father Rebullida's... Promise me that...

"I can't promise you anything." Pedro calmed down. "I was given orders to deliver The Mute in Chirripó, not to leave her with Rebullida. I'll take care of her that far as if she were my sister. I can promise you that much. I don't think Lorenzo would dare do anything... He's scared to death of Rebullida."

"And another thing, besides, you mustn't ever leave her alone at night. That's what Gerónima told me."

"Who knows what goes on with that Gerónima...? Look, Juan...I should have had a talk with you a long time ago and explained certain things to you about life. I give you my word, I'll do it when I get back. Now, get going. I'll take good care of your Mute, better than you can. When I get back, you and I are going to have a long conversation, man to man. I can see that there are sides to your education that have been seriously neglected. Go on...give that girl of yours a kiss if you want to, and then get going. Go ahead, give her that kiss on the lips you weren't able to on account of Lorenzo interrupting you. Kiss her, and let's see if that will exorcise the devil that's gotten in under your cassock."

Juan took a step toward The Mute, then hesitated. Pedro put his hand on his back and nudged him forward. Juan's kiss was fleeting as the brushing of his sandals along the stony road, startled butterflies taking off downhill and disappearing from sight in a swish of his cassock.

Juan had forgotten his knapsack, in which Pedro found a jar of honey, a chunk of meat, a cabbage, three prickly squashes, and a wheaten loaf. He loaded it on the mule and the group continued on its way to the snickering and remarks of the lancers, Hernández's indifference, and The Mute's perplexity.

That night a farmer gave them permission to sleep in his granary. Pedro arranged a bed on the newly harvested sheaves of wheat, fresh and fragrant, Hernández and his guards lay down on the ground in the opposite corner. Pedro gave the prisoner his tonic and, lying down near the Indian girl, said to her, "I hope you won't be flying off on a broom tonight."

After the hooting of the owls, the silence was broken by the sound of the field mice nibbling on the wheat that lasted till cockcrow. They ate their breakfast ration and Hernández received his dose of bull-semen tonic after which they set out on the road with the mule impatient to begin the trek home.

Something mysterious must have gone into the making of that potion. Hernández came back to life before their eyes, his steps now firm and elastic. The lancers grumbled to one another, put out by the prisoner's sudden vitality, and fell silent whenever

Pedro approached. The mule trotting easily, frisked ahead, obliging everybody to run in order to keep up with her.

The Indian girl's suffering in her muteness was evidenced by the vacuity of her hollow smile, her pretty face framed in a curtain of straight black hair. Her slender figure hidden under the crudely sewn tunic and her little round face would have been charming were it not for that vacant look—a sort of cave in which there floated disharmonious, disordered thoughts—which aroused consternation and uneasiness in anyone who sought to sink into the depths of those eyes.

The lancers began to be difficult. They would walk sluggishly, allowing the lame but briskly trotting mule to put distance between them, and cast reproving glances at Pedro's lustrous boots. He pretended not to notice but could not prevent his boots from becoming the target of their antipathy. Hernández, taking deep breaths of the crisp country air, indifferent to the current of envy that was generated, walked comfortably on his wide feet protected by a thick sole of callous. At a moment when Pedro and the lancers had tied up the mule and gone to investigate whether a turn they had taken that the mule wanted to bypass was wrong, Hernández, despite his hands being tied, managed to rummage in Juan de las Alas's knapsack, pull out the chunk of roasted meat there, and gobble it down by the time they came back. Pedro was angry and never let him out of his sight again. However, after traveling a distance it turned out that the mule had been right and they turned back. It was a long, winding trail on which they met only an occasional cart loaded with sugar cane. The mule then turned down another path that led to a hanging bridge over a furiously roaring river that lapped the underside of the precariously loose boards as they crossed. On the other side they plunged through a dense tunnel of vegetation to enter into the shadows of a gothic cathedral, where shafts of light pierced stained-glass windows, seeking the diminutive carpeted world at the foot of primitive trees. The sunbeams picked out brightly-colored little flowers spreading among vine leaves that crept to the heights of great trunks covered with lichens and moss. Pedro stopped to watch a bird the size of a chicken, all green with a red breast and very long tail feathers. Captivated by its beauty, he fell behind. Hernández and his guards had gone on keeping pace with the mule. The Indian girl, who had been in the rear, passed him, pushing through the curtain of vines as though heeding a distant summons, pursued by a beam of light that shone upon her round backside, exposed because she had hiked up her skirt to keep the thorns from snatching at it, flesh the pale-gold color of the leaves on the tree that had called to him through the window in his prison in Seville. Recovering from his astonishment, he hastened to lower her skirt lest Hernández and the lancers see her innocent nudity.

The sun was at the zenith when they emerged from the forest. Irritated at Hernández because he had eaten the meat left by Juan de las Alas, Pedro imposed a fast on him. The prisoner muttered that it was not his fault, that the medicine made him very hungry. One of the lancers called Pedro aside and told him to suspend the potion since they had been advanced pay for a five-day journey and had no intention of going further than that. He added that it would be better to let Hernández die soon than for them to be faced with the alternative of doing him in. Pedro angrily let him know that his mission was to take him to Chirripó where he also had to turn over The Mute; it was his agreement with the Commissary of the Inquisition and the Superior of the monastery. He explained that he didn't know why the Governor had paid them for only five days, even less why it should have been as an advance, and warned him to stop making demands and bothering him with their whining. He advised him that they'd better move their butts and get to Chirripó sooner than later and promised to see to it himself that they were paid what was coming to them. The lancer threw him a contemptuous look, as if questioning his authority for making a promise of any kind, and went off to consult with his colleague.

The trek continued with all in bad humor except the mule, who must have been enjoying the thought of getting home, and The Mute who was smiling vacantly. Pedro, expecting trouble, kept his eye peeled on the pair of shifty half-breeds. Hernández kept complaining that he was hungry and thirsty, and that it was not Christian to be killing him that way, that it would be better to hang him from a tree and get it over with for if they didn't give him food and drink he wouldn't be answerable if he chewed on the mule's skinny, hairy haunches. The mule, as if it had been listening, hustled off into the bushes, the lancers and Hernández after her. Pedro wanted to run ahead, but The Mute, whether tired or simply because of a whim, had sat herself down on the root of a gigantic tree to wait until things returned to normal. When Pedro managed to get her up to follow the others, they were already out of sight. Not being an experienced woodsman, Pedro lost his way, went about in circles, wishing them all in hell, including The Mute. However, on hearing the sound of running water he followed it. Had it not been for that, events would have taken a very different turn for he reached the stream just in time to catch the two lancers about to drown Hernández by holding his head under the water. Bellowing loud enough to scare off a flock of parrots, and cursing at the lancers, he was able to rescue the prisoner. In the violent argument that ensued, the two alleged that they could not go on because their feet were skinned raw and that they had been paid for a job which they were now doing, that two days and two days were four days, round trip, and one day's rest. This they claimed was the agreement they had made with the Governor and Angulo, which was the reason they had volunteered since nobody else was willing to undertake a trip over the mountains with a madman, a convict, tried and sentenced by Father Angulo's Holy Tribunal as an incestuous blasphemer, who by no means deserved having anybody run the risk for him of dying of a snakebite on a naked heel with no boot to protect it, and threatened by scores of ocelots and mountain lions, waiting to pounce.

Worn out, Pedro opted for suspending Smiles's medication, considering that a natural death for the prisoner was preferable to what the lancers might do to him. He resigned himself to the idea of returning to Cartago with The Mute and accepting the fate La Chamberga had in store for him, turning himself in once and for all to Avendaño and confessing that he was a fugitive from the Inquisition.

Relations tense, no one talking, they went to sleep out in the open that night. Pedro, clutching Agueda's machete, fighting exhaustion and the annoyance of the crickets' constant chirping, stayed wide awake. The Mute was left to her own fate because Pedro had forgotten about her, concerned as he was in keeping watch over the lancers and Hernández, who kept complaining about not being given anything to eat or drink, despite all the water he had swallowed. At daybreak, still fighting sleep, he tied Hernández to the mule which was submissive, as though ashamed of having run off the day before. The prisoner was not given his potion, but although tied to the mule, he managed to get hold of the bottle and gulp down its entire contents. Hernández had lost all sense of prudence and discretion. He was not the same miserable wretch who had been slapped into the pillory, not the human floor mop that dragged himself naked on his knees to the altar, green candle in hand. Nor was he any longer the man who wept, clutching his daughter's skirt, begging pardon for having— as the Commissary said—"destroyed her virginity." Perhaps what happened was that he was recovering his customary bestial aspect and so between him and the mule there was no choice, for she was a thousand times more human.

Pedro's thought's were turning in that direction when suddenly Hernández dropped out of their sight. The mule was shaken but held her ground. Pedro and the two lancers went to the spot where he had been and saw Hernández hanging below the lip of a steep ravine, suspended from the rope around his waist. Pedro laid aside his machete and began trying to pull him up as he yelled to the two half-breeds for help. They gave no sign of moving and Hernández, panic-stricken, could be of no help to himself. Pedro wanted to make the mule pull and tried to convince her to go forward but the taut rope around the animal's belly was threatening to slip off her and down to her legs. Suddenly the rope slackened and the mule, freed, fell to her knees. Below, Hernández looked like a puppet caught in the branches of a small tree that had broken his fall. The half-breeds looked at the body below and Pedro at the rope severed by a machete stroke. The prisoner had begun to move slowly and awkwardly, clutching at the thick foliage, swimming in the sea of leaves, then left the tree, and tried making his agonizing way upward. Pedro removed the rope from around the mule, undid the knot and threw the end to Hernández. The rescue was not an easy matter. After half an hour, he managed to reach the top. Now, Pedro realized that the lancers had taken off, politely leaving the machete and him all alone in the midst of the forest with a convict, a lame mule, and a foolish mute, not knowing how to continue on his way or how to get back. With an irresistible urge to throw Hernández back over the cliff, he sat down near the ravine and banged himself on the head with his fist. He tied Hernández, quiet and chastened, to the mule again.

Finally, having decided that the most sensible thing to do was to return to Cartago, Pedro turned the mule around. However, belying her reputation for gentleness, amiability, and cooperation, she refused to retrace the course and insisted stubbornly on going forward. In view of this, he decided to change his mind and putting his fate in the hands of the mule, let her continue on to Chirripó. And so night fell and the now placid beast shut her one good eye and rested. Tired out by the turmoil, Pedro prepared to go to sleep, After tying Hernández to a tree, he lay down with the machete under him, and immediately dozed off, unconcerned as to whether The Mute would follow suit or not. At sunup he was awakened by the mule's braying. Pedro finished the wine and divided food from the saddle bag three ways. Provisions were giving out. Never had he regretted anything as much as this, but he took courage at the thought that they had already covered so much ground that Chirripó couldn't be too far away now and, they resumed their journey. Before long, they were brought to a halt by a swift flowing river swollen by the rain. The mule hesitated, then led them to a higher beach where they waited for the current to abate.

As he sat down to devour the poor remains of their meager rations, which hardly placated his growling guts, Pedro cursed the luck that caused him to undertake this frightful adventure for fear of La Chamberga and Avendaño. In his disgust, he picked up the empty bottle of Hernández's potion, poured out what was left of the mosquito-bite remedy, threw the two bottles as far as he could into the river, and watched the current carry them away. Finding little reason to go on living but with desire to do so unabated, he got up to find something more to put into his stomach. As he foraged the edge of the river, his attention was attracted by movement among the bushes, possibly of a monkey or large animal on its way to the river. Gripping his machete he stood still and waited. It was a plump, stocky friar, carrying a rounded object by its handle. As it drew closer to the water, Pedro recognized Gerónima and the iron ladle in her hand.

Pedro's relief at seeing the cook in this remote spot was so great that he ran to embrace her without pausing to consider what had brought her there. He hugged her like a drowning man a life preserver. Stiff and taciturn, the Indian woman accepted the embrace, not returning it, not loosing her hold on the ladle. Pedro's effusiveness abated; she explained her presence in a few words. Since Juan de las Alas was not allowed to go along with them, it was up to her to do so, for her mute sister could not be left to wander about alone in bad company.

When the current had slackened, they were able to cross the river, and that night Gerónima lay down next to her sister, one arm over her breast. Snoring placidly, the two slept soundly. Pedro, as he nodded off, was considering that once The Mute was installed at the Chirripó mission, he would go straight back to Cartago with Gerónima for he had come to the conclusion that the danger posed by La Chamberga and Avendaño paled in comparison to the very thought of a snake slithering between his legs.

After the third day in the mountains, Pedro began to feel the trip was taking too long but asked no questions for fear that Gerónima would get angry and go off on her own. She, an Indian, was demonstrating her capacity for survival in the forest, picking bananas and berries, finding edible roots and plants. Hernández consumed these with gusto, apparently indifferent to the length of the trip. He was so recovered that he made no effort to dissimulate his lecherous leers directed at The Mute. Gerónima, now her sister's guardian and keeper, took on the task of checking the ropes and knots that restrained the prisoner during the night. Pedro, uneasy but happy to have her along, climbed craggy slopes, the machete at his waist, ignorant of what he might face on the other side. His skin had darkened and there were great circles under his eyes from the long nights of vigilance against surprise attacks by wild felines. Rents in his shirt exposed areas of skin resembling the bark of a blighted olive tree, pitted with scrapes and insect bites. He climbed upwards, clutching at roots and branches nature placed there to aid him in the ascent. His stomach was inflated and his guts irritated by the raw diet to which he was unaccustomed. Totally repentant at having gotten himself into such a fix, he yearned for the security of his monastic cot, the refectory table at the monastery, and even his desk at the city hall. Starving to death, he took tree bark for smoked ham, sausage, blood pudding, and Extremaduran salami. He speculated about what the lancers might have told on their return to Cartago, reproached himself for having fled from La Chamberga instead of standing up to her, and lamented not having gone to the city of León to talk to her—a safer and more civilized trip—and find out why she was looking for him, instead of clambering about on all fours like a monkey, terrorized by snakes, and accusing himself of being an inept coward and a congenital idiot. And so, half dreaming, his thoughts hopped ruefully from codfish in tomato sauce, roast mutton with fixings, fresh white bread, cheeses, sour pickles, chicken in marinade, to wineskins, barrels, hogsheads, cascades of red wine. The more Pedro was weakened by these illusions, the stronger Hernández grew on his diet of roots and green bananas. Desperate and envious, Pedro dragged himself painfully in his tracks among rotting tree trunks, giant tree roots, and lianas, the beards of primeval trees, hanging from on high.

The two Indian women walked nimbly beneath the forest canopy, treading almost noiselessly through the undergrowth, their quick, sure hands separating the lianas as they went. Chimeras, appearing and disappearing through the dense greenery as separate waist-high figures, lower bodies, legs alone, they moved in space and time disobedient to the laws of nature. It was inhuman to be able to pass so effortlessly over obstacles that Pedro had to strain so hard to negotiate. When he was approaching the end of his endurance, and all he could think of was lying down on a soft, springy, surface where there were no ants, they reached a third rushing river. They saw it from above and had to descend through a sheer pass to a valley that seemed a great green, gnarled hand, partially obscured by low clouds and intermittent mist—vertical slopes going straight to the rushing river, foaming at the gorge. They went down and down till stopped by the angry waters.

This river was not among those indicated by the monastery that they would pass on their journey. Pedro suspected as much and now he was certain. Gerónima had led them astray from the route to Chirripó so he had no idea where he was or where he was going.

Furious, he grabbed the woman by the hair and began shaking her. Hernández laughed, a lunatic expression on his face, and The Mute looked on without interfering. The mule, which had been looking at the river with a calculating eye, turned it on the commotion and shook her head with scornful patience.

"Where do you think you're taking me, tell me? Where? Speak you damn Indian! Speak!"

Gerónima let him shake her, then, tiring of Pedro pulling her hair, she loosened his grip on her with a powerful push and threw him to the ground, neatly and without great effort.

"Be quiet, Spaniard," she said, smoothing her hair, "you won't get hurt. We go to Urinama to see Rebullida and deliver this man and my sister. Then we go back, us two, to Cartago."

"To Urinama! Without supplies and carrying twenty wax candles I don't know how to light and a sack of damp wheat!"

"At least you have boots," answered Gerónima, picking up the ladle she had dropped during the encounter, "the fathers walk there on their bare feet... You're not as good as a friar."

"I'm hungry," said Hernández, "want fish to eat."

To Pedro's astonishment, Gerónima left him to go into the thicket from which she emerged with a long stick, coolly asked Pedro for his machete to make a spear, and with it went to the river. Wading in up to her waist she was soon back with a large fish. Pedro, unused to raw meat, to say nothing of fish, could not eat it.

Having thrown the last fish bones into the water, she pointed towards the source of the river and indicated, "It's rained up above and will rain here. We'll wait for the water to calm."

After this statement it was clear, without further discussion, who the leader of the group was. Then she took Pedro's machete and handed over her ladle, which he accepted without any idea what to do with it. The Indian then went deep into the forest, returned with an armload of leafy branches and spent the rest of the afternoon fashioning a shelter suspended by two poles on one side and fastened to the ground on the other. There they took refuge when it suddenly started to rain. Gerónima's superiority now stood clearly established. The next day they waited to cross until afternoon when the water level had receded, each hanging on to the mule's tail, until all arrived safely on the other bank, including Hernández, whom Pedro would have preferred to see drown, for he had become an unbearable burden. That crossing spelled the end of the sack of wheat but the candles survived, as did Pedro. He was the last to emerge dripping on the opposite shore to be confronted squarely with the naked mute wringing out her tunic, indifferent to Hernández whom her sister at that moment was tying up with his hands behind his back.

Then followed the long uphill climb, arduous and dangerous, for it was over a trail that went along the edge of a precipice. Before long, however, they came to an empty hut where they stopped for the night. In one corner there was a pile of dry logs, gourds, bows and arrows. That Indian dwelling seemed to be there waiting for them.

Moving easily about the place, Gerónima came upon sheets of *mastate*, a tree bark with a leather-like texture which she laid out on the dry floor. Pedro was familiar with it from around Cartago. Then she made a little pyre of the logs and proceeded to patiently rub two sticks together on top of the letter the Guardian had sent to the catechizer of Chirripó, which now served no purpose, until enough heat was produced to ignite the paper. It was none too soon, for the stars could now be seen, closer and colder than Pedro had ever seen them, and bright moonlight shone through the openings in the roof, illuminating the room as if it were day. Hernández lay down and was soon snoring. Gerónima stretched out, her arm across her sister's chest. Pedro sat close to the fire warming his bones and mulling over his anxieties.

Unable to sleep despite the day's exertion, he continued to bemoan the untenable situation into which he had gotten himself. On the one hand, despite her treachery, Gerónima's presence made him feel secure, like a small boy with a trusted aunt. On the other, his inexperience at coping with the wild and his weakened physical condition led him to think that not Hernández, but he, Pedro Albarán would soon be on the receiving end of the prayer for the dead, lying in the ground in a place where carnivorous beasts prowl and cannibal plants sprout. Then, he consoled himself for a while by reviewing in his mind's eye the vision of The Mute, naked, wringing out her tunic next to the river, the sun warming her budding body. One day—he said to himself in an effort to recover his old-time equanimity—one day, she will be a beautiful woman. Would be, were nature not so unfair as to create a beautiful, perfectly proportioned body, and fail to put anything into its head. The poor decerebrate was deep asleep, under her sister's protective arm, her body possibly a bundle of nerves that functioned autonomically like those of a decapitated chicken.

He approached them. Gerónima slept heavily, snorting like a seal through her broad nostrils. The Mute lay on her back, her face turned toward the moonlight. Pedro noted that she slept with her eyes open in a vacuous stare lost in the limitless time of a dream, focusing on nothingness towards a point on the ceiling. He was fascinated by the emptiness in the stare of the sleeping eyes and bent over to gaze into them. The iris was black, round, speckled with infinite golden rays. He felt as thought he were sinking into an incalculably deep pool, a subterranean well from which her dreams were emerging materialized in the form of strange, unknown creatures, mysterious primordial beings, forgotten, relegated to the opposite extreme of collective memory, mythological animals, and innocent, naked men and women... The burgeoning of fantastic images was a shock that plunged him into a melancholy state. What dreams could that head be dreaming? What absurd, bizarre images were ingrained in her? He thought of how when Juan de las Alas was caught in the kitchen he had tried to justify his behavior by saying that he was looking at goldfish in Catalina's eyes.

Fearful of being half-crazed, his nerves and reason frayed by the outlandishness of his situation, Pedro moved away to his place and kept watching her from there. What he was now saw seemed a shared dream. The Mute sat up, reached out as though to touch Pedro's face, tracing its outline in the air. He apprehended and could feel it. He could feel the gentle touch on his taut cheeks, sliding softly over the bridge of his nose to the contour of his lips. Responding to the invitation, he raised his hand and let it trace in the air the round little face, the short nose, feeling under his fingertips not nothingness, not the chill of the mountain air, but warm throbbing flesh. Abruptly, Gerónima awoke and the eucharistic communion dissolved with the dispelling of sleep and all reverted to what it had been moments ago: The Mute, asleep under the iron shaft of Gerónima's arm; Pedro, a hand lost in emptiness limning a mirage in nothingness. Something impalpable as whispers faded into the silence, then the ear picked up the sound waves of ripples and a sea of moonlight brought infinite calm.

Pedro faced the new day upset, out of sorts, frightened of himself, worried and fed up, as though thrown off balance by an external force impossible to control. He wanted his machete back for he felt helpless without it, but Gerónima would not return it and that further irritated him. He was walking an insecure tightrope in the effort to keep from losing his grip on sanity and it was taking its toll. He managed to survive the day's walk, unable to conquer a sense of having gone astray, of missing his true self, surprised when Hernández called him Pedro, feeling as though an unknown identity would assert itself and argue with the old personality that had accompanied him all his life.

He was letting himself be led, swept along by a force it was useless to oppose, struggling furiously to hold himself in leash and not kill them all, Gerónima, Hernández, and The Mute in particular...to go on alone with the mule, more human, in any case, than the strange characters around him now.

He got behind the mule, seeking respite from his disturbed mental processes in the swaying of her rump, in counting the hairs in her tail, reading messages in the wiggling of her ears, endlessly checking Juan's knapsack, now filled with wild fruits, to make sure it was secure. Uphill and down again, until a peak was reached which gave on a glorious landscape of giant ferns, a valley patterned with many rivers cutting their channels into the hills. They made their way down along a wide trail that bore the tracks of traffic winding down towards the valley and the rivers.

Pedro, walking behind the mule, focused his gaze mainly on his feet in order to avoid meeting the eyes of the others. Gerónima had turned dumb as her sister and Hernández opened his mouth only to demand food.

They continued down the slope in that way until suddenly Hernández stumbled, fell in a sitting position, hands tied behind his back, slid into Pedro knocking him over, rolled under the hooves of the rearing mule, to slam finally into a thorn bush. Its spikes inspired in him a fusillade of oaths and blasphemies, and he outdid himself in foul language and curses against everything divine and human until Pedro and Gerónima came to help him up. "I piss and shit on God and I'll see you all in hell! Untie my hands, damn you! What kind of a Christian would put a man to walk these fucking, sonofabitch gulches with both hands tied? Fuck the Virgin and fuck you all!" And so, in order to shut him up and cease shocking the tame little birds of the forest, they untied him on condition that he walk a distance in front of Pedro and behind the mule. And, in that way, they reached the flatland. And so the prisoner was enabled to escape, a fulfillment of Pedro's most ardent desire that he should get away and be eaten by wild animals. He allowed that without the slightest remorse for by then he had lost all moral bearings and command over his actions.

The valley was very hot and humid. Pedro took off the rag that was once his shirt to mop his salty, itchy, sour sweat, then threw it into a puddle of stagnant water with a feeling of liberation. Gerónima, however, picked it up, wrung it out, folded it, put it in Juan's knapsack, and set it on the mule's back, with no comment. Pedro started to remove boots and underdrawers, as well, but Gerónima stopped him, explaining that without clothing the mosquitoes would eat him alive. Then she plunged into the jungle and came out with some berries which she squashed with her fingers, making a paste that she smeared on Pedro, turning him red. This was done in the nick of time for a little further along the way a swarm of mosquitoes attacked the group, spread over Pedro's lean flesh and would have left him more crucified than Christ if not for Gerónima's protective measure.

"More annatto, Gerónima, more annatto!" he shouted, slapping at the voracious insects and swinging his arms like a windmill in a hopeless effort to drive them off. They entered his ears buzzing furiously, pierced his eyelids, bit and stung, pestering with such relentlessness that Pedro lost what little control he still maintained over his wits.

The infinite hordes of insects seemed to be waiting there to torment him, all in collusion to frustrate his trip to Talamanca of the heathen Indians and obstinate missionaries. Carnivorous ants climbed into his boots and flocks of yellow butterflies beclouded his vision. Because his eyes were fixed on the ground, searching out other enemies, he hit his head against a wasps' nest, arousing the creatures whose fiery stings left welts that were to last for days. All this insect world had come into being around a patch of fermenting fruits on the trunks of enormous trees that exuded a sweet sap. Guerrilla columns came from everywhere, crawling, flying, long-legged, proboscidian, even toothed, others with sting, antennae, and diminutive jaws, crawling or fluttering over the rank sexuality of the lush blossoms—all color and no aroma—partaking in the orgy with tiny long-beaked birds that plunged with unbridled lustfulness into the exuberance of fleshy petals. Stupefied by the orgiastic abandon of these mutually dependent existences, by the fecundation that seemed to have no starting point, by the obsessive reproductive drive in which the most diverse species participated in an immense collective pairing, Pedro emerged from there erect, he, too, a part of the bacchanal. Since he could not assuage his urge like a hummingbird, he felt impelled to throw himself upon Gerónima, or The Mute, or even the mule herself, to transfix anything with the pecker that had left Cartago in a downcast state and was now coming back to life awakened, perhaps, by the aphrodisiacal venom injected by the insects.

Inevitably, desperation was beginning to close in upon him. He realized it, and after having found somewhere to bathe himself and alleviate his compulsions by grace of cool water, he lay down in the shade of a refined and narcissistic tree that stretched its branches over a placidly flowing stream to reaffirm that it was still handsome. He remained there dozing peacefully for an indeterminate time, resting until he awoke feeling renewed and eagerly looking forward to the return with Gerónima at the helm.

But his incursion into the world of insects and flowers had affected him strangely. In a world where anything is possible, there is no reason for rationality to reign, and so he began to sing at the top of his lungs, dancing and scratching himself at the same time, indifferent to the point when pain turned to pleasure and pleasure reverted to pain, stamping with his boots upon the sylvan life underfoot, challenging the trees and their fauna with upraised fists, pirouetting before an audience of monkeys as he roared with laughter at himself until Gerónima fetched him a smart slap in the face that snapped him back to sobriety, ashamed. He mopped his sweat on the mule's tail, a liberty she permitted him, as if she understood very well that he needed all the support he could muster.

The sunset found them in the hollow of a gigantic fallen tree trunk. Not until the hand that held the ladle brought him back to reality did Pedro become aware that Gerónima had lined it with leaves and branches that would evict the current dwellers. She had dripped vegetable juice of some kind onto his lips which he swallowed without hesitation and quickly fell into a deep refreshing sleep. Eyes rheumy, members numb, brushing aside the cobwebs of unconsciousness, he made his way back to alertness, squeezed into the bed-like tree cavity. Bewildered, he marveled at finding himself in such a place and still himself. If instead of arms and legs he had seen cockroach feet or squid tentacles, his surprise would have been no greater.

He had no desire to talk, and grateful for his companions' silence, devoted himself on the next lap of the journey to picking flowers which he would attach to the mule's ears, fix in Gerónima's hair, The Mute's hair and his own, his beard, his chest hair and any other place that seemed to him worthy of adornment. And he followed along with the two women, letting himself be led, with no concern as to where, how, or why they were taking him. Had Gerónima so desired, his head could have been lopped off with the machete long before. When there was nobody and nothing else to serve as a flower receptacle, he began to weave garlands, alternating long, thin leaves with round, plumper ones, the first one going to adorn the mule's head. Running off at one moment to gather materials, like a faun, his head wreathed in leaves, he stumbled upon a heap of rags concealed in the weeds that turned out to contain a feverish, delirious body.

It was a man, not yet dead but close to it. He took no notice of a procession of ants that filed over his body, up one side and down the other. Judging from his beard and color he appeared to be a Spaniard in deplorable condition. Taking him by the ankles, Pedro dragged him to where he could get a better look at him. Had the man been able to see this would-be Dionysius, half-naked, with a leafy crown on his matted hair, he might have imagined he had crossed the Styx and was being received on the other shore. He was filthy, tattered, and carried nothing to identify him. His hands were claws clutching to his breast something evidently precious to him, his knees drawn up protectively.

Removing the wreath from his head out of respect for the dead, he leaned over and tried to separate the man's hands. The man showed that he was alive by resisting and mumbling unintelligibly. Putting his ear closer to the lips, Pedro heard him repeating: "It's mine...mine..."

"Yes, I know it's yours."

Pedro had never seen a living body in worse condition, yet this wasted creature was trying to lift his head and speak. "I found it," he was saying, "I did... I myself... I..."

And he clutched whatever he was holding as he breathed his last, eyes veering as life faded, to roll finally whitely upward in their sockets. The bundle of rags heaved once convulsively and the castaway was left beached at the edge of the road and of life.

A few minutes of silence passed. Gerónima and The Mute looked on, and the mule, as well. Pedro then recited the prayer he had prepared for Hernández's death: "Take leave of life, brother, and be consoled that now you rest in peace..."

They had nothing with which to dig a grave and so covered the body with branches over which Pedro sprinkled a symbolic spoonful of earth before leaving it in the knowledge that the jungle and the animals would dispose of the remains. Soon after having taken to the road Pedro was his old self again, gratified that chance had brought them to the stranger in time to send him on his way to the other world with a prayer for the dead. (The man was fortunate under the circumstances that someone showed up in such a remote place to be with him just moments before death claimed him.) Then it entered Pedro's mind that fate was manipulating the strings of the future and that the encounter was not casual; he was prompted to turn back and examine the body more closely. Removing the branches that covered the body, he noted with repugnance a funereal froth on its lips, on which the flies had settled to feed. He was particularly curious to know what the man held in his hands and pried apart the fingers. A river stone came to light, round, smooth, and gray. Its secret at that moment was known only to the flies that were sucking up the dead man's spittle. He replaced the leafy shroud and went on his way.

With the stone in hand, he pondered its mystery, turning it over and over, unable to find that it possessed any singular property, thinking: It's not a precious stone, no diamond, emerald or the like, nor topaz, chalcedony, or even agate. However, it could be some stone that had a medicinal property like those prized by the Arabs—the stone of Armenia or of Tripoli, or of Goa, the Judaic, or lodestone. Perhaps it might be bezoar, famed as an antidote against all poisons, a preventive against plagues, and a neutralizer of depressions...those so common among mountain climbers... If it were bezoar, it would have had no effect on the stranger whose glance was that of a madman. Besides, bezoar does not occur in any river, which is where this stone evidently came from; it is in the intestines of ruminants and must therefore have a different appearance. Nor is it lodestone, which is obvious at a glance. If it were, he would have brought it as a present for Smiles who had once told him that mixed with white lead, olive oil and turpentine it is excellent for treating purulent bubo and carbuncles, and under the mattress it favors lovemaking and protects against lice... Lost in contemplation of the mystery of the stone, Pedro reviewed everything he knew about stones. He discarded the idea that it might be an altar stone: it was said that gathering a stone from each of seven altars, pulverizing and dissolving them, will cure madness and diarrhea at the same time, and mixed with powdered staghorn, is an infallible cure for melancholy, and immediately restores movement to paralyzed members... yes, much has been said and written about stones. Plato discoursed upon their properties, as did Theophrastos, Dioscorides, and many scholars and alchemists... However, the little stone in his hand had nothing in common with its miracle-working relatives: there was no mistaking its ordinariness and plebeian origin—a riverbed.

Annoyed with himself for wasting time on idle speculation, he pantomimed throwing it far away so that nature might take over the task of swallowing up in the undergrowth the dead man's last property along with its secret—and he suddenly found himself slammed face down on the ground, where he lay, immobilized by a heavy body kneeling on his back and a pair of hands around his neck trying to strangle him. He struggled desperately and futilely until he began to lose consciousness when he heard a loud thud and felt the hands relax at his throat and the body drop off alongside him. When he had caught his breath and turned around he saw Gerónima, bending over Hernández, ladle in one hand, machete in the other. Pedro, still dazed, considered that it was poor judgement on her part to have used a ladle on him when there was a machete available and that had he been in her place, there would now be a proper distance between the Spaniard's head and his body, and an expeditious solution to the problem.

They tied the convict up and waited for him to regain his senses, which, to Pedro's regret and that of sylvan scavengers, did not take very long. The man came to his senses, weeping and begging forgiveness, explaining that he had not intended to kill Pedro but only to disable him long enough to bang The Mute a few times, which was the reason he had been following them. The justification was that Pedro was to blame for his needing a woman so badly, that the tonic he gave him so heated his blood that his cock stood up and he had been going around for days unable to control it.

They allowed him to go on unburdening himself until he passed without transition from pleading for mercy into a litany of curses. His outburst so annoyed a troop of white-faced monkeys that, indignant at his foul insults, they bombarded him with rotten fruit and branches. The attack grew so furious that Pedro thought for a moment that if their aim improved, and the missiles grew heavier, the white-faces would be carrying out the sentence the Church had imposed. However, they soon tired of the sport and swung away through the trees. Pedro, considering him the cause of the entire unfortunate chain of events leading up to the latest outrage, had no choice but to make Hernández march in front of him.

Gerónima did not agree and warned Pedro that if the prisoner had escaped, it was because he was capable of surviving on his own and that it would be better to tie him hand and foot and leave him to his fate. When Hernández heard this he fell to his knees before Pedro and beseeched him to take him along as far as the Urinama mission where he promised to serve the friars until his debt was paid. And in the midst of his laments and appeals to Christian charity he came out with a surprising proposal, something that had not occurred to Pedro and which in a single phrase clarified the mystery of the dead man's stone.

"Take me along," said Hernández, "and I'll show where the gold is..."

Since Pedro only stared at him in surprise, he went on. "What else is a Spaniard after, anxious enough to risk his life for it? What else would a Spaniard be looking for in this godforsaken wilderness but gold?"

And he proceeded to go on at length about a mine named El Tisingal, supposedly located precisely in this region, often mentioned in Cartago, sought since time immemorial. It was the source of the gold that the Indians used for the jewelry that so captivated the Admiral when he landed at the grape-shaped island...

"Gold, gold in great quantity that gave the province the name of Costa Rica, rich coast, rich in gold..."

"Siren songs," snorted Pedro. "I wouldn't believe you even if you had the mine right here under my nose."

"Listen, what's there to lose? If that dead man went out hanging on to a stone that way, not wanting to give it up even after he died—I could see what it cost you to pry it out of his fingers—it was because it is worth something...is worth something. There's nothing to lose in finding out. I promise not to bother the girl and to chill down the urge in the river when we check it over. It can't be far from here. I think I can hear it, it must be almost within earshot. See? If we find nothing, drown me, if you want...drown me!"

They started out with Hernández walking ahead, hands tied behind his back. Soon, in fact, they came to a river with a swift current and dangerous whirlpools in the center, to say nothing of rocky banks, enough to discourage anyone. At the edges there were stones similar to the one Pedro lost when he was attacked by Hernández. A couple of crocodiles, long, lazy shadows, floated nearby which seemed to be waiting patiently for some hapless traveler to mistake them for floating logs.

"I told you so! I told you so! There's the river!" shouted Hernández, pointing with his chin.

Gerónima stared at the crocodiles stolidly and they at her. Pedro gazed at them paralyzed with fear; never before had he

seen such enormous, ugly creatures. He recalled something he
had once read about running zigzag if they chased you, it being
difficult for them to break away at an angle because of their long
heavy tails. As though guessing that here there was no easy prey,
they took off awkwardly, carried by the current, floating
indifferently out of sight. The river seemed to be blaring
announcements of all kinds, from warnings of danger to seductive
whispers calling attention to treasure in its entrails. Hernández
went on shouting, "This is, this it! I can see it glittering! Let's go
into the water, Pedro. There's nothing to it. There at the edge,
stick your hands in. Millions of nuggets, stick your hands in..."

Gerónima had gone upstream to see if there was a ford where
they could wade across and returned to say there was none and
she would go downstream to investigate.

Pedro sat down to skip stones into the water and watch the
splash and concentric ripples that formed and dissolved into
wavelets. There actually did seem to be something shiny on the
bottom and if they waited for the water level to go down, there
would be nothing to lose in sneaking into the giant river's bed
and seeing if there weren't something hidden under the mattress.
As Pedro cast one stone after another into the water, following
the ripples that widened and widened until they disappeared into
nowhere, he envisioned himself returning to Spain wearing a
velvet jacket and lace shirt, bribing officials, for that's what gold
is good for. And he imagined himself in a book-lined library,
himself stretched out on a couch next to a small table on which
there was a flagon of wine and snacks of sausage, leafing through
a book published in England, listening to music played on a guitar
by a woman in a patio of orange trees in bloom...

"Oh, shut your damn mouth, or I'll heave you in the river," he
shouted at Hernández, annoyed with himself for getting
distracted by thinking nonsense, and he went on skipping the
stones in the river until Gerónima returned to say that she had
found narrows down below and that they should cut bamboo and
reeds to make a raft, for hanging on to the mule's tail would be
too dangerous because of the crocodiles.

Hernández had another fit of rage and refused to help,
demanding that his hands be untied so he could look for treasure

on his own since Pedro was being such a jackass and idiot in refusing the riches right there at arm's length.

Building the raft was a simple task and when it was finished they dragged it to the water and floated it down to the place Gerónima selected. Hernández refused to get on and put up no little resistance. It was necessary to threaten him with throwing him in the water to be eaten by the crocodiles. The mule was the other one who resisted getting on the raft but, in the absence of carrots, she finally let herself be convinced by a couple of handfuls of succulent grass. The Mute got aboard and so did Pedro and Gerónima, carrying a long pole. She pushed off from shore with no difficulty and the raft floated to the middle of the river and downstream, carried by the current. Then, all at once, Gerónima lost hold of the pole, the light cane structure was caught in a whirlpool, crashed against a boulder to the unearthly shrieks of the mule and the howls of Hernández, split in two, and the half with Gerónima and Hernández on it continued downstream. Pedro and The Mute, clinging to a chunk of the raft, were swept into a backwater and onto land. The other part with its passengers was carried away swirling in the current until it disappeared from sight around a bend. Pedro tried to run after it but a family of crocodiles made him turn right back to where The Mute was waiting for him, naked as the day she was born, wringing out her dress, smiling, indifferent, unafraid, and vacant. Pedro gripped her by the shoulders and shook her, shouting "You idiot, you idiot, your sister is drowning, is drowning!" The girl let him shake her until, breathless, he dropped to the ground shuddering at what happened and thinking only of how much he needed Gerónima— more than he had ever needed his mother—to be able to continue their journey. The Indian had caused him to revert to a time long ago when he was an infant sucking on a breast, and he latched onto the ladle as to a teat when he chased after the foundering raft. Never did he hate anyone as he hated The Mute at that moment, with her witless smile, naked without shame, wringing out the jacket that served her as a tunic, more silent and removed than ever.

Perhaps in one of its meanders, the river would have cast the remains of the raft towards land. Or, perhaps, Gerónima would have leapt into the water and swum ashore—that is, if she was able to swim and if there were no hungry crocodiles close by. In any case, Pedro could do nothing but wait, and he remained sitting there skipping stones over the water and watching the ripples come into being and disappear. The Mute spread her tunic out in the sun and sat with her legs crossed, a little Buddha, her pubis quite exposed.

Hours went by and Pedro remained where he was tossing stone after stone into the water, waiting for a sign of the castaways that never came. Shadows began to lengthen and night closed in. When it was no longer possible to see or to distinguish shapes beneath the moonless sky with few stars, Pedro, not having eaten and not hungry, lay down on the still warm ground and without any invitation The Mute lay down beside him. As though he were Gerónima, he placed his arm across her breast, but all at once withdrew it. Taken aback by the sudden tumescence that seized him, he could not restrain his arm from moving with a will of its own to curl around the girl's waist. The mute, with the guilelessness of a child, turned her back to him, pressing her compact little rump against his abdomen. Aroused by that intimacy, he sent his hand over her body in a slow trek of urgent desire, stroking, with no resistance from her but with neither her compliance nor participation, she made herself impervious to touch, invulnerable, frigid, giving no sign of pleasure or repulsion, signaling simply indifference. She was unmoved as his hand tensed over her lemon-shaped breasts, squeezed her small, firm bottom, caressed her peach-fuzz flesh. No rebelliousness, no cooperation, not even an acknowledgment of receipt. She received his caresses like a mirror, a reflecting pool, unresponsive to external stimulus, inert, glacial. There was no other way for her, and having her was the same as not having her: the Mute lacked feelings and attempting to seduce her was a waste of time. Pedro's impatience brimmed over. He turned her face up and mounted her without further ado with the intention of taking her by force before her impenetrable detachment caused him to lose the impulse, for he felt that she was draining him out, that his urge was dispelling like the widening ripples made by the stones he had been throwing into the river. Even now she showed no resistance, allowing her legs to be parted, not willingly, not unwillingly, submissively, turned inward, as though the violence was not involving her, she a split personality, impassive, neutral, and despite everything, dreadfully tepid...

He gave up, lay down sprawled out, languid, surrendered, limp, feeling like an idiot, pride wounded, lust frustrated in anger and fear.

The Mute was left as indifferent as she had been before. Pedro, even more offended, if that could be said, sat up to restore his dignity, and, though he was unable to see her eyes in the darkness, he knew that she was looking at an indefinite point in empty space, plunged in a deep dream filled with golden things.

Pedro woke up in the morning, and it took him time to understand why he was lying next to the sleeping girl on a river bank. He entered the water together with the reflections of dawn, amazed that crocodiles had not eaten them. He gathered up his scattered and disjointed emotions stemming from the episode of the dying man clutching the stone, Hernández's attack, the raft accident, and his frustrated attempt to violate The Mute. He went into the bordering fringe of vegetation to hunt for something edible and was lucky enough to find some wild avocados. When he returned she was sitting in the lotus position, looking in the direction where the half raft carrying Gerónima had disappeared. Feeling guilty and ashamed for what happened between them he put his hand on her shoulder, in a friendly, consoling gesture, and quickly withdrew it almost as though he had touched a wasps' nest; the contact reawakened his original, earliest reaction to the girl, his mistrust of her disembodied eyes. There was no other woman quite like this one. Her beauty made her perverse and dangerous. Keeping his distance, he handed her an avocado, turned around and went off toward the river. If Gerónima had not drowned she would find a way to reach them, would do the impossible to return to her sister. His anxiety was eased by the thought and he decided to wait for her until midday and give her up for dead if she did not appear by then. The Mute would be a burden he had no choice but to assume.

He walked a distance upstream to explore and returned. The Mute was seated in the same place, legs crossed, expression of vapid ingenuousness unchanged, eyes staring at the river downstream. Pedro then went off in that direction to explore and after a short walk came upon a path with recent footsteps marked in the mud. It appeared to be a frequently used way for the Indians to get water. He was not sure whether to be worried or pleased at the sight. Not wishing to move any further away, he returned to The Mute and sat down beside her as he pondered what to do next. The sun was soon beating down and he sought a shady spot. No sooner did he resume his game of skipping stones in the water than he heard crackling sounds in the underbrush. He jumped to his feet holding his breath, ladle at the ready. The Mute remained impassive. A moment later a loud braying could be heard and the mule emerged from the jungle, still lame, still one-eyed, carrying no load but still possessed of her one good eye, her marvelous instinct, and looking beautiful with her coat clean and glistening. Pedro received her with a joyous shout which was choked off by the sight of Hernández, his hands free, bruised, a jagged cut on his face, hunched over.

His story was that when the raft sank the current swept him against rocks until he was able to grab onto a tree root and pull himself out of the water and that he met up with the mule when he walked back upstream.

Hernández seemed crazed, his jaw slack, his bloodshot eyes wandering from The Mute's nude body to the river, without fixing on either.

"The river is full of gold nuggets," Pedro told him. "Look at them there. See how they glitter right there at the edge of the water... You'd better get to work right away before Gerónima comes back and ties up your hands again."

The madman hesitated. The sun struck golden reflections from the wet stones in the river bed and The Mute's skin, too, had the sheen of pure gold.

"Gerónima is coming," Pedro insisted, "and will make you keep walking to the mission and give you up to the friar who will put you to hard work and make you pray two hundred Our Fathers every night with a hair shirt on. If you don't obey him, Father Rebullida will turn you over to the Indians who will chop you into small pieces and eat you raw. Look at the river, at the way it glitters. All you have to do is stick your hands in."

The madman stumbled to the river edge. Pedro put The Mute's tunic on her, lifted her to his shoulders (My Lord, how light!), gave the mule's ears a tug. She limped behind him until they reached the trail which she followed as Pedro took a last look at Hernández, kneeling at the river edge, his two hands plunging in and out of the water.

"You've gone out of your skull, you foulmouthed blasphemer... May the crocodiles take pity on you, you sonofabitch...!" he shouted but there was no answer.

He set the girl down and no sooner did her feet touch the ground than she turned and ran off towards where Hernández was. Pedro roared with rage, took two steps in her direction, stopped and yelled, "To hell with you!" and without another backward glance, set out into the jungle after the mule, which seemed to know exactly where the path led.

Of how Agueda Pérez de Muro
helped Pedro reconstruct a part of
his life intangible as a dream

At a certain moment, particularly when in profile, perhaps due to a certain tilt of her head—as she was now, bending over serving the chocolate—Agueda still possessed the initial bewitching quality of my lady of torment before the earthquake, before her buck teeth came into evidence. A tight scarlet bodice encased her once wasp-waisted form, made more ample now by time. A sheaf of blonde locks falling off the shoulder onto her brown holland blouse, had a golden luster in the candlelight. The gesture with which she poured the cinnamon-scented brew into the majolica mug decorated with blue flowers had lost none of the seduction of the bejeweled little hand holding up her brocaded petticoat that inspired Pedro to copy out sonnets, quatrains, sestinas, and rondelets from the works of others onto sheets of paper he used for the monastery accounts.

Agueda Pérez de Muro had finally completed her mansion on the southwest corner of the main square, a handsome building, its sloping hip roof covered with tiles, a long porch roofed on three sides and open in the front towards the main square, with heavy vines of blue flowers entwined about its cedar columns. There was an elaborately carved bench there from which the council and city hall buildings could be observed, as well as the window at which Pedro had once sat behind his scribe's desk. It crossed Pedro's mind that perhaps Agueda would sit upon the same bench to gaze at that window. The thought touched him deeply...he had softened with the years, turned sentimental.

"Wait, Pedralbarán," Agueda was saying to him, now, "my hand trembles at the thought of what could have happened to that poor child, all alone, at the mercy of that madman... But don't be in a hurry, the night is long and has just begun. I don't want to lose a single detail of your marvelous adventure. Extraordinary things are said about you in Cartago, people weave incredible tales about your life and fantasize you as the prisoner of a dragon and a witch who bedazzled your wits..."

Agueda handed Pedro the Toledo mug, steaming and fragrant. He sipped the warm chocolate, smiling melancholically at the thought...nothing could be further from a witch than the gentle, sweet-natured Mute. About Gerónima as a dragon...well, possibly. It isn't true that time erases all pain. There was a keen throbbing deep in his breast and, a never fading nostalgia. "Nostalgia is the desire to possess something, fed by the memory of that thing." Who wrote that? I can't remember. He repeated the saying aloud and Agueda just chuckled.

"Spinoza," she said. "Baruch de Spinoza, the Dutch Sephardic Jew. Devotional books aren't the only ones you will find in this house. I also read things Father Angulo does not approve of...books my husband brought me from Guatemala as an apology for his long absence." There was a chill note of bitterness in her voice... "You loved her very much, didn't you? Tell me Pedralbarán."

"Very much," he replied, feeling infinitely old, infinitely tired. His eyes wandered over the room: upholstered chairs, a Spanish credenza inlaid with mother-of-pearl and tortoise shell, silver candelabras set out on a long table, expertly calculated to illuminate all corners of the room. There were tapestries of Chinese silk everywhere and in one corner a lovely icon of Saint Agatha upon a silver pedestal, fresh flowers lying in homage beneath. The perfect floor tiles smooth and shining. The ceiling covered in a symmetrical design of white cane. The door to the street shut, the one to the inside garden open, through which the scent of the flowering plants entered the room. Agueda, watched him, her feet on a velvet cushion making little movements of satisfaction, as she explained, "We finished this house four years ago, except for a few details. The oratory still lacks a number of things because I wanted the altar to be gilded but we haven't been able to get the gold leaf... After Serrano left, foreign trade has not been the same."

She took a leaf of tobacco from a small chest, rolled it, and lit the end from a candle, the odor of the tobacco momentarily displacing that of the tallow. Seeing her smoking, Pedro thought that Agueda had become an interesting woman, one who read Spinoza and sent up more clouds of smoke than a blacksmith.

"Well," said Pedro, "I came back because I couldn't come to terms with the thought of that brute shattering her innocence. The mule continued on its way. I retraced my steps and there she was again, sitting there like a little bronze Buddha. Hernández's hands moved in and out of the water scratching for gold. That was when I saw Gerónima on the other side of the river, unable to cross to this bank. The water level had indeed dropped overnight but even so it was still impossible to wade across or even swim. I watched her walk back and forth, entering and coming out of the water, the crocodiles always a danger. There was nothing I could do. After a while she made signs to me indicating that we should continue on our way and I, thinking that she had decided to go back to Cartago, put The Mute on my shoulders as before and set out on the trail, a footpath opened by the presence of man, still bearing fresh prints of bare feet. There was no sign of the mule and so I forged ahead with my burden, trying not to let despair overtake me. After walking for some three hours, to my great surprise, I came upon a kind of temporary shelter covered with palm leaves now dried out and rotting, and somebody inside. It was...Gerónima! She wouldn't tell me how she had been able to cross the river and by that time I was so exhausted and so relieved that I set The Mute down and collapsed on the ground. Fate had brought me back again into the inestimable company of the Indian woman. I know, now, that Gerónima crossed the river comfortably in a boat belonging to the Indians... The Indians! It seems incredible but in all that long trek I never saw one, and they had been following us all the way!

"We plunged on through this world, so difficult to describe, a constant flux of life and death, the closest thing to the idea of eternity that a human being can conceive...species intermingled, one with another, in an eternal spiral of decomposition and recomposition, millions of living creatures devouring one another, linking together the vegetable and animal kingdoms, overreaching the frontiers of sap and blood, a chain in which each link is the last segment, as well as the first in an endless sequence... I felt myself an intruder, an outsider, an invasive canker inflamed by the heat, the mosquitos, and the damp; inflamed particularly by my irrepressible fascination with The Mute which again possessed me with a force I had ceased to resist. I woke up one morning before reaching Urinama. She was before me, bathing in a stream, the sun gilding her body. I emerged from my dream and saw her figure burgeoning upward and downward, buds suddenly ripened, skin burnished copper, contrasting with the cool tones of the vegetation and the sky. Denizen and contour of the forest, forest herself, in harmony with her surroundings, her natural frame encompassing her... I approached slowly trying not to frighten her, so that I might share her bath. And so I had her close to me, could see into her slanted eyes filled with living things; in them reflections of the trees, the badgers, the ants, the butterflies, the monkeys, and a deer, and I thought that this is what Juan de las Alas was looking at when Lorenzo surprised them. Her smile was inviting, gracious, warm, brimming with encrypted messages, secret codes and tenderings.

"The short time it took to embrace her imposed a renunciation upon me. What I was renouncing, I have yet to be able to determine. I was impelled by her terrifying beauty, her silence, and everything that had happened previously, even the panic provoked by her strange way of being. When I reached her, I was, if I may so describe myself, one sole sensation, pure feeling and emotion, passion, delirium, ardor... A melange, a totally entangled skein, I lost myself in her. A better description of her than mine could be had from the frightened little fish and the startled small creatures that went to drink water and saw her trembling beneath their thirsty mouths: white foam and warm streams of life breaking the smoothness of the surface rippling with waves of interminable ecstasy... I was not aware that I had crossed a frontier and thought that everything would revert to the way it was. She emerged from the water as though I had never stepped over the threshold of her innocence, with her usual look, filled with animals and empty of concepts. And, as for me, I was concerned only about one thing, whether Gerónima had seen us and, if she had, why she allowed it.

"That same afternoon we reached San Bartolomé de Urinama,

the last redoubt, a small clearing in the dense forest, with two huts and a very small hermitage with its cross. The place looked deserted, and I expected to find nobody there, but all at once who should appear to welcome us but the mule! After her came dark-skinned Cristóbal, and behind him the ghostly, ragged figure of Rebullida, a cassock dancing upon his bones. Rebullida was looking over my shoulder, which made me turn around to see if someone had followed me, but no one was there, just The Mute and me. Gerónima had disappeared.

"It was a little while before I realized that San José should have been at the mission with the sixty soldiers. They were the ones Rebullida was looking for, and when I explained that I had come alone and that San José should have arrived with the escort in Urinama some time ago, he was very disappointed."

"San José never got to Urinama," reflected Agueda, laughing.

"Never... Poor Rebullida was wild with impatience. If he was glad I came, he concealed it well. Perhaps he had grown accustomed to the grim loneliness and the only thing that concerned him was starting at once on his project for bringing Indians out of Talamanca and over to the other side of the cordillera. Black Cristóbal was the only one who asked questions about Cartago. He told me that the Indians fled from them and that he hadn't been able to get a single one to move near the hermitage. 'But where are the Indians?' I wanted to know after not seeing any. 'Out there it's loaded with Indians,' he told me, making a sweeping gesture with his arm. All I could see was forest and more forest... When Rebullida became convinced that something out of the way had happened to delay San José, he looked at The Mute and wanted to know why I had brought her. I explained everything, telling him of Angulo's decision, of Hernández having to expiate his sins at the mission, of how he had stayed behind hunting for gold in the river... The only answer he gave me was that I should write the priest Angulo and tell him not to be sending sinners to the mission to expiate their sins for he had enough on his hands converting the heathen without straightening out the twisted souls of Spaniards...

"Then, he led me to what he called 'the monastery,' a very primitive structure standing two spans above the ground in which there was a straw mat upon which he slept and a table with some books piled on it. It would be hard to imagine more abject poverty! Then, his glance lit on The Mute who was squatting on the floor, and he commented with a note of rancor in his voice: 'So, this Indian has caused disturbances in Cartago, too. I don't understand how a friar could lose his head over her.' 'Juan de las Alas is a lad,' I said, feeling like one myself."

Rebullida hadn't answered. He kept looking at The Mute strangely, with repulsion one might say. After a long silence, he spoke. "I don't want her here. Her parents don't want her, either. It would be best for her to go back. She can't stay here, scaring the Indians, and me, as well." The friar made the sign of the cross. "The devil has refused to leave her. I have exorcised him three times." He coughed a dry little parenthetical cough. "I took her to Cartago because I hoped that, away from this place where Satan holds sway, and under Our Father Saint Francis's pious protection, the devil would flee from her... The powers of hell are weakened in a monastery, they retreat and abandon the possessed."

It was Rebullida who seemed bedeviled, with his bulging eyes, hooked nose, scrawniness, and madman's appearance. Pedro would have liked to know why the Indians didn't want The Mute, whether they were rejecting her because she was dumb or because her eyes were wells whose source was in another world, another dimension. But he said nothing of that. The one he did ask about was Gerónima.

"This girl's sister came with me, but she disappeared. I couldn't return without her."

"She is surely visiting her family," Rebullida answered calmly, as if it was the most natural thing in the world. "She never leaves her sister alone. She will show up when you begin the trip back. I imagine the Father Superior gave her as a guide."

"That's right," lied Pedro.

"She is the guardian angel Divine Providence has placed beside this child to foil the designs of the Evil One. An excellent woman, loyal, submissive, very Christian."

Pedro's concept of Gerónima was quite different, but he did not contradict the friar.

Rebullida sent The Mute to the hermitage to sleep beside the simple altar decorated with large flowers and an effigy of Saint Bartholomew who looked cross-eyed because of the apostasy of the termites; they had made a path precisely for the purpose of eating out the pupils, after having gorged on all the fingers of the right hand and part of the vestment. The missionary strung a hammock for Pedro who had never slept in such a strange type of bed and who abandoned it to breathe fresh air because he was half-choked by the smoke of the fire Rebullida had laid to drive away the mosquitos. Outdoors, the forest sang its cantata of feline footsteps, vegetal sobs, and insomniac owls. The half moon stabbed down its rays to the treetops, illuminating the wooden cross of the San Bartolomé hermitage and the humblest of solitary campaniles waiting out with Franciscan patience the installation of a bell. Above was a sharply outlined shadow balanced starkly against the dark sky. Pedro thought it might be a weather vane set up there by whim of the missionary to keep check on the direction of diabolical winds—Rebullida being capable of the most outlandish things—but that was unlikely since he could not remember having seen a weather vane, and besides the calm was heavy and enervating; there was no breeze, the trees were still, and the heat smothering. The other possibility was an animal, a fox, panther, or, perhaps, a monkey. The silhouette moved very slowly, walking along the ridge pole cautiously but with assurance and then stopping and moving no longer. Pedro waited. Whatever it was up there remained still. Pedro hurried to the hermitage feeling his way in the shadows of the small space. His eyes gradually adjusted and in the faint moonlight examined all the corners. There was nothing but the image of the saint. The Mute was gone. He went out and looked around the building, but she was nowhere to be seen. Up above along the ridgepole of the roof, the figure moved again, going from one end to the other, and stopping next to the campanile, leaning against the cross, and then he saw it clearly. He wanted to shout and call for help, to find a ladder, but as he hesitated, The Mute climbed down clinging to the supports of the rickety bell tower while Pedro, paralyzed with fear, stiff as a statue, waiting until she had come all the way down and brushed by him, her eyes open in the unconsciousness of sleep. He followed her. She walked into the hermitage, lay down on the dirt floor and was peacefully asleep without closing her eyes. He lay down beside her and put his outstretched arm over her breast, tranquil now that the mystery was solved: The Mute was a somnambulist. Which explained everything: that Rebullida should consider her possessed by the devil, that Gerónima never left her alone, and that for the Indians, in their beliefs and superstitions, The Mute, a sleepwalker, was to be repudiated (apparently there were no somnambulists among them). Beyond that, she was strange, exceedingly strange, unlike anybody or anything there is. Filled with tenderness, he slept next to her until on being awakened by a mooing cow he hurried off to his hammock so that Rebullida should not think he had spent the night with her.

And so, Rebullida took leave of him as he had received him with a word of advice that was at the same time an order: to go down to the coast and continue on as far as Matina to investigate what happened to San José. Whatever information he was able to obtain Pedro was to communicate to Cartago for them to take the necessary measures. The mule went with them loaded with wild fruits and cooked vegetables. As the friar had predicted, no sooner had they left the mission than Gerónima appeared, the inescapable ladle in hand and a cagelike crate containing a mysterious load carried on her back with a headband.

"Why didn't you tell me your sister walks in her sleep?" Pedro asked her, and without waiting for a reply took advantage of the opportunity to get things off his chest. "It's a natural thing that happens to some people and has nothing to do with the other world. I consider it outrageous that they gave her to Rebullida just for that reason... It is just as stupid as Rebullida believing your sister is possessed of the devil. Honestly, Gerónima, I didn't know that the Indians were as foolish and ignorant as the Spaniards. I thought they were more practical and wiser...

"It's not because my sister walks in her sleep... It's because she doesn't let the stones talk."

"Stones don't talk. What nonsense!"

"There are stones that answer questions and they told me I will never go back to Cartago."

"Then, if magical stones told you that, you are both wasting your time because we are bound for the coast on the way to Matina on the shore, and from there as fast as possible to

Cartago. It seems that Father Rebullida also talks to stones, out of being lonely and out of his mind, and he doesn't want your sister at the mission and is returning her to the monastery. The Father Superior is going to throw a fit when he sees her again and what he'll do is send her to Esparza or Granada or give her away to anybody because the law says he can't sell her."

"And my sister will never go back to Cartago... The stones said so," continued Gerónima sadly. Pedro was annoyed because now he recalled that San José had spoken to him about stones that the Indians hold in the palm of the hand to ask them things.

"That stuff is witchcraft," he said angrily. "Spells are just foolish talk. My head tells me we should get moving as we have a long journey ahead of us to Matina and from there we'll connect up with a mule train or detachment of soldiers who will take us to Cartago. So, let's get on with it!"

Agueda had been waiting for a while for Pedro to continue his tale, which was interrupted before the point where The Mute climbed the campanile in her sleep.

"Rebullida's only distraction," he went on, "his only entertainment, other than going out fishing for heathen souls, was to walk about the mission with a line for laying out parallels and verticals for the future city that the Spaniards would found there. At sundown, he would take a carbonized stick and a piece of white balsa wood and draw plan after plan without ever saying where the church and the main square would be located. The Sunday I spent there, he came out to give the call to mass which he did by banging on an ancient conquistador's stirrup with a knife blade but nobody came.

"When I left him, I met up with Gerónima and together with the mule we set out for the coast on the way to Matina. We descended in a straight line north, avoiding all Indian villages, which seemed to me an aberration of Rebullida's overheated imagination since I still hadn't seen a single Indian or dwelling. The few conversations I had with him made me suspect that he was living completely alienated from reality, lost in a fictitious world, as out of his senses as the dead man with the stone, as Hernández, as San José, as I, myself... Rebullida was lamenting that the Virgin Mary had not seen fit to appear to an Indian in the mountains, and dreamed of a Virgin of Talamanca, like the Virgin of Guadalupe or Los Angeles, and other dark-skinned saints who are most effective in attracting the worship of the Indians. As I listened to his yearnings for a Virgin to appear and so facilitate the conversion progress, I told him, 'Why not invent one...?'"

"What an irreverent thing to suggest! I'm shocked!" said Agueda in a tone of mock indignation."

"He answered very seriously that he would never use My Lady as bait, not even if it meant saving the soul of a thousand Indians..."

"Adamant..."

"Adamant! Then, he added that it was unnecessary to pretend miracles because Mother María de Agreda had foretold in those years that Saint Francis would be victorious and that all the heathens would be converted by the mere sight of his cassock."

"The little nun was quite mistaken."

"No doubt she was. However, I'm convinced that Rebullida believed her to the end, to the last breath.

"To go on, we proceeded towards the coast and one day later we met up with two little blacks who had white spots on their skin. It didn't surprise me because nothing surprises me anymore. They were under a *chilamate* tree holding on to each other, not having eaten in any number of days. They were pure blacks, two little slave boys who knew no Spanish, more or less ten years old. I was worried about the strange spots being leprosy. Years later when they were able to tell me their story, I learned that they had been kidnapped from Africa. Their settlement was surrounded, some were able to escape, but they and their mother were captured and put on a ship which foundered off this coast. I am no slave expert and had no idea what caste they were, whether they were from Angola, Congo, Arara, or where... Nor did I know their names, and so I baptized with what they sounded like to me, one Babí and the other Bugalú."

"Bugalú?" Agueda lit a second cigar, expelling a cloud of smoke and gathering up her skirt to place her feet more comfortably on the velvet cushion.

"Yes, Babí and Bugalú... Who knows what could have happened to them! Who knows!"

"They tried to run away but Gerónima held them by the hair while I practically had to force yucca and bananas from our supply into their mouths. The mule sympathized with them from the very beginning and with her nose helped Gerónima hold them down. They looked at me in fear, undoubtedly surprised that no birds were nesting in my beard. I took them along. That night I made love to The Mute for the second time: the forest was bringing its discords into harmony, the praying mantis hurrying to finish pairing before daylight when it would have to disguise itself as a leaf to confuse voracious nomadic ants which at this time were sleeping in a swarm at their bivouac... Without my realizing it, The Mute was swaddling me like the pupa of a butterfly in its cocoon. My appearance couldn't have been less attractive, I had blisters on my feet, you could count my ribs, and my beard looked like an oriole's nest. We descended, the entire journey was downhill... Suddenly, I could feel the scent of the sea in the air. I climbed a tree to scan the horizon and could hardly contain my joy when, beyond the green mass of the woods, I was able to make out a blue fringe that separated the sky and the land... There, less than a league away was the ocean, the sea of the North, the same sea that had brought me to America, that separated me from the Spanish peninsula, from Europe... My nostrils filled with the ocean scent and I shouted "Water, water!" My legs became light and agile and I climbed down nimbly as a squirrel. I slashed my way through the guts of the jungle with my machete, not paying attention to whether I was chopping the tails off snakes or the heads off lizards. And I didn't stop until the roar of the waves and the screeching of sea birds was very close, right nearby, music to my ears. I reached the beach at a point where the jungle fights the sea over every inch of sand, where when the tide is out, thousands of blue and yellow crabs, with red legs and pedunculate eyes, come out to welcome us among giant turtles and other creatures hidden under the shells of pink snails... On the still warm afternoon sand, the crabs and wrinkled old turtles brought a sample of the loving kiss of the waves and approached with curious eyes to look at us. We must have seemed a strange and intriguing group to them. I doubt that they had ever seen a man with as big a nose as mine, a woman as homely as Gerónima, two little blacks stained like a checkerboard, a mule as ungainly, and a woman as lovely as The Mute..."

Pedro was embarrassed at being so carried away in making this last remark and Agueda looked at him sideways as she readjusted her feet on the cushion and took a long, sensual drag on her cigar.

Intoxicated with joy as he was, Pedro forgot the uncertainty of his future and the way to Matina. Delighted at the infinite vista of the sea, he knelt among the crabs, which lifted their claws, undecided whether to nip at his dark flesh or scuttle away from him. Red monkeys screeched at the visitors from the tops of the tall trees. A lone pelican, finding himself displaced from where he meditated upon the enigma of life, flew out toward the horizon, and the snails sensed unfamiliar waves with their tentacular ear. Pedro took off his rags and plunged into the water, marveling at it for he had never experienced such warmth and transparency. Splashing about like a grampus, he cleansed body and spirit, scrubbing himself down with seaweed, floating on his back and then on his face to soak his beard, imagining the while that he was on a route of navigators and that very soon the captain of a sailing ship would lower a boat with able-bodied oarsmen to put him on a ship that would sail him to Cádiz, far from this noxious jungle world, its stench of rottenness, its maniacal and addled people, to return to civilization, to the cobblestoned streets of Seville, to the libraries, to the drinking companions and women with deep cleavage and indulgent smiles... He would return to La Chamberga's tavern which would now be run by a new proprietor—or proprietress. Dreaming in that way, completely oblivious to the fact that he was a fugitive from the Inquisition and that he could never return to Seville, he sported in the sea, waving to nonexistent ships and captains, and diving into the water so that there wouldn't be an orifice of his body that went unwashed. He was thrilled by the coral reef and all the deep-sea life, the varicolored little fishes, black sea urchins with long spines and white, round ones with short spines. He admired the marine flora that looked like mushrooms and cabbages, sea beds that simulated lace and needlework, and

other indescribable wonders never before seen... When he
emerged from the water he saw his four companions standing
with the mule far from the water, very frightened, undoubtedly
thinking that it was by way of the sea that all calamities, all
perversities, all the iniquities of the slave traders, the
conquistadors, and the colonizers came.

Clean, wet, and lighthearted Pedro looked into The Mute's
eyes, scanning her feelings, discerning there that he would be
unable to go anywhere without her. Although, dumb as always,
she could articulate nothing, he knew that, without her asking
anything of him, nor pleading, not demanding nor begging, not
insisting, he was imprisoned between two horizons, that of the
ocean and that of the depths of her almond-shaped gaze. It took
only a second or two for him to make up his mind: if he had to
plunge in and navigate, he would have to do so first in the pool of
her two eyes. He lifted her in his arms (My Lord, how light!) and
dove into the sea with her before the terrified eyes of Gerónima
who surely was thinking that the immensity of that expanse of
water would gobble them up never to release them again.

That night The Mute, seasoned with salt and flavored with
seaweed, was more delicious than ever. He journeyed through her
most recondite labyrinths, and came to realize that she possessed
the property of never satiating, which seemed to him the best
antidote to boredom.

That night, Catarina began to live without anybody realizing
it, not herself or her mother.

"I'm going to serve a dish of snacks," said Agueda, aware that
Pedro's reminiscing had made a nostalgic jelly of him. She clapped
her hands and Bárbara Lorenzana appeared, her head twisted to
one side. With the years, her skeptical expression had grown more
pronounced and now, it was not only her wry neck, but her full
body, that gave her a distrustful air. The expression on her face
seemed to question the integrity of life itself. She had become
stout and luxuriant, but had produced no offspring for her
mistress as Rafael Fajordo, the auctioneer, had pronounced for
her future when he sold her to Friar Lorenzo for eighty pesos,
which were never paid. Bárbara went out and returned with a
tray of tempting-looking tidbits: chicken thighs, chunks of pork

and beef, fried yuccas and potatoes, surrounded by delicious little tomatoes. After settling the tray on the table, she replaced the partly consumed candles, all done with a graceful economy of unhurried movement, her neck twisted to one side, dubious as to the effectiveness of her work, her mistress's orders, the guest's intentions, the house's stability, the light issuing from the little flames, of herself, and even the presence of the door through which she disappeared.

Pedro, bewitched by The Mute and the sea, remained to rest on the beach for a few days, enjoying them as a real holiday. The weather was fine, without rain; the breeze off the ocean was not only cool but drove away the mosquitoes.

A quarter of a league southward he found a broad beach of warm white sand where he put up a shelter with the help of Gerónima, who was uncomplaining and agreeable to everything. Food was a simple matter in view of the abundance of turtles and lobsters which could be caught merely by reaching out into the water. Let San José wait, thought Pedro as the days went by. The two slave boys had become friendly and cooperated in foraging for food and rubbing sticks together to make fire. Pedro would steal away with The Mute to the shade of a tall almond tree, a leafy and hospitable bower for lovemaking and resting afterward as they gazed upon the lovely, placid bay, watching the great long-legged cranes fly over shoals of iridescent fish. Pedro used his machete to fashion harpoons but hardly needed them for the abundance of fish was such that they could easily be caught by hand in the little caves of the coral reef, an effective barrier to the sharks whose fins could be seen in the distance.

Pedro spent one week in idleness, unable to summon the will to continue on the journey. The mere thought of beating his way back sickened him, and he justified himself with the argument that all were overtired and needed to restore their energies. The two mottled black boys raced about the beach, capturing among the rocks little creatures which seemed to be seeking escape from the overpopulated waters. By the beginning of the second week, the weather changed, the sea became rough, and there was a heavy downpour that threatened their makeshift shelter. Pedro considered that to resume the journey under such conditions was foolhardy and that it would be best to stay right there until conditions improved.

When the storm was over and the sea calm, Gerónima had woven a hammock which she hung between two palm trees. Pedro was lying in it, swaying in the breeze, when he realized that he had not the slightest desire to return to Cartago and was ready to stay there at the edge of the sea until driven off by sheer surfeit. None of them was important enough to prompt a search over such difficult terrain. Even the reefs made access by sea difficult. He shored up their shelter, and every time he chopped a slender pole, he thanked Agueda for her gift. He explored the surroundings and discovered a small freshwater lake inhabited by a mythical creature with breasts like a woman, a face like a cow, and the rest of it a huge fish. He would always see it hugging an offspring in its fins. Years later he learned that the curious creature was a manatee. Another inhabitant was a huge, old, drowsy crocodile. In order to have no dealings with him, he found that since it rained at night he could get enough water by digging a hole and lining it with banana leaves. The forest behind them provided an inexhaustible larder of vegetables, and all of those things together constituted an edenic escape from life's tribulations. Pedro had no compelling reason to stay nor any for leaving, and so continued letting the time go by between feasts of fish and lobsters, encouraged by the thoughts that La Chamberga would tire of looking for him, Avendaño would be about ready to leave Cartago, the Superior at the monastery would have found another bookkeeper, and the Governor another scribe. More than anything he was delighted at the idea that Lázaro de Robles had no one to annoy with his unbearable buffoonery.

For the first time in his life Pedro was feeling truly free. He had no ships to burn, nor permits to request, no safe-conducts to present, nor academic credentials to obtain. He could do without all of it, even without his own name, if he chose. And he was able to do whatever he pleased, making love with The Mute to the point of prostration, for example. He was younger and stronger than he would ever have credited, and he had the invaluable companionship of Gerónima and the pair of black boys: they were a small community, living freely and simply by their own efforts.

And he stayed on, without purpose, without dates, for no

other reason than that he was having a very good time. Laughing at himself and his brazenness, he said to Gerónima, "Your stones were right, I'll never return to Cartago."

"The stones didn't say that you would not go back to Cartago. I didn't even ask them," Gerónima replied, and told him that the mule, evidently bored with the endlessly monotonous expanse of sand and the pathless nature of the great ocean, had taken off without a goodbye.

Pedro considered the implications of the loss of the animal, calculating that perhaps it was better that way for she would probably have returned to Rebullida's mission and he would be assuming that they had had a mishap and perhaps even died. Better to be taken for dead by the world. Much better!

Busy organizing his wild and primitive life, Pedro was forgetting La Chamberga, the Inquisition, the people of Cartago, governors, commissaries, and superiors. What he sometimes missed were his goose quills and papers for he would have liked to keep a diary, a journal. However, he forgot even those when Gerónima advised him that summer was ending and the rainy season beginning and that the community's shelter was going to be inadequate.

"I got busy building a proper house... I can't even begin to tell you how useful the machete was that you gave me. I always thought of you while using it and thanked you for it from the bottom of my heart."

"I'm glad," said Agueda, skeptically, for she didn't believe that Pedro thought of her for one moment during his sojourn on the beach. "A place like that would bore me to death," she added.

"When food and shelter are matters of immediate necessity, boredom never comes into the picture, especially in a place as beautiful as that. And there was nothing monotonous about it, if that's what you are thinking. Of course, there were no luxuries, but life is full of surprises. When I finished the house, which was comfortable and had a tight roof, I took on myself the job of teaching the two blacks the few secrets of the sea that I knew. Babí turned out to be a great fisherman and Bugalú quickly proved himself a talented hunter. With instruction from Gerónima, I made bows and arrows and our diet was enriched with the meat of small mountain animals. It was then that the black kids found Torquemada, the jaguar kitten, and brought him to me. He couldn't have been more than a few weeks old and must have been abandoned by his mother or perhaps she was killed. He came to stay with us when The Mute was causing me great concern; now that her pregnancy had apparently cured her sleepwalking, she was obsessed with climbing to high places. Despite her bulging belly and breasts swelling in anticipation of motherhood, she would move among the branches as agilely as a little monkey. Torquemada helped me weather the scares that The Mute gave me with her aerial mania. The little animal with great yellow eyes was as playful and mischievous as a gentle, furry kitten. During the season when the turtles came to lay their eggs in the sand he quickly learned to dig them up and eat them, chewing through their soft shells, and had to be shut up in a corral before his voracious appetite left the beach looking like the aftermath of a battle. He grew rapidly and never have I seen a more splendid animal, his fur sleek, his muscles powerful, his eyes intelligent and cruel, turning tender when The Mute entered his corral to bring him a lobster or other food.

"He and I had playful wrestling matches inside his enclosure during which he kept his claws sheathed and I worked off some of my excess energy. Our battles could grow quite furious and it was during one of those moments that he went out of control and I lost half a finger. I'm sure you noticed, Agueda, that I lost part of the little finger on my left hand. Torquemada was the first to eat the unfamiliar creatures that Bugalú brought in from the mountainside and Babí from the sea. He looked forward as I did to our playful but fierce encounters which always ended with him pinning me to the ground as he emitted roars of joyous victory. I soon realized, however, that his stay with us would have to be terminated but I didn't want to set him free until The Mute had given birth, for our game served to relax the buildup of my tensions. Poor Torquemada!"

"Poor, why?" asked Agueda, absently. She had noticed that the chocolate pitcher was empty and said, "I believe the moment has come to turn our attention to a jug of wine that I bought at the port of Caldera." And she added, roguishly, "It happens to come from Peru..." With which she rose and went in her bare feet to a cabinet out of which she took two blue glass goblets and a bottle in the shape of an onion, evidently made in England. She set everything on the table, went back to her seat, clapped her hands, and waited while Bárbara, her eyes heavy with sleep, came in.

"Serve us the wine," she ordered. We looked on as she filled the goblets, handed one to each of us, and left.

"What were you going to say about the jaguar Torquemada?"

"He died defending my life when I was ready to set him free. It happened shortly after San José arrived, who appeared like Christ, walking on the water. I spied a spot on the horizon and knew that, on account of the reef, no ship could enter my bay. It had never occurred to me that the crew would be able to get to my beach simply by walking over the rocks and dead coral. Besides, I was convinced that San José must have reached Rebullida's mission by way of the Sixaola River. When I saw him advancing through the waves, his cassock blowing in the wind, followed by a procession of evil-looking characters, I felt as though I was looking at an illustration out of the New Testament come to life, and that the twelve apostles were visiting me in the midst of a crowd of the Hebrew people...San José had seen the roof of my hut in the morning sunlight and came on as big as life and as hidebound as ever I knew him. Following him were Corporal Juan de Bonilla and the soldiers of the escort who had not deserted during their incredible adventure.

The friar appeared to be gratified at seeing me and, actually, it was neither the time nor the place to be reliving old quarrels and holding grudges... He told me that on the first attempt he was unable to find the mouth of the river and had continued on his way as far as Admiral's Bay where he went down to see some Indians he knew. However, they received him in a hostile manner, and he lost two soldiers and three slaves in the conflict. He turned back and this time found the river mouth, but it refused him entrance. 'That Sixaola is an atheist,' he told me. Accordingly, with the escort considerably reduced, he returned to Matina, and from there to have another go at reaching Talamanca via the Sixaola. I warned him that he had missed the river mouth again and that he would have to fall back because the Sixaola was much further below where he had now arrived. When he left, after having taken on fresh water and a stock of turtle meat, neither he nor I could foresee that he would never achieve his goal of entering the Sixaola."

Agueda laughed. "He never made it. For two years he went from Matina to Portobello, from Portobello back to Matina, until the crew, including Corporal Juan de Bonilla, deserted, leaving him alone at the mouth of the atheistic river... Here, we assume that he set out to walk in Rebullida's tracks, covering half of Talamanca on foot without finding him and, walking continuously, he came upon a cargo of blacks, castaways from a pirate ship, whom he tried to sell in order to replenish his capital with the idea of buying another sloop. He came to Cartago with several of those blacks but he was intercepted at Turrialba and arrested for smuggling. Before he returned, the Corporal had already reported that he was insane. The Franciscan friars took him out of Guatemala and he was never able to return for there was a warrant out for his arrest... Cartago gossiped about that for a long time."

"And Rebullida kept waiting for him..."

"Yes. Until they sent Father Andrade to him with another escort...but overland!"

Agueda rolled another cigar and leaned over one of the candles to light it. The wrinkles on her neck showed up against the flame.

"Oh, that mad San José!"

Pedro had not rejected his embrace and gave no sign of pent-up resentment. And San José, with his obsession of reaching the Urinama mission by way of the Sixaola River, asked no questions and didn't even notice The Mute's bulging belly, nor did he give any indication of surprise when, before the entire troop, she climbed a palm tree in order to drop some coconuts so that Pedro might offer his strange visitors a drink. San José was interested in absolutely nothing unrelated to his idée fixe. As naturally as if he were at the monastery in Cartago, he turned to Gerónima and asked for a fire on which to dry his cassock. He talked and talked of his project to conquer the river, paying no attention to Corporal Juan de Bonilla's angry face, nor the scowls of the soldiers. The Corporal caught Pedro's eye, raised a forefinger to

his temple and made little circles, in full view of San José. He
asked no questions, either, but later in Cartago, talk went the
rounds that the former city council scribe was living like a playful
dolphin gamboling with a pregnant siren among the waves of a
Talamanca beach guarded by a barracuda: Gerónima.

After they left, life resumed its normal course, the hours of
sunlight, the phases of the moon, The Mute at the bursting point,
the baby trying to force its way out through her navel, her ears,
and particularly her eyes, which had become so gentle and
velvety with the tiny creature moving in the depths of their dark
pools. It was the change in that glance, the shock and the fear,
that Pedro saw when "The Flying Dutchman" came, and The
Mute together with Gerónima ran into the house to hide. The
vessel approached, coming in from the outer sea, growing in size
as it neared. It did not stop as San José had. More experienced
and skilled sailors avoided the coral reef and arrived safely and
undamaged as far as the beach itself. Pedro saw them coming
and, though at first he thought it was San José, foiled again by
the stubbornness of the river, he was soon able to recognize some
black, brutish-looking individuals and the blonde head of a
European.

"Torquemada died when the pirate arrived," Pedro said, staring at
his empty goblet.

"What pirate?" asked Agueda, as she went for the wine bottle
herself this time to fill the two glasses and then settle back in her
seat to continue listening, as she puffed contentedly on her cigar.

Pedro considered that the woman was thinking of other
things and asked the question without real interest, so he did not
reply.

"What pirate?" Agueda insisted. Pedro saw her staring at him
curiously through half-closed eyes.

"Oh, yes! The one I called 'The Flying Dutchman.' Actually he
was an Englishman. I named him that because of his strange
story. I had gotten used to seeing distant ships with absolutely no
interest or yearning on my part in their approaching the shore,
for I had no desire to talk to anybody, to have any contact with
the outside world or to go anywhere. By the time those people
arrived, Gerónima had taken off, which she did frequently without

telling me where she was going, I taking it for granted that she had her contacts on the mountain with those ghostly Indians I had never seen. She always returned with bunches of medicinal herbs, gourds, and wooden knives which came in very handy because the machete was now quite worn down. I never asked where she had been and she never gave me any explanation. That was our way of each preserving status and living together without friction. She seemed to accept my relation with The Mute as being outside her scope and approached life on the seacoast to some degree as a challenge since she was from the mountains, the jungle, the rain forest..."

"But what about that pirate?"

"As for the pirate...one day The Mute came to me, her eyes wide with fear, and I saw a dot on the sea coming directly towards us, skillfully avoiding the coral reef. It was not San José. It was a piragua with a crew of eight, all black but one. I gripped what was left of the machete, and waited for the invaders. The two women hid in the house while Babí and Bugalú made for the forest with the idea that the ship had come for them. They had left me all alone to face those fierce-looking people, the European carrying a carbine. My appearance couldn't have looked very reassuring to them, a beard down to my chest, hair like a pelican's nest, skinny, hairy legs, naked as a jay bird except for the remaining sleeve of my shirt doing duty as a loincloth, and balsa-wood sandal-soles tied to my ankles with reeds since nothing was left of my boots but the memory. The men beached the boat, jumped out, and removed a large and apparently heavy chest from it. The European, a blonde braid hanging down his back, approached me, a grim expression on his face. I, with my back to the house could not see that Gerónima had opened the gate to set Torquemada free. Racing happily towards me, thinking it was another game, he leaped onto my shoulders knocking me to the ground to pin me there and raise his head in a roar of victory, only to receive a bullet in his brain. Stunned, I lay there, spitting out sand, when I heard the man's voice speaking in abominable Spanish. 'You owe me your life, Spaniard,' he said.

"I got up to see two blue eyes looking at me out of a red face and Torquemada's body beside me. 'You sonofabitch,' I answered, 'that jaguar was my friend.'

"Torquemada's agate eyes stared up at the sky, blood dribbling from his open jaws.

"The pirate picked up the machete that had fallen a few feet away and examined it with an amused expression. He then pointed at the blacks who had placed the chest in the shadow of the almond tree where The Mute and I had made love in the summer nights. It annoyed me to see them standing there staring at me curiously. He then motioned me to follow him and as we walked towards the tree he explained haltingly that he had heard of me in Matina and wanted to show me something that might be of interest.

"He told me that he had lost everything in an earthquake at Port Royal and that he was now doing business on the sea but that things had gone badly for him in Matina because of the competition. He threw open the chest for me to look. Inside was a variegated tangle of velvets, silks, red woolens, and taffetas which the pirate spread out on the sand for my appreciation. While extolling the beauty of the embroidery, stripes, lace work, and fringes, he offered to trade with me for Indians, cacao, or whatever I had of value. When I told him I had no Indians, slaves, cacao nor anything that could be of interest to him, he looked at me skeptically and said that he knew that I had two Indian women and two black boys and ordered his men to search the house. They found no one, for Gerónima had run off to the mountain with The Mute. This infuriated the Englishman who ordered his men to skin Torquemada and take the hide and ordered me not to move from where I was until his men found the Indians and slaves. He cursed and complained about the devil being after him, that the earthquake left everything he had under water, that business was going against him, that he had no money to pay his men, that he had invested what little he had left in the contents of the chest, that he even owed for the rental of his piragua, and that to top it all, The Flying Dutchman had appeared to him the night before, an experience so horrible that it nearly caused a shipwreck, and he almost drowned. He related all this to me as he put the materials back into the chest without folding them, while I watched two of his men tear off Torquemada's golden skin, leaving his remains for the crabs. The other five disappeared into the forest to track down my people while I tried desperately to think of something I had that might be of value to this marauder. My only wealth consisted of the two Indian woman and two black boys. A short time passed and the pirates did not return. The Englishman kept talking. I offered him a coconut that had fallen at our feet. He opened a hole in it with the battered blade of my machete and drank and then sat down with the carbine across his knees.

"'Last night,' he told me in a hushed tone, 'The Dutchman appeared to me. Haven't you ever seen him flying over the sea?'

"'I never saw anything except birds flying over the sea,' I replied, trying to be pleasant in case his men found my people, and I had to beg for them to be left alone.

"'So, you never saw The Flying Dutchman?' he repeated.

"'The only Dutchmen I know were bankers in Seville, and they were as rooted in the ground as their vaults,' I assured him.

"'The one I'm talking about,' he lowered his voice even further and pausing to look behind him, continued, 'the one I'm talking about appeared to me in the dead of night, five cable's lengths from my piragua, on the waves, all red and green...sails spread...hellish flashing lights...horrible men, skinny as corpses clutching onto the timbers of the bowsprit and the foreyard, staring at us...and he, HE, was on the foredeck...so close that I could perfectly make out his loose leather boots, slashed doublet, and Burgundy-style hat...and he was laughing, showing all his teeth, his lower jaw hanging loose...his skull...and the ship glaring in the night all its lights on and sinister, off-key music blaring, as if there was dancing inside the ship... It was sailing right for us, straight, and—this is what's unbelievable—it was like it was made of fog, it went through us from prow to stern, then rose up into the air and went off towards the moon... Horrible...! Horrible...! Do you know who that was?' The Englishman stared at me, his eyes glaring, the same look I knew well having seen it in Rebullida, in the unknown man with the stone, in Hernández...madmen's eyes.

"'Do you know who that was?' he repeated. 'It was Vanderdecken, the Accursed! who sold his soul to the devil to escape the Cape, where he was caught in a storm! Condemned to sail the seas for all eternity...!'"

"'Man,' I asked, trying to calm him down, 'couldn't it have been a play of mirages in the water, a cloud of glowworms, Saint Elmo's fire?'"

"Infuriated, he looked at me, and shouted, 'Do you think I'm crazy? That I don't know what I'm seeing? I saw it! I saw it!' As he talked he held his index finger up to his eyes and sighted along it. I, thinking that he had been driven out of his mind by the earthquake, thirst, loneliness, bad luck, offered him more coconuts and went along with him and told him that yes, of course, there are ships that fly, that have a crew of corpses, that even kidnap people and bring them back with no memory of anything, that work in cahoots with Satan, sirens, and devils that ride the clouds, tritons that jab Christians with their tridents. In short, I invented all sorts of wild tales so as to stop him from keeping the carbine trained on me. Finally, I saw the black pirates coming out of the forest empty-handed. They had found no one and wanted to know whether to continue searching until the next day or what. I then had the brilliant idea of offering the Englishman an infallible charm, proposing, in order that he should believe me, to exchange it for a new machete. And he accepted."

"An amulet?" asked Agueda sarcastically.

"It was a stone that I had found in a deer's intestines, a bezoar, which I was saving to give to Smiles if I were ever to see him again...," answered Pedro a bit shamefacedly.

"Ah!" said Agueda triumphantly. "That means you were thinking of returning to Cartago, of not remaining there for the rest of your life, as you said."

"Well...yes...maybe. Meaning that I was thinking that such happiness could not last forever."

"Well, I showed the pirate the stone and, on the spur of the moment invented how to use it effectively against the evil eye, phantoms, earthquakes, the black pox, and for favoring sales, good business and calm seas... I told him that the Celts and Druids used those stones to attract energy from the planets and that they were highly prized in ancient Syria. To make a long story short, it didn't take much to provide historical background for my story since the Englishman was of such crass ignorance that he accepted it all very seriously. He gave me a machete with a new blade and left with the stone and Torquemada's skin. I gave the animal a burial worthy of a dear friend."

"The lands here in America are a nest of maniacs," Agueda commented to fill the pause that followed Pedro's last rueful remark. "How are our descendants going to recover the wits lost in this enormous insane asylum?"

"Lunacy is worldwide," Pedro answered, suspecting that both he and Agueda could be counted among its inmates.

"The plain truth... We didn't know who was king. Spain was divided and the British seized the opportunity to grab off Gibraltar...and here...here, meanwhile, Serrano is arrested and they send us an interim Governor, the same person who was the force behind the missions... But you were telling me that The Mute was going to give birth... Wait, I'll be right back." And she went out the door to the patio. Pedro could hear the splashing as Agueda urinated. She did not return immediately and her footsteps could be heard going off to another part of the house.

The Mute gave birth one night. Gerónima had built a little hut near the manatee's stream in which the water murmured reproachfully against the fate that sent it on its way to be swallowed in the salty sea. Gerónima walked there slowly, The Mute following, her heavy belly a retort in which sun and moon boiled, an incubator containing the raw materials provided by Mother Nature, elements fed in the warmth of the crucible for nine months—the gentleness of patient heat—that brings about the birth of the red baby, the white baby, the chick, the Opus never, ever surpassed...

The moon came out, round and punctual, above the sea. Pedro who knew nothing of those delicate situations, appointed Gerónima the midwife, humbly acceding to her every request, and what she requested was that he make himself scarce and go for a walk on the beach and wait for it all to be over. He went to converse with the waves, and they told him of a mysterious process in which The Mute's womb would open to allow passage of a being destined to seek the reason for life in the justification of its existence. "The Mute is giving birth to a child condemned to die," the waves told him. And Pedro sought philosophical motives for exempting himself from such an infamous responsibility.

A rustling of silk could be heard and Agueda entered with a shawl over her shoulders for the night had turned chilly.

"The Mute gave birth to a little girl, Catarina," said Pedro laconically.

"Catarina is a charming child," said Agueda emphatically.

"I was disappointed when I saw her. With her prominent nose, she was something that looked more like a tadpole. That's how I knew it was my daughter. She couldn't have inherited such a nose from anybody else."

"What an ingrate! It's true that Catarina has a big nose, but it lends her distinction."

"To tell you the truth, I didn't see her until she was a month old, which was when Gerónima allowed me to. All that month, she had me running around after the strangest things... She asked me to bring her the eye and the claw of a parrot so that the child would be intelligent; a small hawk so that she should travel a lot; the claw of an anteater so that she would be firm in her convictions; a monkey to be agile... I buried the umbilical cord under the almond tree so that the child would return to where she came from. Maybe it was because Gerónima didn't ask me for anything that had to do with beauty that poor little Catarina is so plain."

"I don't know what you consider beauty in a woman..."

There was a suspicious note and one of resentment in Agueda's tone. Pedro, thinking of her rabbit teeth and how they had chilled his former passion for her, avoided the subject.

Catarina, a strange and delicate little creature, spent her first year of life riding on her mother's hip or back. The Mute, making no distinction between her individuality and the child's, continued climbing to heights with the child clutching on to her hair. Had Pedro not been so carried away in conjuring up the image of the mother and child in the palm fronds, he would have noticed the gleam in Agueda's eyes.

"After she gave birth, The Mute recovered all her former agility even though she was nursing the infant. Then, she began to indulge another whim, of going out on a cliff that projected over the sea, to dance, teetering at the very edge of the rock with the child on her back."

"What was she like?"

"The little girl?"

"No, the mother." Agueda's eyes were on the candle flames and she seemed to be groping for something vague and fleeting that might escape in an instant if she relaxed her concentration.

Pedro was slow in answering. He was taken by surprise even though he had asked himself the same question countless times. To speak of The Mute, it was indispensable to be a poet. The Mute was indescribable, even in another's verses.

"You want to know what she was like? I don't know... It was difficult to put one's finger on it. She was not retarded as I thought when I first knew her... Rather, at times she seemed a treasure house of wisdom. She had a quality of seeming to possess the secret of things, as though she were always seeing through to the bottom of everything. And she had...that smile...that sweetness...that way of being that made one feel...as though...as though..."

"As though what?" Agueda insisted eagerly, petulantly.

"As though the world...life...everything had order, that all things were the same, you, me, the trees, the sea... One single, great unity... At the same time, it seemed to me that the best image, the best example that could explain her, if any explanation for her were possible, was the silent depths of the ocean, that unknown space that sailors dread because they have not seen it... Beings that no human eye has ever seen, and that no consciousness, no intelligence can determine... Creatures that refused to come to the surface at the onset of genesis and are there, way down, hidden, rebels against the command of light, of transparency, of unblemished nature, of the comprehensible, in the depths, absorbed into the aqueous shadows, not emerging, perhaps because they are too weak, perhaps too vulnerable to the assault of reason... Fearful because we do not know them. Fearful...dreaded by sailors because with respect to them the compass, the mathematics of sailing vessels, are useless....Because they can emerge suddenly and nobody is prepared to deal with them, to conjure up nature from out of the depths, from the cavities and strangeness, from other eons, dark, inaccessible, unpredictable..."

"The Mute was a human being. An Indian, but a human being. She was a woman. I think you are exaggerating."

"She was"—Pedro paid no attention to Agueda's comment—"she was...chaos, I now think."

But Pedro had said "chaos" in the hermetic sense of the alchemists: "the chaos from which all the wonders of nature arise." He made no reply and Agueda remained looking at him askance while he lost himself in reproachfulness towards The Mute. He could never forgive her lack of signals. The mutes Pedro had known before her were extremely vociferous with their guttural noises and restless hands. But this one, his Mute, kept her hands still and hadn't the slightest intention of breaking silence with them. And she was always remote when he looked at her with desire, and she received his caresses detached from the warmth of the bodies, from their beauty, from the symmetrical blending of their members. Detached also from their irresistible seductive power. In despair because she rejected any attempt to define her in a way that would set her within the locus of familiar attributes. Pedro had tried to call her darling, sweetheart, but it was as if she hadn't heard, and it was the same when he called her pussycat, little monkey, little mouse, squirrel. She responded only to the name "Mute." And as useless as her voice was, so keen was her hearing. She always sensed the coming of the rain over the sea long before anyone else and would run to take shelter in the house.

And there was a host of other things about her that Pedro didn't want to tell Agueda because they belonged to a realm of more intimate sentiments. He said nothing, for example, of The Mute's second pregnancy, the most closely kept secret of all.

Pedro figured the expected date by measuring the diameter of her navel but he was wrong for she gave birth a month earlier. She was weaving a wicker basket as he sat, lazily toying with her hair, arranging it in a bun on the nape of her neck, when she suddenly doubled over and a stream of warm water ran out of her upon the sand. Gerónima came running at her cry, saw that her sister was going to give birth before time, and went to prepare her midwife's accouterments. Catarina looked on, tugging on her Medusa hair, her little black eyes dancing with excitement, watching Gerónima help The Mute who walked clutching at her abdomen as though to hold the infant back from coming into the world before its time. Pedro went off to pace the beach. Catarina, her sidewise glance so much like her mother's, followed after until Bugalú picked her up in his arms. Later they went into the hut along with Babí, for night was now falling.

The Mute had a predilection for giving birth at night—said Pedro to himself—as he sought the moon, aware that it was at its minimum phase. On the darkened shore, the crustaceans wandered about like souls in purgatory, uneasy at the silence, for they had grown accustomed to human voices. The misty, dewy evaporation—terrestrial liquid and dampness, humus, and vegetal exudations—had remained in suspension in the air since there were no ocean breezes. Not even the tiniest wave broke the surface, the sea heavy and gravid in expectation of winds that clear the evil humors of organic beings. Pedro walked, wondering whether San José were still traveling from Portobello to Matina, if the English pirate had met up again with the Flying Dutchman, if nobody would ever land on his beach again. He climbed up to the cliff on the brink of which The Mute would teeter, and there he remained, enveloped in the darkness of his scattered thoughts, until he heard the cry.

It was a shout without words that seemed to rise from the depths of the earth. It rose, cutting through the fog like a knife edge, interminable, guttural shrieking of an animal in agony, a howling appeal to a departing life. Pedro leaped from the rock to land on the sand and run along the edge of the sea, stepping upon small creatures on his way, and nearly colliding with Catarina and the two boys who had come out of the hut, terror-stricken. Without stopping, he crashed into the lying-in hut to see Gerónima in the light of a pine-knot torch, a wooden knife in her hand, leaning like a witch over her sister's body flat on its back, legs drawn up. Pedro leaned over The Mute's chest. Her heart was no longer beating. Gerónima was saying something but he was in no condition to hear her. His eyes wandering wildly, he could see a fluttering in her abdomen and then he lost his senses. Pedro's hands were rigid as he pressed the beloved head between them, the fingers like two great claws. He was unable to see Gerónima cut apart the flesh of the dead woman, and in a spasm to expel a sob caught in his throat like a shark bone, he did not hear the cry of the newborn so violently wrenched into the world. In his desire to stem with his own body's warmth the waning warmth of her body, he did not feel Gerónima's hand resting on his shoulder to call his attention to the infant. Time disappeared and pain marked the hours, a stopwatch that never ceased, brief stabs of consciousness, time an eternity.

Pedro disappeared from this world to float in a limbo without tears until the sun came out again and the morning found him stupefied and unable to understand what had been totally absent from his projects and was beyond any amending. Something irreparable had taken place, something that had no remedy and no treatment. No trick, no skill, no effort, no sacrifice was of any use. Dazed, unable to come up with an explanation behind which to barricade himself against the black thing that had crashed over him, he watched numbly the narrow column of ants struggling to cross a puddle of blood to reach the great open wound; he looked without seeing at the green, voracious flies; listened without hearing to the roar of the fierce, noxious beast that had scented a tasty morsel. He had eyes and ears only for the waves, and tamely let himself be led by the two slave boys to the sea, where they submerged him in their lulling to return him to his senses, and then they stretched him out in his hammock after giving him a bitter, benevolent liquid to drink that put him to sleep.

While he was consoled in the unconsciousness of slumber, Gerónima wrapped her sister in a bark sheet. When Pedro awoke, she prevented him from seeing the body and told him that she would take it to the top of the mountain where she would leave it to rot and, after a certain time, recover the bones, clean and burnish them, put them in a bag that she intended to hang from the roof of the hut. Pedro paid no attention to her and dug out a hollow with his own hands at the base of the almond tree, and between its roots settled the peach and copper skin, the breasts filled with useless milk, the gentle curve of the rump, the smooth, damp, elastic grotto in which he had planted the fruit that caused her death. The Mute had left him in ultimate silence. Never would he really know who she was nor why he had loved her so deeply. The enigma lay buried beneath a heap of coral, all hope gone of ever resolving the mystery of her essence.

Pedro had loved the unknown and for that reason would go on remembering her till his own death, the desire unsatisfied of hearing her voice, without ever knowing the thing she wanted to tell him, without a clue, a sign, a lead to follow in order to reach her. All was brutally interrupted; from then on, he would have to search for her in Catarina's eyes, in the marine abysses, in the shadows of the forest, in all the places where the keys had been lost to the subterranean, hidden nature of the woman that had caused him to drop anchor so far from the books and taverns of Seville.

Gerónima had shown him the baby, a lump of reddish flesh lying on a banana leaf. He turned his head away.

"He's hungry," she said.

"But you have no milk. Let him die."

"No animal lets its young starve to death."

"Then, take him away, far away. I don't want to see him!"

Gerónima plunged into the forest with her leaf bundle of flesh making for the mountain, disappearing, the faint sound of the infant's wails, fading. Pedro's eyes were dry, his heart empty. When Gerónima returned days later, he asked no questions, she offered no explanations. Pedro had enveloped himself in the self-centeredness of his sorrow, crouched like a mummy next to the coral grave, looking out toward the unfeeling ocean that responded to no questions nor asked any, the sea broad and remote with its unplumbed depths, its abysses of blind fish.

He stopped eating. Blue circles framed the dry lids of his staring eyes, as he slid, unresisting into a pit of depression. He neglected his daily tasks and now paid no attention to Catarina. If he did look at her it was only to search, fruitlessly, for her mother's features, seeing only himself in the skinny legs, and curly head. He would regard her and say, "Poor little thing, how ugly you are!" Rejected, she would seek Gerónima's lap or go walking with the slave boys.

Pedro remained alone, left to his fate and his own devices. They would seek him out at mealtime, forcing bits of fish into *him, the bones carefully removed, giving him coconut milk to drink, making him swallow, so that he should not die. Deafened and self-blinded, he turned inward, cut off communication with the others and with the world, to submerge himself in the mystery of The Mute's disappearance, seeking her at the top of the palm trees, at the cliff edge where he killed the days beneath the sun and rain, splashed by the waves and befouled by the pelicans.*

He paid no attention one stormy night when the tide rose to the point where it undermined the posts supporting the house, which collapsed, the roof timbers not taking the trouble to fall in upon him. They pulled him out unscathed but mortally wounded in spirit.

Pedro had turned into a blurred copy of himself and life went on without him. Indifferent to everything, he crawled within his misanthropy, permitting depression to do the work of sapping his spirit. There was no telling how long he might have survived such melancholia if a piece of news had not suddenly shaken him to the core and back to life. One day, when the two black slaves returned from one of their frequent forays into the mountain, they informed him that they had seen a man who had hair the color of corn silk and green eyes who was walking about naked, talking about a kindly God who loved all people. His garment was made into a sack in which he kept the herbs that he picked on his way, without ever eating any, his feet covered with sores. The boys followed him about for an entire day watching him from a distance.

Agueda, unaware of the flights of Pedro's thoughts, asked, "What did The Mute die of?"

"She died in giving birth to her second child," replied Pedro laconically and then lied. "The baby was born dead. It was a short time afterward, maybe months, that I heard Juan de las Alas was going about preaching at the settlements in Talamanca. It was Bugalú and Babí who told me about seeing a man with hair the color of honey and Gerónima identified him as the young friar who was looking for goldfish in her sister's eyes, the same one whom I didn't let come along when he met up with us that early morning after we left Cartago... Juan's presence had the effect of shaking me out of my depression after the death of The Mute. I realized then how time had passed, how Catarina had grown, that the two boys I had found as children hiding in the hollow of a *chilamate* tree would soon be men... Juan brought back to mind that childish Indian girl that the friars of Cartago had disguised under a Franciscan cassock and suddenly I felt all the weight of my grief over her loss pressing down upon my shoulders..."

"How old was The Mute when she died?" Agueda asked.

"I don't know exactly...sixteen, eighteen..."

"Then, when you first knew her..."

"Twelve...eleven...thirteen...something like that."

"Well, after all," observed Agueda to cover up her shocked expression, "Indian girls mature very young..." And she stared at the end of her cigar.

"When the blacks told me about Juan de las Alas, and Gerónima backed them up, my surprise and joy was so great that I never thought at the moment that Gerónima was hiding information. I had ears only for what the boys were telling me about Juan... Wonderful things. They said that when he crossed the river, the crocodiles held their tails in their jaws to make a bridge for him and the snakes made a rope of themselves to help him down the ravines... My urge to see Juan de las Alas gripped me as powerfully as my depression had. Then, I began to question Babí, Bugalú, and Gerónima. That was how I learned that they had kept in contact with the Indians of the mountain who were very uneasy about a detachment of soldiers that had arrived to escort Rebullida... What I never imagined, what never remotely crossed my mind, was the uprising the Indians were planning under everybody's noses. It never occurred to me because as far as I was concerned the Indian population of Talamanca at the time consisted of The Mute and Gerónima. I had never even seen them come to the sea to get salt, which I later found out they did."

"How is such blindness possible?" Agueda couldn't believe it.

"Remember, I was living in isolation..."

"And with eyes only for The Mute..."

Pa-brú Presbere is entrusted with a mission by the Kapá

The sun would soon be coming up to lick the golden palm of the Recul houses.

Seated on a river stone, the Kapá spoke, his eyes clouded with early morning mist. He had been up all night with the divining stones and was now questioning them beside the flowing water. His body was very still, hands upon his knees, heels tucked under his lean backside. The shadow of the Golden Eagle upon his old breast was barely a tone lighter than the dark-bronze color of his skin.

"The sun is coming out," he said, "and the women will soon be arriving to bathe their children, and all sleeping things will be awakening. The time has come for us to wake up, too.

"You were my mother's favorite grandchild, my sister's most beloved son, whom I have watched over like a father, you were the one designated to wear my face..."

He paused to hear what the fish under the water were saying and seemed to understand something for he continued with determination: "The order of things has been broken. So that equilibrium may be restored, you must make the journey to Viceita. Viceita has fought too much, and love for their lances and pikes is stronger than their love for me; they no longer wish to call me Father... I shall speak with your mouth and tell the Chief Warrior that this war is a war between gods which must first be fought under my command. When the first part is fulfilled and the men of the cross are dead, the other war will then come, of soldier against soldier, and that will be the moment for Viceita to take up arms, not before."

At the Kapá's last word, the laughter of the women was heard and the river filled with naked bodies and sunlight.

Days later, Presbere set out on his journey to Viceita. Accustomed to the lightness of his loincloth, he felt the weight of the Golden Eagle upon his breast. He descended through the gorge of annato trees, passed by the place at which the hawk bathes, and entered the area where the trees abound whose sap turns the skin black. For three days and three nights he fasted there, then climbed mountains, scaled cliffs, and reached the heights of Viceita, the nation of warriors, where the sacred city of Surayom was, the place where Sibú sowed the first grains of corn, two by two, from which the Indians sprang.

The Lari River's winter current detained him. He sat on the bank, waiting, so they might see him and that he was on his way. He let the rain paste his hair to the nape of his neck, to his shoulders. He waited all that day, all that day and that night. The next morning before daybreak, when it was certain that the weather was clearing, he entered the water and swam without haste. On reaching the other side of the river his heart was quiet, his spirit serene.

He did not proceed along the open path upon the mountain; he waited for them to come for him.

"You wear the Golden Eagle..." said the Warrior when he welcomed him. "Is the Kapá dead?"

"I wear the Eagle because I come with Kapá's face over mine, and he is telling you that there will be war."

The Warrior moved his lips without looking at Presbere, nor at his wives squatting beside the fire in the center of the house. The Warrior wore bamboo tubes through his ear lobes and a red bone in his lower lip.

(He has a forked tongue, thought Presbere.)

"War...against whom?"

"Against the men with hairy faces like monkeys."

"Why? They have come here, are peaceful people. See this..." He showed him an illustration of the Crucifixion. "They say that this is a more powerful god than Lord Sibú-Surá."

"That is what they say...it is for this reason that the Kapá commands that we the people of the Coén River be the first to make this war: god against god. Afterwards, when the first part is fulfilled, Viceita's men will take up their lances, their shields, and their arrows, against the soldiers that will come."

"The foreigners have powerful arms," the Chief Warrior objected. "How will the people of the Coén River fight? The foreigners drove the Teribes out of our lands with those arms. We have only thanks for them."

"They will also drive Viceita out of your land... Now, before it is too late, listen to the Kapá's plan."

Presberé spoke at length, had much to say, and the Warrior listened in silence, dipping fingers into the boiled yucca on the fire.

"The Spaniards," said Presbere, "are shrewder than the Teribes. First, they send those men who wear a rope at the waist, who confuse us with gods and words. After those men the color of ticks, come the mouths of fire. Now, listen: I will go down to Urinama for the friars to pour water over my head..."

"Do you not fear their power? Do you think you are stronger than their god?"

"I am the envoy of Sibú-Surá. I spoke with the stones and wear the face of the Kapá. That water can do me no harm... The stones were consulted, and they have said that this part of the battle will be won. When the Spaniards are dead, when the survivors have fled, many soldiers will come from over there, from afar, to take revenge. War will then be great! Then, Viceita can draw their bowstrings so that no foreigners shall come out alive from Our Land."

The Chief Warrior said nothing. He was thinking. His cheeks, painted red, were immobile as the ocelot about to spring. He squinted his eyes: "You are no warrior... Wars are the responsibility of Viceita."

One of the women stirred the fire and a column of smoke made a cloud between the two men.

"Nevertheless," the Warrior said to Presbere, "I cannot disobey the Kapá. I will do as he has said."

Such was the meeting with the Chief Warrior of Viceita. Now, it was necessary to go and confer with Comezala, the ally. The Kapá's command was a box of stones. "How many rivers, how many ravines, how many disagreements will have to be negotiated before beginning? It will be necessary to go to Sichaque, Namatz,

Cachaveri, Ujambor. It will be necessary to return to Suinse, to his house, to elect his chiefs. And then, it will be necessary to go to the friar's hermitage to be baptized..."

This was the grave responsibility of the nephew of the Great Father, the possessor of the wisdom of the ancients, the only one who could talk to the Keeper of the Seed, to the Lord of the Underworld, where the brave and the good go over a bridge of ropes woven by the singers between Our Land and the setting sun.

It will be necessary to speak with Comezala and send couriers everywhere. It will be necessary to ascertain many things, such as: the real names of San Miguel, San Agustín, Concepción, Santo Domingo, Santa Cruz... In Viceita there was a pine cross and under it a woman painted on a piece of wood holding a little girl on her lap. The Warrior had said that the woman's name was Saint Anne and the little girl is the mother of all the gods.

"And so, the Kapá has assigned you a mission," said Comezala, looking at him with due respect.

Presbere accepted the whipped chocolate Comezala offered him, drank, and explained: "Usekar's nephew, my peer, Our Land is in danger. I come to tell you what you already know: your people, my people, the chiefs, all the clans, the old people, the little children, all the people will die far away from the Grave Digger, the Singer, the Chocolate Maker, and there will be no drums to accompany us on the final journey."

Comezala agreed: "Aoyaque died far from Aoyaque... Now, Aoyaque is called San Bartolomé, that one with blue eyes painted on a piece of wood that the friars have... What happened to the Aoyaques? They took them by deceit, by force. They disappeared like the peoples who had toads of gold, frogs of gold... They broke their vessels, stole their jade, disturbed their dead... Now the Aoyaques are dying of the cold because they had to deliver over their cotton to the Christians, deliver over their honey and their corn, and now they have no ink for their pens nor cord for their hammocks."

"You know them well!" exclaimed Presberé, surprised.

"I have them close at hand. In San Bartolomé Urinama they baptize them with the point of a sword, and with firearms, in the place they call San José Cabécar."

"Comezala," Presberé's heart was alight, "we are still many, we can still defend those that remain. Let us join forces, let us call the clan of the Valley of the Deer, of the Owners of the Beehives, of the Owners of the Crane, of the Gourd Tree, of the House of Fleas, of the Quetzal Bird, of the Moon, of the Clay Pitcher, of the Fireflies, of the Majagua Tree, of the Brook of Surá, of the Brook of Gold, of the Brook of Green Water...we will call them all together..."

They were now silent and thinking, thinking alike...

"What I think," Comezala said, "is that when the crosses are toppled, soldiers will come from the valley they call Cartago to take revenge. They will come with horses, with firearms. Some from Chirripó, others from Boruca."

"How do you know that?" asked Presberé.

"Because the cow-meat eaters always make a cross. But they will be given help. More arms, more horses, more crosses will arrive by sea. That king whom they say is very powerful will send them."

Presbere smiled; now he was the one who knew better. "Listen. Two kings are fighting on the other side of the sea, in the nation they call Spain, that we so fear. Those two kings need their arms to fight the war between them and to defend themselves against their enemies, the English. The English are the ones who come and steal people and cacao, who come by sea in ships."

"How do you know?" asked Comezala.

"I have spies," Presbere said, smiling, showing his even, white teeth, and the two laughed like elated children.

Agueda listens closely to Pedro's story and the description of his meeting with Juan de las Alas

The information that Juan was going about preaching in Talamanca shocked Pedro out of his stupor and there was no way, no effort, no device, that could halt the torrent of tears that poured from his eyes or hold back the sobs that burst out, wrenched from the dark debris of grief that had lain pent up at the center of his breast. And so, he threw off his heavy burden, freeing himself completely from the horror of the loneliness into which The Mute's absence had plunged him, and was astonished at finding that he had survived the hopeless loss. Then, gathering Catarina in his arms, he spoke his first words as a resuscitated victim: "On your feet, Pedro, and see how the world turns. Tomorrow, I'm off to visit Juan de las Alas. You two boys will come with me and Gerónima will stay to take care of Catarina."

Gerónima took a dim view of Pedro's proposal and warned him that she knew the way better than the slaves and suggested that she accompany him and they stay with Catarina. She explained that Juan de las Alas was not in Urinama but with another friar in a place the Spaniards call San José de Cabécar.

Pedro then realized that while he was lost in limbo, Gerónima had remained very much apprised of happenings beyond, far beyond the sandy borders of their world. He did not leave the following day but waited until the start of the dry season for the climb way up to the Cabécar mission was very steep and difficult. He finally set out with Catarina riding on his shoulders, and Gerónima with the machete that the Flying Dutchman had traded for the bezoar stone Pedro was saving for the shoemaker. Babí and Bugalú stayed behind guarding the only metal they possessed, the old iron cooking ladle from the monastery, so rusted by the sea air that it spent more of its time greased with animal fat and hanging from a roof beam than carrying out the duties for which it was intended.

Pedro returned after all those years to plunge once again into the wild jungle exuberance. Breathing the bracing salt air, invigorated by a healthful diet, he felt buoyant, thoroughly recovered from his melancholy. The Mute had become a cleanly healed scar, accepted as dear and ineffaceable for the rest of his life. There was so much to talk over with Juan. It was hard for him to think of him as a man now, so many years after his boyish infatuation with The Mute. Certainly, he would not have forgotten her but he wondered in what way he would have remembered those feelings. He looked forward to their grieving together over her premature death.

Led by Gerónima's sure, steady pace they covered the terrain over mountains and through canyons and some stretches of open trails, Pedro preparing himself along the way for the meeting with Juan. He remembered nostalgically the apple-cheeked lad, constantly getting into trouble, climbing forbidden trees, being scolded by the friars. It would be very like him to emulate Saint Francis and preach in the nude. How to explain to him about The Mute? Juan would understand, he was sure. He would invite him to come down to the coast to visit the coral grave. The Mute's death was an agony that had to be borne and Gerónima did what had to be done. It was for the best that she had taken the child to where the full breast of an anonymous Indian woman would give him nourishment. It was for the best. The remains of The Mute were a skull and a bundle of bones whitening between the roots of the trees; she was transmuted into fertilizer, flowers, and fruits, and her decomposed flesh fed new lives, tender leaves... Her blood became sap. And he retained the material remembrance in the little child he carried upon his shoulders. Catarina's future was now to be his responsibility. Pedro considered growing cacao for dealing with the pirates, and building a boat in which to transport it to Matina for that would be a way of earning money enough to lead a more civilized life. Catarina should not have to spend the rest of her life on a lonely beach with a pair of spotted blacks and a closemouthed Indian woman. There were no proper schools, convent or otherwise. Thinking of the future, Pedro wondered whether Catarina, so lacking in either charm or a dowry would ever manage to attract a halfway passable husband.

They came to the bank of an immense, wide river and Gerónima, indicating it, told him that it was the great Sixaola River whose mouth would not permit friar José de San José to enter.

"How do you know it wouldn't let him enter?" asked Pedro, who thought San José had been at the missions for a long time.

Gerónima shrugged and went toward the river bank looking for something. Finally she found what seemed to be a boat that was apparently left there for the use of travelers. It was a long narrow canoe hollowed out of a tree trunk. Skillfully wielding the paddle, she maneuvered the little craft into the rapid current and across to the other side without mishap. Pedro and she pulled the prow of the boat securely onto dry land. Pedro looked about, uneasy at being in this strange place, a score of questions on the tip of his tongue which he refrained from asking for he knew he would get no reply and so, as always in the past, he consigned his fate to his companion's ever capable hands. Peering through the dense foliage into which they plunged, Gerónima in the lead, he was able to distinguish a single thatched roof but could neither see or hear any sign of inhabitants.

As Pedro trudged along, Catarina upon his shoulders seemed so inevitable a weight that his thoughts were constantly occupied with her. Plans and projects concerning her future raced through his mind; he knew they would mean returning to the life he had left behind him, before it was too late to put them in practice.

The temperature kept dropping as they climbed. When Gerónima finally announced that they had arrived, Pedro's lips were blue and he began to feel the first of the sharp rheumatic stabs that were soon to become a torture. Catarina's teeth were chattering, and she whimpered with the cold. When, all at once, the cross of the hermitage came into view, Pedro's spirits rose, and he felt prepared to be at one with the community of Spaniards.

The Cabécar mission had several buildings and a central street hacked out of the jungle by machete. Pedro was not long in discovering that authority there was invested in the mouth of the harquebus and the edge of the sword. He came upon the first member of the escort, a mulatto on guard, sitting with a lance across his knees, his two hands busy searching his clothes for lice. He stood up, surprised and nervous, at the sound of Pedro's calling out, "Guard, hoy!" to identify himself before the guard should become confused. Having shouted that, he felt thoroughly foolish for if naked, hairy Pedro was a deplorable sight, the stinking, tattered mulatto went him one better with his dark skin tinted green by the light off the mountains. The man fell back a few steps, distrustful when Pedro identified himself as a Spaniard who lived at the seaside. Gradually, the guard, regaining his aplomb, lowered his lance, and loosened his tongue to say that he remembered him as the scribe at the city hall whom he had seen around The Mother of Visitors place, and asked if all the surprising rumors about the strange Spaniard who lived on the beach were true.

He explained that he was a mulatto from Darktown and a sadder and wiser man for he had been offered a golden future and eight silver pesos to sign up, of which he had gotten nothing so far from the adventure his poverty had driven him to undertake but tribulations, misery, constant panic, and abominable food. As he spoke, he kept eyeing Pedro from head to toe as though expecting to witness a sudden transformation, such as crab claws growing out around his waist or his disappearance into thin air, while Pedro, who had no inkling of the lengths to which popular fantasy had gone in embroidering a myth for the credulous around his simple, hermit-like life, asked for Rebullida, Juan de las Alas, the escort, San José and all the other people with whom he had lost contact since he had removed himself from the society of man. He learned from the mulatto that San José had never reached Talamanca (which was all he knew about him). However, he also informed him that Rebullida was still in Urinama, wearing ornaments around his neck and anxiously awaiting the relief contingent but that no soldier wanted to leave Cartago for Talamanca. "Gutless Spaniards," said the mulatto, spitting on the ground, "who left their balls with the Cartago whores, so they send nothing but coloreds out this way."

Once he started talking, the guard took it upon himself to give Pedro a detailed report on how Rebullida launched an all-out conversion and pacification campaign which was so successful that peace was made between the Teribe and Viceita Indians through the supernatural arbitration of Saint Anne, whose hermitage he had erected in Viceita. "Every hermitage with its saint and rosettes, as is proper," said the mulatto who made no bones about his admiration for Rebullida. "Friar Pablo keeps the devil on the hop, even though the evil ways of the Conquest officer makes it difficult for him... "The Conquest officer," the mulatto dropped his voice here, "gets drunk on corn liquor, swears and blasphemes all over the place, and keeps molesting the Indian women. And, all the while, Father Rebullida, sick from going about barefoot in the mud and puddles of foul water, is breaking up heathen rites and undoing hellish conspiracies, his nerves on edge on account of that pig of an officer..." He went on and on about the man until Pedro interrupted to inquire about Juan de las Alas. Annoyed at having his complaint cut off, with an ill-humored gesture in the direction of the hermitage, he muttered that a mass for the dead was being held and then resumed his litany even as Pedro was walking away, complaining that it was of no concern to anybody that he, the guard, had to remain for four days in the heat and rain at his post where he could be run through by a heathen Indian at any moment "which it seems is what that sonofabitch Conquest officer is looking for."

Pedro walked up the lonely roadway towards the church. A little tower perched on the roof of the Lord's house like a dovecote housed a bell that was made to ring by the wind—winds from on high, a galleon bell with a melancholy, shipwreck tone—and, below, at the door, a barefooted, ragged congregation with an air of pirates about them shared the space with pious pigs and disorganized hens pecking at lumps of manure. When Pedro came into sight there were some shouts of joyous welcome which were quickly stifled when it was realized that the half-naked man with a child astride his shoulders, followed by an Indian woman, could not be the long-awaited relief contingent. A hesitant, curious silence ensued, and when Pedro introduced himself in a low voice to avoid disturbing the mass for the dead being conducted inside, one of the men who was holding up his trousers with one hand, for lack of anything else, told him, "That makes five dead, now," and invited him to enter, but Pedro would not. He set Catarina down and handed her over to Gerónima. He was anxious to know what was happening, why people were dying, afraid that there was some epidemic there that might endanger his daughter. "No," another man explained, "there's no epidemic. One died eaten by a crocodile, another from snake bite, another from a worm-infested leg, a fourth from a pus-filled bubo, and now, this one from relapsing fever." Another chimed in, "We all have the fevers. Nobody knows how they come and the friars forbid us getting treated with herbs because they say the devil pisses on them."

Pedro entered alone, making his way through the miasma of the soldiers. Indians knelt inside. A friar in a chasuble, or more exactly, an evocation thereof, officiating at a rickety, makeshift altar, his back to the congregation, turned around. Juan de las Alas's hair was a long, dirty, tangled mane, plastered to his temples with the sweat of months, his eyes a green flame, his expression fevered, skirting the edge of delirium, and his loose lips hanging sadly, half-hidden by an untidy beard.

Pedro did not recognize him.

Ad Deum qui laetificat juventutem meam.

And Pedro said to himself that God had sacrificed Juan's youth to obtain a bitter, prematurely aged man.

An infant in arms began to cry. A man, nerves unstrung at the noise, seized the Indian woman's arm, forcing her to her feet.

"It's because of these miscarriages that we have to be here," he yelled hysterically beginning to push the woman out so that she fell on her side without losing hold of the infant.

Interrupting his stream of Latin, Juan de las Alas called out, "Enough of that, Solana! She has nothing to do with it!"

Somebody helped the woman up as the man named Solana made an obscene gesture toward the altar with his fist as he shouted, "Fuck you, fuck the Indians, and fuck the Governor! They're going to bury us all here just like Quiróz and Mendoza and Chavarría!" And the man passed by Pedro on the way out, his face contorted with fury.

"Go to hell, Durán!" yelled another Spaniard, and when it quieted down, Juan went on with the mass: *"Deus, cui proprium est misereri semper et parcere, te supplices exoramus pro anima famuli tui..."*

A man spit on the dirt floor next to Pedro, who looked at the yellow gob streaked with blood beside his feet and moved fearfully away. The mass for the dead continued and Pedro, listening to the muffled voice, translated from the Latin to himself: terrible day, day of wrath that turns the world to ashes...we all shall tremble...death and nature are aghast... Day of grief, terrible day, *lachrymosa dies illa qua resurget ex favilla, judicandus, homo reuse,* and Pedro looked at Juan, a wounded little bird, a prisoner in his tattered chasuble, head bowed toward the ground upon which he knelt; earth tamped down by the feet swollen with fungus of the escort stationed there to protect him against the rage of the Indians.

Shame, suffering, and dusk were in Juan's eyes when, at the end of the sacrifice, he turned to the people whose eyes were fixed upon him and he closed with: "*Ite, Missa est.*"

"*Deo gratias,*" responded a few as they moved forward to the dead man stretched out upon some boards, covered with a rag. Juan's restless glance lit momentarily on Pedro but he gave no indication that he had recognized him.

"How did old Juan react when he realized who you were?" said Agueda.

"I would even say he was shocked. He never expected that I would ever be visiting him or imagined that I would have any interest in doing so. It is through him that I got to know all the strange stories that were circulating among the Spaniards who were saying that I had been bewitched by an Indian sorceress who had the power of transforming men into sucklings, at the same time that I was sinking ships on the high seas; that I had been seen closely guarded by two devils who had the peculiar ability of changing the color of their skin; and that I wasn't able to escape the witchcraft because at the slightest sign of my trying to, another small devil whose head is a nest of vipers follows me everywhere, tangling me up with his strange locks tighter than the chains on a warship's anchor... I was blamed for shipwrecks and storms... We talked of the time he spent in Guatemala studying theology and conversed about many things before either of us mentioned The Mute. I don't know who was the first. I didn't want to look at him because it seemed to me that he was blushing or perhaps it was just an idea of mine. I told him everything, absolutely everything. All that I had never been able to tell anybody. He listened to me without a word, stroking Catarina's head with deep affection, very tenderly as I went on talking and talking...I don't believe I ever talked that much before in my life.

"You've talked quite a bit right here, too," commented Agueda.

"True," answered Pedro, thinking that it was not the same thing because he had told Juan everything, holding back nothing, while telling only a part to Agueda and not revealing much. That was because among the things he told Juan was the story of the second child and in this way it was a sort of confession and enabled him to unburden himself by sharing with another the uncertainty of not knowing what had happened to it.

"Why don't you ask Gerónima?" Juan had said to him.

Pedro couldn't explain to him that he wasn't able to ask her because he would have broken an agreement. Pedro wanted the child to die and Gerónima had taken over its life and the child no longer belonged to Pedro. That's how it stood and there was nothing to be done about it.

Juan remained silent and pensive for a time after Pedro ended his long and painful story with a description of The Mute's burial beneath the corals, dead as she. He then launched into an account of the status of the mission, the problems caused by the vileness and brutality of the soldiers, and the tolerance of them by his colleague at the mission, Father Andrade, who was away at the moment visiting Rebullida in Urinama. Rebullida was chronically ill and no longer ranged Talamanca as he used to in pursuit of lost souls. He also told Pedro that Father Lorenzo had sent him to Guatemala and that Father Zamora was now in Chirripó.

"I've heard tell that you talk to the animals," Pedro said teasingly.

"My brothers are to blame for such rumors," said Juan. "They think that it will be easier for them to make converts if I become known as a saint. They say that it was my God-given gift for attracting the souls of the heathens that prompted a formerly very rebellious chief by the name of Presbere to accept subjection and voluntary servitude and baptism by Friar Pablo. The truth is very different, though... I had nothing to do with that chief and the Indians run away from me. Do you know what they call me?

When they see me coming, they take to their heels, crying out, "We don't want priests the color of ticks!' That's what they say, and they shut their doors or throw stones at me... That's why I shed my habit, so they can see me naked as themselves. The flesh does not represent sin to them and that's what Rebullida is unable to understand: that blessed innocence! Yes, Pedro, that's how it is. The Indians laugh at us, humiliate us. They told Father Andrade that if he was going to heaven they would sooner go to hell than have to see him."

"Very sad," said Pedro. Conversion of the Indians was about as important to him as radish leaves, but he felt obliged to say something sympathetic. *"And the ones I see here, these women with their children..?"*

"They were brought here by force and violence, and if they are not under guard day and night, they run off to the mountain the first chance they get."

Agueda, busy rolling herself a cigar, asked, "Did Juan know about Rebullida's project for taking Indians out of Talamanca?"

"Of course, he knew. What's more, he told me that he had tried to warn Rebullida that it wouldn't work, seeing that those Indians were tribute payers to the Crown and when they were brought anywhere near a settlement of Spaniards, they would steal them. But Rebullida answered that in any case the English were stealing them and that once Christian communities were established, a way would be found to maintain tribute to the King, at the same level of payment. In Juan's opinion the real reason for displacing the Indians far away from their lands was the failure of the missions; it was the final attempt to weaken and disorganize them in order to impose the gospel and payment of tribute."

"Possibly, possibly... After so many years of running a mission in Talamanca since the days of the venerable Father Margil, the end result has been nothing but enormous expenditure of time and money... Yet, it seems to me that the attempt to remove them from their lands was a sound move. What good were useless vassals to the Crown? All those hands wasted in the jungle. Apart from the backwardness in which they live, their rebellious nature is a constant source of danger."

"Juan de las Alas had quite a different idea."

"Juan de las Alas is a mystic, and I am a practical person," answered Agueda, puffing rather nervously at her cigar.

Juan was fascinated by what he was learning about the Indian's pagan religion. Fired up, he explained with gusto that the Indians believed in a hereafter below the earth. "They say," he explained to Pedro, "that it is from there that the trees are born and the plants come, and that people have their roots there, too, for they were sown like the kernels of corn. Therefore, God is not in the heavens as we think, but down underneath in a world below, subterranean, from which life originates... Not a bad idea, don't you think?"

And Pedro listened warily for Juan was uttering incredible heresies. At the same time, he was enjoying himself, because Juan had not really changed that much, after all. Basically, he had remained the same mischievous, rebellious kid, whose youth the Guatemalan theological seminaries had not succeeded in withering away. He told him so. Juan smiled—he was missing two teeth—and recalled when the Superior had the little tree cut down by which Pedro had made his nocturnal escapades. He confessed to him that one time he followed him to The Mother of Travelers place and hid himself among the horses to watch the gaming and found it boring

"Incidentally," said Juan, "somebody, I can't remember who, told me that a woman was looking for you in Cartago and had finally stayed on living with The Mother of Travelers, waiting for you to come back." And throwing him a glance of ingenuous impishness, added, "A very pretty woman, wearing a chambergo, I think they said."

Like a phantom that suddenly materializes, La Chamberga had thrust herself violently into the world of Indians' beliefs and Juan's afflictions, bringing with her all the fears and uncertainties that Pedro had by now forgotten: Avendaño and the Inquisition. Oh, what foul luck! La Chamberga in league with The Mother! Who knew but that the two of them were wagging their tongues and now all Cartago, including Inquisitor Avendaño would be aware that Pedro was a fugitive from the Inquisition. Fearing that there might be a knowledgeable soldier among the sinister contingent of cutthroats, he had an uncontrollable urge to get back to the beach immediately. It was already late. When these same soldiers returned to the city they would make it their business to advertise that they had seen him with the Indian woman who was the monastery cook. As soon as he had recovered from the initial shock, he told himself that gossip on their part would not change matters. That, after all, José de San José and the Flying Dutchman had already taken it upon themselves to tell about him and to fabricate a fantasy replete with medusas, devils that changed color, dragons, witches, and spells.

Juan had not noticed the silence into which Pedro had lapsed for he was pulling worms out of a puppy dog for Catarina's entertainment. Gerónima had gone off to visit with the Indians of the mission.

When Pedro told Agueda that Gerónima had mixed with the mission Indians, she remarked, "Naturally. Spying, of course."

"You can be sure of it. She must have been busy as a bee counting up soldiers, weapons, and supplies right under our noses," he answered.

Pedro hoisted Caterina to his shoulder and set off to make his way back to the coast, promising himself never to return to the mission nor to any place inhabited by Spaniards. Juan had promised to pay him a visit. Pedro had changed and this trip had made him begin to realize it was a fundamental change that had built up in him subtly from day to day as a consequence of his simple way of life and his association with the Indian women and the black boys, impossible to be reversed, unless he resumed his former existence in Seville. Perhaps not even then. The deep marks etched into his being, especially by his association with Gerónima, were definitive. Without going farther afield than the matter of the fire, for example. Many years had gone by since Gerónima first lit it by rubbing stones together over a little pile of fine dry grass, and it had gone out very rarely since then. The fire burned in the center of the house, brightly during the day, banked during the night. The attitude of a man who wakes up at night in fear that the fire may have gone out is not the same as that of one who has flint and tinder at hand. Nor does he who goes looking for the claws of an anteater for a newborn have the same outlook as the one who goes to the market to buy it a rattle. Without Pedro realizing it, Gerónima had obliged him to conform to the habits and customs of her people. At the mission, Juan de las Alas had placed a pewter spoon next to Pedro's tin plate but he ignored it, preferring to use his fingers like an Arab to pick up the chunks of meat and vegetables he was served.

The candles had all gone out and Agueda dozed in her chair. Pedro had not opened his mouth in some time and it was now after midnight. He would have liked to go to sleep but preferred not to be impolite to the woman who had provided him food and lodging, who was going out of her way to be attentive to him and Catarina. Pedro coughed. Agueda emerged from her lethargy, clapped her hands and Lorenzana, her eyes heavy with sleep, appeared with fresh candles. Agueda ordered more wine.

"Didn't it occur to you that the Indians would oppose Rebullida's project?" Agueda inquired, smoothing the wrinkles of sleep from her face with her two hands.

"It never crossed my mind. Actually, the Indians remained unknown beings to me... Except for Gerónima and Catarina, of course, who began to tell me strange stories she heard from her aunt. And through her I became aware of an incomprehensible world of mysterious beliefs and an unusual way of conceiving the world, life, and death... As I approached the frontier of the impassable, a chasm opened at my feet and behind my back a tragedy was brewing... I attempted to plant cacao with the idea of shipping it to Matina but made no effort ever to build a boat and the beans rotted... I was bogged down in laziness. I was no longer concerned about Catarina's future, and in order to pass the time taught her to read and write, elementary arithmetic, and a bit of natural history. She learned quickly and readily memorized what I wrote in the damp sand before the tide came in and washed it away... One day Bugalú went off to the mountain and did not return. I went crazy looking for him without anybody to help me. Gerónima and Babí took it very calmly, while I was in despair, thinking he had died in the jungle, abandoned and alone..."

"He'd gone off to join the uprising and the others knew it."

"That's what happened, and I had no idea. Gerónima had recruited him. Bugalú was an expert bowman. And where he might be now nobody knows. I don't understand how I could have been so shortsighted nor why Rebullida wasn't aware of it."

"Rebullida was obsessed with his project. Besides he must have been very worried by the news coming from abroad. The allies had taken Madrid. Holland, England, and later Savoy, and Portugal had gone over to the Austrian side and, as you know, Spain lost Gibraltar. Who could have imagined all Talamanca rising up in arms? Everything seemed at peace here and we thought that the pacification work of the missionaries was proceeding effectively. Blas González Coronel alone thought otherwise, and time proved him right."

"Rebullida was deceived by Viceita's submission. I believe that Juan de las Alas had a foreboding of something but never told anybody."

"That's why they were caught unawares. If it hadn't been for you..."

"Not at all, not at all, it was a matter of coincidence, I never pretended... I had nothing to do with it!"

Pedro felt ill at ease. He preferred not to dwell on that. It was preferable and more gratifying to think of the long walks and moments of meditation at The Mute's grave in those years during which his relations with Catarina grew so much closer. He watched her developing, able to shift from one language to another, from his own, to Gerónima's, and even somewhat to Bugalú's. And with the change of language, her mentality changed. Catarina, the mestiza, a duality, thought all the world was like that, for she knew no other way. Pedro began to question whether he was really her model for all the others, or if each was merely a different model and his the worst. Catarina was turning out to be the sum total of them all and for that reason, perhaps, did not consider herself worthy of imitation. Uneasy, Pedro wondered about his daughter's opinion of a father who was inept at fishing, a total loss as a hunter, no cook, and incapable of reviving a fire that had died during the night. Pedro's only achievement worthy of consideration was his having given

Catarina a good basic elementary education, knowledge which in the context of her way of life could not be considered much more than an adornment.

Upset because he had a daughter who knew many more things than he, Pedro went one day to tell The Mute about it. And, seated there on her coral grave, it occurred to him that he didn't have the slightest idea what The Mute thought of him, either. It was something that had never concerned him before. "If I only knew," he said to himself, "through what sort of a distorting lens she looked at me, loved me, and thought of me."

The visit to Juan de las Alas had left him out of sorts. He began to feel alienated, as if the world were inhabited by creatures from another world, and he was the only survivor of a terrible cataclysm. Feeling unbearably lethargic, he lay back in the hammock woven by Gerónima where he spent the whole day under the palm trees with the red monkeys swinging above and grimacing at him, his eyes on the horizon in case the Flying Dutchman reappeared or San José might pay another visit. Then, Catarina came to swing him in his hammock like a little boy and tell him fantastic stories she had heard from her aunt.

"And so, the little girl"—she recited with great seriousness—"was below ground, and she felt a bat bite one of her fingers. It hurt very much and she cried out. The mother heard her voice and got very angry and shouted, 'Who was it bit my little girl?' And lots of people came and they cut the bat in two. One part of the little animal fell up to where Sibú is and it said to him: 'You sent me to eat the little girl and now I am dead. What am I to do now that I am dead?' Sibú answered it; 'Because you carried out my order I am going to cure you but never again will you be with your head upright. From now on you will hang with your head down.' And Sibú sent for the little girl and when she arrived she fell onto the stones and many people came and they jumped on her and stamped and danced all over her until she was squashed into pieces and then her mother also came, and the mother started to cry, and out of her tears were born the mountain lions, hawks, and the fleas, and she accused Sibú of the death of her little girl and he answered that he had done it so as to create the world..."

"Child! Tell your aunt not to be telling you dreadful stories like that any more!"

"But you didn't let me finish. After he ate the little pieces of the little girl, he took a shit, and out of the shit little bushes, little trees came, the flowers grew, and..."

"That's some creation story those savages have!" roared Pedro and he warned Gerónima: "I don't want you to be telling Catarina gruesome stories! You're stuffing her head with death and shit."

Gerónima answered: "Don't the Spaniards nail God on a pole and then, when he dies and is good and dead, don't they eat and drink him? And after eating him, mustn't they have to shit the flesh and blood of their God? If not, then what do they do with it, leave it stuck in their guts?" And she closed out her case by dropping her favorite remark: "I've never seen anything good come out of a Spaniard's shit...only flies."

Defeated, Pedro heaved a sigh, for he had to admit that she was absolutely right, and settled back in his hammock to go on listening to Catarina's fantastic stories. He felt grateful that Gerónima had not heard of the Inquisition's burnings at the stake for she would have said the Christians have a god so terrible that he eats people charcoal-broiled. Catarina, noting that her father was humbly giving in to her, continued to reel off stories as she rocked his hammock, hoping to put him to sleep. They were stories curdled with literary figures, strange symbols, and complex ideas and Pedro whiled away the time trying unsuccessfully to decipher their cryptic meanings, interrupting Caterina from time to time with comments that were shocking to her.

Sibú was a rascally trickster of a god who appeared in all the stories. "And so," she related, "Sibú saw a group of three very beautiful sisters, and in order to find out which was deserving of his affection, he disguised himself as an ugly man. He put on clothing like that worn by Juan's soldiers, stinking and full of holes. The women turned their backs on him and said, 'Why would I want to have anything to do with a man like that?' But he noticed that one of them, the youngest and prettiest of the three, kept looking at him without saying anything. So he asked her if she liked him as he was, ugly and dreadful. That girl's name was Cacao and she said that yes, she did like him. She, however, had been able to notice that there was a very handsome man under the disguise. The sister who had not noticed anything, said to her, 'Cacao, how could you, the prettiest of the three of us, care for such an awful man?' But Cacao did not answer and went with Sibú to bathe in the river and when he took off his clothes the sisters saw that he was very good-looking, the most handsome man they had ever seen, and they died of envy..."

"But, my child," Pedro interrupted her, "what do you know of such perverse feelings? Do you have any idea of what envy is?"

"I envy Gerónima when she goes to the mountain alone and I can't accompany her. I also envy that you can spend all the day lying in this hammock while I have to go and collect dry wood for the fire. And stop interrupting me for I am going to continue the story. All right, now, so Sibú said to Cacao, 'because you like me, you will be always lovely, your beauty will never fade, you will continue to bloom, and you will give forth harvests without limit.'

"And he said to the sisters, 'Because you didn't like me, you two will be cursed your life long.' And to the little wild papaya, which one of them was, he said, 'You will give forth flowers but never fruit.'"

"Tell me another," said Pedro, sleepily.

"All right, I'll tell you another. Once there was a man who went to bed with his sister..."

"No! I don't like the way that story starts out."

"Listen! This man fell in love with his sister and went to bed with her. Sibú scolded them and punished the woman by putting a worm into her body that sucked away at her. But she liked that and hid the worm so that her parent would not see it, because the worm was a man who..."

"That sounds to me like a Boccaccio tale."

"I don't know who that is. She let the worm be there for one month...well, she became pregnant and the family didn't know who was responsible. She hid the worm and took good care of it, even nursing it..."

"I don't want to listen to you anymore! Your aunt is crazy. Go

and let her know that she should tell you nice stories about fairies and elves that live in the forest, because that dreadful thing you're telling me is not a story fit for children."

"Gerónima didn't say it was a story for children and if I tell it to you it's because you are not a child," said Catarina and she went off peeved to ask Gerónima for stories that didn't have to do with worms because they disgusted her father.

Presbere makes ready

The couriers set out, men who had the power to change into squirrels, fish, or hawks. There were spies who had the power to become cockroaches and vultures. The native interpreters who fled the missions and Christian settlements returned, divesting themselves of their parrot and macaw feathers.

There were women who ran like squirrels, their infants on their back. And there were those who had eggs fertilized within the body like the snakes. Some stayed at home making arrows of *pijibaye* wood while others went up into the mountains to practice archery against the stationary target of the sapodilla tree and the moving targets of falling leaves.

Each one in Our Land had something to do. There was great spirit and much confidence. The stones foretold that we would be victorious.

The news went out, flying, swimming, walking. That Our Land was rising up, that all the nations had risen in arms, all covered by a single tapir shield, all united behind a single spear of *pijibaye* palm, so that no one else should be trampled to death by cattle or cringe under the slave driver's lash, so that those humpbacked from the weight of firewood and crocks of water might return, so that all the people of Our Land might live by their customs, planting corn, planting cacao, weaving cotton, firing clay, hunting the wild boar, fishing in the rivers, dancing at their fiestas, seeking a mate, making love to the mate, bearing children, dying when their natural time comes, and so that they might be brought to the World Below, as ordered by the Sower and Maker, Lord Sibú-Surá.

A tremor from below shook the earth throughout all the surface of Our Land. The friars were officiating in their useless churches and noticed nothing.

Sunai, the basket weaver, came running with the news to the

House of the Masters. The artisans stopped working, set the unfinished baskets aside, the rolls of pita fiber, *guarumo* canes, palm leaves, and *tibourbou* cordage on the ground, the needles of deer bone in the hands of the astonished old women, suspended, unthreaded.

"Presbere is coming here! He's on his way over the brook of clear water, is now passing through the macaw's ravine, now getting close, now he's climbing, now his necklace of macaw feathers is coming into view."

The eldest mother went out to welcome the Prime Mover of the Earth, the Engenderer of Man who was wearing the face of the Kapá. When Presbere entered the house, he asked everyone to sit at a distance from the fire so that the smoke would not obscure their words.

Sunai's eyes were wide for Presbere was not as she had imagined him. She had expected a young man slim as a laurel, and this was a mature man and sedate as a fig tree, his face grave in expression, under the skin the muscles weaving nerves like the cords of a hammock.

What brought Presbere here? He came to ask for ropes. They had to be thick as half a finger, the length of a forearm, tightly braided and with fifteen knots, the last of which to have a strand of thread colored red with achiote dye.

The artisans worked all that morning rubbing the *tibourbou* cords against their thigh smeared with cacao oil, a red strand in the last knot.

The messengers waited in Suinse's great house. Each was given a rope: one for each clan chief: this for Comezala, this for Cachaveri, this for Suchaqui... None for Viceita. For Viceita, no. Presbere will go to Viceita when the friars are dead, when Our Land is rid of foreigners. Afterwards Presbere will go and turn command over to Principal Warrior to make war against the soldiers who will be coming from Cartago. Gods against gods first. Then, soldiers against soldiers.

The messengers asked no questions. They were told that they must untie one knot for each day of travel. The first attached fins to his feet and jumped into the river; another with hawk feathers flew into the air; and one who had deer feet scampered off towards the sea...

Agueda nods and Pedro relates how Gerónima's departure took him unawares

She made the announcement without preamble: "I'm leaving and not coming back anymore. The best thing for you is to get out of here, too."

"But, why? Why?" Pedro exclaimed. "We've lived together for so many years and, now, suddenly, without any explanation, you're off, abandoning us, knowing very well that Catarina can't live without you."

Not only Catarina, he couldn't exist without her, either.

And Gerónima, stone-faced, was going off, like nothing, as though it were the most ordinary thing after all those years, after having shared so much life and so much death, so much love for Catarina. She was leaving and nothing in her seemed to regret the utter abandonment in which she was leaving them. Such ingratitude was not possible. She had always been sparing of words, almost hostile, impervious at times, but effective and devoted. And brave. Ungrateful, as well, for he could very well have had turned her in when he was at the mission with Juan de las Alas and sent her to Rebullida or back to the monastery at Cartago. By now, she would have been enslaved by Rebullida or stewing in the Father Superior's kitchen... He, however, had given her freedom and never interfered with her disappearances into the mountains for days at a time. For Gerónima came and went as she pleased. And if she had stayed with Pedro and The Mute, with the black slave boys and Catarina, it was because she wanted to. And now she was casting off, just like that, without a thank you for having been rescued from the altars with rosettes and saints with painted eyes, perhaps from being dumped on her back in the brush and taken by force by the Conquest officer, or thrust violently into a friar's bed, compelled to life as vassal of a king on the other side of the sea, to bearing unloved, servile, hypocritical, submissive, shifty, exploited mestizos, that ungrateful hussy! "Oh, woe is me!" Pedro lamented, "Now what am I going to do without her, on my own, with a black boy for company whose skin is spotted, who will also probably end up one day leaving me in the lurch...what am I going to do now in this wilderness abandoned even by the pirates...?"

Gerónima left, taking nothing with her, without giving a last embrace to Catarina, who watched her, dry-eyed, as she left, having been given as a remembrance a length of rope that had knots and a bit of red string on it. (Who knows what sort of toy that was? It looked like something that had to do with witchcraft.) Pedro did not admit that what gave him the most pain was Gerónima's having taken away with her the secret of the whereabouts in that jungle fastness of the son about whom he had never inquired and, now, suddenly he was anxious to know where, how, and with whom the boy was. But not even as she departed did he ask for him. He watched her disappear among the bushes and primeval green giants, swallowed up by the red canna flowers and the leaves of the wild plantain tree. And she was gone, a blow without impact because of the suddenness of it, leaving a play of light and shadow, a void of loneliness.

Through Agueda's window, the night appeared at its darkest, as dark as it can get when dawn is about to break and shadows are at the point of losing their daily battle with the morning light.

"It's understandable that she should have left so abruptly," said Agueda, yawning. "I couldn't really tell you why. She was answering the call of her blood."

"She might have given me some hint of the impending danger..."

"What about the cord with the knots that she left Catarina? Couldn't that have been it?"

"I have no idea. Who knows what that piece of rope might have meant? Very odd, don't you think?"

"Who can understand those Indians? Who will ever be able to?"

And so Gerónima was gone, and only Pedro missed her rough presence, her harsh manner, her chunky body, and unappealing features. He pictured her likeness in the flames of the home fire, saw her reappearing as he scanned the jungle. He awoke in the mornings to the aroma of beaten cocoa and the smell of boiled yucca, but it was never Gerónima but Babí bustling about, as indifferent as when his brother disappeared. Catarina continued running about playing her games in the sand, never asking for her. Gerónima's absence was enveloped in heavy silence.

Life became disorganized. Pedro tried to take her place in the kitchen with unsatisfactory results. The black proved even less capable and so occupied himself with makeshift fishing tackle to provide flapping, gasping fish for supper. Everything was in a muddle. The solar schedule established and enforced by Gerónima for all duties went by the board and morning became short because the three easily fell prey to indolence and negligence and seemed to be living on the edge of pure inertia. Catarina became disobedient and refused to eat the undercooked or warmed over fish that Pedro served her on withered leaves. Babí balked at going into the forest to gather tubers and fruits. Nobody obeyed Pedro. The little community suffered a vacuum of authority and Pedro, annoyed at his inability to deal with the situation began leaving them to their own devices while he took long, fruitless strolls in the hope that he would discover something to justify an existence that was becoming irksome. Although he had already made up his mind to go, he took no action for he had no idea what else he could do. Going back over time he reckoned that it must now be the year 1709, figuring that Charles the Bewitched died in 1700, the British took Gibraltar in 1704, The Mute died the following year, and he went to see Juan de las Alas... He wondered how many years had gone by since he visited the Cabécar mission. How old Catarina was. He wasn't sure whether she was six or older, which meant that the boy would now be one, two, three because Spain lost Gibraltar in 1704... The strain of going back over the years and making the calculations soon tired him out. The rains had started, and he was forced to take shelter in the house and there, curled up before the fire to ease the rheumatic pains in his joints, he pondered the pointlessness of his existence.

The days rolled on and, in keeping with his indecisive character, he reached no decision. He wanted to go, but not while the rains were so heavy nor without knowing exactly what it was that he would like to do with himself. He was awaiting a sign, a signal, a nudge from fate, and fate obliged with a violent storm of hurricane force. The old almond tree under which The Mute's bones lay buried was toppled, taking many other smaller trees down with it. It was a catastrophe of epic proportions that shattered the habitat and lives of all the living creatures of the place, from which even the smallest had no escape. Falling branches scraped Pedro's house without destroying it, a notification, a warning, or so Pedro interpreted it in his anxiety for something to prod him on his way. It happened during the night and, the next morning, when the rain stopped and the wind had died down, Pedro made up his mind to leave, for even the trees around him were dying. Now, nature herself no longer wanted him.

That same night Pedro decided to remove The Mute's remains and rebury them wherever his future dwelling was to be so that they might share the same grave. Saying nothing to the others, he summoned up the courage to try and gather the bones that would have been scattered by the storm among the roots of the almond tree. He had to go into what had become a quagmire, avoiding snakes, among the smashed bodies of chipmunks, squirrels, iguanas, sloths, skunks that had launched their ultimate defense with their last breath, along with birds' nests, destroyed eggs and all the orphaned fledglings... He saw crabs crawling, unexpected travelers at the top of the tree, and heard the melancholy cheeping of an oriole unable to find its ruined nest. At the base of the trunk, the giant's roots exposed themselves to the sky, in a shameless, naked, obscene tangle torn from the enormous hollow in which they had lain hidden for a hundred years. The center of the almond tree was hollow and it appeared that a second birth had been taking place inside it: womb, crucible of death and decay, where The Mute's bones, the bodies of the animals, and vegetal excrescences were being transmuted into God knows what...The tree, axis mundi...mythical center, now on the ground, humiliated, vexed, its ramified members stretching towards an inferno of death and suffering.

Pedro had to hunt for The Mute's bones in this disconcerting, rotting place. Pedro, grave robber... At the jagged pinnacle of his last wish, he yearned for the first time to have her skull in order to satisfy himself that she had not been a hallucination of his delirium, an invention, an illusion, a tropical fever. To confirm the materiality of her skeleton, to touch her chill tibias, clavicles, and ribs, her femurs, occipital bones, so tangible, oh, so tangible...

There were bits of dead coral here and there. He searched, digging in, pulling out, going under, diving in, covering himself with dirt, sand, decomposed flesh, guts of birds, foul-smelling things, but there was nothing left of her. The Mute was hiding from him, camouflaged in the disorder, avoiding his eager hands busily, insistently, removing branches, roots, mud. The Mute did not want his hands to find her, was fleeing his sad, amorous eyes, fleeing the fingers that had once felt the softness of her flesh. And he, tirelessly raking for her until he was forced to accept—a certainty from which there was no appeal—that his beloved's bones would never come to light because they had been ground up and pulverized by the same timber that had served as the tombstone for her grave.

He had no valises, baggage, or anything to take away with him. He had no passport, no papers that he needed. He would be leaving just as he arrived, a loincloth between his legs, a machete, its edge now dulled, at his waist. Five had arrived and now three were left. At one point they were nearly seven, but The Mute's death spoiled everything.

When he announced that they would be leaving by way of Cabécar, the black refused to go. They fought, and Pedro won out. It was the only road he knew. He would arrive at the mission in time to join up with Juan de las Alas and a group of soldiers of the escort who were bound for Cartago. And he himself was in no condition to walk along the swampy shore to Matina. He had no idea what rivers had to be crossed, what obstacles were there, what dangers might be lurking in the area. The uphill climb to Cabécar would be difficult during the rainy season, but he at least knew the way and did not wait for the weather to change. They left in the midst of a downpour, which seemed to dilute his sorrow. Catarina walked beside him and the black followed with a package of smoked fish, their only food. The crabs that had welcomed them years before retired into their caves—selfish hermits—and the turtles swam out to sea, leaving the beach looking gray and deserted as it received the last three pairs of fresh footprints, the toes pointing away. The solitary house and the footprints pressed into the sand before being erased by the sea were the only remembrances left for the cranes until they took flight over the coral banks in search of schools of wandering fish.

His knees weakened by intermittent pain, Pedro kept his grief under control by battling the jungle. He lost his way and found it again, delaying arrival at the Cabécar mission by constantly going astray. He would lose reference points: a particular mountain peak, the position of the sun, a river he had not crossed before...or had he? And so, braving the crocodiles and exhausting himself in order to avoid thinking, at times believing he was being watched, he finally arrived almost on his hands and knees, the black carrying Catarina on his shoulders. The ordeal of his poor aching bones assailed by the dampness made him forget for a while the distress of his bitter failure as a founder of ports and civilizer of wild beaches.

Pa-brú Presbere attacks

At San Bernabé de Urinama, Father Rebullida gave the letter he had just written to the Governor a last reading and signed it: "the same nothingness," folded it, placed it under a piece of polished wood he used as a paperweight, carefully wiped off the pen, corked the ink bottle with a chunk of corncob, blew out the candle, and lay down on his mat, hands resting upon his chest. When he finished praying, he said to himself that the Governor could not refuse him this time, for the men were tired out, ill, and no good for very much anymore. Once the relief contingent of fresh, well-fed soldiers arrived from Cartago, he would begin getting Indians out of Suinse, Tuina, and Ujambor... He imagined the transferal and willed the rapid arrival of replacements bringing a supply of salt and biscuit, candles, sacramental wine, and wheat flour for preparing the Host. He was exhausted, too, so tired that he had suspended flagellation in recent months because he fainted after the first few strokes of the scourge. His eyelids drooped and he fell into a profound sleep.

It was three o'clock in the morning and a new moon hung in the dark night sky. Neither Rebullida, nor the two soldiers who slept in another hut, heard them coming. Nor, even if they had been awake would they have heard the rustling of the dry leaves and crackling of twigs.

He was awakened by the soldiers' agonized screams, as spears were jabbed through their ribs. Rebullida, the Baptist, knew that the secretly hoped-for moment of his martyrdom had come. He ran to the makeshift church, knelt at the altar under the little icon of Saint Bartholomew, opened his arms, and was just able to say "I thank thee, my Lord, I am thy servant, thy will be done..." before a club crashed into his skull.

His head was cut off and an Indian carried it out clutched by the beard. Rebullida's eyes were closed as he went.

The prayer book was ripped apart, some sticking the torn pages into their hair like feathers. The dead letters fell, the *gratia plena*, the *mea culpa*, the *misere nobis*, the *ora pro nobis*, all fell, dropping like wounded doves.

Saint Bartholomew was taken off his pedestal and smashed to bits. The ciborium was pulled out with the hosts, which they ate. When they saw that nothing happened to them, they danced around decking themselves out with whatever ornaments came to hand. Then, they took down the cross, and attacking it with hands and feet, reduced it to a pile of splinters.

Having done this, they took brands from Rebullida's fire and threw them onto the roofs of the houses.

The hermitage burned, Urinama burned.

Comezala assembled his people to the cry of "Chirripó!"

Presbere gathered his people and waited...

When the fires had died out after many hours, the pigs came out of their hiding places and threw themselves upon the charred bodies.

Comezala went to the high hills of Chirripó. He found Zamora celebrating mass, his back to the door. Comezala's men entered slowly; not one of the Indians there uttered a sound. The friar didn't realize what was happening until he saw the point of an arrow protruding through his tattered cassock.

Presbere had been waiting on the banks of the Tarire River while this was going on. He was waiting for the full moon, waiting patiently.

The night of confidences ends and
Pedro has a fit of jealousy because of
Bárbara Lorenzana

"Juan de las Alas was overjoyed when I arrived for he never expected to see me again. The mission's work had intensified over the last few years. The war in Spain had brought on financial problems and, as Juan explained, the wheat crop was being monopolized by the military. Cerdeña and Menorca had fallen to the English and the Pope was teetering between King Philip V and the Archduke of Austria. All of this had its effect on the colonies and Cartago was seriously concerned. News arrived months behind time and nobody knew if Madrid had fallen into Allied hands again or whether Philip was still in power.

"Juan's behavior toward me was very concerned and affectionate, and he even gave up his own bed to me. He rubbed lard into my legs to ease my rheumatism, filling me in at the same time on the latest information that had come in. 'That's all the news of the world I can give you,' he said. 'As you know, nobody remembers that this place exists.' 'Juan, I've lost track of time. Do you know today's exact date?' I asked. 'This is September 15, 1709.'"

"Oh! exclaimed Agueda, absorbed in his story, "that was just the day before San Bartolomé Urinama was set on fire."

"You'll see..." Pedro commented, "communication was so irregular that Cabécar didn't know or suspect anything. You must remember that the rain is very heavy at that time of year and it's impossible to cross the rivers."

"Not only that, nobody was left there to tell the tale."

Juan de la Alas had lost other teeth, and as he spoke the words were accompanied by a slight whistle. Little by little, he had begun to take on aspects of Rebullida: the feverish eyes, scraggly beard, sickly skin color, prominent bones. He had not set foot out of Talamanca in all those years, during which he suffered sickness and hunger. He told macabre stories of massacred Indians, raped Indian women, soldiers who on the day of arrival began counting the days until replacements were to come: a litany of cruelties, sins, crimes, aberration and desperation. Soldiers would be transferred, survivors returned to Cartago as others came in anxious to cooperate with the evangelization only to end up in complicity with the devil. The atrocities were at such a pitch that Pedro forgot about himself in his sympathy for others, the muted memories stirred up of the time long past when he felt for the unknowns howling in the San Gerónimo tower of the Inquisition. It seemed incomprehensible, impossible, that of all the Indians in the mountains he had only known two. Juan explained to him that entire communities had been transported to the other side of the mountain range and that the Indians were to be exiled from the banks of the Coén River to the outskirts of the central valley where Cartago lay. Relief and replacements would be coming. "Father Rebullida and Father Andrade were requesting large contingents," Juan told him, "to remove the people and transplant them to the Christian communities from which the Spaniards took them to work their cornfields, sugar refineries, and cacao plantations."

"A natural consequence of the period. Just imagine, Juan, Spain is too caught up in its civil war to have any energy left over for its overseas colonies, and the settlers take advantage of the situation to obtain labor for their enterprises. You can't do anything about it. It would be better for you to give in. Otherwise, you'll lose heart and go out of your mind fighting impossibility."

"I can't accept that, Pedro. I can't... I know that neither God nor Our Father Saint Francis can accept it. But it seems that I am alone in seeing it this way. Rebullida, the friars at Cartago, all believe they are acting in the name of God and for that reason have rights over the lives of these people... I sometimes think that God has forsaken us..." And he lowered his voice, "I sometimes

think...have come to think...that God...either does not exist or has grown old, and like old men, gone deaf."

Pedro smiled. "An atheist missionary would be a novelty."

"Don't make fun. Jesus died on the cross, and it seems to me that now I am seeing the most innocent and defenseless of his children being crucified. We are worshipping a God of death, not a God of life... Eternal life is not sufficient justification." Juan stared at his habit inlaid with patches. "If our holy mission is to save souls for eternal life, must we do so by murdering the bodies? At times, I feel the urge to shout: 'Run away, run away, all of you from my lying promises!' Just like that. To drive them away so that the soldiers won't find them."

Spent by his confession, he clasped his hands together over his rags and shut his eyes; fighting the devil of doubt, tortured without letup, he went on. "Jesus sacrificed himself in vain. His Father had abandoned him the moment he was born. We baptize with water, and what is left of that water? It runs off, dries up, leaves not a trace."

"It would be too expensive to baptize with wine..." joked Pedro who, however, was deeply concerned by Juan's words. "You are going to end up in the flames, if anybody overhears you talking like this. Besides, I don't believe the good Lord has anything to do with it. You must remember that the money-changers hide behind the Gospel."

Juan did not reply and Pedro looked through the doorway: a world divided into two violently opposed parts could be observed outside where three Indians were dragging a huge tree trunk while a pair of soldiers sat on the ground playing dice. The green landscape faded off toward the grayness of the cloudy sky. His glance turned to the monk, his head hanging. The simpleton of the scapulary, of love among mankind, of the love of God, of tolerance and solidarity, had no words with which to console him. Juan was an employee of the Crown and was not properly carrying out the duties for which he was being paid. He was betraying his Franciscan habit—or was he? To whom should he have been faithful, to Francis or Fray Pablo Rebullida? He wanted to ask what difference there was between the saint of the Seraphic Order who preached in the nude and spoke to the animals and

Rebullida, blind to the body of the Indian. But Pedro asked him no questions. Poor Juan had enough with his sweltering tick-colored habit, tied with a cord more tormenting than the hair shirt, set down in a no man's land, because his brothers in Saint Francis regarded him with distrust and the heathens rejected him as an accomplice in murder, cruelty, and injustice. To the Indians, Juan was an invader.

"They don't even have gold with which to arouse covetousness... So poor! With their girdles of seashells, their feathers, their articles of wood, of reeds..." Juan lifted his eyes and let them roam in search of an answer.

"They have land."

"Yes. Land on which the Spaniards intend to graze their cows."

"And don't forget their labor which is the most important."

Disheartened, Juan dug into the folds of his cassock to transfer a louse to the blanket where he let it roam freely.

"You're going to infest me with lice!" Pedro protested.

Juan burst into the laughter he seemed to have lost, and for an instant, his toothless gums notwithstanding, he was again the mischievous little friar who dreamt of being a missionary for the greater glory of God, amen.

Near them, Catarina played with a broken rosary. Outside, the rabble soldiers waited for dark to stretch out on their filthy straw mattresses, reeking as if all the concentrated sweat of the Conquest had seeped into them and the foul rags they wore. Their energies restored and hatreds refreshed, they prepared for sleep and the next day's manhunt.

Juan left and Catarina remained alone with Pedro. And she lay down beside him to thaw his chilled bones with the warmth of her little body. Before nodding off, he asked himself uneasily why Juan had fallen silent when he spoke to him of The Mute, and answered himself: "Maybe because all have a right to protect their most precious secrets."

When he was sound asleep he had a most unusual dream. He dreamt of The Mute for the first time. His dreams practically always revolved around things experienced, recently lived, matters of urgency. But this one was of a different kind and must have taken place around daybreak because he was awakened by the voice of the Conquest Officer. In the dream, he could see himself lying face up on The Mute's grave, the sharp edges of the corals digging into his back and kidneys, but unable to move, for his arms and legs were heavier than lead. The Mute's big, warm, luminous eyes looked down at him from the crown of the great almond tree, tall and luxuriant as in its best times. Then, the head, the long, straight black hair, the prominent cheekbones, the little, turned-up nose, and full-lipped mouth, materialized bit by bit. Her body, wrapped in a kind of white gauze, looked like a chrysalis. Her bare head lay upon a bundle of filmy transparencies. Driven by a mechanism like that of a music box, The Mute's head began to rotate and Pedro heard music in his dream. And he said to himself, "I am dreaming because I am not familiar with that music, have never heard it before, don't know what the instruments are, but it is music." The head continued to spin, accelerating until it was impossible to distinguish the head from the neck. Then, the music became transformed into an intense blue color, and the speed of rotation began to diminish. Pedro, still lying face up, was very happy that it was happening in this way, and he said to himself, "This is a good dream, it is very beautiful and very sad, too." And he heard The Mute's voice, which emerged from her mouth like pink crystals and he saw but could not decipher the words because they were in Catarina and Gerónima's language, but by making a great effort he was on the point of understanding the meaning of the crystals when a shout of "Sonsofbitches, on your stinking feet" shook him harshly out of the dream. Everything grew blurred and the next thing he heard was, "We'll be slaughtered like pigs the day they attack."

Pedro got up painfully, dismayed and deeply depressed, and accompanied Juan to the celebration of his mass. He was annoyed that his dream had been interrupted and upset at having to take part for friendship's sake in a ritual that disgusted him. Not only that, but he had to share the frugal breakfast with Father Andrade who had returned from Viceita the day before, having gone there under orders from Rebullida to negotiate peace and submission. He and Rebullida were diametrically opposite physically and in character. He had a robust constitution resistant to privation and overflowed with zeal in fulfillment of the task assigned him by God and king. Having the instincts of a shopkeeper, Andrade kept track in a small ledger of souls saved for the holy cause, jotting down baptisms, marriages, and extreme unctions. He deceived himself by recasting, with an artist's skill, the scenes of horror into views of grateful Indians and pious soldiers grazing like sheep on the bucolic meadows of the Gospel.

Catarina and Babí's baptism was scheduled for that morning, and as Juan de las Alas was finishing mass before the sleepy, bad-tempered troops, Andrade was pouring the water from the baptismal font over Catarina, changing her name from Catarina to Catalina because the former—he said—smacked of sectarian heresy. Babí disappeared and was nowhere to be found even though they went into the mountains in search of him. Pedro didn't care. The affection that had developed between them over the years on the beach had dissolved at the mission, and he resigned himself to the black lad's flight, thinking that it had been prompted by his having looked upon the baptism as a horrifying evil spell cast upon him.

After Babí's disappearance, Catarina fell into a state of lassitude and apathy out of which she could not be drawn even by Juan's games. Pedro's depression worsened, and he began wishing even more ardently than the soldiers themselves for the relief contingent to arrive. He felt the jungle closing in on him, smothering him, the wild mountain ring tightening, stifling breath and good humor. He would awake every morning to the officer's "sonsofbitches," his daily wakeup call, rain or shine, still drunk from the night before or sober. It was impossible to ignore, for the cocks roused up, chorused after him, followed by the mooing of the cows and the cursing and swearing of the troops marching to mass.

The month of September was shedding its days and its end was drawing close. Pedro kept count of the days until the arrival of the new escort when they would join the group being returned to Cartago. Some of the men were unable to withstand the delay and fell ill one after another with spasmodic fevers that left them weakened and immobilized.

Once again, Pedro dreamt of The Mute. She was hanging among the branches of the almond tree in her chrysalis envelope, he below, as before, the dead corals digging into his back. He watched as a cold green fire that seemed to come from inside the wrapping, broke through it, followed by a rain of white bones, smooth and lustrous as the purest marble. They floated down gently between the leaves brushing Pedro like caresses. He awoke spontaneously and found himself sitting up in bed, his arms stretched out, with such an overwhelming sense of sadness that he could not hold back a sob. He walked about all that day feeling sorrowful and alarmed, keeping Catarina close by his side, and at the same time so out of sorts that when Juan approached to ask what the matter was, he snarled at him, "Now, don't be pestering me with your theological doubts. Better go lay one of the Indian women in the bushes. Maybe that'll take care of your problem."

No sooner did the words leave his lips than he regretted having said them. Juan replied calmly, overly restrained, "You may be right. I ought to be out there enjoying women instead of pumping them full of false hopes."

Annoyed with himself, he took Catarina by the hand and took a turn around the compound, retracing his steps over and over again until he was quite familiar with the layout and exact dimensions of the place.

There was a full moon, making everything look bright as day, and he was behaving like a lunatic. It rose over the mountains shedding a milky light upon their bodies. It was so bright that Pedro could have read Juan's breviary if he had had a mind to. He left Catarina asleep and went off, his mind at ease, on one of his aimless, leisurely strolls. The shadow cast on the ground by the cross of the hermitage seemed an invocation for a pagan ritual. He stood in the center of the shadow where the four arms of the cross met contemplating the luminosity that rose along the curve of the sky, recalling nights like this on his beach listening to the constant murmur of the sea, tranquil and hardly perceptible at times, playful so often. The jungle was silent. Not a sound could be heard, not of the night birds nor even the screech owl, nor the passage of the big cats, nor the crackling of the boughs under the weight of the raccoons. The silence was oppressive; all the world was asleep, even the Conquest officer, thank the Lord. He returned to the hut that had been assigned to him. As he stepped over the threshold, he saw a dark shadow *hovering over Catarina. He leapt forward and seized the intruder by the hair. In the dimness, he recognized the rugged features and fearsome stare of Gerónima. Shocked, he let go of her and she moved so rapidly that he later wondered if it had really happened. His mind registered the push with which she thrust him from her, her silhouette in the doorway, and nothing more. Catarina remained asleep, unaware that her aunt had tried to kidnap her. Her life would have taken a very different turn had she succeeded.*

"She might have struck you and taken the child if she was as strong as you have described her," whispered Agueda, moved by the story, "but she didn't because that would have raised an alarm, and she put concern for her people first."

"In any case, she was taking a great risk. If I had come later and found Catarina missing, I would have called for help."

"What did you do, then?"

"I embraced Catarina for the longest time, so shocked I couldn't move. Then I calmed down and decided to notify the officer. I went to the barracks where the soldiers slept and found the guard outside dead, with a spear in his chest. Then, the sound of drums, very far away, scarcely audible. I woke up the officer..."

The officer searched the mission and found nothing. All the Indians had fled. Not even the cooks were there. Cristóbal, the mulatto, who was in Cabécar at the time, said, trembling with fear, that the drums were signaling war. The officer lost his head, shouted orders one minute and contradicted them the next. It was Andrade who took the decision to retreat to Urinama. Pedro followed the troops on horseback, Catarina astride behind him. The five sick soldiers were left behind, abandoned to their fate.

Whipping the horses they rode northwest. From the mountain height they saw the flames and imagined the attackers with their clubs, shields, and shell necklaces, stamping with their short, stocky legs on the rosettes of the altar and the body of Christ that had been left behind, forgotten in the sacrarium.

On remembering, Juan dismounted and knelt to weep and bemoan their sinful negligence, imagining the hosts strewn on the ground like little, white coins. But there was no time to lose and Andrade, scolding him for his useless lamentation, made him get back on his horse. They looked for the last time at the fire and, as if they were at the scene, saw the pigs run off, the cows with their legs broken and throats slit, heard the death cries of the soldiers, sacrifices of the officer to the Indian's blood lust, killed, nobody knew how, among the red tongues of flame that rose to heaven invoking the power of a God impotent to prevent the horror.

"It was thirteen days after Urinama was burned..." Agueda was leaning over, her legs drawn up, arms clutching her body.

"Yes, thirteen or fourteen... We didn't know about it although before long we suspected as much. Then we found the ashes... Rebullida's body was half charred and half devoured by animals... We could not find his head. To tell the truth, we didn't look too carefully. We were anxious to get out of the mountains and to Chirripó as soon as possible."

"The same thing happened there."

"Zamora was dead...before the altar. It seems he was holding mass. There were bodies of a soldier, his wife, and their child...I suppose..."

"The fourteen hermitages of Talamanca burned. There was nothing left of the work of the missionary fathers. Their entire sacrifice! So much effort, so much devotion! All that courage for nothing..." Agueda crossed herself and remained staring into a dim, vague corner.

On the Way of the Cross, some mounted, most on foot, on hands and knees, dragging themselves along the peaks of the fearful precipices, with accidents constantly happening. Andrade broke a leg on a fall from his horse and a hammock had to be improvised to transport him. Four soldiers were hit by arrows from Indians who were following them, herding them out of the mountains, as it were, hustling them on their way. Hunger gnawed at the empty stomachs, and when there were no bananas or wild roots to be found, they chewed on their boots in an effort to deceive their guts. One gravely wounded soldier could not take the strain and fell dying against the hammock in which Andrade was being carried. The priest, stretched out, injured, had the courage to pray a response. A shallow grave was being dug and leaves and branches gathered to put over it in order to give him Christian burial, when an Indian burst out of the thicket to throw himself on his knees, sobbing, in terror, before Andrade, begging for protection. The officer lost no time in grabbing him by the throat to interrogate him. He was a Christian Indian from the Chirripó Christian community, who was running away from the uprising. He related how the priest in charge of the parish, Zamora, was celebrating mass when Comezala and his warriors entered and killed the friar from behind, an arrow transfixing him between the shoulder blades. The officer shook him violently demanding to know why nobody had interfered.

The man, his eyes bulging from their sockets, his hands clenched together, begged for clemency, saying that it was because Comezala had been sent by Presbere. Presbere, he explained, as though uttering the very name scorched his lips, was the most feared one in Talamanca, and wore the face of the Kapá. Presbere was the envoy, the appointed one, chosen by the Kapá to drive the Spaniards out of Talamanca. The corporal seized the man, battering him with questions as to how the Indians of Chirripó knew of that Presbere, who he was, where he lived, and where he was. But the Indian, teeth chattering, suddenly tore loose from the corporal and ran off toward the forest. However, the officer caught up with him and before he could be stopped plunged a knife into his throat.

"Thereby losing a most valuable witness," said Agueda.

"Exactly. The officer was more crazed than that Indian. The name Presbere was impressed upon us, and it seemed to me that I had heard it somewhere at some point, but could not remember."

It was impossible to forget that name. Many days followed without rest until they reached Tuis. Long days and endless nights husbanding bullets as though they were sacred charms. In the last ambush they underwent, neither Pedro nor Andrade was able to hold Juan back from throwing himself bodily into the forefront of the attack with arms widespread. They saw him fall and spent the last of their ammunition in driving the Indians off. When they picked Juan up, the point of the arrow that hung from his chest had stopped miraculously between his ribs and they were able to withdraw it easily. Juan's life was saved but a round, open wound remained.

"Juan had definitely lost his mind," Pedro related, "and went about continually in the same bloodstained cassock..."

"Crazed and naked, too," added Agueda. "They told me that you could see the clean, round wound..."

"Round and fresh. It looked like a small hole made with an awl."

Caterina on his shoulders, he waded rivers and streams that he had once crossed with The Mute. The mud and dampness did not daunt his resolve to come out of this adventure alive and provide for the child. So driven, he was able with the other survivors to reach an Indian village where the chief came out to greet the shattered, hairy band, mouths hanging open with hunger.

He had left behind him the jungle through which he had borne the small body of his daughter, keeping her alive with the fruit of the pijibaye palm. And added to the punishment his body had undergone was the torture of Catarina's questions. It was impossible for him to tell her that the Indians were savage people because she had known only a loving mother and aunt. Nor was he able to explain why Juan wandered about stark naked, eyes sunken in, mumbling incoherently, now in Latin, now in the Indian language.

"I don't know how we managed to survive, nor where the strength came from that enabled us to keep going on that frightful journey, without provisions and the Indians on our heels all the time," said Pedro, as the first rays of daylight filtered in through the open patio door.

Agueda did not comment. She got up, snuffed out the tiny flame left in the dying candle. The fine wrinkles in her face could be counted under the dawn's pitiless light. She was first to say goodnight and leave for her bedroom. Pedro remained in his chair recovering from the exertion of his narrative and in expectation of he had no idea what. Agueda had gone out with a vague and ambiguous smile that could have been interpreted as implying affectionate understanding, or just as easily, veiled mockery. And he felt ill at ease, very uncomfortable, for he had unburdened himself to her at length of many confidences, and she had gone off without a sign of sympathy, taking a chunk of his life along with her and leaving him only that enigmatic smile.

Pedro got up heavily from his chair, his legs cramped. He went out through the same door she had used, rounded the patio in the corridor that led to a second patio where there was a small guest room. The door to Agueda's room was a little ajar, and he could see in as he went by. Seeking her tangible, physical presence to counteract the feeling of desolation in which he had been left, he committed the indiscretion of peeping into the room. She sat on the edge of her wide bed with its canopy of striped, blue silk, the flowered velvet bedspread turned back to expose the sheets with embroidered, lace-trimmed ruffles. He could see in the morning light her clothing, petticoat, tight-fitting bodice, Brittany-cloth blouse lying folded on a bench. Bárbara Lorenzana went over to the bed and sat down beside her mistress who was wearing a long white nightgown. The contrast of her skin and the African's was striking. Agueda lowered her head to the full, round breast of the slave, who began to slowly undo her golden braids, baring the pale nape of the neck. Lorenzana's twisted neck no longer had the expression of cynicism that made it so special but rather one of tenderness and compassion as the Spaniard abandoned herself with sensual languor to the combing of her hair. In this foreshortened view of the two female profiles Pedro sensed a strange and inexplicable intimacy, something that he had been denied. At the same time, this aroused a fit of jealousy in him against the pair, without his knowing why, a jealously that was as stupid as it was ridiculous. He cautiously retreated to the impersonal coldness of the guest room where he plummeted onto his bed, regretting once again that Agueda had put a bed in her children's room for Catarina.

Presbere talks with the Kapá for the last time

The oracular stone on the palm of his hand did not move. The Kapá blew on it three times, taking a long pause between breaths. The stone was not moving. It appeared remote, cold, and alien in the warm light of the fire. When the Kapá began to sing, the cavern did not reply, the echo was deaf. Why had the world gone sterile? Why were the gods silent?

"My time is at an end," said the Kapá. "You will have to continue on to Viceita alone. My face can no longer accompany you, it will return to the World Beyond Below and, so that it may go in beauty and splendor, you must notify the *Atabal* Drummer, the Gravedigger, and the Cacao Dispenser Woman."

"Impossible," protested Presbere. "If Our Land loses the Hidden One, who speaks with the lords of the other worlds and the secret things of the earth, the struggle will die out, no one will fight, it will be a fatal omen."

"I can do nothing to prevent that, and you know it. I told you that my time is ending, as with all borrowed time. No one is the owner of his time."

Troubled, Presbere asked, "Have I done anything wrong?"

"You have done everything properly and well. But this is a world of appearances, and no one can span all the spider's threads except the lords of the World Beyond Below. There, at the last of the worlds, at the final tier, is the knot that ties up all fates, and my sight does not reach that far. I am only a man."

For the second time in his life Presbere felt the terrible gnawing of doubt. His entire task, entire struggle against the Christians had followed a perfect plan, down to the last detail. All the rituals had been observed; he had been careful to a fault in his service. And the stones had spoken favorably. Now, the stones were silent. The cavern silent. The Kapá fallen silent, too.

"Hurry," said the Kapá. "When my body is on the mountain peak, before my bones, no longer in decay, are clean and lustrous, you must go to Viceita so that the Chief Warrior may carry out that which was agreed upon."

"The Chief Warrior speaks with a forked tongue," murmured Presbere.

"Yes. That is true. But be confident. Do you remember what we asked the stones?"

"We asked if the Spaniards would be leaving Our Land."

"And they left. Is it not so?"

"But they will return and take revenge for their dead."

"We also asked if the people of Our Land would live in peace when the Spaniards were gone, and they said they would."

"But we did not ask how long peace would last."

"One does not ask that. As I have told you...time is borrowed."

Pedro takes a crab for God and
finally learns why La Chamberga
was looking for him

He didn't come looking for me at my shop. I was the one who
went to see him at Agueda Pérez de Muro's, who took him and
his little daughter in. When Pedro did not return I could not
understand why. The Mother and I often discussed the matter
without arriving at any explanation for the mystery of his
disappearance. We knew from the lancers that he had insisted on
carrying out the mission of taking the prisoner Hernández and
The Mute to the Christian community at Chirripó. They also told
us that he was half out of his mind. Since the Indian cook of the
monastery also disappeared, we figured they must have gotten
together and made some arrangement. In any case, we kept
kicking the question around and rejected the possibility that he
had fallen off a cliff and died or been killed by an animal in the
jungle. Why did we reject it? Because The Mother read the cards
and the dregs of a cup of chocolate and said that she saw him
alive but could not tell where. That's The Mother for you! She
knows her magic but can't give an answer for everything.

Later on, rumors were brought in by people coming from
Matina, strange stories about a Spaniard who was living in a hut
next to the beach. Then the returning soldiers of San José's escort
told even more outlandish tales: that the city council scribe had
been seen in a place by the sea living with a witch from
Talamanca. The Mother and I even went as far as considering a
rescue operation, but never got to it. Then, the new Governor
Granda y Balbín arrived and life in Cartago became very rough;
everybody had to shift for himself and memory of Pedro began to
fade, to lose importance. Granda is the absolute opposite of

Serrano. It's not for nothing they call him "The Monster." The province couldn't recall a worse governor in its entire history.

Pedro returned sad at heart, on the run from the Indian horde. Very sad! As Doña Oliva Sabuco wrote, the sad of heart dry up and are consumed without fever, or they are paralyzed for being caught between the soul wanting to die and the body to live. Pedro's body was covered with sores. The sad of heart catch skin conditions, like buboes, lice, scabies, and abscesses. He became somnolent, for the sad of heart sleep more than joyous people; each period of wakefulness drains them, and the juice of life that flows from the brain dries up. He was suffering as well from love sickness; the love that merges the man with the beloved woman causing him to lose awareness of his own self. The affection of love can kill creatures other than human beings. When the male pigeon sees that his mate is missing he goes off into a corner and stops eating. To lose what one loves can be torment, can cause unspeakable anguish. I read that an Athenian youth fell in love with the marble statue of a woman; he wanted to buy it, but the senate refused permission, and the young man, in despair, died by his own hand. Human beings sometimes fall in love with nonhumans: Semiramis is said to have loved a horse, Ortensio a moray eel, Jerges, a banana palm...

Perhaps Pedro was in love with The Mute because he thought of her most as a being who belonged to the kingdom of nature. It is also possible that some become enamored of their own longing... Love and desire belong to the type of affection that does not produce ill humor, but which waste the creature in love without chills nor fever...it withers away. Since all understanding is concentrated in that which is loved, on losing the loved one, there is no enjoyment for the lover in anything, not in food, in drink, nor even conversation. And this happens because the discord between body and soul upsets the body. It is said that what inspires man to love is nature's perfection, and this is called...I don't know how...don't know what...or in what way.

Pedro arrived in the condition I described, with chill and dampness in the bones besides. Agueda Pérez took him and his daughter in. Catarina was a very bright child, too serious for her tender years. It was difficult to get her to speak.

I gave Pedro a pair of boots and made slippers of fine leather for her. She never put them on. Her feet, like those of the Indian women, were wide. I taught her how to give her father massages with a special unguent I prepared to soothe his swollen joints. I have no idea whether it was because of the salve or the girl's hands, but the fact is that Pedro's condition was eased.

The first time I came to visit him, I entertained him with an account of how Serrano was finally sent to Guatemala, for neither Father Angulo nor José Pérez de Muro, Agueda's father, was able to raise the amount necessary to make good the deficit on the books owing to the King. His place was taken by a governor who promoted the missions because he was convinced that the friars would succeed in pacifying the Indians of Talamanca, but he did not last very long. Then Granda took over. Granda marched into Cartago as though it were a battlefield in Flanders. Military discipline took over, and he put the whole population into a straitjacket with heavy fines for the Spaniards and prison and floggings for the others. There was no longer freedom of any kind. Notices were posted every day on the pole outside the city hall of his new good-government, proclamations flatly forbidding certain things, which to us was outrageous: dice and cards illegal; The Mother's gaming house closed down; bearing arms outlawed; cohabiting outside of marriage prohibited; no work other than slave labor permitted in Matina. Also, the owners of cacao plantations were obliged to defend their property against the pirates at their own expense. Since Granda had made it illegal to do business with them, the pirates stole the cacao which they had always exchanged for goods.

I can't tell you everything Granda declared illicit. He even clamped down on sorcery which almost involved me because the ignorant brute mistook my science and pharmacology for witchcraft and spells. The jails never had so many tenants before nor was the square ever so crowded with spectators for the lashing of blacks, mulattos, and Indians. When the cacao growers began to rebel—for no governor had ever treated them so harshly—to win them over, Granda approved the circulation of cacao as legal currency. This was a serious error. The cacao producers tended to raise its value and the merchants coming from Nicaragua and Panama to depreciate it, which has created instability that affects us all. In any case, Granda was not able to win over the cacao growers, who for the last year have been petitioning the Supreme Government to bring Serrano back. The rumor now is that Philip the Bold has already appointed a successor. However, since no news is arriving because of the civil war, it is hard to say what the next months will bring. Furthermore, the Indian uprising has added a new dimension to this free-for-all.

When I saw Pedro somewhat improved, in order to cheer him up, I took him to a joint run by a fat-assed little *mulata* that was camouflaged as a broom factory. It had absolutely nothing in common with The Mother's place, of course, absolutely nothing. The Mother closed her gaming house on orders of Granda, went to live on the slope of a volcano and is no longer in business. She operates a still there but just for her personal use and the occasional friends like us who visit from time to time. Pedro and I went in past stacks of brooms to the back where there was a ratty makeshift barroom. There were just a few customers because everybody is scared of Granda making a roundup and their being dragged off to jail or the whipping post. Pedro sat down, looked around the place vaguely, and began throwing back the rum like there was no tomorrow, and as he swilled his drinks, he spilled his story. When he came to the end, he said, "God and nature are one and the same." That sounded like heresy to me and I said to him that nothing can be considered as perfect as God because we humans lack understanding of the absolute. I began philosophizing on the subject as Pedro listened to me, letting it in one ear and out the other. I told him he'd get sick if he didn't let up, and he answered that he drank because he had once known perfection and that it was something absolutely impossible for a human being to endure.

"God does exist," he mumbled in a rum-soaked voice.

"He exists a little, a lot, or not at all," I answered. "As far as I'm concerned, too much."

"You're drunk," he said, his tongue thick. "God exists and has the form of a blue crab. He walks sideways and has one claw for tearing the flesh off people."

I got scared. Nobody was listening to us, but you never can tell, so I quickly changed the subject. "Captain Casasola's wife is spoiling you too much. She always went overboard for you. Watch out, Captain Casasola is a dangerous man."

"Forget it! Agueda has rabbit teeth, and besides she's old and wrinkled as a bagpipe."

"Not really... She still looks like a juicy piece to me..."

"I'm not interested in women anymore... You don't get me. You didn't understand a word of what I told you. Agueda is a good woman who was touched by my daughter. And she's going to help me find a job."

"Where?"

"In the government."

"With Granda?"

"Yes."

I figured whatever it was that the fat-assed *mulata's* rugged rum was letting me figure. "That means Casasola is looking to put somebody he can trust close to Granda. Granda will never accept you."

"You're mistaken. He already has."

I was still able to think. "Which means that Granda is looking for a way to win over Casasola."

"For what?"

"What do you think, my friend? You don't know which end is up, anymore... To win over the cacao growers so they'll stop going to Guatemala looking to get Serrano back."

"And why now? Why hasn't he done it already?"

"Because there was no Indian rioting before, jackass, that's why. Because Granda is in very bad shape between pirates attacking Matina and Indians in rebellion. Because if he doesn't come out on top in this tight spot, he'll lose his post which will be a black mark against him for his future." I could see he had no idea what I was talking about. "Your brains, Pedro, are completely rusted out. Granda has found a way of keeping his bridge from collapsing for when he has to cross it..."

"Does Casasola have that much power?" my friend asked, sounding surprised.

"That much or more. After his father-in-law died, he became one of the richest men in the province. He has enemies among his own people, though...remember López Conejo?"

"From Malaga. A bachelor. Played cards at The Mother's on Fridays."

"That's him. He's not as loaded as Casasola and maybe that explains why he's committed himself to Granda all the way, like old man Mier Ceballos... Now, Blas González...remember Blas González of the Royal Bank? Well, Blas, as usual, is playing a double game. He broke with Granda because he wanted to relieve him of the chief magistrateship of the Inquisition. The two posts are incompatible, you know. And González spent nearly a year hiding in a monastery while Casasola was in Guatemala, where he was sent by the city council to push for the removal of Granda. It seems, however, that Casasola filed no appeal before the Royal Tribunal and González cannot forgive him for it. Granda cooled down when Casasola got back without having done anything and canceled the warrant of arrest pending against Blas González. There is a bitter rivalry now between Blas and José de Casasola. They can't stand the sight of each other but there they are in the same boat so they have to keep up appearances...but there's something very amusing about a side of Granda's personal life...he has illicit lovers flogged, while he cohabits with a personal mistress himself, besides which he has a daughter by her. Can you guess who she is?"

I figured he wouldn't care so I let him know: "Nicolasa Guerrero."

"Who?"

"Nicolasa...that Nicolasa! The girl from Ujarrás you were falling for once upon a time, the one with the thick eyebrows, very black hair and very white skin."

"Such a young thing with that old fellow? I understood he was not a young man."

"Check the numbers, Pedro. Nicolasa was about seventeen when you left. That would make her twenty-four or five or so, now."

"How about that!"

I could see a dark, rum-soaked cloud settling in over him.

Hurrying to change the subject, I asked him, "How come you haven't asked me yet whether or not I got hitched?"

"That's true. Well, did you?"

"No. But I did hook up with someone for a time, and they tell me there's a little coffee-colored kid running around who resembles me, but I'm not at all that sure he's mine. Then, the woman got mixed up with Carranza, the silversmith, and I preferred to step aside. Triangles were never my favorite figure. I'm alone...very much alone."

Conversation drifted. The little *mulata* filled our gourds again, whispering at the same time that she couldn't make ends meet just on her sales of rum. Neither Pedro nor I had any interest in a woman that night, so we kept on just drinking.

"We now have a fine bordello," I commented, "adobe, and all tiled and elegant, but with nobody inside..."

Our mood turned melancholy and little by little we began losing the thread of what we were talking about. The last I remember there is that I was leaning my head against Pedro's shoulder and he was wiping my tears away with his shirt sleeve. He was snuffling and talking nonsense until the little fat-ass threw us out in a very unfriendly manner, yelling that she didn't want queers in her joint, that it was bad for her business.

I got Pedro back to the Casasola house on the southwest corner of the square as best as I could and propped him up there against a column in the hall with a bunch of blue flowers on his head. A momentary clearing must have opened in my alcoholic fog for suddenly remembered that I hadn't told him everything I meant to and had left out the most important of all.

"Pedro, psst, Pedro, wake up. That woman was here looking for you...La Chamberga. Ask The Mother because she was staying with her and left you a letter."

* * *

He preferred to go by himself to The Mother's house on the slope of the volcano. He wanted no witnesses to what The Mother would be telling him, and to read the letter alone. The shoemaker explained to him how to find the place, and soon after climbing the path he met an Indian half-breed who was driving a pair of calves up the same hill. He walked with him through scattered settlements, past cultivated fields and pastures. Then, between cottony clouds, The Mother's little house, red-tiled roof and thatched porch, came into sight, looking out toward the valley, the entire city at its feet. He went through a little gate where he had to defend himself against the inconsiderate threats of a group of unfriendly geese until The Mother appeared on the porch and shooed away her feathered guards.

The Mother, her vast bulk wrapped in a simple shawl, her eyes lost in a sea of kind, cushioned plumpness, threw open her arms to enfold Pedro like a great eiderdown quilt. Moved to tears by the heartfelt display of her affection, Pedro let himself be overwhelmed by the joy of seeing her again, realizing at the same instant how much he was consoled by the *mulata's* very presence. She then held him away from her like a wisp separated from a haystack, as she planted a sonorous kiss on each cheek.

"You must know that I closed the gaming house," she said as she caressed his hand, "for my head is more important than a deck of cards. Don't you agree?"

She showed him in and took a bottle of a clear liquid out of a little cupboard, saying, "It gets very cold up here, and this reunion calls for a celebration."

"That sounds great," said Pedro, smiling, happy, and the two sat on a pair of small benches, half of one of the mothers' buttocks overflowing the edge of her seat.

"And so, I am now busy at other things," she said, serving the drinks in two small pewter mugs. "I'm growing potatoes and onions and can't complain. I'm doing well."

"I'm delighted," smiled Pedro, swallowing the liquor scorching his tonsils on its way down.

The Mother burst into hearty laughter. "Burns, doesn't it?" and added, "I still have my Barrio house. If you need it, it's at your disposal."

"Thank you, but I'm staying at Captain Casasola's."

"Well, one never knows... Some time ago I felt I wanted to do something to help when I learned of the terrible things that had happened to you. What a frightful thing to think of you having been locked up in an Inquisition prison. Why didn't you let me know? I could have done something for you."

Pedro gave a start. "How did you find that out? Who told you?"

"Your friend, La Chamberga."

"And how did she know? I left Seville without having talked to her."

"Oh, what an innocent you are, my dear. La Chamberga knew all about it and went looking for you to let you know... She left a letter for you. I'll fetch it right away but first you must tell me about yourself. What terrible things you went through and how you suffered. I suspected that you were running away from something very ugly and sinister... Now, I understand how you could have been such a fool. Small wonder!" She saw the expression of terror on Pedro's face, and her tone of voice immediately changed to one of sweetness. "Don't be alarmed, La Chamberga is no gossip and my lips have been sealed. Don't get that look in your eyes, nobody is overhearing us except the geese, and all they know how to do is cackle. Wait just a minute. I'll be right back."

She pulled herself up and went to the rear of the house. It was remarkable how that palm-tree body of hers could have put on such an accumulation around the hips. She left the room rolling languidly like an overloaded ship and returned, bearing an envelope sealed with wax.

"She waited a long while for you but finally tired. Time kept dragging on, and it began looking so uncertain that she gave up and went off with a Galician who had a mining claim in Honduras. He was a good man and promised her his love and the mine, besides. La Chamberga was a very special woman and loved you very much. She crossed the ocean and traveled leagues to find you. She even wanted to look for you at that place on the coast where they said you were living, but I talked her out of it, because all sorts of disturbing gossip was going around about you. They were saying that the place where you lived was a Garden of Eden in the form of a woman's breast. And there were rumors that your house was a fabulous compound filled with fantastic creatures who guarded you; frightful monsters, gryphons with the body of a lion and wings of an eagle, dragons that spit flames, and elephants with fish tails... It was also being said that this strange kingdom of yours was being run by a woman who made you drowsy with her songs, who was seen coming out of the water with the body of a siren, followed by giant squids and immense black and white marine centipedes that walked among gorgons covered with scales that had tusks like pigs, and medusa snakes growing out of their heads... La Chamberga did not believe those stories and said that Spaniards always had wild imaginations that distorted the world and that, knowing you as she did, the only true part was probably that about the breast."

That was undoubtedly a true picture of La Chamberga, hardheaded and foulmouthed. Said Pedro, wanly, "She was right and she was wrong. Yes, there was a woman who held me there, but she had little breasts, like lemons."

He was completely disarmed by the tenderness and understanding in The Mother's eyes, as she patted him on the shoulder, and said, "Tell me the story, all of it. You'll feel better."

And Pedro told her what he had told Juan, all that had been weighing upon him for years, that he had not told Smiles nor Agueda during that night of unburdening. He spoke of the rejected son whom Gerónima had taken away. And then he described how deeply he had suffered when The Mute died and, in putting her into words, he began to babble.

The Mother took his two hands in hers and said, "Yes, I can understand, I can understand." And he, imbued with her warmth, confessed, repented, and the Mother absolved him, saying. "What else could you do? It was not your fault. Life was to blame."

By the time Pedro convinced himself that the great villain was life itself, so mean, always so cruel to the poor human being, so vulnerable, so weak...and poor me, oh, misery me, how ashamed I am of myself, the mist had penetrated into the room where they were seated, but The Mother's great body was impenetrable. She was massaging his icy hands, soothing him, forgiving him all his misdeeds, justifying his actions, finding an explanation for the most outlandish things, with her honeyed voice, warm flesh, eyes glowing with generosity in her rotund face, exuding love, all-forgiving, brimming over with forbearance.

"Well, now," she exclaimed, standing up and leading him into the kitchen, "life goes on and we must be courageous and live it."

A big pot filled with potatoes was boiling on the fire.

"God is a crab," remarked Pedro.

"If that's what you'd like to call him, do so," she answered. "I'm conducting an experiment with potatoes that a former customer of the gaming house brought me from the south of

Chile. They call them *coraílas* there, which sounds like a name for a woman. But I don't know if they'll grow in this climate. I distilled the liquor I gave you from potatoes. It's very strong, isn't it? And now, here's the letter La Chamberga left for you. Go ahead and read it, I know you're anxious to."

Pedro took it and gingerly broke the seal. He repeated that God was a crab. The Mother smiled. The letter was from his maestro Servando, in his unmistakable handwriting.

"La Chamberga told me one other thing," the Mother said, noting his hesitancy, giving him time to collect himself. "She told me that when you get drunk you are capable of the worst foolishness. You're not drunk, now, are you?"

"No, and I'm not going to do anything foolish." And he turned to the letter which read, as follows:

"I haven't much time to write all the things I would like to because your friend La Chamberga is leaving in a little while to follow your trail in the New World, to tell you all about the things that are in this letter. She was trying to reach me for a long time but I didn't want to see her because it seemed strange for me to be hearing from a tavern-keeper and I was suspicious. I will tell you what you should know and more that would be of interest.

"The day you caused the fuss in La Chamberga's tavern, if you will recall, you said, among many other ill-considered ravings, that "To have a French king would be a fine thing." The Inquisitor Mendoza, knowing what Portocarrero was up to, was going around with his ear to the ground, and thought that you were an agent of the Cardinal trying to influence public opinion in favor of a French King. So he had you picked up and brought to Triana Castle to be interrogated by a confidential censor of the Inquisition.

"I found this out some time after you left, when the death of the King loosened many tongues. I also learned that your famous phrase came to the ears of Cardinal Portocarrero. He was very concerned that you might be on to his machinations and bribed a jailer to keep harassing you in the hope that you would come out with something about the plan for putting a Frenchman on the Spanish throne. But you, my friend, couldn't confess anything because you didn't know anything. So you escaped and they kept hunting for you under your real name. I say your real name because when they picked you up you were registered under the pseudonym of Pedro de la Baranda. I am ashamed to admit that my lack of imagination prompted me to get you papers under that same name.

"Since the Inquisitor Mendoza lost out (a fresh King for a dead King, a French one in this case), he has become much more circumspect, and you can return to Spain without fear and resume the activities that previously concerned us..."

Servando's letter went on to relay bits of gossip of the kind he was so fond: how María Luisa de Saboya, upon her marriage to King Philip V refused to go to bed with him until after the fourth day of marriage; how the Queen's first lady-in-waiting, a certain princess of the Ursinos, an ambitious old woman, had their majesties completely under her domination through the black arts, and how that same old crone governed Spain in connivance with Madame de Maintenon the morganatic wife of Louis XIV. Servando closed his letter with one of those quips he was so given to: "Spain is a stew cooked up by a royal pirate crew with assorted side dishes made by a pair of supercilious bitches."

Having read through the letter twice more, Pedro remained sitting with it in his hand for a long time. At last, he understood why the Inquisition seized him and, then, thinking of Servando's closing words, he smiled.

Observing her visitor as she sat next to the fire, The Mother waited placidly for his reaction as she said, "I hope this letter that's been here expecting you for so long will bring a little peace to your life."

Pedro allowed himself time to digest the news Servando's letter brought him and to reach a conclusion as to whether or not it really spelled peace for him. On the one hand it cleared up the past, but the future was as dim as ever. Finally, he said, without looking at The Mother, "Imagine this, Mother... A barrel of wine is to blame for my being here!"

"Don't tell me you drank the whole thing!" The Mother's eyebrows arched upwards. "A whole barrelful!"

"I didn't drink it. It was what I read from it."

"What's that, now? Tell me how it happened. I can read cards and the dregs in a chocolate mug, but I never heard nor much less imagined anybody could read wine."

"It was actually the wine barrel. Somebody had written 'Piss for the French' on the side of it."

"Then, it wasn't the barrel that was to blame but the rascal who wrote that and you yourself for paying attention to such a nasty thing. Aren't the French our allies?"

"Now, yes, but they were our enemies, then. And I didn't repeat what I read. I said, "I hope they give us a French king.""

"What's so bad about that. Our king is French, isn't he?"

"Yes, but before... Never mind, there's no point in my explaining it to you. The whole business is too complicated. And, another thing. My real name isn't Pedro de la Baranda, it's Pedro Albarán."

"What do you mean? I always thought it was Pedro Albarán."

"Oh, what a mess! I don't know where I'm at anymore! Now that this letter has cleared up everything for me, I'm more confused than ever. My life and myself don't make sense to me anymore."

Pedro held the sheet of paper out to the flames which devoured it enthusiastically as if anxious to learn the latest court gossip.

The Mother then accompanied him out to say goodbye. Pointing to the valley, she said, "Look. Look at that world down there and tell me what you see."

"I see...the crosses of Saint Nicholas, of La Soledad...the bell tower of the parish church, the roof of the city hall and, over there...that must be the monastery."

"Now, tell me what it looks like to you."

"What can I say? Kind of small!"

"That's why I like living here. The world down there looks tiny. In comparison, my geese look huge."

As he walked back over the path that had led him to the solution of a mystery, Pedro felt a desire cropping up to see Juan and share the news that had come in the letter, if his head had straightened out in the meantime.

He had not had time for a long talk with the Father Superior of the monastery, although he had spoken briefly to him. He was now a very old man with a handsome white beard, his hair turned completely gray. The Father had obtained a pair of spectacles from Guatemala but, obviously, they did not correct his problem for he was always looking over the tops of them. Pedro was told that he had become more absentminded and more prone to ignore disorder in the monastery, but his impression was that he had grown more kindly and tolerant than ever before. This meant that the monastery was rolling along on its own impetus. Few changes had taken place in the city over the seven years he had been away: Three more streets paved, the bordello, Agueda's house, and a small increase in the population of the Barrio of the Coloreds. Most noteworthy, however, were the changes in day-to-day living wrought by Granda y Balbín's repressive measures. The quality of life was not what it used to be. The easygoing atmosphere of live and let live, the gossipy chitchat of the days of Serrano were missing, the pleasant rubbing of elbows on the street corners, the little get-togethers after High Mass, things of the past. Mules were no longer to be seen grazing in the main square. In their place stood the whipping post, sinister and menacing, bloodstained. Pigs and chickens no longer had the run of the dirty drainage ditches and the mud in the streets. People retired early and were not often to be seen in public places. However, the impact of the changes forced on the inhabitants of Cartago by Granda was felt most in the Barrio of the Coloreds, now silent and moribund...no more strumming guitars and rebecs, no sones no vihuelas, no wild dancing, gone the nostalgic and sentimental songs that made the whole city vibrate. The little mulata's joint where Pedro went drinking and sharing confidences with the shoemaker was a sordid and gloomy place where even the drunks had to put a damper on their carousing.

On the highroad, never for a moment empty of smugglers and mules laden with goods, not even ghosts of the pirate Morgan, the Headless Horseman, or the Wagon Without Oxen were to be seen. After six o'clock, when the sun had set, a black sheet of silence and fear settled in over the streets and houses, broken only by the lugubrious clanking of lances and sentinels' shouts, measures instituted by Granda to forestall a coup by members of the city council, or the nobility, or even the church, because he wasn't very fond of either the priests or Angulo, now a vicar. Granda himself was spending almost no time in Cartago, holed up in Ujarrás at the house and sugar mill he had provided for his concubine, Nicolasa Guerrero.

The people were saying that Granda had eased off to some extent since the arrival of the survivors from Talamanca. The shoemaker remarked to Pedro that there was nothing like a common enemy to bring together the bitterest of enemies, an observation which was not off the mark. The general dismay, aggravated by the fact that everybody had believed in the success of the mission as reported by Rebullida, turned all eyes to Granda. The news of the native uprising must have come as a great shock to him for he closed himself inside Nicolasa's house, would see no one, and ignored all the complaints that arrived from Cartago demanding his appearance.

José de Casasola called a meeting at his house for a group of important Spaniards, to which he invited Pedro, so that they could discuss what to do about Talamanca. Very annoyed because he wanted no involvement in any decision about that, Pedro suggested that Andrade and the Conquest officer be invited. However, Andrade's broken leg kept him confined while the Conquest officer had caught the tertian fevers, and there was no moving him on account of the uncontrollable convulsions and delirium that kept recurring every third day. Pedro, then, had no choice but to attend Casasola's meeting as an observer. Rafael Fajardo, the auctioneer, who sold Bárbara to Lorenzo, who knew Talamanca very well, having been an officer with the previous relief contingent, arrived shortly after he did. He was followed by: the priest Angulo, who had undoubtedly made a pact with the devil in view of the extraordinary youthfulness of his ever-present spit curls; López Conejo, fiftyish, but well-preserved, sturdy, with a slight paunch, and a gray mustache that lent him an air of gentility; José de Mier Ceballos, fortyish, content with life for he had lost his infertile wife and remarried a fertile one the same year. He looked healthy and his blonde hair, typical of the Burgos mountains, aroused a certain feeling of insecurity among the others in view of his well-known ties to the President of the Royal Tribunal of Santiago de Guatemala.

They entered, one by one, took seats and listened to Rafael Fajardo, who seemed gratified at having been included since he was not exactly a member of the inner circle of soirée organizers

and cacao plantation owners. Fajardo was relating his experiences
as a Conquest officer in Talamanca and giving his opinion on
what should be done if it was decided to send out a force to
punish the Indians. In his fifties, but still strong and active, he
oozed self-satisfaction as he described appropriate sites for
ambushing. The Polo brothers, now much more subdued than in
the Golden Gang days when they thundered their horses into The
Mother's patio, listened to him with thinly-veiled expressions of
scorn. The topic had been under discussion for some time when
Blas González Coronel arrived quite late. Pedro noted Casasola
tense up at the sight of the man as he passed through the room, a
twisted half-smile on his lips. The only visible change in him was
the spectacles on his vulperine nose. Impeccable, he had not
gained an ounce, his expression of cunning and cynicism perfectly
well-preserved. He seemed to be walking with his head three feet
above the heads of the others, not because he was taller than
they but because he felt himself above them. Courteous and crafty,
he quieted the assemblage as he took a seat, every inch the former
cavalry captain, former public scribe of the city council and the
administration, current magistrate of the Inquisition, Deputy
Director of the Royal Bank, also permanent familiar of the
Inquisition, and still Sergeant Major, resplendent in the sacred
halo of his branded herd in Aserrí, his cacao in Matina,
Tucurrique and Tuis, his fourteen slaves, the inconsolable
widowhood of his erstwhile wife Doña Bernarda de Fonseca, and
his current spouse Doña Juana Arburola; passionate lover, as well,
of a certain Micaela Solano whose physical attributes had been
described in detail by the shoemaker when he was bringing Pedro
up to date on the deeds and misdeeds of each of the notorious
gentlemen of the Very Noble and Loyal City of Cartago.

José de Casasola sat at the head of the table in full awareness
of his own considerable halo of accomplishments—not to be
outshone by those of Blas González nor Mier Ceballos—namely,
councilman, Chief of Militia, familiar of the Inquisition, and son-
in-law of Don José Pérez de Muro (absent for reason of interment
in the parish church cemetery.)

Pedro was amused to see the bluffing game that developed
between Casasola and Blas González in the light of what Smiles
had told him about them, namely, that the city council had

entrusted Casasola with the mission of going to Guatemala to petition for the removal of Granda while the other waited in the monastery for him to return. Casasola finally returned after a year in which he accomplished nothing and Blas González left his refuge in humiliation.

Sitting next to his host, Pedro examined his profile out of the corner of his eye. Agueda's husband, no longer young, still maintained a certain youthful arrogance, his hair wild but somewhat more subdued and darker in color, his mouth curiously feminine. Casasola glanced over at someone made unrecognizable by the passage of time, a beautiful youth, black as ebony, who was decked out in an absurd velvet coat, lace collar and cuffs, gilt buttons, and pants so tight that his thighs seemed on the point of bursting open the cloth. This handsome little black was Jose Canela, the same slave child with the spike in his leg that Agueda's mother had bought on the day Lorenzana was auctioned off and given to her son-in-law to be his page. Casasola motioned to the boy who limped to the corner of the room where there was a crock of water. He limped not because one leg was shorter than the other but because his foot was deformed. He filled a silver mug and brought it to his master.

"Gentlemen," said Casasola, "Spain is going through one of its worst periods. I have received news that Louis XIV of France is attempting to negotiate peace with the Archduke and his allies behind the back of his grandson Felipe, our Catholic majesty."

"But José," said Blas González, drumming on the table, "did you bring us here to inform us of what's happening on the Peninsula or to let us know what we are going to do about Talamanca? I'm in a hurry and would like to get straight to the point."

Casasola covered up his annoyance by sending José Canela for more water, after which he said, "Very well, down to brass tacks. The Indians have risen up, killed two friars and ten soldiers, and wounded many. All the hermitages and monasteries in Talamanca are in ashes. Nobody knows for certain what the savages are planning, whether they will be satisfied with what they have already done or if they intend to push on to Cartago in alliance with the half-breed pirates."

A snicker from Blas González could be clearly heard. Pedro

saw Casasola's fingers clench and stretch towards his rapier. Pedro wondered why he was wearing a weapon in the house. His hand then relaxed and returned to the table top, as he said, "Why don't you take the floor, Don Blas González? You're interrupting me constantly."

"Come off it, José," he replied, "I have no intention of interfering with what you have to say. But I would like you all to know that I am here only as an observer."

"For Granda?" asked the priest Angulo, squinting at him.

"Yes. He asked me to inform him what was decided here."

"And why doesn't the sonofabitch put in his own appearance?" yelled Casasola in a rage.

"Keep a cool head, man. Granda is disposed to support the decision reached here. And that is precisely what we should do...take measures."

"I have already made my decision, and it is to march straightaway to Talamanca and punish those heathens... Gentlemen, Matina is abandoned, the cacao is rotting there, and we are all losing a good opportunity to do business with the French."

"The problem," Mier Ceballos put in, "the dilemma, lies in the fact that Granda will never agree to pulling out Indians to serve in Matina because they belong to the crown..."

"That is precisely the point I wanted to explain when Blas interrupted me!" Casasola banged the table once triumphantly with his fist. "Gentlemen, with the situation on the peninsula so serious and so unpredictable, the colonies are left on their own. Governor Granda is not the one to decide what should be done about Talamanca. He has been here too short a time, barely two years. It is up to us! We, the people of this city are the ones who must take power into our hands and settle the matter ourselves."

"I already told you, José, that Granda agrees to support any decision we may make here," Blas González said patiently. "So, you don't have to go into that matter any further."

Mier Ceballos smiled and the Polo brothers, thoroughly disconcerted, stared at Blas González. The priest Angulo took advantage of the pause to pull out a handkerchief and mop his forehead. The room had been made oppressively hot because of a brazier sent in by Agueda.

"Can't that brazier be taken out?" Angulo wanted to know and asked José Canela for water.

"In any case," said Mier Ceballos, pursing his lips and letting his eyelids droop, "it seems to me that the Royal Tribunal is going to protest if those Indians are removed from their lands..."

"But isn't that precisely what the missionaries were doing?" asked Lopez Conejo.

"Yes," seconded Ceballos who was also a defender of the Indians. "Yes, but to remove them for purposes of colonization, not for working in the Matina cacao plantation. They are the king's tribute-paying Indians, dammit!"

"Piss on the king! If we fall on our faces being respectful, the cacao plantations will be ruined and so will we. Or maybe you expect the Bourbon and the Austrian will come over and harvest the cacao for us?"

Casasola was so irritated that he got up and began to pace around the table. Pedro, amused, watched the heads all turn toward Blas González waiting for him to speak. Adjusting his spectacles, he finally came out with "But, José, I don't see why you can't understand me... This is the third time I'm telling you that Granda will agree to whatever is decided here."

"And what has to be decided," said Angulo, apparently bored to death, "is when and how to go into Talamanca and punish the assassins."

"There has to be an incentive." Fajardo raised a finger asking for the floor, and said, "There has to be an incentive for recruiting the necessary forces... Allow me to make a suggestion: offer as slaves the Indians they take prisoner in a just war."

"That would be very difficult," put in Mier Ceballos. "Slaves of a just war come under the laws of 1534 and the new digest of 1680 establishes that..."

"Perhaps it would be advisable to suspend this meeting," interrupted Angulo, getting to his feet. "Let us wait for His Lordship of Ujarrás to arrive and discuss the matter with him. We are not going to come to an agreement today."

José Canela opened the door, Angulo went out, and Pedro took advantage of the moment to slip away to his room. The last words he heard on the way out were: "...according to the laws of 1680, only Araucans, Mindanaos, and Caribs may be enslaved..."

The new secretary of the Governor's Office entangles himself in his own contradictions as war preparations build

The main office of the city council looked very different. Pedro's desk had been shifted away from the window to a corner in the rear and was piled up with papers and useless articles. Over the rectangular stain on the wall where the portrait of Charles II the Bewitched, had hung, there was now a painting of a man with a normal-size jaw—Philip V, who shared the space with his wife María Luisa de Saboya, the same lady who had refused to sleep with him until the fourth day after the wedding, as Servando had said in his letter. In Pedro's opinion, the two portraits must have been copies of Mexican originals, judging from the portraitist's personal approach to art and poetic sense of humor, which had given the queen a large scarlet disk on each cheek and a mouth so red that she seemed on the point of bursting into a bawdy roundelay. The national colors stood guard beside them and above the lintel on the door to the armory hung the shield of the city of Cartago: *FIDE ET PACE.*

The last winter showers were falling on the roof tiles and though it was early the room felt chilly.

The shutters were half-closed and a man sat in shadow at the end of a table beneath the portraits of the two monarchs. He stood up, walked around the table and stopped to stare at Pedro. Pedro launched his examination of the man—starting at his feet, his gaze traveled up from the toes of the deerskin boots, counting seven solid silver buckles as it went up the calf; climbed the tight-fitting moss-green trousers; skimmed the binding along the edge of the jacket as he counted the buttons, also of silver; spanned his waist strangled by a sash; estimated the count of gray hairs protruding from under the open shirt collar; skipped to the narrow forehead; then ventured to descend to the bloated face, the cruel, stony eyes and the thick, whitish mustache that hung over the thin, compressed lips. Granda y Balbín wore his hair long, caught up in back with a short bow. When he opened his mouth to speak, a choked-off, barely audible voice emerged as though from a prison cell in which the vocal chords acted as the bars.

Pedro tried hard to maintain his composure and refrain from collapsing with laughter upon the meeting-room table. It was utterly ridiculous to hear a man so notorious as authoritarian, tyrannical, dictatorial, and cruel talking in that way, stretching out his neck to ease the painful expulsion of sound.

"You can sit...at this desk...starting tomorrow."

The Governor made the sound "orrow" as if it were costing him his last breath.

It was tragicomical. How could this character provoke such dread? Pedro watched in astonishment as he bent over the table, took up pen and paper and wrote a note which he handed to Pedro. It said: "Don José Casasola told me you were the city council scribe, so you already know the job. Report to my Lt. General Don José de Mier Ceballos for further orders."

That was the entire extent of his interview with Granda y Balbín. Curious about his inability to speak normally, Pedro walked over to Smiles's shop. The shoemaker laughed and explained. "He talked normally when he arrived but he began losing his voice right away. Now, you can see he's getting thin. Before, he couldn't hide the bulge of his belly even with his sash and now you can't even see a bulge when he buttons his jacket. Granda runs the government with slips of paper. That way he doesn't have to show up anywhere in person and can spend long periods at Nicolasa Guerrero's. You know how the written word is feared in these parts, so it's a very effective procedure. Nobody likes to see things in print. If you look into the files you'll see them filled with Granda's little notes. They say the old fox has copies made of them which he takes to his house in Ujarrás. Yes, indeed, Granda's bits of paper sow panic."

"Everything about him sows panic," agreed Pedro, "until he opens his mouth."

"Yes, he looks like an iguana with eyes like an evil old witch.

Frankly, I can't understand how Nicolasa can go to bed with that decrepit old wreck. Certainly not for love. The gossip is that old Guerrero offered him his daughter when Granda spotted her one afternoon at a celebration of the Virgin of Ujarrás. The Guerrero family is now enjoying great prosperity."

"I'm worried," Pedro said. "I don't really have any idea of how to maneuver between Granda and Casasola."

"Bah! Don't be imagining trouble! If Casasola got the old guy to give you the job, it's because they will be working together in the Talamanca campaign. He wants to distinguish himself so's not to be removed and, feeling ill now, he wants to govern in peace. Casasola and his crew, on their part, need hands for Matina. The fit couldn't be more perfect."

"But what's going to happen to the missions? What will the King say?"

"Bah! They count for nothing!"

* * *

That's what I told him...they have no weight. Because that's the size of it. Things in Spain are all too uncertain and the country is drifting. Granda is losing control, and the cacao growers are taking advantage to govern for their benefit. Another thing: looking at it cold-bloodedly, punishing Talamanca would be to my benefit. It would be a good chance to find the apprentices I need, get myself a couple of young Indians and build up my business. I decided to enlist but didn't tell him Pedro a word. I was pumping him about what it was like there in the mountains, if there were lots of snakes, whether the Indians were as savage as they say, if it was possible to get enough food should there be no beef available. To make a long story short, I was asking him so many questions that he began to suspect that I thought the idea of attacking Talamanca wasn't all that bad and so his attitude towards me began to change. He clammed up, became distant, grouchy, unfriendly and actually disagreeable. By then Pedro had been working at the city council for about a month under Mier Ceballos and was in charge of recruitment.

* * *

Returning to his old desk was unpleasant. Pedro had no complaints about Mier Ceballos who left him pretty much alone, not interfering in his work except to give simple, direct orders. Perhaps it was the very situation of being left to his devices that bothered him. He would have much preferred simply taking orders.

Besides, he no longer had anybody to talk to. Smiles was now taken up with the idea of enlisting to go to Talamanca and finding himself a couple of Indian apprentices. At least, that was what he claimed. Pedro did not feel that was the whole story; rather he believed that the shoemaker was keen on the war for its own sake. Perhaps he was fed up with his unstimulating trade and its daily grind and for that reason saw the war as a new experience, an exciting adventure. In any case, the fact of the matter was that Pedro and Smiles were estranged. Nor was he able to talk to Juan de las Alas. Since his return to Cartago, the little friar spent hours in silence contemplating the roses in the garden, speaking to no one. Catarina was the only one who could draw him out of his introversion. Juan passed the time with Catarina, killing plant lice, driving away ants, and weeding the garden, doing their best to protect the roses against their natural enemies. There was always a small, stubborn, dark stain on his cassock at the height of the nipple, the site of the Indian arrow wound that refused to heal over.

As for Andrade, when his broken leg had mended, he left for Guatemala to appeal for support in punishing Talamanca. Juan, then, was the only missionary eyewitness of the Indian uprising; confused and melancholy he was a quite ineffectual one. He had not recovered from his compulsion to go naked and every now and then would strip in the monastery corridor, as if the cassock interfered with his destroying the plant lice. One day, Agueda's sister Doña Josefa happened to come by on her way to confession just as one of those episodes was in progress. Screaming with horror, she raised such a row that a ray of lucidity entered his foggy brain and, on his own initiative, he hurriedly dressed himself. That was the last time women were allowed to enter by the garden wall. To keep Juan busy, the Father Superior wanted to return him to his former duties in the kitchen. However, the cooks, two black slaves, reported that all he did was weep and stand staring like an idiot into the cooking pot. To the friars in the monastery Juan was a brother with a screw loose and to the kindly Superior he was a victim of the devil's machinations. Andrade, consumed by rancor, had left for Guatemala to demand revenge for Rebullida. Juan, driven by no sense of rancor, languished, alone, victim of buried woes. When Pedro visited him, the bluish cast of his flesh took on a faint pink tinge, and he would smile, revealing the desolation of his empty gums. That was the only sign he gave that he was enjoying the visit. He would sit down next to his visitor, then get up and wander off, eyes fixed on a point beyond the monastery walls, and no question, no cajolery, could bring him back. It was impossible to have a conversation with him, for he would only babble, lost in thoughts of things beyond his consciousness. He was a child returned to his mother's womb to be lulled by the beating of her heart.

Only Catarina held the key to reviving Juan. It was a joy to watch the two of them bending over the plants in the garden, absorbed in the task of exterminating pests. The mestiza's almond-shaped eyes, so like her mother's, had the power of seeing that which is hidden from ordinary mortals, and she recognized things in Juan others could not. They talked to each other, sharing a universe with its own sun and moon, floating in a gaseous constellation, weaving about between luminescent planets inhabited by beings named—as far as Pedro was able to distinguish—Sibú, Surá, kings of the animals and sister tapirs. Matters human and divine, incomprehensible in themselves, became even more so because they mixed languages together so that they ended up with one that must have been the language The Mute would have spoken, had she not been dumb.

December was coming to an end, and preparations for the Christmas festivities merged with those for war. Agueda's kitchen was in an uproar with conversations on things culinary, and in the dining room Casasola and Rafael Fajardo bent over a map discussing routes and military tactics for squelching the rebellious Indians. That closeting of the two men took place in secret, apart from the official meetings in the city hall with the Governor participating. He sat in a fine leather chair at those meetings, the seat and back upholstered in velvet stuffed with cotton batting, which he had brought all the way from Hungary where Granda had achieved the height of military glory in battle against the Turks by snatching the flag from the standard bearer and slitting his throat. People snickered when Granda's Hungarian chair was mentioned, whispering that if it were true that he who kills by the sword dies by the sword, Granda was already losing his head in that very chair, starting with the vocal chords.

Seated at his desk, Pedro took note of the decisions and measures regarding the punitive campaign, feeling shocks of horror up and down his spine every time that Granda, instead of writing little notes, spoke in that voice which Smiles compared to that of an old bagpipe or out-of-tune guitar. There was little opposition to the proposals on the Governor's part. He made no objection when Casasola suggested approaching Talamanca by the old missionary road with López Conejo coming by way of Boruca. However, he was very upset when Casasola suggested that he remain behind in Cartago because his age and weaknesses would prevent his going on the campaign. Granda, his chin trembling, wrote in a note that he sent around from hand to hand: "My only weakness is in my throat, not my ass. There's nothing to prevent my riding a horse."

The most difficult problem to cope with was that of recruitment. Pedro reported that despite the announcements and proclamations, very few appeared even to ask for information, and even those refused to sign up when they learned that there was no guarantee that war booty would be available.

Casasola became impatient. He said that both he and Fajardo had said repeatedly that volunteers would be promised Indians as slaves in addition to respectable pay. Granda was shaking his head and the other remained silent. Mier Ceballos ventured to suggest sending a courier to Guatemala to enable the President of the Royal Tribunal and its Judges to decide whether a promise of that kind could be made. However, he said this without conviction because he knew that such an appeal would be rejected or delayed for so long that it would be tantamount to a refusal. Casasola waited, leaning back, teetering in his chair. A smile beginning at the bridge of the Roman nose extended over his patrician face, the carefully shaven square jaw, the corners of the artfully arched mouth. The Captain had let his hair grow stylishly long and now wore it, like Granda and Blas González, lying on the nape of his neck tied back with a black cord. The sound made by the legs of Casasola's chair striking the floor as he rocked back and forth was really irritating. Since nobody would speak, the Captain stood up, his long arms dangling at the sides of his woolen jacket, the slight contraction of his fists lending him the same simian aspect Pedro had observed the first time he saw him, the day a glimpse of Agueda's petticoats almost drove him into delirium. Casasola now seemed a handsome ape who had dyed his hair in order to differentiate himself from the pack, challenging the old male's power. The Governor had clenched his hands together, the knuckles whitened by the tension, as he struggled in the sepulchral silence to find an honorable escape. Blas González pushed the inkwell towards Granda. Pedro, who had been using it, quickly hurried to hand him a pen and a sheet of paper, which he waved away without taking his eyes off Casasola for a moment, his shoulder hunched over the table top. When Granda opened his mouth to speak, all the others could clearly be heard drawing breath and holding it in as they waited. "Let them be offered Indians taken prisoner as slaves for ten years," he said, enunciating with great difficulty, "plus ten silver pesos. Consult Guatemala afterwards."

Mier Ceballos cast an alarmed glance at Blas González who shrugged his shoulders.

As the participants were leaving, Pedro listened to old Nicolás de Cespedes, the oldest of the councilmen, saying that the life of an Indian in captivity was no more than five years, as personal experience had proved to him. Casasola who was also on his way out but heard him, answered, "In five years production in Matina and trade in cacao will have normalized." And from Pedro's desk where Blas González was reviewing the notes that had been taken, he muttered, "And the struggle for the throne will have ended..."

When the city council room had emptied, and he was alone and at peace, Pedro dropped into a chair to order his thoughts. The shoemaker had once diagnosed him as suffering from a cold liver, but it was now heated up nearly to the boiling point. Something much more serious than Serrano's smuggling was involved. The Law of the Indies was being violated here: turning over Indians, property of the Crown, as slaves was a crime from which there was no appeal. No good could come of this, and he wanted no part of an affair which was of benefit only to others but could get him into trouble. He carefully cleaned his pens, shut the inkwell, then proceeded to sew together the pages of notes on the meeting. Nobody had ordered him to take down Granda's last statement, so he had not done so.

For some reason he did not want to leave the city hall. He had a sensation that resembled fear of the outdoors, of going into the street. He struggled briefly against the distress brought on by the mere sight of the table and chairs. A feeling of horror and disgust began to take possession of him until a sudden breath of air ruffled the flag and caused shrieks to rise up from his guts to his heart: "I don't want them to kill Gerónima! I don't want my son to be enslaved!" Of course, he hadn't opened his mouth, but the sensation of having screamed was so intense that he clapped his hand over his lips and pulled himself together.

There was nothing he could do to stop it. Belated remorse over the son he never knew served no purpose. Perhaps the boy was already dead. As for Gerónima, she had asked for it. Now it was crystal clear that she had taken part in the uprising and done nothing to protect him, Pedro, from becoming a victim of the insurgent Indians. Nor was it any use to lament the fate of the two black boys who had chosen to follow their own path. All in all—he said to himself, calmer now—Catarina was in Cartago by his side, and she represented everything in the world that mattered to him. Besides—he smiled—he was now free. Not only was he able to use his true name but nobody and nothing could stop him from moving to any spot he chose in the Empire, in America, the Iberian Peninsula, or the Philippines, if he so desired. For a moment he entertained the idea of traveling to Mexico, Lima, or Santiago de Chile. The world had broadened, grown vast, was filled with opportunity. His smile faded when he remembered that travel of any kind called for money and his pockets were empty.

Finally, as he was preparing to leave, the shoemaker barged in. Pedro frowned. The last thing he wanted to hear was commentary on the preparations for the attack on Talamanca.

"I didn't come to bug you just because I felt like it but because

I just found out something I had to share with somebody, because I can't stand it," said Smiles. "I just got through talking to a trader on his way from Realejo. He stopped by my shop to offer me toolmaker's dies, but I couldn't buy them because he turned down my cacao, saying it was musty. He also had a load of cotton he wanted to exchange for mules to take to Panama to exchange for Peruvian coin, and he was going on from there to El Salvador to buy indigo, and..."

"Enough!" howled Pedro, unable to keep his nerves in check.

"Let me finish," answered the other, quite self-possessed. "...but, he wasn't going to continue on to Panama because he found out about the Indian disturbances and was afraid to go through Boruca. What the fellow told me was that they threw the Nuncio out of Madrid." Smiles waited for Pedro's answer.

"I don't believe you."

"Well, I don't figure a dealer like that had any reason to lie. What he told me specifically was that the King broke off relations with the Pope. That is, Pedro, between Spain and the Holy See..." he said, making a slicing gesture through the air with his hand. "Coming from Realejo, the man told me that the Archduke of Austria entered Rome with his army, surrounded the Vatican hill, put the Pope between his sword and the walls of the basilica, and told him, 'Either you give me your support or I set you down from the saddle of Saint Peter's.' Well, now, something like that must have taken place because when Philip found out that the Pope had made a public announcement of his support for the Archduke of Austria, he hit the ceiling in royal and majestic rage and right then and there said to the Nuncio: 'Tell the Pope he can go fuck himself and as for you, pack up and get the hell out of here...'"

"Stop fooling. If that's true, it's very serious."

"I spiced it up a bit, but basically that's the story, King Philip V broke diplomatic relations with the Holy See. Things look very bad on the Peninsula... The dealer also told me that this year of 1709 that's about to wind up has been named the Year of the Famine for the peasants are eating their own children in order to survive... Eh? How do you like that tale?"

"I don't know. I can't get my head straight."

"Well, I'll tell you what. Nothing is going to stop Casasola and his gang now, not even the Bishop."

The day that Pedro nailed the proclamation on the post of the city hall, Diego Malaventura, the town crier, in the usual deadpan and secretive manner with which he practiced his trade, announced throughout the city that all Indians taken prisoner-of-war in Talamanca would be made available as slaves for a period of ten years and each soldier would receive payment of ten silver pesos on return from the campaign. By the time Diego had completed his round and turned in his stand and trumpet, the first volunteers from the Barrio of the Coloreds were already on the way to Pedralbarán's desk.

When recruitment had not been completed by Christmas, Diego Malaventura came back for his stand and trumpet and went to the neighboring Indian towns to seduce them with the promise of other Indians as slaves. The trick worked: mestizos, Indians, and ladinos[7] came to the city hall to register under their Spanish names. Pedro was surprised at the large number of Indians named Diego. It was as though there was no other saint's name or the priests all had attacks of amnesia during baptism.

At midnight mass on December 24th, the priest Angulo took upon himself the task of fulfilling the recruitment quota by delivering an impassioned sermon in which he called for justice for the murdered missionary fathers. Angulo did not refer to the Indians as senseless savages, as José de San José called them. He was much subtler, using terms like apostates, traitors to the Catholic faith and both majesties. In this way Angulo legitimized the war against the Indians, justifying enslavement of the prisoners, inasmuch as—he explained in the course of the sermon—apostates must be snatched from the clutches of the devil and be made to abjure apostasy in order to save their souls, and to deliver themselves up to the benevolent hands of the Spaniards so that they, through love and patience, could bring them back into the fold. The following morning, despite it being a holy day of obligation and the birthday of a King who had sought to save humanity through a message of peace and love, there was a lineup of poor Spaniards asking to be enlisted to march off to war.

The populace forgot about the scarcity of meat when Diego Malaventura took to the street with his musicians to call for

7. Spanish-speaking mestizos born in America.

turning over the best cattle, the fattest, biggest-uddered milch cows, the youngest calves, to feed the troops that would be off inland to Talamanca. Moved by the message of the town crier, written by Pedro himself, these very animals were removed from the slaughterhouse to travel with the soldiers. The enlistment of livestock under the slogan of "A cow for the King," was a great success. In a way, Pedro was relieved because he was publicly making mockery of the war but nobody seemed to realize it. Actually, his original idea been "A cow for God" but all too aware of the hellish fate in store for the poor creatures, he changed it so as not to offend them.

However, it was not just in the city hall that he had to put up with disagreeable tasks. At meal times in Agueda's house, Casasola was continuously demanding that he tell him again and again what the attack on Cabécar had been like, what he had seen in Urinama, how they had managed to escape, what the Indians of the Chirripó Christian community had told him about Presbere, what the rivers were like at that time of the year, where the best places were for ambushes, and whether he knew anything about the fighting tactics of the Talamancans. Agueda listened, playing the while with a napkin that had a huge letter "A" embroidered on it. Pedro took his time swallowing his food, wiping off his lips, and responding in the politest and least precise manner possible, dwelling mainly on the misfortunes of the flight, Andrade's broken leg, Juan's wound that refused to heal, how difficult chewing shoe leather turned out to be, with harness even worse, hunger's effect on the guts, the madness of a person under pursuit, the uneasiness of going off to one side to shit, the stampeding horses, the shadows in the foliage sensed at twilight and the sleepless nights, the dread of enemies lying in wait, being able to count every rib, and, particularly, water, from above and below, with the never-ending rains, the constant dampness, the rivers, the ground without a dry square inch underfoot, eyes blurry, clothing sticking to the body, mud puddles and snakes slithering through them...

But the Captain was stubborn and the entire horror that Pedro went out of his way to describe in the liveliest and most sinister manner possible didn't daunt him. With a smug little smile of self-sufficiency, he confined himself to remarking how strange it was that the Indians hadn't killed everybody since they had the fugitives outnumbered. And he hit the nail on the head because that was precisely the question Pedro was asking himself. They could have killed everybody but didn't. It could be said that we were being herded by them...herded out of Talamanca towards the city, like sheep to their corral...

Against his will, Pedro had to be present when Rafael Fajardo and López Conejo came to the house and they were all leaning over the map spread out over the dining room table. Under the beady eyes of the Madriz brothers and the Polos, the Conquest officer—now recovered—was tracing out imaginary lines with a dirty, stubby finger. Rafael Fajardo and the Officer, Francisco de Segura were in agreement that López Conejo should enter by way of Boruca, taking the Viceita route because the chief of the town was beholden to the Spaniards for having driven their enemies, the Teribes, out of their territory to the other side of the mountain range. Fajardo was the only one who had even a vague impression of Presbere since he was in Urinama when the Indian arrived to surrender. The idea that his submission and acceptance of vassalage was nothing but an act enraged Fajardo. He could not recall whether Rebullida had baptized the Indian but thought so and that he had named him Pablo. It was all quite vague because Fajardo could not describe him, had no idea whether he was tall or short, fat or thin, young or old. After racking his brain unsuccessfully, he ended up saying, "Those savages all look alike."

Casasola was unable to piece together all the elements he needed for a clear idea as to where he had to go and whom he had to take into custody as the leader of the uprising. Fajardo's vagueness was particularly annoying to him, and he was commenting about this at the dinner table one day when everybody was taken aback by impertinence from Catarina, a child who was always so sweet and well-behaved. The Captain had remarked as he folded his napkin and wiped his fingers on the edge of the tablecloth that Fajardo's inability to describe Pablo Presbere was deplorable.

"His name isn't Pablo, it's Pa-brú," said Catarina.

"And how do you know that, my little witch?" asked Agueda, a benign lilt in her voice.

"Pa-brú means king of the macaws," the child answered and

turned her attention to licking her silver spoon and wiping it with the tablecloth.

Agueda's older son José Manuel who was already showing signs of the Inquisitor he was later to become, rapped her on the knuckles, saying, "That's not done, dirty little girl. Besides which children are not supposed to address their elders, especially when they're mestizos." Catarina put down the spoon, got up from her chair, and stalked out of the room, her stiff little braids bouncing against her ruffled blouse. Pedro's felt his heart sink and his face turn red with rage as he choked off an impulse to slap the nasty boy's face.

Catarina stopped in the doorway, turned around, and looked at the Captain. "All Indians aren't the same," she said, with a slight tremor in her childish voice. "My mom didn't look like my aunt. Presbere is from Suinse and the Suinse people belong to the macaws. Like the macaws, Presbere must have very bright feathers in the tail."

"How do you know all that?" Casasola was intrigued.

"It's just little girl talk," Agueda defended her. "She imagines an Indian with a tail like a bird. How cute!"

"Suinse. Where is that?" the Captain insisted.

"It's in Our Land. My aunt told me."

"Right. But where? Next to what river?"

Catarina lowered her eyes and would say no more.

"Let her alone, José. How should she know such things?"

"It won't hurt to remember that name. Suinse, Suinse. I'll ask Fajardo, he must know."

Pedro had just taken down the proclamation from the post in the corridor at the city hall when the shoemaker appeared. The two of them saw the crumpled paper land in the same irrigation ditch into which Lázaro de Robles emptied Pedro's inkwell, and watched it floating in the stagnant water until somebody emptied a chamber pot farther up, causing a current to flow that carried the proclamation a short distance till it was trapped for a few moments by a clump of yellow flowers and then continued on towards the West.

Pedro had not spoken to Smiles since he enlisted in the punitive expedition. The shoemaker had no idea why Pedro was angry with him and sought stubbornly to worm out the reason.

As a pretext for opening a conversation, he asked, "Is Granda in?"

"He's in Ujarrás," Pedro answered curtly, starting off to his desk but Smiles held him back, herding him into taking a seat beside him on the steps. At that moment a pair of women strolled by and they could overhear one of them complaining that the next thing "that French King" was going to forbid was the wearing of mourning.

"His grandfather's influence," the shoemaker commented to keep the ball rolling. "Louis XIV always hated the color black, novenas, funerals, prayers, and the cult of carrion... They tell me that everybody is now wearing a wig at court... As for mourning dress, it seems to me that it really boils down to a practical matter of business... Have you ever stopped to think of what people spend on candles alone?"

Pedro couldn't take any more. "If you came to waste my time with this kind of talk, I have to get back to my desk. I have a lot of work."

"What's with you? Why have you got a bug up your ass? I know you have it in for me, and I'd like to know the reason."

"Look, I'll tell you the truth, I don't see why you had to enlist for the war."

"Oh, man...! It's true that I'm your friend, but I don't get it that you should be so concerned about my neck."

"I don't give a shit about your neck. What I can't stomach is your looking forward to joining a war that has nothing to do with justness and to go killing Indians for the sport of it."

Smiles was left with his jaw open, unable to understand Pedro's vehemence as he watched him stalk off into the city council office and shut the door.

In the middle of January the shoemaker marched off with Casasola's squadron. Granda had received four thousand pesos with which to hold back the pirates and punish the Indians. They had four thousand rounds, some swords and a small cannon brought from Matina. That was their entire arsenal. The two hundred enlisted men were all untrained novices because Granda did not want to mobilize the regular company on the grounds of needing them for defense against a hypothetical attack by half-breeds. The raw recruits had received intensive training but were ignorant about mountains, had had no experience with rocky ravines, had never seen ghosts hiding among giant leaves. Pedro wondered whether Casasola might not end up with an arrow through his elegant officer's jacket and what Agueda would do as a widow. He imagined her in mourning, dressed in black, wearing a veil, shut in at home, passing in her palanquin behind dark curtains on her way to Carranza, the silversmith's workshop.

Agueda would not remain a widow for very long. Buck teeth or not, her huge fortune guaranteed a new husband of her choice. In the light of her sugar mills, herds of cattle, cacao plantations, and mansion who would even notice her teeth? Besides, there was no denying the fact that Agueda was still handsome, in full possession of all the charms a woman could need. From a distance she was splendid, her figure full but well-proportioned, opulent without overflowing, compact. And she dressed expensively and elegantly, her taste impeccable. Pedro smiled as he remembered the rustic outfit she wore for seducing Serrano—peasant blouse, plain skirt, espadrilles—the day she appeared at the city hall on her father's behalf to obtain release of the jugs of Peruvian liquor...modest, simple, no hint of the *grande dame*. And she succeeded. However, it did Serrano no good to have condoned the illegality, for Pérez de Muro could not or would not make up the amount missing from the till, and he ended up removed from office and banished to Guatemala. Could the gossip be true that Serrano had managed to get himself reappointed and continue governing in Costa Rica? Pedro had seen royal decrees addressed to Serrano dated 1709 in the archives which was very strange since he had left Cartago in 1704. Serrano had always been against the Talamanca missions and predicted failure for them.

Pedro's thoughts turned to those matters in order to keep from being upset at Smiles's departure. The shoemaker, standing next to his mount, wore a very serious expression, his gut sucked in, a bottle of brandy peeping out of his back pocket raising up the skirt of his leather jacket, a knapsack on his back. He was holding his buttocks so tightly drawn up that he appeared to be making a titanic effort to restrain a fart.

Angulo held mass at daybreak for the troop and their families. When it was over, the people poured into the main square, waving hats and shawls in farewell, with cheers of victory for the defenders of the faith, punishers of murderers, executioners of apostates. They was so carried away that they seemed unaware of the appearance of that inadequately armed group of some hundred beggarly, barefooted individuals, their clothes patched, sad, small bundles slung over the shoulder containing corn tortillas and, at the best, bars of bitter chocolate, and a chunk of jerky. In the imagination of all in the main square, there flamed the image of the white robes of the Knights of Saint James, the red cross of the Templars across their broad breasts...horsemen, faces flushed in the early-morning chill, setting out for Jerusalem, two by two on a single mount to exterminate not poor, naked Indians, not at all, but fierce, arrogant Saracens! A few among the crowd, who ventured to make fun of the sorry aspect of the mules overloaded with sacks of salt and flour, were brought up short by the officials. Casasola was to leave by the old missionary road as Pedro had done together with Hernández and The Mute. López Conejo and Governor Granda would take off the following day along the route to Boruca. The two groups would make a pincer movement to trap the macaw, the multicolored bird climbing the hills of Viceita at that moment.

Opinion among those not going off to war was that Casasola would be getting the worst of it. Granda, in the corridor beside the Spanish flag, twisting the ends of his mustaches as he savored some malicious thought skittering behind his narrow forehead; he waited in the seat of honor for the Captain, now in command of infantry, to turn the insignia over to him. Caracoling on a white mare with slender legs, braided tail, and mane clipped in front, Casasola received the flag. With the first rays of the sun, the first drum rolls could be heard together with the off-pitch, but nonetheless heroic, trumpet call. José Canela on foot, held the reins of his master's horse, the contrast between the white of the steed and the black of the servant striking a discordant note of beauty amidst the motley accoutrements. As the captain rode by, Pedro noticed an old, dilapidated conquistador's helmet bouncing on the horse's rump. It was the remains of a suit of armor Pedro had seen before at Agueda's house. It once belonged to an illustrious forebear of hers on her mother's side, the Governor of a Province, Juan Vásquez de Coronado. Pedro amused himself by macabrely imagining Casasola literally baked within the contraption, and a wasp's nest inside.

Old Nicolás Cespedes, in the town hall corridor next to Pedro, brought his hand up to his bald spot and then rested it on the railing, saying, "They'd better not bring back any Indians over forty years old. They can't take the work. I know from experience."

Blas González overheard the remark and added, "They should ask for their birth certificate before plugging them. They don't have much ammunition and if there are eight thousand unruly Indians as that blowhard Andrade claims, they'd best line them up by twos so the bullets will last."

"Cartago and Spain forever!" shouted Casasola, returning the flag to Granda's hands. Cries of "Long live King Philip the Bold," could be heard coming from among the soldiers and from the observers, "Kill all the heathens! Wipe out the scum!" Casasola kissed the edge of the flag, presented arms, and rode to the front of the formation at the head of which were Fajardo, the de la Madriz Linares brothers, and Tomás and Andrés Polo. One woman burst into tears and another called out, "Spare the children! The children are innocent!" Slowly the troop moved out, starting with Casasola's mare, the advance spreading like a shudder of impatience as far as the cows that made up the rear. The Spaniards went by, the mulattos and blacks of the Barrio, the mestizos and the Indians. After them, the mules weighed down by their loads of salt meat, tobacco, wheat flour, honey, and sugar cane. Last of all, the cows, dejected and silent, behind them the little cannon obtained from Matina which, as was later known, fell into the Reventazón River because the hammock bridge could not bear the weight. A swarm of kids, running about and playing, followed the tiny army.

Pedro returned to his desk thinking of The Mother and what she would have done if... Surely, she would have cried, so dearly did she love the shoemaker (for all the attention he would have paid). In any case, Smiles's going off to war was an act of unbelievable stupidity.

Where Is Presbere?

Presbere's men moved out to confront the Christians now balancing precariously on the precipices as they advanced along the top of the cordillera, their horses having already trodden the grasses of the plateau.

A murmur that beat its wings like a wounded dove, an evil omen, fluttered on lips that no longer spoke the chieftain's name. The birds, frightened by the approaching danger, fell silent. The water jaguar bared its fangs on the river bank; the sloth and the angel of the banana grove looked at one another, bewildered, distressed, hanging on to the topmost fronds with their curved claws.

Ready yourself, Surá, Master of the Seed, to receive your favorites, the braves whose fists grip the bow that lets fly the arrows against the thieves of bodies and souls, the looters of sweat and blood!

Presbere had been taken prisoner by the Chief Warrior, and his hosts, dispirited, alone, faced the Spaniards approaching in cavalcade. The animals, frenzied by the spur, had trampled the sacred leaves of the *sahinillo*. Terrified, the hills fell silent at their galloping, and the springs shut off their waters over the divining stones now indifferent to the fate of the Indians.

The red bone that pierced his lower lip did not tremble, his cheekbones painted with annato did not move, as the Chief Warrior said between clenched teeth: "People of the Coén River clans, sons of the Kapá: The Kapá is dead... Since time beyond memory the Viceita clans have made war. Go forth, then, obey, and head off the Christians. Wait for them at the rivulet where the serpent bathes, your spears pointing West, for it is from there that they come."

Presbere was not there. Anguished by the Hidden One's death, they obeyed unaware that the Chief Warrior had taken him prisoner to be exchanged for the freedom of Viceita.

And they thrust themselves against the fierceness of the Captain, fury against fury, the flying arrow in unequal combat against the fire spewed from the guns.

Watching them approach, Captain López Conejo thought of Malaga, of promotion, of Christ's cross, of the salvation of his soul. What he saw was a horde of naked heathens coming on to kill him and spurring the horse cruelly forward, yelled "God is with us!"

A tear trickled slowly from the sloth's eye and the angel of the banana grove hid his reddened eyes.

Captain López Conejo dismounted, examined the marks made by the horseshoes in the tapir hide of the ineffective shields and the bodies of the fallen.

The fallen, wounded as they were, never faltered in defense of their land. Near death under the horses' hooves, paying honor to their torn-out guts, with their last breaths they screamed the words, "Drink blood, Christians, drink blood!"

While the war rages Pedro storms Captain Casasola's wardrobe

As the summer advanced, tidings of the campaign were slow in reaching the city. The news in the letters that arrived in the mud-stained, water-stained saddle bags was confusing. The couriers staggered to the door of the city council like war-wounded, stinking of sweat, shit, and fear. Mier Ceballos and Blas González fell upon the damp papers, fighting to be first in learning what had happened.

Blas González laughed as he read. The Governor had finally remained in Boruca. It seems that he stayed in Ujarrás longer than should be...Nicolasa's embraces had tempered His Honor's belligerent zeal inasmuch as—the document indicated—he sent López Conejo to cross the cordillera with only eighty men. It remained to be seen how the Malagueño would fare in his new role of Sergeant Major of the campaign. The most martial action taken by our Governor had been to issue a proclamation in Boruca...

"I have a copy here," said Blas González and proceeded to read it.

"In the town of Boruca, on the 15th day of February, 1710, Don Antonio de la Granda y Balbín, in fulfill...etc., etc. I herewith make it known to the residents...that whoever comes to swear obedience to the Governor and Captain General of the King, Our Lord, I herewith offer to pardon him, on his royal behalf, for any crime he has committed. And those who do not so come forth, I proclaim to be rebels, traitors to both Majesties, worthy of being burned alive, as will be done to them in the war, which I, of course, do proclaim..."

Blas González passed the sheet to Mier Ceballos. "I don't know if you are aware that Nicolasa's brother Juan Guerrero was recruited and appointed Conquest Captain there in Boruca... The courier just told me so, but I will not acknowledge it until I receive notification from Granda and who knows when that will be, because I'm sure Guerrero won't be charged the *media anata*.[8]

"He appointed Esteban Nieto General Adjutant."

"Nieto will be reliving his heroic campaigns against the Araucanos... José Casasola will throw a fit when he learns that the President of the Royal Tribunal, Don Toribio del Cosio, has replied with unusual speed that he has denied the right to deliver captives as slaves and orders that Indians removed from Talamanca be sent to populate for the Crown and pay tribute."

The arrival of this document from Guatemala made Pedro very happy. He was imagining Casasola in the midst of the jungle, hungry, wet, eaten alive by mosquitoes, in a foul frame of mind because the Indians had not met him head on but had retreated to the deepest recesses of the mountains, leaving the soldiers hung up along the way and with little appetite for chasing after them. And so, under those conditions, Don Toribio's premature and inopportune decision was an ill omen and to carry on the war under such conditions would utterly demoralize the troops.

Pedro sent off the decision from Guatemala to Talamanca on the same day it reached him. Casasola had not yet received the communication nor had any notion that the Royal Tribunal had deprived them of slaves when he found it necessary to request more cows. He was in desperate straits for the ones they had brought with them had fallen off cliffs, been bitten by poisonous snakes, or perished for a variety of other reasons.

Mier Ceballos had Pedro prepare a proclamation requesting the donation of cattle. However, the euphoria of the initial days had subsided and now with the announcement that there would be no captive slaves, there was little if any enthusiasm left.

When Agueda learned of her husband's predicament, she had fifty cows brought in from her Bagaces hacienda and sent to him and paid the drovers out of her own pocket. Besides, she sent along tobacco, and two jugs of wine. The latter—Pedro was pleased to assume—would have little possibility of reaching the Captain's gullet.

---

8. A tax amounting to half a year's pay.

In the same letter that Casasola had requested the cows, he reported that he was "combing Talamanca," already had taken a hundred prisoners, and was surprised that the Indians had not come out in the open to fight. Evidently, it had not cost much effort to take those captives.

In the Captain's absence, Pedro was accorded the honors of master of Agueda's house. He was served the fullest plate, the linen was changed on his bed every day, and there was a whole new candle beside his bed each night. It was during this period that Pedro began to impart confidences to Agueda though he did hold back certain ones which he later told The Mother in less than half an hour. It became a routine for him to remain chatting about this and that with the mistress of the house indifferent to whispering on the part of neighbors, including certain allusions of a very sarcastic nature on the part of Blas González, who lived next door, as to whether the reason for lights being on in the living room until all hours of the night was that some member of the Casasola household was pregnant. After inquiring after the health of the family, he wanted to know whether Doña Agueda was not upset by the absence of her husband, the poor fellow, off in the wilderness fulfilling his demanding obligations to King and Church.

Had González known that in addition to conversing all night long with Pedro she had placed a hot brick in his bed to prevent his feet from getting cold and bringing on a new rheumatic attack, he would have taken it upon himself to poison her husband's mind by sending him an anonymous note together with a set of cow's horns. Pedro, however, was not about to confide Agueda's attentions to anyone. He was very discreet in that sense, but where he did lose his head was in the matter of Casasola's wardrobe. The couple slept in separate bedrooms. In his, there was a wardrobe containing militia officer's jackets on wooden hangers and underneath them a trunk in which underwear, shirts, stockings, and handkerchiefs lay carefully folded and sprinkled with camphor. Agueda had Pedro's only jacket washed and suggested that he put on one of her husband's. Pedro chose one with a captain's insignia and arrived at the office of the city council feeling very comfortable in it.

Astonished at seeing him arrive so decked out, Blas González adjusted his glasses, examined the captain's epaulets, and commented, "The title of militia captain is befitting Don José Casasola y Córdoba... He has left his house alone and a Cordovan appropriates his jackets..."

After having read the letter Servando had sent him with La Chamberga, Pedro regained self-confidence and his old bravado and answered, "Come off it, González! What's with you? You know very well that 'He who leaves Seville, is no longer king of the hill.' Your Honor is cunning as a Jesuit..."

Blas González smiled wryly.

"You have nerve, Pedralbarán... Much for a certain prisoner who fled with fear from a certain Inquisition judge..."

But Pedro was not intimidated. He had been wanting to exorcise his past and retrieve his true identity. Now to his surprise, he was losing his fear.

"How well-informed you are, Your Honor Don Blas. So you are now aware that I was unjustly put up in Triana Castle. I assume the Inquisitor Avendaño was the one who informed you."

"You are quite mistaken, Your Honor. Avendaño had no part in it, no part... Avendaño was a spy of the Archduke of Austria who was enlisting followers of his treacherous case and succeeded in pulling the wool over everyone's eyes, even Father Angulo's, in passing as an Inquisitor of the Holy Office. But he didn't get very far. He was taken by surprise in Cartagena de las Indias distributing propaganda in favor of the Archduke to some passengers who were embarking. After two days in prison he was hanged." Blas González paused momentarily to weigh Pedro's reaction. His eyes glittered behind his spectacles with malice such as Pedro had never before seen. "Affairs of the Inquisition are not as sluggish as those of the State... They are lightning quick! You should be grateful for Charles II's testament, for..."

He went over to a wooden box with a large lock, the key for which never left his person, opened it, poked among the bundles of papers until he pulled out some files that bore the emblem of the Inquisition and opened one in which he could see a long list of names. González shuffled through the pages wetting his finger lightly with saliva.

"Here you go. Read this for yourself, Pedralbarán." *Pedro Albarán, Cordovan, resident in Seville, grandson of an Arab heretic, suspected of conspiring with the French against the Inquisitor General Mendoza, prisoner in Triana Castle under the name Pedro de la Baranda.*

Blas González returned the file to the box, double-locked it and pocketed the key.

"You are a very lucky man, Pedro Albarán! Divine Providence has taken a special fancy to you, for this information arrived in the same post that brought the news of the King's death and, out of prudence, I decided to wait out developments before reading the messages. Now, plotting with the French is no longer a crime and intriguing against a partisan of Austria such as the former Inquisitor General Mendoza is meritorious!"

From that day on, Pedro didn't put on Captain Casasola's insignia again. There was nothing, however, to stop him from wearing his Brittany cloth shirts, not even the whispering of the neighbors, for he did so in the light of Agueda's amused and tolerant smile. The tête-à-têtes with Agueda became more frequent.

Though there were limits to his confidences with her, he thoroughly enjoyed her company, particularly since Juan de las Alas was crazy, the shoemaker was off to war, and The Mother of Visitors lived in a remote place. He needed her and at one point was about to brave the journey to the volcano, but the very thought of her bewailing the shoemaker's departure caused him to desist. He had no other friend than Agueda at the moment and his giving of himself was reciprocated by her in a thousand charming ways. For instance, she did not suspend placing the hot brick in his bed until the weather became unbearably sultry.

Then, one night she entered Pedro's bedroom wearing a nearly transparent nightgown, the lace collar open at the throat, her long blonde hair hanging loose down to her waist. Pedro saw this apparition, all pink and white, approaching, and there could be no doubt as to why she was there. Neither one said a word, but he quickly shifted to one side of the bed to make way for her. He would have preferred the candle to have been left burning, but she blew it out. Better, for the darkness obliterated her buck teeth, and just her body was there, perfumed with fragrant herbs, bespeaking meticulous preparations. *Agueda never improvises*, he thought before entrusting his prolonged abstinence to the ministrations of this woman who had so carefully allowed her action to mature, in the way her husband had conducted himself in planning his military strategy. In the same way that Casasola traced the course of the rivers with his index finger upon the crude map of Talamanca, so did Agueda explore Pedro's body, moving over it with the caution and prudence of one anticipating the possibility of a surprise attack. The educated touch of her fingers set Pedro on fire, but feeling somewhat inhibited, he let her proceed, turning over command of the skirmish until he was left as emptied as Blas González's royal coffers. But, then, in a final encounter in which he emerged the victor, he sank down into a cove of sweet repose from which he watched Agueda slip on her lacy nightgown and warily leave the room, closing the door gently behind her.

The following morning, the Agueda at breakfast wore the same unbiasedly affectionate expression of friend and confidante, permitting none of the emotions of the night before to show through. Bárbara Lorenzana moved about the table with a pitcher of chocolate, bending her neck in a disquieting way. Or, at least, it seemed so to Pedro.

On his way to the town council, he was wondering where Agueda had learned to play all those guitarist's grace notes and whether Captain Casasola's red hair did not bespeak an ardent temperament well disguised by his chilly arrogance. Be that as it may, Pedro felt pleased and contented. Because of his current enjoyment of Agueda's favors, the Captain could frown as much as he liked and, for all Pedro cared, Blas González Coronel could send him the horns and anonymous note if he so desired.

But Blas González must have enjoyed, all on his own, a vengeance he had not sought but which was none the less sweet for that. A long letter from Casasola had arrived in which he indicated no awareness of an adulterous affair between Agueda and her house guest. He did, however, report that the President of the Royal Tribunal, Don Toribio del Cosío had refused to allow him the booty of captured Indians because he was against their enslavement. Casasola reported that the news had struck a very sour note among his men. Their disappointment was so great that he had to call an immediate council of war to deal with the unfortunate matter. As a result, the officers announced that

"Either we are given Indians as slaves or we are getting out of here and fuck the war, the King and the Church!" (Of course, not in those words but in rather more elegant terms befitting a good loyal Christian subject.) In short, Casasola wrote that since the Governor had made a promise, he must live up to it, and square accounts later on with Don Toribio del Cosío. The captain also reported that seven hundred prisoners had been taken, including children and adults and that he was waiting for López Conejo who was at that very moment dickering with Viceita about the turning over of the chief Presbere so that he and López Conejo could return to Cartago together triumphant and with few casualties. The Captain was certain of victory since, as he said, the Indians had offered little resistance, and the only thing lacking was the head of the leader of the rebellion with which to close the book on the war.

Mier Ceballos forgot the serious conflict afoot with the Royal Tribunal, Blas González his antipathy for Casasola, and both set out to notify the priest Angulo of the good news and to request that the bells be rung to summon the populace to hear the announcement. The request was immediately complied with, and a large group gathered from the four corners of the city—particularly the Barrio of the Coloreds—at the atrium where the tidings were received with rejoicing for the heroic champions who would be on their way back with booty of hundreds of captives.

Pedro, at the window of the council chamber, was deaf to the tolling of the bells and jubilation of the inhabitants.

Angulo, standing in the middle of the atrium, arms upraised to the heavens, gave thanks because the heretics had been given the punishment they deserved to the greater glory of God and our Majesties, may He protect them.

The friars came running down the street from the monastery with the Father Superior at the head, Juan de las Alas not among them.

The war ends and Pedro is left entirely in the dark

The Mute's body was a gateway opening on an infinite universe. Agueda, on the other hand, ended precisely at the moment she put on her nightgown, left the room, and closed the door. Making love with The Mute was the exploration of an inexhaustible world even long after the two bodies had separated. When Agueda was gone, Pedro turned over and fell asleep, satisfied like a dormouse until he awoke at cockcrow to think of all manner of things except the woman who had spent a couple of hours with him during the night.

Pedro lost interest in Agueda after the arrival of Casasola's letter. Not that he rejected her, it was simply that she no longer excited him the way she had. Or perhaps he was too uneasy to give himself up to fornication as fully as he had.

He became very nervous, particularly after Granda sent a courier at full gallop to report that the war was over and Casasola and López Conejo were on the march to Cartago with over seven hundred prisoners and the chief Presbere, who had been turned over by the Viceitas.

Agueda went into his room that night in her street clothes. She left the candle burning on the bed table and sat down on the bed. The two looked at one another. She sighed and said: "Captain Anchieta brought me a letter from José this morning. He says in it that he is fully gratified because the last of the resistance was squelched by the capture of the Indian Presbere and that now that the war is over, it will be up to Granda to keep his promise to make Toribio del Cosío recant... But I didn't come to give you a military report... You know very well that I am fond of you and have tried to be hospitable... I think it would be a good idea to ask the Father Superior for lodging because it is not advisable to have José find you here. Bárbara and my slaves are silent as the tomb but that doesn't hold for the neighbors, especially Blas González. I would like you to go as soon as it's light, and you can leave Catarina here. You know that I am very fond of her."

She leaned over, kissed Pedro sweetly on the forehead and left, taking her candlestick with her. Pedro's candle had been out and so the room was pitch dark. What manner of woman was this who was able to fit together so neatly the pieces of life's jigsaw puzzle? He had not offended her, no. Nevertheless, a sudden feeling of humiliation brought the blood rushing to his face. Agueda had a solution for every problem, quick and effective. Naturally, to stay there after having slept with her would put her in an uncomfortable position and possible a dangerous one were her husband to learn that she had been unfaithful to him with her guest. However, Agueda could have gone about getting rid of him with a little more consideration, and not so suddenly, at the first crack of dawn, without his even knowing if the Superior had space for him.

Before daybreak, while it was still dark, instead of going to the monastery, Pedro sneaked like a thief into the children's room and took Catarina out of the house with him. His plan was to take her to the shoemaker's shop for the two of them to hole up there until Smiles returned. After that he would see what could be done. He had to force one of the window shutters because the front door had two great planks nailed across it. Inside, there was an unbearable smell of mold and damp leather. He lit a candle with a view to making a bit of order in the place and opening a window to ventilate it. He started piling up espadrilles in a corner when Catarina began to scream. Huge rats had jumped on the bed where she was sitting. Seizing the three-legged stool he had sat on the first day he came to Smiles's workshop, he tried to drive them off. In a few moments it was hard to distinguish whether the child or the rats were screeching louder. The noise grew so loud that Pedro was afraid they would attract the attention of a patrol, and he and Catarina climbed back out of the window. He had no idea where to turn, whether to huddle together with her in the atrium of the church, return to Agueda's house, or to seek refuge in the monastery. It must have been about four o'clock in the morning, and he couldn't be bothering people at such an hour—people who would in any case be curious about what went on at Agueda's house that she should have put them out on the street in such a fashion. Carrying Catarina asleep in his arms, he made for the church where he thought a door might have been left open but no, they were shut tight. He was considering going to the monastery to wait at the door like a tramp until it was light when he thought of The Mother's house in the Barrio of the Coloreds. Nobody would be living there now, and he could try to force his way in. He set off for the Barrio with the absurd hope that The Mother might have come back to the city. He could confide his situation to her, and she would be unquestioning in her acceptance of them. But, no, the place was shut tight. With Catarina deep asleep in his arms, he crouched in the doorway to wait for morning. With the first rays of the sun, hinges creaked and a very sleepy, very black woman came out of the neighboring house. Seeing the two next door she approached and asked who he was and if, by any chance, his name was Pedralbarán. When he told her that it was, she handed him a large, heavy brass key, saying, "The Mother told me, if you came by one day, to give you the key to the house, that you might need it."

Moved by the mulata's foresight, without further ado he opened the door with the key and entered. The black woman returned with a supply of candles and a paper folded in four. Pedro lit one of the candles and read: "As I have seen how mean fate has been to you, I thought somebody should outwit the old crab."

When word came that the conquerors were fording the wild Reventazón River—transformed into a placid brook by the terrible drought of recent months—his reaction was icy, and he refused to go out to meet them as many in Cartago did. He stayed in The Mother's house, opened the window facing the main street, and waited there, looking out in expectation of a sight of the victors and vanquished as they passed. Nor did he want to go to the town hall for he could not stomach the sight of Mier Ceballos pulling a strand of hair over his bald spot, nor that of Blas González looking over the tops of his spectacles in a way that made it impossible to tell what he was thinking.

The first exhausted contingent shuffled its way through the dusty road past The Mother's house. Scattered, undisciplined, the colored militiamen looked like survivors of a bloody disaster rather than the heroes of the glorious victory described in the dispatches. Emaciated, indescribably filthy, they staggered along, staring as though without seeing, eyes coated with rheum. Some, however, revived by the first sight of home, danced, limping with joy.

Behind these came the officers. Rafael Fajardo was the only one who had been able to keep his horse alive; the others rode on the backs of the mules, Casasola making a supreme effort to keep from falling forward over the animal's neck. José Canela, his orderly, was not riding with him, and the conquistador helmet he had left with was also missing. He had a tangled beard, long matted hair, was crawling with lice and looked like a derelict.

They were a walking doctor's sampler of buboes and boils, pustules and running sores, ghosts seeming to have risen up out of the clouds of dust raised by the skirts of the women who ran to meet them. Following the officers shuffled another disorganized contingent, faces swollen with mosquito bites, stinking of urine and feces. Only the blacks seemed in good shape, but they were many fewer than had set out. Alongside them shuffled the valley Indians, trying to fend off the boys who were swarming around them, trying to snatch away their machetes.

Pedro, looking for Smiles among the Spaniards, was dazed by the shouting, the jumble of ragged scarecrows, and the mass of people swirling about them, celebrating the return of their relatives for no other reason than that they were back. But there was no sign of Smiles in any of the groups. Nor did he see Agueda, or any other wives, nor the priests or friars. They were all in the church singing hymns, ready to come out when the returnees reached the main square, where the Spanish awaited them. After that they would be going to their homes where a wooden trough with hot water awaited for them to wash off the accumulated filth. Some women stood in the road waiting for the stragglers who were escorting the captives. Pedro lifted Catarina down from the window and moved away himself. He didn't want the little girl to see what remained to be seen: the captives.

Sitting on the bed with the child, he was telling her the story of Boabdil, the Moor, who wept as he left Granada forever, when the sound of hundreds of pairs of feet could be heard outside, a faint, slow, muffled sound. In silence, they listened to what seemed like a procession without human voices.

"They got no tail," one woman shrieked.

"Sure, in front they got one," called out another.

"You mean that?" yelled the first.

A shapeless, homogeneous, compact mass passed by the window. Catarina opened her mouth to ask a question and then closed it. Boabdil, the Moor, continued to weep.

The dog days make Cartago
unbearable. Hundreds of macaws roost
in the bell tower of the church and Juan
de las Alas glows with an inner light

They brought Presbere back in a covered wagon with a thatched roof. Nobody could see him because he was locked up under close guard in the Governor's tool house. The lancers reported that he spent all day and night squatting on the floor in the darkest corner of the room.

The captives were taken to the corral where the cattle auctions were held. Granda returned to the city a week after López Conejo and Casasola, with Juan Guerrero at his side. It was soon after—nobody knows the exact day—that a flock of macaws flew over the city and roosted on the city hall roof. Nobody had ever seen such a thing before, and the people gathered in the main square to gaze in amazement at the sight of the rooftop carpeted over with the incredible multicolored feathers, angrily blue, insolently green, aggressively red. The birds fixed their round, unblinking eyes on the gawkers standing below, admiring the clamor of colors, the haughty beaks pecking under the wings to smooth the fine down, combing the boisterous rainbow of their plumage. Some of the more daring boys tried climbing the posts of the corridor to catch one to bring home. However, they defended themselves valiantly, and such an uproar was created with the screeching of birds, the cries of the crowd egging them on, and the boys' howls of pain that Granda and the city council came out, interrupting their meeting on urgent matters concerning the end of the war, and ordered everybody to disperse. The macaws grew frantic, creating a deafening uproar, much worse than that of the parrots during the mating season when they are at their rowdy, shameless lovemaking up in the trees on the square.

Captain Casasola was confined to his house, feverish, his hair cut short, skin taut over his cheekbones. He was much too weak to spend his scant reserves of energy in discussing anything not immediately related to the one thing that concerned him: the distribution of the captives. Granda and Blas González, casting about for pretexts to delay the matter—the former, because he didn't want to incur the wrath of the Royal Tribunal before time, and the latter, because in his post as Deputy Director of the Royal Treasury, he was obligated to protect the interests of the King— saw an excellent opportunity for wasting time in driving off the macaws on the basis that it was impossible for the city council to meet because of the disturbance created and because they were pulling up roof tiles leaving holes in the roof through which their gaudy feathers could be seen against the sky. The more Granda and Blas González waved their arms, the more irritated the birds became. Finally, when it became clear that nothing would scare the intruders, the Governor gave orders for the police to try shooting at them. However, they were informed that what little ammunition was left in the armory had to be saved for guarding prisoners.

The lancers climbed up ladders with their spears, the crowd below roaring with emotion as they watched them trying to keep their balance on the ridge pole while the birds flew at them beating their wings and using their powerful beaks to tear off strips of shirt as well as bits of flesh. The hubbub made people forget for a few moments that there was a copper-colored, defenseless mass of captives awaiting their fate in the stables of the corral. Never had a flock of macaws been seen before, let alone on the roof of the city hall. The council could not meet that day nor the next. On the third day, the birds flew off—for reasons unknown—to the bell tower of the church. When Sunday came the bells could not be rung because the macaws had taken them over, and the faithful had to be summoned by the dreary sound of cowbells.

The meeting room was quiet, but one seat at the table was empty. Captain Casasola was bedridden with intermittent and malignant fevers that kept rising and falling. Bárbara Lorenzana told one of Blas González's slaves that her master's eyes rolled up into his head and that he shook all over with terrible chills and convulsions even with ten blankets of Guatemalan wool covering him.

With Casasola absent, Granda and Blas González took control and won the support of Mier Ceballos, Ocampo Golfín, and Nicolás Cespedes with respect to forbidding the distribution of the captive Indians until an affirmative reply was received to the petition Granda had presented before the Supreme Government in Guatemala.

It was Mier Ceballos's idea to hold preliminary hearings on Presbere and his underlings until such response was forthcoming. López Conejo agreed reluctantly, having no choice but to give in, reassured by the promise that once Presbere was executed, the distribution of the Indians would be made whether or not there was a reply from Don Toribio del Cosío. Discussion went from one extreme to another and the fate of the seditious Indian passed from Granda's control to López Conejo's, one holding back to gain time and the other pushing for speedy trial and execution.

It was at this time that Pedro saw the door of the shoemaker's shop open and two huge rats run out under a hail of espadrilles. Thinking that some intruder had taken possession of his friend's house, he went to investigate. The man inside had no pot belly so he couldn't be Smiles, but ravaged appearance and all, it was Smiles, busily moving rolls of leather, sweeping up dust, and chasing vermin. On seeing Pedro, he brought his hand up to cover his face, and as if he had seen him only yesterday, said: "Can you imagine? Not even private property is respected in this town any more! Somebody broke in through my window and moved my things around."

"It was me," admitted Pedro.

"And who gave you permission to enter my premises?"

"I'll explain... But... How come nobody saw you return? I thought... that is, I was beginning to figure..."

"That I was dead? I am dead! And, now, I'd like you to do me a favor and leave me alone. I'm very busy, as you can see. So just get out. I have a lot of work to do."

And he made a gesture of dismissal with his broom which had nothing left of it but the broomstick. In other times, Pedro would have just laughed at the absurdity of the situation, but he refrained. He just shrugged, excused himself, and was starting out when the shoemaker took his hand away from his face, revealing a great gash that exposed cartilage where his nose had been.

Watching Pedro's expression of horror, Smiles lowered the broom. "For your information," he said, icily, "it's mountain leprosy. How do you like it? Now, go." Then, lightening his tone, he added, "You'd better. It may be contagious."

"No, I'm not going. I'm going to heat up water so you can take a bath. You smell like a monkey. How did you come into the city?"

"Don't be asking foolishness. If you want to help me, there's a big basin in the corner and outside you'll find enough wood. Get a light from the neighbor but don't tell him I'm sick. Get me some clothes. The rats took care of what I left."

Pedro watched as he undressed. He removed his drawers which fell apart in his hands and threw the remains in the fire together with his shirt and the strips of leather that were once his jacket. The water was beginning to steam. Smiles's skin was greenish in tone and covered with scratches and welts like a mended old boot. He was a pitiful sight, the poor fellow, a shadow of his former self, a wreck.

"It all started with a mosquito bite, an insignificant little sore that began to eat away my flesh, going deeper and deeper... Oh, but I'll take care of it. In a couple of days I'll be like new! The rest of my body is sound, as you can see. I have nothing serious anywhere, just superficial scratches. An evil creature stung me, is all, and I'll find the cure. But I need you to get something special for me."

It was painful to be there right in front of him, seeing him so disfigured. He had a little snub nose before, but now...! Why didn't the mosquito sting him in the ass?

"Casasola is a monster," the shoemaker said, bitterly. "You can't imagine the things he did out there... No, you couldn't!"

Pedro made no comment and the shoemaker, looking at him sideways, went on, fuming, as though Casasola were responsible for his misfortune, "Among other bestial acts, he burned an Indian alive to make others come out of a house where they were holed up."

"We Spaniards, as you know, find that bonfires have a particular attraction for us. And did the ones inside come out?"

"No, they didn't... So, Casasola tied the Indian to a post, piled fire around him and said that he was burning him for being an apostate, a heretic, and a traitor to both Majesties... But those inside the house did not come out. And then...have you ever smelled the odor of human fat burning? I never did. Not until that moment... The stench had not left before he put the house to the torch..."

"And, so they came out..."

"They came out...yes, they did..."

"And..."

"Some of them are here, prisoners. The others...well, you'll be able to see what the lancers did to them. Run through, like...! Well, how should I know like what?"

The water now hot,. Pedro took the basin off the fire, and Smiles began to wash his body carefully, stripping away the muddy crusts that covered his sores. None of them looked serious. After passing the washcloth over his face, he threw it into the fire. It sputtered, sending up black smoke and was finally consumed. Seated on the pelt over his bed, he said: "When The Mother finds out I'm back, she'll want to come and take me to her house on the volcano, but I don't want to go there."

"She'll take care of you, you'll get some rest, proper food."

"I don't want to go up the volcano. You know something, Pedro, out there in the Talamanca mountains, seeing the things we did, I thought to myself it's impossible for so much sin to go unpunished. God will make that volcano explode and burn us all up, like Sodom and Gomorrha, none will be spared!"

Smiles looked down at his bare feet, the grime removed, and said, solemnly, "I vow that since I came out of this alive, I will become a priest and expiate my sin."

Pedro could not hold back a sardonic chortle, suddenly aware that it was a long time since he had laughed, and said, "A priest, you?"

"Yes. I am going to found the 'Order of the *Virgen de los Angeles*,' the members to be called '*Los Angelicales*.'"

His expression was one of such seriousness that Pedro did not laugh again. He had had enough for the moment and left, telling Smiles that he was going for food and clothing. He crossed the square and knocked on Agueda's door. Bárbara Lorenzana answered and told him that her mistress was at the Captain's bedside for he was suffering an attack of his quartan and tertian fevers. When Pedro asked her for clothing and something to eat for Smiles who had returned from the war very weakened and in poor health, she bent her head in compassion and returned quickly with a package of food and trousers that had been José Canela's.

"Canela died in an ambush," she said, handing him the trousers. "Because of his limp, the poor little fellow couldn't run fast. They are small, but if the shoemaker is as thin as you say he should be able to use them."

They were an excellent fit. Smiles's body was now like that of a youth. He shut the workshop and when The Mother learned that he was back and came to see him, he refused to receive her. That same day, she returned to the heights of the volcano from where she looked down upon the people and their foibles, small and insignificant. Had Pedro not brought him food every day, Smiles would have died of starvation or been bitten to death by the rats which returned to their nests in the uncured hides.

It was difficult to obtain what the shoemaker asked for, but Pedro resorted to Diego Malaventura, who spoke to an Indian who lived in Juan de la Herrera, and that man brought it in a jug, the opening of which was sealed with a piece of corn cob pierced so that the snake could breathe.

Removing it from the jug, that is to say, letting it come out (for he didn't touch it) the shoemaker exclaimed, "A *tamagá*, and nice and small! Thanks, Pedro, exactly what I needed." He then caught it with a forked stick and returned it to the jug. "Now," he continued, "listen very carefully for the success of my cure depends on exactness. Bring me four raw potatoes and as many lemons as you can. If you can't get lemons, banana vinegar, but lemons are better, and be here tonight, ready to stay through till morning and take care of me."

That night, having arranged with his black neighbor to look after Catarina, he went to the shoemaker's shop with the potatoes and lemons. The first thing Smiles did was to squeeze out the lemons, leaving the juice at hand in a brass pitcher. He then took the snake out of the jug again, arranging it so that he could grasp it by the head and make it bite the potatoes, after which he put them into a stone mortar. Next, after returning the snake to the jug he mashed the potatoes to a paste with the grinding stone.

"Now," he told Pedro, "You will have to tie me to my bed with a rope and then put a stick between my teeth so that the neighbors won't hear me scream. Then, using a very clean little stick you will pick up some of the potato, being careful not to let any of it touch your hands—remember it contains poison—and you will spread it on my lesion. But only on the lesion because if you let it go over the edges it could destroy all the way through the bone. You will have to stay and watch me all night because you can never tell how a person will react to snake venom. Once I am tied down and have the stick between my teeth, you must go to the window and watch until you see two bats pass by flying together. Then, you must bar the door and shutter the window and smear the potato mash on me. And you must pay no attention to whatever I do when the poison hits my blood. If I am still alive at daybreak, I will be practically cured of everything and only lacking the lemon juice. You will give it to me to drink for then I will have no strength to scream or break the bonds. And if I die...a copy of my will is over there in that little book by Doña Oliva Sabuco de Nantes. I am leaving everything to The Mother."

"You mean to say you are going to cauterize it with the poison of that snake?" asked Pedro in horror, seeking a way out of taking part in the experiment.

"It's the only cure for what I have. So, do as I say if you are really my friend. If you don't want to, go on your way and let me rot alone. Don't give me anything but lemons until I come back."

"Back from where?"

"From the other world, jackass. Where else?"

The worst of it was the sight of Smiles wearing the trousers of the departed José Canela tied to the bed with a stick between his teeth. Pedro, his hands trembling, covered the lesion, the patient's eyes following his every move. Smile began to sweat and blood ran from his nose and ears. Racked with pain and fever, his body shook the bed so violently that it threatened to fall apart. Towards dawn, his condition was so serious that Pedro repented having paid no attention to the matter of the bats for he did not fancy standing at the window like an idiot because of a stupid superstition.

He had to go to work at the town hall and leave the shoemaker alone, his face horribly swollen, sweating blood, his gaze vacant, biting the stick so hard that it nearly broke. He took it from between his teeth before going out, making him swallow lemon juice without letting him catch his breath, and then putting back the stick. He repeated his drastic treatment each time he was able to get away from the town hall. When the patient fell into a stupor of exhaustion the lesion was covered with a black stain.

Towards midnight of that next day, Smiles opened his eyes, their expression now one of a person returned to sanity. He spit the stick out and asked for water. Pedro gave it to him mixed with the last of the lemon juice. After that, he wanted to eat and confessed that the ordeal had been terrible, that he would prefer to die rather than go through anything like it again because he had such frightful visions, and his body was as hot as if he were not on his bed but on Saint Lawrence's gridiron. He had Pedro bury the remains of the potatoes in a safe spot in the yard. However, the mash had disappeared and the mortar looked as clean and empty as the shop was of rats. A few days later the vultures also died of strange convulsions.

Smiles snipped a piece out of José Canela's trousers—the cleanest bit of cloth that could be seen in the place—and passed it carefully over his nose. There was something indescribable there now, a black and pestilent swelling up to the white bony arch. The shoemaker could not see himself and asked Pedro to give him the exact details of what was there. Smiles was completely happy with what he heard and explained to him that new skin, smooth and clear as a baby's ass, would soon grow in and mercifully cover over the raw flesh.

"Now I will be able to fulfill my vow to become an angelical priest," he said gleefully. "The goal I will set for myself and my followers will be to treat those with a pestilential disease and give sandals to all who go barefooted. A good cause, worthy of pardon for all our sins, don't you think?"

"It seems so to me," Pedro responded, thinking that treating pussy bubos and foul infections and devoting one's life to shoeing the shoeless called for careful consideration.

The truth of the matter was that after two nights without sleep and the nervous tension he had undergone, he was so thoroughly exhausted he couldn't have laughed even if he wanted to. Everything was exhausting right then, even the weather. The rainy season was late in coming, and the earth was drying out. The drainage ditches exuded the stench of wastes thrown in by servants and slaves, and the rivers could be waded across at ankle height. The wells supplying the city had given out, and potters labored day and night on vessels for the water carriers who had to cover enormous distances to provide enough.

This made the invasion of the macaws even more mysterious for nobody ever saw them leave the bell tower to drink water. The superior ordered High Mass to be held in the San Nicolás de Tolentino church since the parishioners were complaining that the birds befouled them as they were entering the church and the racket they raised made it difficult to hear the services.

While the shoemaker was convalescing—remaining shut in for fear that the children would run away from him in the street or that the authorities might banish him as a leper to some distant place like Tucurrique—the town council put the finishing touches on Presbere's preliminary hearing, his death sentence having been pronounced even before he went on trial.

Casasola's followers came to his bedside to inform him of the steps Granda was taking, but the Captain's condition had worsened. He was extremely weak and listened to them, his eyes wandering, as attacks of the fever came and went. He would only repeat the same words over and over again, referring to Presbere: "Hurry up and kill him."

The entire city was aware of the preparations for the execution. Granda had initiated an unsuccessful search in cities, towns, and villages for somebody who knew how to apply the garrote. The murderous instrument had never been used in Cartago.

The administration was engaged in these tasks when Blas

González, anticipating the date when the distribution of the captives was to be made and with no reply forthcoming from Guatemala, cautious as he was, decided to make a count of the captives in order to have an exact number to enter in the books; he instructed Pedro to accompany him to the cattle corral.

This unnerved Pedro. He had considered slipping into the place on his own account many times without admitting to himself why. But he very well knew that the reason was to see if Gerónima and the black boys were among the captives. The inkwell slipped from his hand twice as he was putting his implements into their bag. Finally, with paper and a board on which to write, he set out with Blas González in the scorching heat.

"We shall see how many prisoners are left... Plenty of people will be interested in stealing them in case Toribio del Cosío decides that they must be released. After all, Talamanca belongs to the Crown," Blas González was holding forth as they went. "I wash my hands of it if it turns out later that the number that should be there aren't there. What concerns me is that the Royal Treasury must be in order. That is my responsibility."

Francisco de la Madriz, who was in charge of the prisoner camp, frowned when he saw them approaching, his face a study in suspicion, alarm, and disgust. Making a show of authority, he ordered the Deputy Director of the Royal Treasury to turn in to him the pass issued by the Governor, alleging that he had received instructions from him not to allow anybody into the area. It was a makeshift stockade with a fence of posts a couple of yards tall around it. Blas González disregarded him high-handedly and ordered the lancers to force their way in, which they did. Infuriated, Francisco de la Madriz muttered an oath in a low voice, but loud enough for the other to hear.

Inside, packed into a small space, the captives sat hunched in awesome, apprehensive silence, their knees drawn up to the chest. Not an outcry from anyone, not a sniffling child nor a sobbing woman. As Pedro and González entered, hundreds of heads, hair matted and filthy, were raised, papaya-seed eyes fixed on them. Pedro sought refuge in some indeterminate inner sanctum, but the stench of blood and death made any evasion impossible. Blas González gave the order for all to stand and the lancers began to wield the sharp points of their spears left and right, particularly at the women, who got to their feet with their infants pressed between their naked breasts, their arms crossed protectively over them. A wave of suffering seemed to break over the corral, but not a sound emerged from the stubborn throats.

Squinting his eyes in calculation, González commented, "My educated guess would put the number here at some five hundred. And seven hundred were supposed to have been brought. A greater mystery than the Holy Trinity."

Francisco de la Madriz, who had dogged González's heels, acted as though he had not heard the remark, and shouting wildly, ordered the lancers to herd the women and children to one side and the men and boys to the other.

Pedro took his scribe's implements out of his knapsack, asked one of the lancers to hold the inkwell, placed the papers on the board and began to write, dividing the page into three columns, marked men, women, children; he waited for the count to begin. He avoided looking around him, not wanting to meet Gerónima's eyes, or catch sight of the blotched skin of the two blacks. He kept his head lowered in the hope that if any one of them was there, he would not be recognized. The lancers went to work, using their weapons to divide the prisoners. Some remained stretched out on the ground. Blas González ordered that they be checked to see if they were dead or feigning. None of them rose. They were dead, even beginning to decompose, flies and ants on the bodies. Pedro saw Indians suddenly aroused, eyes blazing with hatred fixed on Blas González. He did not react and raised his hand, beginning the count, as Pedro took note. He finished with the men and started on the women. Pedro was overheated, the sun was fierce, and flies circled his pen. With his eyes cast down, he saw how the Indian women sought to hide their infants, the older ones burying their faces between their mother's legs. Blas González was not interested in faces. His finger flying from one to another, he counted: "One female with two; another with one," and so on. Suddenly, his steady gait halted and Pedro could hear him laugh and say: "Some pirate must have been involved here." Involuntarily, he raised his eyes to see what had caused the interruption. It was a youngster, apparently by himself, a boy with curly hair, his skin a lighter color than the rest.

Amused, he repeated, "Some pirate must have been involved here. Just look, Albarán, at his green eyes." And he continued on his way, taking the count. Pedro, obliged to keep writing, could not stop to have a closer look at the boy. The count finished, they left the camp. On the way back to the city, Blas González criticized Francisco de la Madriz for not having a tub of water for the poor creatures, saying, "They'll die before the reply arrives from Guatemala. He'll have to see how he can account for that."

Pedro didn't listen, lost in the search of his memory for the color of his mother's eyes. Were they green? He could no longer remember. Nor his father's. Unless the boy was a pirate's son as Blas González believed...the English had blue eyes, and also green. In any case, that boy was a mestizo and he was alone. And it was possible that he could be the one The Mute gave birth to when she died. Or he could have been the product of a momentary loss of control on Rebullida's part, an idea quickly discarded by Pedro the moment his mind's eye tried to bring into focus a picture of the priest with an Indian woman on his petate, caressing her naked body, his prayer book alongside them. He muttered something, and Blas González turned around, intrigued. Anyone could have fathered that boy, any pirate, any Spanish soldier of the escort, any one of the friars. Pointless to be upset about the boy. His fate was in the hands of the Governor and the councilmen. The liberating letter that was to come from Guatemala releasing the Indians belonging to the King had not arrived and possibly never would. What assurances were there that the courier carrying it had not been intercepted as he boarded the boat on the Río Grande?

One thing was definite—Gerónima was not among the captives. Pedro did not examine the women closely, but he knew that if she were there she would be spitting in his face and calling him terrible names. There were only strangers among them. Two blacks would have stood out. Perhaps Gerónima was able to hide with The Mute's child and Babí and Bugalú in some safe place. She knew the Spaniards well and saved herself in time. Or they killed her. In either case, it was not worth his getting upset. There was nothing to be done. She might also have been among the Indians kidnapped by Francisco de la Madriz or somebody else, or even the lancers who were supposed to be escorting them.

On June 20, Casasola made an effort to get out of bed and attend Presbere's trial but did not even make it across the square. He passed out near the spot where the whipping post was installed and had to be carried back home. Agueda put him back to bed and covered him with additional blankets for he was seized by an even more violent bout of chills and fever.

Wild with excitement, the populace couldn't wait to see the Indian that had managed to elude capture for so long. There were not only crowds from the city but many from remote places attending the trial. The people of Ujarrás came to stay with relatives and friends in Cartago and peasants arrived from Barva and Asserí. Granda was to pass judgment on the insurgent behind closed doors, but nobody was willing to miss the execution. Nobody had yet been found who knew how to apply the garrote, and it was rumored that the prisoner would be given the honor of execution by firing squad.

Nicolasa Guerrero arrived on that same June 20. It was the first time Pedro had seen her after all those years. She held a little girl in her arms, Granda's daughter; the people were tickled at the idea of a Governor with a mistress who had no compunctions about appearing in public with the fruit of his life of sin. Nicolasa had developed into a beautiful woman, her form elegantly enriched by maternity. But she had lost her air of innocence, and it was said that she had a swelled head and behaved as though she were the Governor's legitimate wife, that she had, in fact, become haughty and arrogant. She pretended not to know Pedro, had never seen him in her life before, and was insolent to him, even appropriating his chair for herself and settling down in a doorway from which to observe the prisoner. Now, instead of long, black braids, Nicolasa wore her hair in a bun, and the ingenuous glance beneath thick eyebrows had turned cold, unpleasant, and snobbish.

Granda's baton of authority, thought Pedro, as he harked back nostalgically to what she had once seemed to him, must have an erotic attraction for her since there was no other explanation for the tenderness with which she looked at her decrepit lover. Besides that, it was understandable that Nicolasa should be grateful to Granda, for thanks to him she owned a beautiful house in Ujarrás, a sugar mill, considerable acreage, and four slaves.

Granda y Balbín had lifted the entire Guerrero family out of poverty and he—as gossip had it—fell all over himself in his attentions to her. The glances they exchanged in the doorway as she leaned back in Pedro's chair, the infant in her arms, called up the grotesque perversity of a grandfather and a granddaughter in the throes of a wild passion. The onlookers smothered their laughter as they watched the fierce warrior of Hungary and Flanders cooing and smirking at the girl like an adolescent.

Mier Ceballos and Blas González had not wanted to be involved in Presbere's trial, which was being held without notification to the Royal Tribunal or request for its approval. Nicolás de Céspedes, seated next to the Governor, was proceeding lackadaisically. Such was not the case with Francisco de la Madriz who had instructions from Casasola and López Conejo to hurry things along. Juan Sancho Castañeda was also hoping for speed, for pirates had recently attacked Matina and left him without a foreman or workers, who had all gone off and joined the marauders. In the absence of Mier Ceballos and Blas González, Granda was obliged to face the cacao growers alone, and they were demanding a rapid solution to the distribution of slaves. His time was running out, Presbere was to be condemned, and the Governor would no longer be able to delay making good on his offer of prisoners plus a reward of ten silver pesos per soldier. Had Casasola not taken sick, there would not have been a single Indian remaining in the corral by now. But according to Bárbara Lorenzana, after his effort to get to the city council to push the Indian's conviction, his condition got so bad that Agueda had sent for the Superior.

The mulatto Cristóbal, who was to translate, appeared when Granda ordered the doors closed for, as was usually the case, a noisy crowd had formed and the usual unruly boys were spitting down from the trees in the square. With the guards outside, the first witness entered the room that connected with the Governor's residence. Pedro had prepared a large bottle of ink and six pens, but he was annoyed that, in accordance with Granda's instructions, the proceedings had to be recorded on unstamped paper. The name of the Indian brought in was Siruro, a man about thirty years old. When instructed to make the sign of the cross, he did so in a form that indicated thorough Catholic indoctrination. The mulatto Cristóbal did the simultaneous translation of his testimony from which it was learned that he was from Urinama and had seen Presbere come with his men, heavily armed with spears and shields. Siruro considered him the most feared man in all of Talamanca and declared that he had immediately fled on learning that they had clubbed Pablo de Rebullida to death and that the chief Comezala had killed Father Zamora in Chirripó.

When Siruro finished testifying, he was taken out of the room and one Bocrí brought in, a younger man than the other and so unsteady on his feet that he seemed about to fall at any moment. He also gave assurances of having hidden for fear of Presbere when he knew that he had come with his men and was burning hermitages and killing friars. Finally, the Indian complained that Captain Casasola had unjustly taken him prisoner and brought him to Cartago.

After him came Uruscara. He was middle-aged and resembled the others so closely that they could have been related. All were Christians wearing well-made crosses, dreaded Presbere, and were innocent of any offenses. He claimed to have been very far away in a sector known as Breñon when Presbere appeared, burning up the mountain in his fury.

They seemed actors in a play. One Indian exited and another entered, all making the same declaration in the same words. At the end, one 'Betuquí' appeared who corroborated everything said by the others. He was evidently the same person under another name as 'Bocrí,' who had testified at the beginning of the concocted farce.

Granda sent for an Indian named Daparí to be brought from the prisoner camp and adjourned the meeting. It being afternoon, Pedro went to visit Smiles and give him a report on the proceedings. The visit was a long one, and he did not keep track of the time. When he returned to the city hall he was surprised to see the square empty. Evidently, the crowd had grown tired of waiting around for information and not getting any. Only the macaws were there on the bell tower making a show of their resistance against the fierce and exhausting heat.

When Pedro entered the meeting room, late and in bad humor, there was a man at the table. He was an Indian, middle-aged, who stood there with all the dignity it was possible for him to muster, dressed as he was in ragged trousers that exposed his powerfully muscled thighs. His hands were tied behind his back, and the first things Pedro noticed as he entered the chamber were the way the veins in his forearms stood out like the cords of a hammock and the long black hair that hung down below his shoulders.

From the doorway where she was installed, Nicolasa, now without her child, stared at the man, her jaw dropped, a dazed expression on her face. She was wrapped in a shawl of such strident colors that had she climbed the bell tower, she could have been taken for another macaw.

The Indian's stolidity, Nicolasa's open mouth, and the strange silence in the chamber converted the slight noise made by Pedro hurrying to his seat into something like a loud sneeze in the middle of a mass. He could now see the Indian from in front. Something in his rough-cut, stern features reminded him of The Mute even though her sweet and gentle face bore no resemblance to his. Actually, this Indian was more like Gerónima. Yet, the next time he looked at him, he saw The Mute again...it was not a physical resemblance, he noted, deeply moved, but his expression. It was that the glance of this mature Indian, whose prominent cheekbones seemed carved out of wood, transcended the walls of the room and, while not fixed on any point, nevertheless looked within. His was The Mute's look when she was asleep with her eyes open, her chest scarcely rising as she breathed.

Granda coughed and Cristóbal gave a slight start. Activity suddenly resumed, and everybody began to move except the Indian who started to speak, with the mulatto translating. Pedro Rodríguez passed the sheets of paper to Pedro who hurriedly dipped his pen and wrote:

"He says that his name is Presbere and that he is of the Suinse nation, as it is called in the province of Talamanca. He does not know how old he is. He appears to be over forty years of age and is the chief of that nation."

Granda tried to speak, but his voice did not obey. He wrote a note and the mulatto, having read it, passed it to Pedro who transcribed it: "Ask him if he knows that the King, our Lord—

God save him—has installed in all cities, hamlets, and localities, his royal justices to punish evil and reward good?"

Cristóbal translated. The prisoner fixed his eyes on Granda, and the corners of his mouth contracted slightly, in what might have been a repressed smile. He replied briefly and the translator mulatto spoke. "He states that he has heard that said."

Granda did not like the answer. He carefully considered his next question. It was so long and involved that Pedro was having trouble transcribing it till the usual note was put into his hands; it said: "If, you were aware of the contents of the previous question, why did you commit the grave and dreadful crime of conspiring with Indians of the nations brought under the shield of our holy Catholic faith through evangelical ministers, and causing the deaths of Fray Pablo de Rebullida, Fray Antonio de Zamora, ten soldiers and the wife of one of them, in the towns of Chirripó, Urinama, and Cabécar, burning churches, and seizing sacred ornaments, which were found smashed to pieces, indicating contempt for them."

The mulatto Cristóbal, in a bind, started, interrupted, went back, and ended with a phrase that was too short for him to have completed the translation. It was obvious that he was having trouble with it. Granda, saying nothing, waited, lowering his head slightly, like a bull readying himself for the final charge.

Presbere looked straight into Granda's eyes and, his lower lip thrust out aggressively, began to speak, unhurriedly.

"He says," the mulatto translated, "it was because the Indians of Tuina, Cabécar, San Buenaventura, and those of San José and Santo Domingo saw reverend fathers, like Father Fray Antonio de Andrade, and the soldiers who were with them, write notes to this city. And they believed that it was about more Spaniards being sent to take them out of their villages, and news of this spread among them, so they were the ones who joined together and committed the crimes mentioned in the question."

Pedro hesitated before he wrote the word "crimes" because, it didn't seem to jibe with the overall context of the sentence. The mulatto also added things of his own and, all in all, it was odd that the Indian should have been able to understand so well if he didn't know Spanish.

There was a barrage of throat-clearing at the table, and Juan

Sancho de Castañeda requested permission to ask some questions. He was nervous because Granda was writing his, which took some time to be read, and he thought that perhaps the prisoner was taking advantage of that awkwardness. Speaking so slowly that the mulatto lost the thread, Castañeda had to repeat his question.

He said: "How can he deny altogether and in part what the previous question refers to, when the coming of the Militia Commander, José de Casasola y Córdoba and the other officers to those mountains and nations is confirming that he is the one who conspired and is responsible for the deaths he is imprisoned for."

The answer was brief, and again the Indian's slitted eyes were fixed on Granda:

"He says he says the same as was said."

Sancho de Castañeda, irritated because the prisoner continued looking at Granda and not at him, who was doing the questioning, asked "Do you know whether Siruro, Bocrí, Unuscara, Betuquí, and Daparí whom the said Militia Commander brought as captives to this city, took part in the said uprising and killings?"

"He says that he does not know," the Mulatto translated, "that any of the named committed that crime."

And for the second time Pedro saw a flicker at the corners of his mouth.

Juan Sancho ran his fingers through his scanty beard, Pedro Rodríguez Palacios fiddled with a shirt button, and Nicolás de Céspedes fixed a sad glance on the Indian—badly bruised, as they all saw. Taking advantage of the silence, Francisco de la Madriz asked permission to question the prisoner, and Granda made a reluctant motion for him to proceed. De la Madriz who as a youth disturbed the dice and card players with his Golden Gang riding roughshod over The Mother's patio and in general behaving arrogantly and rudely, was now a career army officer. After a stint in the Royal Navy, he returned to Cartago with some honors—whether real or imaginary nobody knew for certain—to take command of a regular company. He leaned forward, rested his elbows on the table, and asked the accused if he had accomplices among the prisoners brought to the city. The Indian shook his head and the mulatto translated what he said: "He says that he does not know nor ever heard that any of those Indians had done anything." That was Presbere's last statement. Afterwards, his answer to all questions was that he had nothing more to say.

He was taken out and Granda adjourned the meeting. Pedro decided to pay the shoemaker a visit and see how he was faring, but Granda sent him to Agueda's house to ask Casasola for his declaration. He hated the idea. It would be very uncomfortable for him to face Agueda in view of her having asked him to leave and his not having said a word of thanks to her for all she had done for him and for her kindness to Catarina. And not only that. She had heard him out on that night of confidences, lent him her husband's clothes, and taken him into her bed. No, not her bed, actually. She had gotten into his bed, leaving him with the unpleasant feeling of something unfinished. In the final analysis, looking at the matter coldly, Pedro was not interested in continuing to go to bed with her, and so the war was over. So what? So, she had called a halt at the precisely the right moment, and done so frankly and affectionately. What irked Pedro—he recognized as much now—was that she was the one who called it quits and not he. It was dishonorable for a woman to tell a man not to come into her bed again unless there had been a fight. That's just how it was. On the way to Agueda's house with the file of papers under his arm, he asked himself over and over again why he hadn't been the one to say to her, "Agueda, the war is over and your husband is back, so it would be best if I left this house."

He made his way through the vine and the treacherous thorns hidden among its flowers and knocked on the door. Bárbara Lorenzana answered, surprised that he didn't come to the back door, as in the last days. She inclined her head, glanced at the sheaf of papers and realized he had come on business, not seeking any favor. She showed him in with a certain air of innocence. He detected a strong smell of dry leaves burning somewhere mixed with a sharp odor of vague and vaporous substances. He asked Bárbara to show him to the Captain's room in the hope that by going there he could avoid having to talk to Agueda. She hesitated and finally led him through the patio corridor to his bedroom. The atmosphere there in the darkness was stifling. Straining his eyes he was able to see the sick man in his great *cocobola*-wood bed with a purple velvet canopy, his body wrapped in a thick woolen blanket despite the sweltering heat. A man, a blade in his hand, stood leaning over the Captain as he hunted for a vein in his arm. Pedro recognized him as a Frenchman, alleged to be a surgeon, who had arrived in Cartago following a supposed adventure in which he had been kidnapped from Martinique by the English but made his escape by throwing himself overboard and swimming to the shore in Matina, escaping sharks and enemy bullets on the way. The moment the Frenchman noticed his presence he waved him angrily out of the room with the instrument. Pedro returned to the living room thinking that if the story the shoemaker had told about him was true, Casasola couldn't be in worse hands. It was said that he had amputated the leg of a black boy who had been mauled by a jaguar; he used a saw and then cauterized the wound with a burning brand. The man had installed his operating room in the corridor of the city hall so that everyone could witness the operation. The victim, of course, died to the accompaniment of excruciating screams, while being held down by four men. Soon, a muffled yell from the bedroom indicated that the Frenchman had succeeding in opening one of the Captain's veins.

Bárbara Lorenzana came through the living room on the way to the outside door followed by the surgeon and a black boy carrying a basin covered with an embroidered cloth. The two left the house. Bárbara motioned to Pedro to follow her and led him to the sick room. Between sheets and lace coverlets, the Militia Commander lay back, his nightshirt open, his chest heaving as though there were a bellows between his ribs, his arrogance totally gone. His pallor was evident even in the shadow of the canopy. If the fever doesn't kill him—Pedro reasoned—the Frenchman will and, sooner or later, the Captain will be a permanent tenant in the parish church or the San Francisco monastery, as stipulated in his will. At a prudent distance, for the patient's smell was not pleasant, Pedro explained why he was there. Casasola turned his fevered glance toward him and in a faint voice, said, "I don't want the governor bothering me...let him question Nieto or Tomás Polo."

Pedro did not hear the rustle of petticoats until Agueda was whispering in his ear: "Let's go out, Pedralbarán." The two went into the patio. Agueda, seeming thoroughly unruffled, wanted to know the reason for Pedro's presence in her husband's bedroom. Amiably, she asked to see the papers he had brought, glanced at them rapidly, and led Pedro back to the living room. She took out paper, pen, and ink from the Captain's credenza, invited Pedro to have a seat, and dictated to him in a low, firm voice: "I, Commander of Militia in performance of my duties in the Province of Costa Rica, in the name of his Majesty, do herewith certify, as best I am able, for the information of those who shall take cognizance of this document, that acting under the orders of His Honor Don Lorenzo Antonio de la Granda y Balbín, Governor and Captain General of this Province, I proceeded with armed men to put down the conspiracy and uprising of the heathen Indians..."

Agueda did not dwell upon the sentences, nor did she pause unnecessarily, nor hesitate over the choice of words. She spoke in an unbroken stream, with absolute command of official terminology. When she finished dictating, she took the page, read it through, and went to her husband's room to get his signature. As Pedro waited, he imagined her holding the paper in place and guiding the sick man's hand as he signed. But she returned with Casasola's signature so steady and clear that it was impossible for him to have done it. Agueda had forged her husband's signature without a second thought. Pedro said goodnight and left the house with conflicting feelings, hovering between disapproval and admiration. Agueda never ceased to confound.

Days later, on June 27, in the presence of the accused, Granda read the sentence in his broken-guitar voice: "My decision is that I should condemn the said Pablo Presbere because the evidence has been against him; that he shall be taken from the room in which I hold him prisoner, mounted on a beast with a packsaddle and led through the public streets of this city accompanied by the town crier announcing his crime and that, outside the city, he be tied to a post, his eyes bandaged, *ad modum belli*, and that he be shot by arquebus, insofar as there is no executioner available here to garrote; and that when he is dead, that his head be cut off and placed on high so that all may see it."

The square was packed with people on July 4. The execution

would be carried out using the whipping post there and not outside the city in order to shorten the work. In any case, the part of the sentence stipulating that he be paraded through the city before the execution was carried out. He was given a grand tour of the streets mounted backwards on a mule. The people had been so whipped up by the priest Angulo in an incendiary sermon that, on catching sight of the Indian they went berserk and began throwing loose paving stones from the street at him until the priest himself, horrified at the thought that the roadway to the church would be left full of holes, bellowed: "This is not to be a death by stoning! Have pity on a poor sinner soon to give up his soul to the Creator should he repent, or to the devil, if he does not reconcile."

The town crier, Diego Malaventura, marching ahead of the condemned, waited for the crowd to calm down before beginning his announcement: "Punishment of Pablo Presbere, Chief of Suinse, Indian of Talamanca, murderer of Fray Pablo de Rebullida, Fray Antonio de Zamora, ten soldiers, one woman, and one child, renegade of the Catholic faith, traitor to both Majesties, public inciter to rebellion, leader of insurrection!"

Thus, repeating his announcement as often as feasible during the course of the tour until reaching the post, Diego Malaventura strode behind the boy who played the bells. The Indian was bound to the stake. They did not bandage his eyes. Pedro waited for the man's legs to buckle, but that did not happen. He remained calm. When Angulo approached him with a crucifix and held it up to his mouth for him to kiss, he bit him in the hand. The priest withdrew it yelping *"vade retro"* and other Latin epithets which the crowd took as a provocation for hurling curses at the victim. Presbere bore the insults of the infuriated mob with indifference. Pedro felt a touch on his elbow. It was Blas González. "Spain won't dare go into Talamanca again for another hundred years..." he said. "The distribution of the prisoners will be made tomorrow, but it's not necessary for you to be there. Incidentally, where did you leave the list we made of the captive Indians?"

"Don't you have it? I'm sure I gave it to you."

"I don't have it and don't recall your having given it to me. Too bad if it is lost. There's no time to take another count."

Pedro felt sick. He was going to ask who would be making the distribution, but was unable to get the words out. Blás González would receive his due reward. He moved away from him just at the moment Mier Ceballos lowered his sword, and the shots rang out as a single volley striking their target. Mier Ceballos mopped his forehead as he approached the riddled body, now doubled at the knees, head hanging. The executioner chosen by Granda, a powerful mulatto butcher's assistant, approached the stake, untied the body, pulled it around till the head rested on a heavy log, where he neatly chopped it off with a curved machete, then impaled it on a pike which he drove into the ground in the center of the square. The headless body was removed and the crowd, no longer with a taste for hurling stones, disbanded, commenting as they drifted away on the final moments of the dead man, what he did and didn't do. Inevitably, there was one who claimed to have seen a stream of black smoke emerge from his chest at the moment of execution, which gave rise to the unquestionable conclusion that it had to be Satan carrying off the renegade's soul.

Pedro was about to leave when he saw Juan de las Alas standing before the atrium, his eyes fixed on the macaws in the bell tower. At first, he seemed to be praying, but be began to wave his arms and, his face flushed, raised his voice, calling out to them, "Brother birds, you have your feathers to protect you, the vast forest where the Lord provides your food, and your wings on which to fly. Why don't you fly? The pure air is your home, not the miasma of the drains. Fly off! Fly off!" And the poor madman ran onto the atrium dancing about as though he would take flight, with a ridiculous beating of the sleeves of his cassock, giving voice to such cries and shouts of "Fly, brothers" that a commotion took place above in the bell tower, a fluttering of all the colors in the world, and the macaws flew off from their temporary nest towards the West, their chicks following along on awkward, inexpert wings.

One fledgling, too young, fell to the ground close to Pedro. He picked it up and was holding it in his hands thinking that he might take it to Catarina when Juan came over and gently removed it. His outburst had faded, and he held the little bird to his breast, his expression overflowing with tenderness. With trembling fingers he caressed its down, his cheeks now as fresh and pink as in his angelic days.

"Pedro," he said, "do you realize that the macaws flew westward? That's because they follow the sun. The sun is carrying away Presbere's soul on its rays to the world beyond below where immortality awaits him."

"Very likely," said Pedro, kindly.

He accompanied him to the monastery, fearful that his demented behavior in the atrium within sight and earshot of gossips would come to the attention of Angulo. Juan walked along very happily, clutching the fledgling to him, talking about how happy Presbere would be once he reached the world beyond below where he would be received with all the honors of a warrior killed in battle. Pedro nodded, without comment, for to him the Indian had actually died in captivity, and it wrenched his heart to see Juan's toothless mouth, smiling, as he caressed the little bird he held in hands, now dead. He delivered him to the Superior, warning him that Juan's mind was wandering.

Pedro tossed in bed that night calling up the warmth of The Mute, Catarina's infancy, Gerónima beating chocolate to a froth, the two black boys returning to the forest. It all came to his memory in a sequence of images that was orderly and coherent and, for that reason, vivid and painful. He shrank from what hurt the most, and at midnight he gave himself up to the memory of the mass on the banana leaf that he refused to look at. He was not aware at what point in his remembrances his eyes became wet, but he let himself go, hiccuping, sobbing his heart out, soaking the pillow with his tears. Deep asleep, with Catarina in his arms, he expelled through eyes and mouth all the dark humors of past happiness and present grief that had prevented him from giving free rein to his feelings. He had stretched out on the bed fully dressed and so got up. He went outdoors. A dark mass of clouds was advancing from the East. "It's going to rain," he said to himself with relief. He started out to the corral, avoiding the armory on the way. It was the time of day when darkness holds tight to the earth before its expulsion by dawn. On reaching the stockade, he slipped around to the southern part, which he had seen was not guarded. Summoning all his strength he managed to loosen a post in the fence. Someone inside helped him open a space underneath. The Indians were awake; he could hear movement inside. It was impossible that the green-eyed boy would come within his reach and looking for him in the darkness was out of the question. He waited, and one after another, noiselessly, they squeezed their way out and disappeared into the darkness.

When he returned he found Catarina as sound asleep as he had left her. He picked her up in his arms, went out to the street, and to the sound of shots coming from the corral, began running; simultaneously, there was a sudden burst of thunder and lightning.

There was only one thing on Pedro's mind. Or, rather, two. One was already accomplished. The other was to force his legs to keep moving, no matter what, and to move them as fast as possible. And he felt the first heavy drops of rain on his face.

* * *

Pedro was no longer there when the flood attained its full proportions. The drainage ditches overflowed, and the noise and disorder in the city hall had no parallel. Wet to the skin, trousers soaked, jackets dripping, everybody was yelling louder and louder when they weren't sneezing, swearing or cursing. The priest Angulo was there, too, his cassock and curls a disaster. The storm and lack of ammunition had hampered capture of the fugitives and those who were unable to flee had to suffer the consequences; they were distributed the same day beneath the torrential downpour. I had not gone out yet and saw none of it but Bárbara Lorenzana gave me the story in all its details when she came a few days later to beg me to make a pair of boots for an Indian boy who had come into her mistress's hands. When Agueda learned that the captives were being distributed, she went to claim the share that was due her husband. La Lorenzana told me that Blas González Coronel had set the boy aside for himself, but that Agueda had snatched him away without a by-your-leave, as she was quite capable of doing, offering no explanation or excuse.

It was around that time that the Father Superior called me in to take Juan de las Alas's measurements for he had become quite thoroughly deranged, and the Superior wanted me to make him a soft calfskin jacket in which his hands could be restrained because he had taken to undressing in public. What I saw on this occasion is something that bears repeating. I even forgot my nose problem and was taken by surprise at the Superior's reaction when he saw what was left of it: a strip of new skin with openings above it.

The Superior and I entered the cell and there was Juan, cassock flung in a corner, arms outspread, floating a span off the ground, completely lost in a state of complete ecstasy, suspended in the air. In the center of his breast was the famous wound, round as though just inflicted and with fresh blood at the orifice, red and healthy. His hair, ever filthy and matted, now hung down over his shoulders shining like gold. And there was a pungent odor of jasmine in the room, a very curious phenomenon for the only blossoms in the monastery garden were roses. We watched him descend slowly until he came to rest, fainting, on the ground, and we put him to bed. The Father Superior, old and addled now, was nonetheless terrified, and told me that I must be sure to refrain from mentioning the prodigious happening we had just witnessed. I, dumbfounded, answered that to put a saint into a straitjacket would be an unpardonable sin in the eyes of the Lord and suggested that it would be better to arrange a little room for him at the back of the garden where nobody would see him and Juan could float naked all he wanted, hidden from the sight of old church biddies and other malicious gossips.

Hearing the word "saint" agitated the Father Superior. He covered Juan with his blanket and remained silent for nearly an hour, but from the movement of his lips it was evident that he was praying. Finally, he raised his eyes, looked at me, asked me to leave and to swear by Our Lord God that I would say nothing to anybody about what I had seen. I made a cross with my fingers, raised them to my lips, and returned to my workshop thinking that the Superior must have come to the conclusion that it would not be convenient for the monastery of San Francisco de Cartago to have a saint, the reason being that it would mean exposing themselves to an investigation by the priest Angulo who, envious, would bring in censors of the Holy Office, and they would be sticking their noses into the monastery's accounts, and even into the kitchen where there were two very attractive slaves, one of whom had two little ones whose complexion was of an undeniably mulatto cast.

Juan is now living in a small cell at the rear of the monastery patio. A roseate glow may be seen emanating from a tiny window too high up on the wall for a passerby to look in. The light is like that of a sunset, and people say that the mad friar cannot bear the darkness and keeps a candle burning permanently. To my way of thinking, Juan has become luminous like the fire beetle and glowworm, which transform themselves into ardent embers of pure love.

We never heard anything more of Pedro Albarán. Some say they saw him boarding a pirate piragua accompanied by an Englishman with a blonde queue. Others, that he sails on a ghost ship, adrift over the seas. Others that they have it from a good source that he is in Honduras working in a shaft of the Real de Minas de Tegucigalpa. There's no lack of stories. Wherever he may be, wherever he may go, his memories will be treading on his heels.

As for The Mother of Visitors, once noted for her discretion, she's now a gossip. It was she who told everything Pedro had confided in her about the boy and other things I had no idea of. I know the lad. He's the one Agueda Pérez de Muro has. The Mother assures me that he is Pedro's son. I don't believe so; the color of his eyes leads me to think Juan de las Alas is the father. But with Pedro disappeared and Juan incommunicado there's no way of knowing.

About how Presbere went, step by step, to meet his end, I learned from a captive, now a servant of Mier Ceballos.

A couple of years after Presbere's death, the members of the town council took Granda prisoner, shut him up in the meeting room, and demanded that Guatemala remove him. He was accused of everything: cruelty to Indians, illicit cohabitation with Nicolasa, being a sympathizer of the Archduke of Austria...even of being dumb. But the Royal Tribunal stepped in, and he was set free. Prison finished him off, though. Shortly afterward, he followed Captain Casasola. They weren't reconciled even in death; the Governor's funeral cost only fifteen pesos, Casasola's forty-three pesos, three reales.

When the King's letter arrived, neither of the two was there to celebrate it.

The King says thank you

The King—Don Lorenzo Antonio de Granda y Balbín, Governor and Captain General of the Province of Costa Rica, in jurisdiction of Guatemala: By letter from my President of that Tribunal Don Toribio Cosío, of date the second of January of one thousand seven hundred and eleven, the news was received of the uprising in *Talamanca* by its converted Indians, deaths brought about by them of two Priestly Missionaries and ten soldiers with one wife and one child, with burning their churches and profaning of their sacred vessels and ornaments, and that you arrived with dispatch upon this lamentable scene propitiously to prevent the black *Zambos* of the island of Mosquitos from giving them support as well as to punish their rebellion, which purposes were achieved by your effective actions in proceeding with military forces to the Province of Boruca and dispatching from that locality to *Talamanca* and its mountains a Militia Commander and two hundred men, thereby achieving the result of thwarting the Indian rebels and taking prisoner five hundred of them together with their leader, the moving force of the conspiracy, instituting without delay punishment of death well-merited for his heinous crime; and, having taken cognizance from what I heard in my Council of Indies from my Inquisitor, that no matter how this is looked upon, it is a remedy to be provided from this time on to prevent such an occurrence in the future, I do issue the appropriate orders by Official Dispatch of this day to my President of the Tribunal of Guatemala: I have determined, with reference to your Person, to convey my thanks to you, which I herewith do, for the timeliness, effectiveness, and zeal with which you assessed the importance of warding off the dangers which this province and that of Nicaragua might have undergone had the *Zambos* of the island of Mosquitos supported the unconquered Indians of *Talamanca*, and for the punitive actions undertaken as a warning to them, the merit of which I shall have well in mind in your behalf; and, because, likewise, all are worthy of receiving my benevolence who continue carrying out their duties in my service, I dispose and order that in, my royal behalf, you convey, especially, to the Militia Commander whom you sent on the said action, that he has merited the recognition of my Supreme Majesty for his effective comportment, for which I extend thanks to him, as well as to all the soldiers and loyal vassals who collaborated in the punishment of the rebels and for the concomitant defense of that Province, assuring you all that I am confident that in whatever circumstances may arise, you, as well as they, will conduct yourselves in my royal service in the manner most expeditious for dealing with them, for which you shall enjoy the effects of my magnanimous Majesty. Given in Madrid, the First of September of one thousand seven hundred and thirteen. — I, THE KING — By right of the King, Our Lord — Don Bernardo Díaz de la Escalera.

The Sor Juana Inés de la Cruz
Literature Prize

In 1993 the Guadalajara International Book Fair (FIL), the Guadalajara School of Writers (SOGEM) and the French publisher Indigo/Coté-Femmes inaugurated the Sor Juana Inés de la Cruz Prize to recognize the published work of women writers. The award was named after Sor Juana since she was the first female writer of Spanish America, and her poetry, theater and journals constitute an important contribution to the literary arts the world over.

The primary objective of the prize is to bring attention to the work of a female writer in the Spanish language; all female writers who have published a novel in the previous three years are eligible.

The prize includes publication and distribution, under a standard book contract, of the winning entry in Mexico by Fondo de Cultura Económica Press and, since 1995, translation and publication in the United States by Curbstone Press. A presentation of the award is held during the Guadalajara International Book Fair, at which time the winner is presented with a commemorative bronze sculpture of Sor Juana designed by the Portuguese sculptor Gil Simoes. The winner is a featured reader in the Los Angeles Book Festival in April, sponsored by *The Los Angeles Times*.

The winner is selected in the following manner: January, guidelines are made available to the general public; May, deadline for receiving submissions; October, decision of the judges is made public; December, award's ceremony takes place during the Guadalajara International Book Fair. Contact: SOGEM, Av. Circ. Augustín Yáñez #2839, Guadalajara, 44110, JAL, Mexico.

Previous winners are:

Angelina Muniz-Huberman for *Dulcinea encantada*
(Mexico: Editorial Joaquin Mortiz, 1992)
Marcela Serrano for *Nosotros que nos queremos tanto*
(Chile: Editorial Andes, 1992)

The prize is sponsored by Tequila Sauza S.A. de C.V.; Curbstone Press, *The Los Angeles Times*, Mayor's Office of Zapopan; The Western Technological Institute for Higher Learning, Jalisco; and General Outreach Studies, University of Guadalajara.

CURBSTONE PRESS, INC.

is a non-profit publishing house dedicated to literature that reflects a commitment to social change, with an emphasis on contemporary writing from Latin America and Latino communities in the United States. Curbstone presents writers who give voice to the unheard in a language that goes beyond denunciation to celebrate, honor and teach. Curbstone builds bridges between its writers and the public – from inner-city to rural areas, colleges to community centers, children to adults. Curbstone seeks out the highest aesthetic expression of the dedication to human rights and intercultural understanding: poetry, testimonials, novels, stories, children's books.

This mission requires more than just producing books. It requires ensuring that as many people as possible know about these books and read them. To achieve this, a large portion of Curbstone's schedule is dedicated to arranging tours and programs for its authors, working with public school and university teachers to enrich curricula, reaching out to underserved audiences by donating books and conducting readings and community programs, and promoting discussion in the media. It is only through these combined efforts that literature can truly make a difference.

Curbstone Press, like all non-profit presses, depends on the support of individuals, foundations, and government agencies to bring you, the reader, works of literary merit and social significance which might not find a place in profit-driven publishing channels, and to bring these writers into schools and communities across the country. Our sincere thanks to the many individuals who support this endeavor and to the following organizations, foundations and government agencies: Josef & Anni Albers Foundation, Witter Bynner Foundation for Poetry, Connecticut Commission on the Arts, Connecticut Arts Endowment Fund, Connecticut Humanities Council, Lawson Valentine Foundation, LEF Foundation, Lila Wallace-Reader's Digest Fund, The Andrew W. Mellon Foundation, National Endowment for the Arts, the Puffin Foundation, Samuel Rubin Foundation, and the Soros Foundation's Open Society Institute.

Please support Curbstone's efforts to present the diverse voices and views that make our culture richer. Tax-deductible donations can be made by check or credit card to Curbstone Press, 321 Jackson St., Willimantic, CT 06226 Tel: (860) 423-5110.